Road Kill

Also by Zoë Sharp

Killer Instinct
Riot Act
Hard Knocks
First Drop

Road Kill

Zoë Sharp

PIATKUS

Copyright © 2005 by Zoë Sharp

First published in Great Britain in 2005 by
Piatkus Books Ltd of
5 Windmill Street, London W1T 2JA
email: info@piatkus.co.uk

The moral right of the author has been asserted

A catalogue record for this book is available from the British Library

ISBN 0 7499 0699 5

Set in Times by
Action Publishing Technology Ltd, Gloucester

Printed and bound in Great Britain by
Mackays Ltd, Chatham, Kent

Acknowledgements

As always, various people generously allowed me to pick their brains in order to write this book. These include Robert J Breden FGA DGA of Banks Lyon Jewellers in Lancaster; medical expert Kate Merriman BMBS MRCS; John Morris, managing Director of Mondello Park race circuit in Naas, near Dublin; John Robinson at Safety Services Agency in Belfast; and former RAF bomb disposal expert, Robert Roper. Thank you all. The facts are yours, but I take the blame for any artistic licence.

Yet more people waded their way through the typescript and pointed out the glaring plot-holes. Therefore, my grateful thanks go to Peter Doleman, Claire Duplock, Jane Gregory, Sarah Harrison, Caroline and Robert Roper, Anna Valdinger, and Tim Winfield. Most of all, to my husband, Andy, who suffered probably more than I did throughout every twist and turn.

And finally, my thanks to my editor, Gillian Green, and my copy editor, Sarah Abel, who added the final polish.

For Andy, the reason I'm still here ...

And Jane, who came to the rescue

Chapter One

I swung the sledgehammer in a sweeping arc over my
shoulder and smashed it downwards into the wall in front
of me, allowing the sledge's own weight and momentum to
do half the work. Every dozen blows or so I stopped to let
the billowing dust subside and to take a breather.

It was hard, hot, backbreaking work. Straightening up was
something to be approached with caution, hearing the snap
and pop as my spine realigned itself. The constant jarring
through my hands was starting to make my left arm ache
where I'd last had it broken, a year and a half before. I
rubbed at it, feeling the calcified ridges on the bones of my
forearm, and wondered if there was still a weakness there.

It was a bright Sunday in early August. I'd been beating
the hell out of the bedroom walls of my new home practically since sunrise and, as therapy went, it was doing me the
power of good.

I propped the sledge in a corner and gauged the time by
the shadow the sunlight was casting into the room's dirty
interior. A little after twelve o'clock at a guess. My old
wristwatch had clogged with grit and finally given up the
ghost days ago and I hadn't yet had the need, or the inclin-
ation, to venture out and get another.

It was during one of these brief periods of inactivity that
I heard the distinctive sound of a motorbike being caned up
the long dragging hill towards the cottage.

1

I crossed to the open first-floor window, stepping carefully over lumps of fallen masonry and plaster that signified my morning's work so far, and hung out across the sill. Easier said than done. The cottage was built somewhere towards the end of the nineteenth century with rubble-filled walls of local stone, a couple of feet thick.

The road was almost straight but it dipped occasionally out of sight. Sure enough, as I looked out I caught the flash of a bike headlight as it rose and fell into the undulations and shimmered through the heat haze coming up from the tarmac.

I leaned on my elbows, grateful of the slight breeze stirring my hair and cooling the sweat on my skin, and waited. The road past my new home went on for only another half mile and then became a farm track. The other two cottages in the same row had been recently revamped as holiday lets and were currently empty. If anyone was coming up here on a bike they were either very lost, or they were coming to see me.

The bike drew closer, the tortured exhaust note rising to a thunder, driving out the peace and stillness that normally surrounded this place. In the field over the road a gaggle of fat half-grown lambs scattered before it, bounding stiff-legged to safety.

The rider snapped into view over the last rise without appearing to slow his pace any. I recognised the distinctive shape of the Norton Commando as he thrashed past and waved my hand. The rider's helmet ducked as he caught the gesture, grabbing a big handful of brake lever.

I held my breath and waited for the inevitable disaster, but it didn't happen. The rider kept the bike straight and upright and brought it to a fast halt. He described a neat turn in the narrow road without having to put his feet down and came to a stop outside my front door, reaching for the strap on his helmet.

I'd already identified the rider by his leathers and by the bike, but it wasn't someone I'd been expecting to pay me a visit. I'd known Sam Pickering for years but getting your-self caught up in the game plan of a murdering madman, as I'd done, has a tendency to put off even the keenest admirer and we'd drifted apart. I certainly didn't know he'd got my new address, that's for sure.

'Hello Sam,' I called down, casual. 'Long time, no see. What brings you up here?'

Sam managed to extricate himself from his old AGV lid. Under it, his beard stuck out at angles and his straggly dark hair was plastered flat to his scalp. 'Hell fire, Charlie,' he said, gasping for breath. 'You're a bloody difficult girl to track down.'

The day changed at that moment, grew unaccountably cooler. 'What is it?' I said.

He looked up at me then. Perhaps it was because he was squinting into the sun that made him look so fearful. 'It's Jacob and Clare,' he said. 'They've had an accident. A bad one.'

'Bad?' I straightened. 'What do you mean "bad"?'

Sam screwed up his face, as though I might decide at any moment to shoot the messenger. 'Jacob didn't make it,' he said at last, heavily. 'They've taken Clare to Lancaster but apparently she wasn't looking good.'

'Wait there,' I said.

I ducked back inside, pulling the window shut after me and headed for the stairs, grabbing stuff as I went. My full leathers were hanging on the peg near the back door, but I ignored them. Suddenly I couldn't hear over the thunder of blood in my ears.

The lean-to off what used to be the cottage kitchen had a doorway just wide enough to squeeze a bike through, so it had become my integral garage. I wheeled my elderly Suzuki RGV 250 straight out into the small rear yard and kicked it into life, letting the two-stroke engine tick over just long enough for me to struggle into my old jacket, helmet and gloves, and slam the Yale behind me.

I fumbled with the awkward latch on the back gate and

3

my temper fizzed briefly, making me lash out at it with my fist. The pain the stupid action caused brought back a measure of sanity. I took a deep breath and tried to force calm on my rampaging heart rate. A morning's hard physical labour hadn't made the palms of my hands sweat. Sam had managed to bring that on with a couple of sentences.

He was waiting as instructed as I wheeled the Suzuki out alongside him. He'd put his helmet back on and now he regarded me with some anxiety through his open visor.

'Let's go,' I said tightly. 'Keep up or I'll leave you behind.'

He managed a half smile, as though I was joking. The Commando's engine was three times the size of my little RGV, but on the kind of twisty country roads we had to cover there would be little to choose between them. Besides, I was in a hell of a hurry.

Jacob dead.

Clare badly injured.

Jesus.

I don't remember much about the ride to the Royal Lancaster Infirmary. Perhaps the only way I could push the bike anywhere near fast enough was simply not to think about what I was doing.

Jacob Nash and Clare Elliot. I'd known them more than five years but never separately, couldn't think of them any other way than together. Two halves of a whole.

I'd been so caught up with the renovations to the cottage that the last time I'd seen the pair of them was nearly a month ago. They'd been the same as ever, teasing, happy, vibrantly alive. Thinking of either of them dead sent me reeling into panic and denial.

Not that I was any stranger to death. I'd seen it, touched it and smelled it, more times than was good for me to remember. I'd even felt it come for me, for those I loved, and then swing away almost on a whim.

4

Maybe that was why I couldn't truly believe the news about Jacob. Why I was making this near-suicidal dash to the hospital. Until I knew for certain that it was hopeless and he was truly gone, I would try to bind him to this life by sheer effort of will.

My mind kept running over and over what might have happened, but Sam had only arrived after the event, so he hadn't been a direct witness. Clare had been asking for me, he'd been told, and he was the one who'd volunteered to try and track me down from scrappy bits of information and hearsay. Just about anything, by his way of thinking, was better than hanging around at the hospital.

The very fact that at one point after the crash Clare had obviously been conscious and lucid filled me with a small measure of hope but I shied away from the possible nature of her injuries.

Besides, what was she going to do without Jacob? Did she even know that he was dead?

I couldn't imagine what kind of self-induced error had brought the pair of them down. Jacob was a seriously fast rider, had raced bikes in his younger days and still pushed hard on the road. He had skill I couldn't even begin to match and a seeming sixth sense for dangers lurking round the next blind bend.

And Clare had too much respect for her classic Ducati 851 Strada to be reckless. In biking, as in all things, Clare just had too much style to do something as untidy as crashing.

So what the hell had gone wrong?

Lancaster on a Sunday was fairly quiet and I totally disregarded the posted speed limits all the way through town. Sam was right behind me when I finally pulled into the car park at the RLI and dived into a space marked 'reserved for consultants only'.

For once I didn't chain the bike up, or even check to see that it was settled fully onto its side-stand. Taking the keys out of the ignition was the most I could manage. Having Sam there made me try for composure, so we walked, rather than ran, into the building itself.

Nevertheless, I hit the entrance doors to Accident & Emergency shoulder first without slowing, punching them open and woe betide anyone unlucky enough to be standing on the other side.

Sam bypassed the reception desk and trotted off down a corridor. I wanted to stop and ask, but at the same time I didn't want to let him out of sight, so I hurried after him with barely a break in stride.

It had been around ten months since my last visit to the RLI – only that time I'd arrived on a stretcher. I felt the familiar tightness in my chest that being inside the place again always brought on. They say the body doesn't remember pain. They lie.

After a couple of corners the corridor opened out into a large recess that formed a waiting area. The three walls were lined with a rake of squat cloth chairs pushed together into benches. In the centre was a low table covered with nervously dog-eared magazines.

There were already half a dozen people in occupation. Most of them looked awkward and uncomfortable in their full race-replica leathers. A row of helmets sat like trophy skulls across the end run of seats.

I had time to wonder who they all were, these strangers. I didn't think I'd been away long enough to be so completely out of touch. Nobody looked immediately familiar but I didn't have time for a thorough inspection.

As soon as we appeared, a middle-aged woman who'd been sitting in a corner jumped to her feet and launched herself in my direction.

Before I knew it I'd been enveloped in a motherly embrace of such ferocity I barely knew how to react. Aggression I can deal with in my sleep. Affection defeats me every time.

I gave in long enough to hug her in return, then managed

to lever myself back far enough to be able to breathe unrestricted.

'Pauline?' I said, suddenly grateful to see her. 'What are you doing here?'

'Sam got them to call me,' she said gently. 'He thought Clare might appreciate a friendly face.'

I'd known Pauline Jamieson since she started coming to the self-defence classes I was teaching around Lancaster a couple of years ago. Then, when those came to a somewhat abrupt end, she stuck by me as a friend.

After I'd introduced them, Pauline had got to know Jacob and Clare almost as well as I did. So, of course she would be here. Unaccountably, for the first time my voice wobbled and threatened to take the rest of my face down with it.

Pauline took one look at me and wrapped me in a big hug again. She was wearing a strappy summer dress that was a bit of a fashion mistake with her ample figure but she had the self-confidence to carry it off regardless. Her hair was a vivid shade of burgundy and she smelt of apples and peppermint.

'Clare will make it,' she said, eyeing me intently. Just when I thought her firm tone meant she'd had an updated report, she dashed my hopes by adding, 'You've got to keep telling yourself that.'

'How is she? Have they told you anything?'

'Only that both her legs are broken,' Pauline said. She was one of the most matter-of-fact people I knew, but just saying the words even she winced. 'Pelvis too, I think. I'm still waiting to hear.'

I blanked my mind to the image of Clare's long artlessly perfect legs in pieces like a jigsaw puzzle.

'Jesus,' I muttered. 'Does she know about Jacob?'

'Jacob?' Pauline frowned and glanced at Sam, then her eyebrows shot up and she let go of me just long enough to put her hands to her mouth. 'Oh my goodness,' she said, a little faintly. 'That wasn't who she was on the bike with,

7

Charlie. I thought so initially – everybody did – but we were wrong, thank heavens. It wasn't Jacob.'

Parts of my brain overloaded and shut down. Anger sparked and flashed over. A gut instinct response, like the irate mother of a just-found missing child. The relief was so strong it actually hurt.

'Oh thank Christ for that,' I moaned, pulling away from Pauline's arms to sink onto the nearest chair with my head in my hands.

'You might want to rethink the celebration a little, or at least tone it down,' said a voice above me, tight with compressed emotion. 'It might not be your mate who's cashed in his chips, but it was one of ours.'

I lifted my head to find one of the group of bikers had come over and was glaring at the three of us in fairly equal measure.

He was black, with high cheekbones and a buzz cut. Probably somewhere in his late twenties, he was built like a gym junkie, bulked out further by the snazzy one-piece leathers he was wearing. On the outside of both knees were hard plastic sliders, stuck on with Velcro. The sliders were well scuffed, so either he had the bottle to lean his bike over far enough to get his knee down, or he fell off a lot.

The leathers were the latest pattern of expensive Nankai gear in white and two shades of bright green. I would have laid money on him having the latest pattern of expensive Kawasaki sports bike to match.

We each of us reacted to his intrusion according to our nature. Sam took a step back, I got to my feet and took a step forwards, and Pauline moved into the middle ground between us, stoutly undaunted.

'Don't you think there's been more than enough blood-shed for one day, young man?' she asked, her voice mild.

To my surprise, the big guy looked flustered at her quiet admonition. He dropped his gaze, hunching his shoulders uncomfortably inside all that Kevlar-reinforced padding as though he'd developed a sudden itch.

'I'm sorry,' I said quickly, giving him a way out with honour along with an apologetic smile. I had to tilt my head back to look up at him and I was no short-stop. 'I've just ridden down here like a bat out of hell believing one of my oldest friends was dead.' I shrugged. 'But it was still thoughtless of me.'

He nodded at that, little more than a ducking of his head. On impulse I stuck my hand out.

'Charlie Fox,' I said. He took it and shook it, gently, his fingers engulfing mine.

'William,' he said in grudging response.

'Just William?'

There was a pause, then his face cracked in spite of himself. The smile lightened him up by about ten years and took him several notches down the threat scale at the same time. 'Yeah,' he said. 'Just William.'

Pauline introduced herself, too, then announced she was going to roust the medical staff again for more news. Sam had been hovering nervously while this exchange took place. 'I'll get coffee,' he offered and scurried away before I could do more than nod and smile at him.

William watched him leave with a shrewd stare. 'I see your mate's enough of a New Man to let you stand up for yourself,' he said wryly. Now he'd relaxed I could hear the culture in his voice, close to the lazy drawl of the wealthy classes.

'Sam knows his limitations,' I said. 'But don't underestimate him. He may not like physical confrontations, but he could beat your computer to death with one hand tied behind his back.'

William nodded and the humour left his face as the conversation died away.

'I'm sorry about your friend,' I said. 'Who was he?'

'His name was Simon Grannell,' he said simply, 'but everybody called him Slick.'

The name tickled at the back of my memory but I couldn't put a face to it. 'So, what happened, do you know?' I asked.

9

'Not sure. We got there not long after,' he said, sounding both tired and angry, running a hand over the top of his scalp. 'Slick was already toast and your lady friend was still lying in the middle of the road. I damned near ran over her, too.'

Despite the heat my arms went cold enough to sprout instant goosebumps. '"Too"?' I said.

'Yeah.' He nodded. 'I'm no expert but it looked like something went over her after they hit the deck.'

'Jesus,' I muttered under my breath. 'I suppose her Ducati's totalled?'

'Ducati?' William frowned. 'What Ducati? Slick's bike was a Suzuki streetfighter. They were on that.'

Slick Grannell and a streetfighter Suzuki. *Now* I remembered him. One of the flashy group of riders who liked to show off at the local bikers' haunt near Kirkby Lonsdale.

The last time I'd seen him was probably one mild dry Sunday in early July, setting off from Devil's Bridge like the lights had just gone green on his own personal drag strip and someone else was picking up the tab on his tyres. An idle thought had crossed my mind at the time that he was heading for a fall. I never expected for a moment that he'd take my best friend with him.

For a moment I said nothing but something started niggling at the back of my mind. Clare had passed her bike test before she learned to drive a car and I'd never known her willingly ride pillion. She hated it. Yet there she'd been, out on the back of this guy Slick's bike when I could have sworn she thought he was as big an idiot as I did.

'What the hell was Clare doing out with Slick?' I asked.

William glanced at me sharply, as though maybe he sensed the implied criticism of his mate. 'I don't know,' he said. He saw my expression and was back to his grim-faced look again. 'I just want to find out what happened to them,' he said, 'and she's the only one who can fill in the blanks.'

Pauline reappeared at that moment and I glanced at her,

10

hopeful, but she shook her head. 'They aren't for telling me anything,' she said.

'Right,' I said, determined. 'My turn.'

'Look, I appreciate that you're concerned for your friend, but there really is nothing I can tell you beyond the fact we're doing everything we can.'

The doctor finished making some illegible scrawl on her clipboard and almost threw it down onto the cluttered desk. She barely seemed out of her teens but she must have passed out top in her class for stubbornness. She was frail and slender and looked tired down to her bones.

The pager in the pocket of her white coat went off and she picked it out, reading the display distractedly, then shut it off. Her attention was already somewhere else. I touched her sleeve, enough to bring her back to me.

'OK,' I said quickly. 'I know I'm not family but to me Clare *is* family. Closer than family. I understand her legs are smashed. Can you at least tell me if it's as bad as I've heard?'

The young doctor's eyes flicked down to where my fingers rested on her arm, then up to meet my gaze again and I saw wariness replace exasperation. I took my hand back. She sighed noisily and pushed a lank strand of hair out of her eyes.

'Yes, it's bad,' she said at last, the admission seeming to sap the last of her meagre energy. She stuck her hands into her pockets, pulling her shoulders down, too.

I shrugged helplessly. 'So – will she walk?'

'That depends,' the doctor said, stony, 'on whether we can save her legs.'

She paused and must have seen the blank shock in my face. She let her breath out heavily, took pity on me. 'Look, your friend came in with her pelvic girdle completely fractured in three places. Before we could do anything else we had to put her in an ex-fix in A&E to stabilise her. You know what one of those is, right?'

'Right,' I said. You can't ride a bike and not have seen

11

people hobbling round with their busted limbs wired back together in an external fixator.

She eyed me for a moment before she went on. 'I won't go into technical details, but basically your friend's left femur is in too many pieces to count. Her right's not as bad but it's still a mess. If whatever vehicle that hit them had run over her torso instead of her legs, she'd be dead right now. As it is, she's got nerve and blood vessel damage to both limbs. If we can't repair it—' she shrugged '—she'll lose her legs.'

I was silent for a moment. 'Would it help if you had the best orthopaedic surgeon in the country to work on her – someone who specialises in motorcycle injuries?'

She bridled at that, waving me away. 'I can assure you that the surgical team here is excellent—'

'As good as Richard Foxcroft?'

She began to form an affirmative reply on a reflex, then stopped as the name went in. 'Mr Foxcroft?' she said and the wariness was back in full force. She threw me a short, assessing gaze. 'He used to be one of the consultants here but I can't—'

I grabbed a pen from her clipboard and scrawled a rapid set of digits across the corner of a sheet of paper, ripping it off and handing it to her. 'That's his home number,' I said. 'He could be here in an hour and a half. Will you at least call him and see what he says?'

She was eyeing me now with outright suspicion, fingering the torn scrap I'd given her. The temptation was clear but she was still dubious. 'And how do I explain to Mr Foxcroft where I got hold of this?' she demanded.

I gave her my most winning smile. 'Tell him it came from his daughter,' I said.

Half the secret of being pushy is knowing when to stop pushing and let the weight of your argument roll all by itself. I went back to the waiting area prepared to dig in for the long haul.

Sam had returned successful from his coffee-gathering foray and seemed to have broken the ice a little with William. When I reappeared they were sitting talking about their own past accidents and lucky escapes, their faces sober.

It was the kind of talk bikers always seem to fall back on at times like these. Any moment now, one of them was going to show the other his scars. I hoped nobody asked to see mine or we'd be here all night.

Sam looked up at my approach, mirroring the hopeful expression I'd worn earlier myself, but I shook my head. I wasn't quite willing to share the news that Clare might be facing amputation, not quite yet. Not until the young doctor had made that phone call, at any rate.

'Where's Pauline?' I asked.

'Gone to see if she can track down Jacob,' Sam said. 'He's not answering at home or on his mobile. Pauline said she'd have a run out to Caton and see if the Range Rover's outside the house.'

The jacket pocket of William's leathers started playing the theme from *Mission: Impossible*. He got to his feet, bringing out a mobile phone, and moved away to take the call before the nurses could pounce on him. I took his seat beside Sam.

'So what are you up to these days?' Sam asked then, handing me a coffee. 'You've been right off the map since the winter.'

I nodded my thanks. 'Not much at the moment,' I said, evasive. 'Apart from working on the cottage, of course. It belongs to my parents, really. I'm just sorting out the renovations for them and in return I get to live there rent free.'

If I'd hoped that might distract him, it didn't work. He was regarding me with those sorrowful spaniel's eyes of his. Eyes that didn't miss much.

'Rumour had it you'd gone off to be a mercenary and were either dead or in prison.' He said the words with a smile that wasn't entirely present in his voice.

13

'Interesting,' I returned, neutral, dipping my nose into my coffee cup again. *And close*, I thought. 'But wrong on all counts.'

'But you're still tied up with that Meyer bloke, aren't you.'

It was posed more as an accusation than a question and there was enough hint of sulkiness in Sam's tone to bring my head round in surprise.

'If you mean Sean, then yes I am,' I agreed calmly, watching him flush and allow our eye contact to slide. 'You seem very well informed on the subject.'

He squirmed a little at that. 'Yeah well, it just seems kind of odd that this guy turns up out of the blue and next thing I know you've gone off gallivanting all over the world with him.'

I refrained from reminding Sam that, not only had I never for a moment given him any cause to believe he was more than just a friend to me, but also that I'd do as I damn well pleased.

'Sean and I were in the army together. We go way back,' I said instead, deliberate, too irritated by his moody behaviour to much care how he put that one together. 'He runs his own close protection agency now. I needed a job. He offered me one. I took it.'

What I didn't add was that my first proper assignment in the States that spring had gone terribly wrong and since then I'd been in a kind of limbo, both with Sean and with my fledgling newfound career. Over the last few months I'd felt almost as though I was watching life from the sidelines without joining in. It was not, I recognised, a state of affairs that could go on much longer.

Sam drained the last of his own coffee and crumpled the plastic cup between his fingers, taking his time over it.

'You've changed, Charlie,' he said then, rather sadly.

I glanced at him.

'Yeah well,' I said. 'Everything does.'

*

14

Sam might have been about to say more but at that moment a mismatched couple came storming down the corridor and burst into the waiting area.

The guy was short and squat with huge sloping shoulders inside his badge-covered leather jacket. He had big hands tattooed with snakes and old engine oil and he looked like a brawler. The scar from what was most likely a long-time healed glassing stretched the left-hand side of his upper lip back slightly, giving him a permanent sneer.

With him was a small woman, so slightly built she must have been able to pick her wardrobe from children's departments. She had a lot of piercings and long dark hair that was scraped back and held tight almost at her crown by a scrunchie. So many silver bangles dangled out of the sleeves of her tasselled leather jacket that she jingled when she moved.

Beside me, Sam murmured, 'Uh-oh,' under his breath and I raised an eyebrow at him. 'Slick's missus,' he added, catching the look.

I hadn't known Slick had a regular girlfriend, never mind someone who was permanent enough to qualify as a wife. He'd never behaved as though he had any commitments, that's for sure.

Now, she came storming across the waiting area heading straight for William, with the big biker stalking in her wake.

'What the fuck was he up to, William?' she demanded, her voice harsh and shrill. She was, I realised, quite a bit older than her first impression. There were deep lines etched in round her eyes and from the outer edges of her nostrils down to the corners of her mouth.

'We don't know any more than you do, Tess,' William said, sounding snappy rather than sympathetic.

Tess was shivering violently. She gave a sniff, wiping her face with the back of her hand. I winced in case the bundle of silver rings on her fingers became entangled with

15

the pewter ones in her nose but, remarkably perhaps, she came away unsnared.

'Stupid bastard,' she muttered bitterly. 'How could he do this to me? Just when he was about to do something right for once, he chucks it all away over some blonde bimbo.'

There was enough blonde in my own hair for me to feel included in that insult. I got to my feet and moved in deliberately. The big biker who'd arrived with Tess took one look at my face and put himself between us.

It would have been easy to dismiss him just as muscle, but the eyes that stared out of his slightly flattened face like two hard grey pebbles were bright with intelligence.

'Leave it, Tess,' he snapped, the way you'd speak to a dog. 'We dunno what happened to Slick.'

William looked momentarily surprised at this reasoned argument. 'Yeah, Tess. Don't say or do anything in haste you might have cause to regret at leisure,' he said, with a meaningful glance in my direction. 'Like while you're having your jaw wired back together, hm?'

A picture floated into my head of Slick's grinning, cocksure face. I would have sworn Clare had been just as disdainful of him. I could see him on that flashy gold and blue custom-painted bike of his, setting off just about every time up on the back wheel. Always close to the edge. This time over it.

'No way would Clare ever cheat on Jacob, so before you start accusing her of anything,' I said, making an attempt to keep my voice level and hearing the sting the effort of doing so was putting into it, 'you might want to think about the fact that Slick Grannell was asking for trouble.'

Tess's face darkened and she took a step forwards, bristling. With the hairstyle and the thin pointed features the overall effect was that of a Yorkshire terrier on speed. It seemed to take her a moment to realise that neither of the two men had made any moves to back her up. She stopped and glared at them, then turned back to me.

'Oh yeah?' she jeered. 'Well, if everything's so lovey-dovey between them, why isn't her old man here by her bedside?'

I didn't have an immediate answer to that one but at that moment I heard footsteps along the corridor and turned, hoping for Jacob himself or, at second best, my father. Instead, it was Pauline who hurried back into the waiting area. She'd clearly caught the tail-end of the conversation and was staring at the group of us, white-faced.

'Pauline!' I said, relieved. 'Did you find Jacob?'

'No,' she said, shaking her head. 'The house is locked up with the dogs still inside, and the car and Jacob's bike were both there but—' She hesitated a moment, uncertain. 'It's like Jacob himself has just, well, disappeared.'

Chapter Two

I sat on one of the chairs in the now deserted waiting area, absently building a stack out of the empty paper cups from the coffee I'd drunk during the last five hours.

Maybe it was just the caffeine that had sent my mind into overdrive, flitting from one subject to another without seeming able to concentrate on anything.

Still there was no news of Clare.

And no sign of Jacob.

Things hadn't been quiet, though. I hadn't quite come to blows with Slick's widow, but that was more down to the intervention of his friends than any particular self-restraint on my part.

That and the fact that the police had chosen that moment to turn up, as I'd known they were bound to do at some point. Two uniforms, laden down with handcuffs and CS gas canisters and body armour, had swaggered into the waiting area.

They hadn't seemed to notice the almost tangible resentment their arrival had caused. Everyone concerned had suddenly turned into one of the three wise monkeys. Tess and her oversize companion, I'd noticed, had slipped away almost immediately.

'Officious bastards,' William had muttered under his breath when the pair of coppers had gone away empty-handed. 'Anybody want to take a bet they're going to put all the blame on Slick for either cocking up or just riding too damned fast?' Nobody was foolish enough to take him up on the wager, least of all me.

When it became clear that they weren't going to get to speak to Clare today, William and his mates had departed. Before he left, William had given me his mobile number and asked me to let him know any developments. I'd had a momentary picture of Tess's sullen face but promised to call him, nevertheless.

Sam had gone not long after, with much the same request. Pauline had stuck it out the longest, but she finally threw in the towel around six o'clock.

'I suppose I'd better go and feed that hound of mine before he eats any more of the sofa,' she'd said, reluctant. 'You will let me know of any changes, won't you, Charlie?'

'Of course,' I'd said, smiling at her.

Now, sitting and thinking while I drank too much bad coffee, my mind went round and round what might have happened until it felt like a washing machine on a fast spin cycle. And, tucked away right at the back was the sneaking guilty suspicion that it might have all been my fault.

Or at least something that I could have prevented.

Sometime during the week before I'd seen Slick Grannell for the last time at Devil's Bridge, I'd had another visitor. One even less welcome and not just for the message he brought.

I'd been taking down the old lath-and-plaster ceilings upstairs, ready for knocking the dividing walls out. My local builder had finally deigned to put in an appearance for long enough to install a pair of whacking great RSJs to prevent the far gable collapsing into the field alongside the cottage. My aim was to have the whole of the front bedroom ceiling transferred into the skip I had parked in the lane outside before I quit for the day. Achievable, if I put both mind and muscle to it.

19

I'd been working steadily all afternoon. I told myself I was simply taking advantage of the extended daylight hours and the lack of neighbours but privately I could admit there was a lot more to it than that. The harder I worked the less time I had to think. And the better I slept at night.

Dr Yates, the psychotherapist my father had cajoled me into seeing, would have been proud. Or exasperated.

I'd heard the car coming and, as I'd done later with Sam's Norton, I'd hung out over the upstairs front window sill and watched it arrive. A large official-looking dark green Rover saloon with a large official-looking driver. I'd recognised the car for what it was without knowing the occupants and had felt the first stirrings of unease.

The passenger door opened and a slim man in his mid forties stepped out, a neat figure with an air of unassuming authority about him, in a sober dark blue suit. He tipped his head back to meet my gaze and a pair of piercing muddy green eyes locked with mine. I resisted the urge to squirm.

'Detective Superintendent MacMillan,' I greeted him coolly. 'To what do I owe the pleasure?'

'Charlie,' he returned, his voice chillingly pleasant. 'I'd like a word, if you have a moment?'

It was politely put, but to my ears it still sounded like an invitation from the Stasi. I had a sudden perverse desire to make him meet me on my own terms so I waved towards the front door. 'Be my guest,' I said. 'But you'll have to excuse the mess.'

MacMillan paused and a smile almost made its escape across the thin lips. 'Burglars?' he asked, reminding me of the first time we'd met, when two men had trashed my old flat on St George's Quay in Lancaster. They'd had a pretty good go at trashing me at the same time.

'No – builders. They steal just as much of your money and wreck the place, but at least they leave the video,' I said dryly. 'Come on up. The coffee's on.'

He left his driver in the car and made his way upstairs without undue haste. He reached the first floor and made a deceptively thorough inspection of the alterations I'd made so far in the time it took me to pour him a coffee from my filter machine and add milk and sugar.

As I handed it over his gaze settled on me, sharp and assessing to the point of unfriendliness. I felt a sudden desire to confess to something.

'You're doing some major work, Charlie,' he said. 'Have you been living here long?'

If he'd pulled my driving licence records or run the bike's registration in order to find me, he would have known that but it was interesting that he felt the need to make idle conversation. The Superintendent was not normally one for small talk.

'Only since the beginning of May,' I said, playing the game. 'I'm turning the whole place upside down.'

He smiled briefly again, little more than a flicker that came and went like a flashlight. 'I can see that.'

'No, actually that wasn't an exaggeration,' I said. 'The views are all from upstairs, so I'm opening out the first floor and moving the living room and kitchen up here. Both bedrooms and the bathroom are going downstairs.'

He frowned, eyes sliding away for a moment while he gave the plan some thought. 'Interesting,' was all he said, so I didn't really know if he approved or thought I was mad.

'You didn't come here to talk about DIY, Superintendent,' I said. I leaned against the partly-exposed stonework of the chimney breast and took a slug of my coffee. 'What have I done now?'

'Why should you think that? Although, now you come to mention it, the last time your name came up in conversation I believe you were at the top of the FBI's Most Wanted list,' he said, and he was only half joking.

When I didn't dignify that one with a reply he took a sip of his own coffee, stilled a moment as though he hadn't expected it to be any good, and took another before continuing. Then he said, 'What do you know about Devil's Bridge?'

21

Not quite what I'd been expecting. 'Devil's Bridge?' I repeated blankly. 'I never saw you as a born-again biker, Superintendent.' And when he frowned at me I added, 'It's just a biker's hang-out. Nothing heavy – no gangs, no Hell's Angels – just a lay-by near the river at Kirkby Lonsdale where we go to meet up on a Sunday. Why? Not been demoted to Traffic, have you? Who did you piss off?'

That smile nearly made it out again, but was quickly snuffed.

'On the road between Lancaster and Devil's Bridge there have been twelve fatal crashes involving motorcycles so far this year and the Chief Constable's been getting stick about it,' he said, his voice flat. 'We have reason to believe there's more to it than just bad luck or bad judgement.'

'Like what?'

'Like some kind of organised illegal road racing. We've put in a number of new fixed safety cameras along that road in the last six months. All of them have been repeatedly and systematically vandalised.'

'Safety cameras?' I said. 'That's an insult to our intelligence. Funny how the increase in cameras just happened to coincide with the regional police forces gaining control over the revenue they generate, isn't it?'

'It's a proven fact that the numbers of Killed or Seriously Injured drops where we site cameras,' MacMillan said, his tone ominous now. If I'd had more sense and less outrage I might have taken it as a warning.

'Yeah, and it's another proven fact that the numbers rise everywhere else,' I said. 'Look, Superintendent, much as I would love to stand here all day and debate the statistics on Gatso cameras with you—'

'Motorcyclists are dying, Charlie,' he said quietly, cutting me off at the knees. 'They go out and disable the cameras and then they race on the public roads, and they're dying because of it.'

I shut up for a moment and stood very still like I was trying to feel fine rain falling, wondering if the news surprised me. After a few moments I came to the conclusion that it did not. 'If you know it's going on and you don't like it, why don't you stop it?'

He came as close as he ever did to shrugging. 'We know people are dealing drugs and we don't like that either, but that doesn't mean we can stop them. These days juries tend to prefer truth to supposition.'

I gave him a shrug of my own and moved across to dump my empty coffee mug into the plastic bowl I was using for washing up. Everything in there was covered with a film of dust. 'So get something a jury will like.'

'It's not as simple as that,' he said behind me. 'We've tried to get a man in undercover but they seem to suss him out every time. What we need, I feel, is someone less – conspicuous.'

I heard the sliver of embarrassment in his tone. I stopped, put down my mug with a sharper click than I'd been intending and didn't turn round. 'No.'

MacMillan stayed silent and then I turned. 'No,' I said again, wiping my hands on a tea towel. 'Some of these people are quite possibly my friends. I won't sell them down the river for you. This is not drug dealing or prostitution or armed robbery. This is a group of lads going out on their bikes at the weekends and riding too fast. And you want me to help you prosecute them? No way.'

He pursed his lips and carefully put down his own empty cup on the window ledge next to him. 'Have you considered that you might be saving their lives?'

'Oh no,' I said quickly, shaking my head. 'Don't try emotional blackmail on me, Superintendent. You'll have to go and find someone else to do your dirty work for you.'

The policeman studied me for a few seconds, his head on one side slightly, then fractions of expression passed across his features. Disappointment and resignation. 'All right, Charlie, this was a very unofficial request and you've made your position clear.' His voice had returned to its usual clipped delivery. He nodded, just once, and that wry smile snuck out for another brief appearance. 'It's good to discover you've survived your recent experiences with your spirit intact,' he said. 'I'll see myself out.'

I followed his progress down the new bare timber staircase. Halfway down he paused and glanced back at me, almost rueful. 'I confess I had hoped for better from you, Charlie.'

'No, John,' I said, almost gently. 'You just hoped for more.'

Now, as I sat in the hospital waiting area and sweated and drank too much coffee, I recalled every word of that conversation. I hadn't consciously known that Slick Grannell was one of the group of road racers MacMillan had spoken of, but when I thought about it I realised that at some level I had been aware of it, nevertheless.

And maybe, because I'd refused to do anything about it, Slick was dead and Clare was smashed to pieces. Sometimes you have to face the consequences of your actions. God knows, I'd had to do that a few times. But it didn't compare to living with the knowledge that I'd done nothing.

The bell had just rung on the second round of me beating myself up about that when my father walked in.

Actually, that doesn't begin to do justice to his dramatic entrance. He swept in, looking tanned and healthy, with the kind of arrogance only surgeons at the top of their game can truly master. I teetered between dislike and admiration of his utter self-assurance.

An entourage of medical staff scurried in his wake including, I noticed, the young doctor to whom I'd given his number. They halted *en masse* in the corridor and let him come on towards me alone.

'So here we are again, Charlotte.' He greeted me with the slightest of wry smiles, although his voice was formal and without inflection. I couldn't really tell if I'd annoyed or gratified him by my interference.

24

I stood, realising as I did so that he and a number of those around him were dressed in surgical blues. I hid my resentment that he hadn't thought to seek me out as soon as he'd arrived by telling myself he'd gone straight to his patient instead. Never one to mistake his priorities, my father.

'How is she?' I asked.

'Being prepped for surgery,' he said, not quite answering the question. He caught my expression and sighed. 'Your friend has serious and extensive injuries, but I feel we may be able to do something for her.'

I nodded, his confident tone lifting some of the weight from my tense shoulders. It made me suddenly tired and only too aware of the lack of food and the excess of coffee I'd consumed since breakfast.

'When can I see her?'

'Now – but no more than a minute,' he said, giving me a firm stare over the top of his glasses. 'I would not normally allow it, but Clare has been asking for you quite insistently. Please bear in mind that she's received a lot of pain relief and things will be a little hazy for her.'

'Thank you,' I said. An inadequate display of gratitude but the best I could manage. 'And thank you for coming.'

'You might like to bear in mind that had I not still had some official connections with this hospital, your request would have been impossible,' he pointed out sternly. He paused, then added in a surprisingly gentle tone, 'I can't always come to your rescue, Charlotte, however much I might wish to.'

Ignoring my confusion at that, he turned and strode away. I was left to be scooped up by the junior staff in his wake. 'This way, Miss Foxcroft.'

'It's Fox,' I said automatically. I got an inquisitive glance in reply but I didn't feel like elaborating. I'd shortened my surname after I was chucked out of the army to distance myself both from my parents and my past, but the reasons were too long and too tedious to go into with strangers.

25

They took me straight down to the prep room outside the operating theatre where they were going to work on Clare. I was given plastic over-boots and a gown and told to scrub my hands before I was allowed in. I found my friend lying on a trolley amid a stack of what appeared to be retro-industrial machinery. She looked pale as milk and about eight years old.

'Charlie!' she whispered, her voice fogged and edgy with the pain. 'God, am I glad to see you.'

I moved in and clutched her icy fingers, mindful of the butterfly drip plugged into the back of her hand. She seemed to be wired up to just about everything.

She was wearing a short hospital gown that left her grossly swollen and misshapen legs uncovered. Both were bathed yellow with iodine and the bruises that were already starting to bloom. My eyes skimmed over her left thigh. It looked unnervingly flattened, like a rubber moulding from which all inner support has been removed. Both kneecaps were clearly dislocated.

I tried to avoid looking at the area around her hips. At the linked thin metal rods sticking out from her abdomen that were holding her pelvis together with all the sophistication of a Meccano set. Her modesty was protected by a piece of light sterile cloth draped across her lower body that resembled a partial collapse at a Big Top.

I swallowed and flicked back to her face.

'Don't worry, Clare. They'll fix you,' I said, my voice fierce with unshed tears. 'I promise.'

She made a sort of fluttering motion with her other hand. 'Just as long as they make it stop hurting,' she said faintly.

'They'll do that, too,' I said. I hesitated, but couldn't put off the next question. 'Where's Jacob?'

She shifted uncomfortably, gasped as a new spasm gripped her body. 'Ireland,' she managed. 'Don't know where exactly. You know how he hates mobile phones. He's travelling. Somewhere in the south. Buying trip.'

She began to cry without seeming to be aware of it, tears

spilling down her cheeks. One of the theatre nurses threw me a sharply reproachful glance.

'You'll have to leave now,' she said.

'I'll find him,' I said to Clare, ignoring the nurse. *It wasn't Jacob's fault. Thank Christ for that.* 'What the hell hit you?'

'Transit van,' she murmured. 'Determined sod.' Her eyelids fluttered closed for a moment then snapped open like she was having to fight to stay with me. 'Take care of the dogs for me, Charlie. They've been stuck in all day. Poor old Bonny. And don't let—'

'You really will have to leave,' the nurse said. 'Right now!'

'I will,' I said, answering both of them at the same time. I leaned forwards, urgent. 'Clare, what do you mean about the van? Determined to do what? Knock you off?'

The nurse grabbed my arm but I shook her loose. Another of the surgical team seized me by the shoulder. I stopped struggling.

'All right, all right, I'm going!' I snapped, allowing them to hustle me outside.

As the doors swung shut behind me I got one last look at Clare. Her eyes were closed again and she lay still and quiet as a corpse against the white pillows.

The same nurse who'd ejected me reappeared after a few minutes and passed me a set of keys. I recognised the key-ring as Clare's and realised the nurse must have been sent scurrying back up to the ward to collect it.

'Mr Foxcroft strongly suggests that you go home and get some food and some sleep,' she said. 'He'll call you as soon as she comes out of theatre.' There was a respectful note in her voice that hadn't been there previously.

I nodded. 'I'll be at Clare's,' I said, and left her the phone number on another scrap of paper. I seemed to be handing a lot of those out today.

I retrieved the Suzuki from the car park where, surprisingly

27

enough, it hadn't been either clamped or stolen. Then I rode sedately through the centre of Lancaster and back out again, heading north.

And all the time I was turning over what Clare had said. The main feeling was one of relief that, no matter what Tess might have insinuated, Jacob could not be involved. I hadn't thought so for a moment, but being able to prove it made things so much better.

And then there was the accident itself. I appreciated that, as my father had predicted, she was pumped full of morphine, but Clare had seemed surprisingly clear about it. She'd known it wasn't just a van, but a Transit, which suggested she might have a clear recall of exactly what had happened.

And then we could find out who was to blame.

I made a considerable detour back to the cottage on the way to Jacob and Clare's place. I was conscious of the passing of time and the fact that I might be missing some vital phone call from my father, but I had to have some clean clothes or even I wouldn't want to know me by morning.

My home looked shabby and depressing when I walked back in. The sledgehammer was still propped up against the wall upstairs where I'd left it and a thick layer of dust had settled over just about everything, like I'd slept for a hundred years. I picked my way across the rubble and felt the weight of the work I still had to do there lying heavy across my shoulders.

At the time I'd agreed to take the cottage on I'd desperately needed something that was physically demanding enough to occupy my mind. And, for a time, it had worked. Now, though, it just felt like a burden.

My parents had bought the place intending it to be a weekend getaway but it had proved a little too rustic for my mother's refined tastes and they'd barely used it.

The idea in offering the cottage to me was that I'd oversee the alterations. Something to keep me out of trouble – and away from Sean. By the time they found out I was actually carrying out most of the work myself, it was too late for them to do much about it.

Now, I stripped off my dirty clothes and pulled on my Dainese leathers, zipping the jacket and jeans together to form a one-piece suit and transferring all the accumulated junk from one set of pockets to the other. I stuffed clean jeans, underwear and shirts into a bag that I could clip onto the Suzuki's tank. The whole operation took less than ten minutes. Then, with a last regretful look at the debris, I pulled the door shut behind me and was back on the road.

It would keep.

Twenty minutes later I was turning into the gateway of Jacob and Clare's house near Caton village. It was big and old and rather beautiful in a faded kind of a way. A remnant of Jacob's ill-fated but prosperous marriage, the house was a sprawling hotchpotch of a place, three quarters hidden by creepers. The driveway swept down from the main road and across a field until it opened out onto a moss-coated forecourt.

Jacob dealt in classic motorbikes and antiques from the outbuildings around the house itself. Because of this he'd always been security conscious and I knew that somewhere in the trees at the top of the driveway was an alarm connected to various buzzers and bells at the house to give advance warning of approaching visitors. I'd never been able to spot its location and Jacob had always refused, laughing, to show me exactly where it was.

As it was, the dogs were already going loopy when I pulled up in front of the house and cut the engine. I could see Beezer, the wire-haired terrier, scrabbling about on the kitchen window sill, her wet nose leaving slither marks across the glass.

Before I went in I unlocked the ramshackle coach house with one of the keys from Clare's ring and wheeled the bike in alongside Jacob's classic Laverda Jota and Clare's

Ducati. And still I wondered why hadn't she ridden her own bike today? Maybe, if she had . . .

The dogs were ecstatic to see me. Poor old Bonneville, the arthritic Labrador, had suffered most from the unexpected confinement. She waddled up to me feathering her tail in anxious apology. I patted her head in forgiveness and fetched some old newspapers from the pile in the scullery to put down over the puddle. Good job the kitchen had a stone flagged floor that was easy to mop.

I left both dogs wolfing down food like they'd been starved for a month and went through the silent house to Jacob's wood-panelled study. I don't think I'd ever seen him actually do any work in there – he preferred to run his business from the scrubbed pine kitchen table – but it was at least a repository for his paperwork. Stacks of it.

I sighed and sat in the swivel captain's chair behind the desk, staring moodily at the mass of scrawled notes and shipping inventories. Somewhere in all this lot might be some clue about where Jacob was staying in Ireland, or who with. Possibly. I knew he tended to keep most things balanced in his head. Good for him. Not so good for me.

The phone was sitting half-buried under auction catalogues. I reached for it twice, pulling my hand back each time, before my courage was up enough to dial. Even so, I wasn't prepared for the call to be picked up on the second ring.

'Meyer,' said the terse voice at the other end of the line.

It shouldn't have taken me by surprise. That was the way Sean always answered his mobile but I had to draw another breath before I could launch in.

'Sean? It's Charlie.'

It was his turn for silence. Then I thought I heard a sigh that my paranoid brain translated as annoyance. 'What is it?' he said at last.

'Look, I'm sorry to trouble you on a Sunday evening—' I rushed on.

'Charlie,' he cut across me, gently this time. Definitely

30

gently. 'Don't apologise for calling me. *Never* apologise for calling me. But you sound stressed out. What's happened?'

So I told him the whole story, from Sam's mad dash to find me to Clare's news about Jacob's uncertain whereabouts. 'I need to find him but I don't know where to start,' I finished, a little lamely. 'I thought maybe Madeleine could help.'

Madeleine Rimmington worked for Sean's close protection agency, mainly handling electronic security, and there was very little she couldn't coax out of a computer. If anyone could track down Jacob, she could.

'Hang on,' Sean said. 'She's here. I'll ask.' And there was the sound of muffled voices in the background.

I recognised the flush that rode over me as jealousy, pure and simple. In my head I knew there was nothing going on between Madeleine and Sean. That there never had been. But in my heart I wanted to scratch her eyes out.

When he came back on the line I couldn't hold back a snitty comment. 'She working overtime?'

'No. Actually, she and Dominic are round for dinner,' Sean said evenly, amusement in his voice now. 'He's in the kitchen – as you would expect. We're having duck. Would you like to speak to him?'

The closest I'd come to actually meeting Madeleine's chef boyfriend was looking at a photo of him. I wouldn't have any idea what to say to him over the phone, as Sean very well knew.

'No,' I muttered quickly, ashamed and trying to make light of it. 'Why would I want to talk to a dead duck?'

Sean laughed, a momentary brightness. Then I heard a woman's voice in the background and he was all business again. 'Madeleine says she'll get straight onto it as soon as she gets home later,' he said. 'Meanwhile, does Jacob keep an address book? If so you might want to try and pinpoint any Irish-sounding contacts and give them a call. If he's in the south, look for phone numbers that start zero-zero-three-five-three. What's he doing over there?'

31

I wondered briefly why it didn't surprise me in the slightest that Sean would know international phone codes off the top of his head.

'Clare mentioned a buying trip. He's probably heard about some private classic bike collection coming up for sale and he'll have nipped over to snap the whole lot up,' I said with a smile.

'Hm,' Sean said, noncommittal. 'If he's hired a van to go over that might explain why his car's still there. Look, he must have a fax machine there. Get a list of likely-sounding contacts to me as soon as you can and I'll have someone check out the local hire companies first thing in the morning. Meanwhile, change the outgoing answering machine message, just in case he phones home. Just tell him to call you urgently and leave him your mobile number. And for heaven's sake leave the damned thing switched on.'

I thought of my recently-acquired mobile which was currently languishing in the pocket of my leather jacket.

'OK,' I said meekly. 'I keep forgetting about it.'

'I know,' he said, and I could tell he was smiling again. 'Whenever I try and call, it's always switched off.'

He'd called. The realisation pleased me far more than it should have done. I found myself grinning silently to the empty room.

'Oh and Charlie,' he added, more sober now, 'when you do finally get hold of Jacob, you might want to work out what you're going to tell him about what Clare was doing out with this guy Slick in the first place.'

'I know,' I said, stripped of my smile. 'I'm hoping I won't have to – that by the time Jacob gets home Clare can tell him herself. I'm sure it's not how it looks.'

He paused, almost a hesitation. 'I realise I don't know them half as well as you do, but you really don't think there might be anything in what this Tess girl said – that Clare was fooling around while Jacob was away?'

'No,' I said, immediate and adamant.

'Think about it for a moment. There was quite a difference in their ages and—'

'No,' I said again. 'You're right, Sean. You don't know them well at all. Trust me on this. She wouldn't cheat on Jacob. And certainly not with a waster like Slick.'

'I admire your loyalty to your friends,' he said dryly. 'There've been times when I wish you'd had the same kind of blind faith in me.'

I put the phone down slowly after we'd broken the connection and leaned back in the swivel chair. *Blind faith*, Sean had said. But it was more than that. It was utter conviction.

But even so there was a finger of doubt poking at me. After all, however devoted Jacob and Clare were to each, and however much I protested on her behalf, Clare had still gone off willingly with Slick while Jacob was conveniently out of the picture in another country.

Chapter Three

That night I dreamed of Sean.

It was a kind of buried longing I seemed only able to give free rein to when my subconscious was in control. Talking to him again, hearing his voice and picturing the face behind it as he spoke, had provoked a reaction so strong it frightened me.

The job in Florida back in March was supposed to have been a new beginning for us, an easy couple of weeks in the sun where we could relax in each other's company. But it hadn't turned out that way.

I'd spent four nightmare days on the run with my teenage charge, all the while believing Sean was dead. And then, when I'd found out he was still very much alive, I'd had to stand by and watch him commit what was little more than cold-blooded murder. I'd had to kill to survive, but not for personal gratification. And not for revenge either, however close I may have come to it.

Sean had accused me of not having faith in him, but it had been five months since our return and I was still trying to find a way to bridge the gulf between us. He'd pulled away from me, or maybe it was me who'd pulled away from him. I hadn't even felt able to ask him to come to me now, when I needed him. And – worse – he hadn't offered.

Then, from somewhere above me a small sound broke

through the outer layers and crashed through my unconscious mind like a falling stone.

I came bounding out of sleep much too fast, with my heart screaming. My eyes snapped open allowing the darkness and silence to pour in. For a long suspended second I struggled there, locked between dreams and reality. Then the sound that had woken me came again, and it was reality that elbowed its way to the fore.

Someone was moving about downstairs. Why on earth the dogs weren't kicking up an unholy stink I had no idea. I was a light enough sleeper to have heard the driveway alarm, too – if it had gone off – which meant no one had tripped it.

For a moment my hopeful brain formed Jacob's name and I got as far as opening my mouth to call out to him. Sense kicked in and I shut it again.

My eyes were adjusting to the gloom all the time. I'd left the curtains open and the moon threw a trickle of thin silver-grey light into the room. I swung my legs out of bed and carefully picked up the old-fashioned alarm clock from the bedside table, squinting at the luminous figures. It was a little after two-thirty in the morning. I suppressed a groan as I groped for my shirt and jeans.

My father had finally called just before midnight with the news that Clare was out of surgery and doing 'as well as could be expected', and I'd crawled into one of Jacob and Clare's spare beds soon after.

I'd used the time before he'd rung to hunt for any sign of Jacob's Irish contacts, as Sean had suggested, feeling like a thief as I'd systematically gone through Jacob's desk and papers. I'd bunged the resulting half-dozen-name list down the fax to Sean's office number. Now it was up to him.

Unless, of course, the stealthy intruder downstairs at this moment was indeed Jacob.

I padded on silent bare feet across the polished floorboards and slowly pulled open the bedroom door, praying

35

it wouldn't creak. At the end of the landing I could see the faint glow of a light on somewhere below. As I tiptoed towards the stairs I reached out and picked up a copy of a bike magazine that was lying on a chest of drawers and took that with me.

I descended with controlled haste, keeping to the outside of the treads. As I went I rolled the magazine up into a tight baton with its thick spine to the outside.

In the hallway downstairs I halted, listening. Over to my left the grandfather clock against the kitchen wall ticked sonorously. Under the study door a thin band of light was showing and I could hear movement inside.

Suddenly, the door opened and a man walked out so quickly we nearly collided. I don't know who was more shocked by the abruptness of the encounter but he let out a surprised yelp and took an instinctive swipe at my head.

I ducked under the clumsy blow and jabbed him in the Adam's apple with the coiled end of the magazine. He staggered back, choking, hands up to his throat. I pivoted sideways and brought the rigid edge of the spine slashing up, hard, onto the inner bone of his right elbow, then jabbed again on the backstroke, this time to the collection of nerves centred in his solar plexus. If it had been a sword I was holding, I would have run him through.

As it was, my attacker went down with a crash, overturning a chair. One of the dogs – probably Beezer – finally began to bark behind the kitchen door, frenzied little yaps that sounded neither big nor menacing. More's the pity.

I flicked on the lights in the hallway and found that my intruder was a young man with longish dark hair, wearing a T-shirt and bike leather trousers. He'd been carrying a backpack that he'd dropped when he'd fallen and he was currently trying to clutch at all the points I'd hit with the hand that still worked. I waited until he had the breath to speak. At least I'd brought something to read.

'Fuck me,' he gasped eventually. It was more of an exclamation than an instruction. There was the faintest trace of an Irish lilt to his voice and something about his face was familiar, but I couldn't place him. Certainly not enough to be able to justify him creeping about in Jacob and Clare's house in the middle of the night, that's for sure.

'Who are you?' I said.

'Fuck that!' he countered hotly. 'Who the hell are *you*?'

'If you'd just answer the question,' I said mildly, rolling the magazine up again, 'we'd get along a lot better.'

'You could be anyone,' he said, wary, rubbing at his throat and not taking his eyes off what I was doing with my hands. 'I'm not telling you anything until I know what the hell you're doing here.'

I sighed. If there was one thing my time in the States had taught me, it was how to communicate with stroppy teenagers in terms they'd understand. This one looked twenty at a push, but I'd be willing to bet he wouldn't be allowed into a nightclub without having to show his ID.

'Tell me what I want to know,' I said, conversational, leaning over him, 'or I'll hit you again.'

He reared back, shocked, then a gleam of laughter appeared and a big grin broke through his natural mistrust. His shoulders came down a fraction.

'Well if you're a burglar, you're the prettiest thief I've seen in a long time,' he said. 'OK. My name's Jamie – Jamie Nash.'

'Nash?' I repeated, confused. Jacob's name was Nash. 'But—'

He nodded. 'That's right,' he said. 'Jacob's my dad.'

I put the coffee down on the kitchen table in front of Jamie and sat opposite, picking up my own cup. He smiled in thanks and, now I knew the connection, I could see Jacob's smile there, Jacob's eyes.

The family resemblance was clear, but Jacob had never mentioned having any children. He rarely talked about his ill-fated marriage to Isobel but I suppose it wouldn't have been kind to do so in front of Clare.

37

'How's the arm?' I asked.

'I may play the piano again,' he said, rueful, flexing it gingerly, 'but I wouldn't bet on it. Where did you learn to hit people like that? With a rolled up magazine, for Christ's sake.'

'Self-defence classes,' I said shortly and didn't add that I'd been the one teaching them. 'It means I'm classed as having had training and if I'd beaten you up with a chair leg they'd have thrown the book at me.' I smiled at him as I took a sip of coffee. 'This way you're the one who gets laughed out of court.'

He snorted. 'Remind me never to ask you to housetrain a puppy,' he said. 'You'd beat the poor little bastard to death inside the first week.'

'So you don't know whereabouts in Ireland your dad might be?' I asked.

He'd just taken a drink of his own coffee and he shook his head vigorously and swallowed before he spoke. 'Didn't even know he was away,' he said. 'Ironic, isn't it? He's over there and I'm over here.'

Beezer jumped up onto Jamie's lap and bounced up and down a few times, trying to lick his chin. He stared at the terrier without really seeing her, ruffling her ears in a reflex gesture. 'Shit this is bad,' he muttered. He glanced at me with an almost fearful curiosity. 'About Clare, I mean. How is she?'

I repeated my father's diagnosis, such as it was. 'Do you know her well?'

His gaze passed over me briefly, then slid away. 'Not really,' he said with an awkward shrug. 'I haven't really seen that much of Dad since he and Mum split up.'

Difficult to know how he'd be expected to feel about his father's girlfriend, I suppose. Particularly as she was far closer to Jamie's age than to Jacob's.

I'd told him only the bare bones of the story. That Jacob was away somewhere in Ireland and that Clare had been in a bike accident in which another biker had also died. I didn't tell him the rumours about what might or might not have been going on between Clare and Slick. As it was he'd taken the news in pale silence.

'So,' I said, sitting back. 'Your turn. What were you doing breaking in to your father's house at half-two in the morning?'

Jamie grinned. 'Got in to Heysham earlier this evening and went round the town with a few mates after we got off the boat,' he said. 'Then—'

'Boat?'

'Ferry,' he explained. 'From Ireland.' And when I still looked blank he added, 'That's where my mother's family hail from, so that's where we went back to. Just outside Coleraine. In the north.'

I reached for my coffee cup again and waved him on.

He shrugged again, still fussing with the terrier. 'Well, I was supposed to be meeting someone but they didn't turn up,' he said, pulling a rueful face, 'so then I didn't have anyplace to stay.'

A girl, I surmised. *And he'd been hoping to get lucky.* 'And?'

'And nothing,' he said with the same kind of easy smile that Jacob was master of. 'I suppose I just thought why should I shell out for a hotel when my dad's place was just up the road, so I thought maybe I'd come and crash here.'

He hesitated, possibly realising that use of the word 'crash' was not the best choice in these circumstances.

'So you bypassed the drive alarm and broke in through the study window,' I said dryly, draining my coffee cup and standing. 'Don't they have doorbells in Ireland?'

'I didn't want to wake anyone,' he said, smiling easily. 'I helped Dad dig that sensor in one summer when I was about ten. And the study window's always had a dodgy catch on it.' He tipped the terrier back onto the floor and got to his feet, too.

'Besides,' he added, following me out into the hallway,

39

'when I saw the car and the bikes were all here I wasn't expecting them to be away – or that I'd be jumped by Lara bloody Croft on the way in.'

I led the way upstairs, turning off lights as we went. At the airing cupboard on the landing I dug out sheets and pillows and thrust them into Jamie's arms, ignoring his surprised expression. I think he was probably hoping I'd offer to make the bed up for him. His mother, I reckoned, had a lot to answer for.

Jamie made straight for the second room on the left, pushing open the door and stepping inside before I could stop him.

'Er, Jamie,' I called sharply. He stopped. 'That's where I'm sleeping and I'm afraid you aren't invited.'

He cocked his head in my direction, taking in my rumpled shirt and jeans in a single sweeping glance that seemed to suggest he was giving me serious consideration. 'Oh well, if you're sure,' he murmured, backing out. 'Although, as that used to be my room, technically speaking *I'm* not the one who's in the wrong bed.'

For a moment I considered offering to move, but he was already grabbing for the handle of the door opposite instead. I shrugged, but slid the bolt on my door once I was safely inside. Then I climbed back into bed and slept like the dead for what remained of the night.

I woke around seven the next morning, courtesy of my in-built alarm clock. A lazy mist hung over the trees and the river, promising another long hot day ahead. I glanced down onto the forecourt and saw a snazzy little race-replica Honda RVF400 with a Northern Irish plate on it parked up next to Jacob's old Range Rover. Nice bike. It seemed that in amongst the rest of the genes, Jacob had also passed on his love of biking to his son.

I slipped into the bathroom first, then climbed into my leather jeans and a clean shirt, glad I'd made that detour. I looked in briefly to the bedroom Jamie had taken but he was spark out, lying diagonally across the bed in a face-down sprawl.

I went downstairs and let the dogs out, then rang the hospital again for news of Clare. Comfortable, they told me, which seemed absurdly optimistic of someone with as many broken bones as she had.

The sun was already throwing out warmth, beginning to heat up the stones of the old house. I drank my first coffee of the day sitting out on the terrace in peaceful solitude, soaking it up. The events of yesterday seemed remote, like a dream. I remembered my conversation with Sean and almost wondered if I'd imagined that, too.

Away to my right came the sound of water running down the drainpipe from the bathroom. Sleeping beauty awakes. I went back inside to put a fresh pot of coffee on.

I was halfway through filling a cafetière when the drive alarm went off. The dogs scrambled out of their beds, barking furiously like they'd been practising the drill. The combination of the two made me jump and slosh hot water onto both the kitchen floor and down the leg of my jeans. Good job they were leather or I'd have been scalded.

When I looked out of the window onto the forecourt, it was just in time to see the post van pull up outside.

'Oh yes, very dangerous *he* looks,' I told the dogs, sarky, as the mail dropped through the letterbox in the front door. They whined and avoided my gaze and looked embarrassed. I wondered if it was the alarm rather than the vehicle the dogs reacted to, like some Pavlovian experiment. Was that why they hadn't kicked up a fuss last night?

Jamie arrived just as the coffee was brewed. He didn't wait to be invited but helped himself, retrieving a mug from the cupboard next to the kitchen door without hesitation.

'Know your way around, don't you?' I said, nodding to the mug.

He paused, startled for a moment, then he grinned at me. 'That's where they've always been kept,' he said. 'Dad's nothing if not a creature of habit.'

41

He was wearing the same leather bike trousers he'd had on the night before, and a clean T-shirt with a designer label on the front. He pulled out a chair from the kitchen table, turned it round and sat astride it, leaning his forearms on the back.

'I've rung about Clare and they tell me I can go in and see her this morning,' I said. 'You want to come?'

He frowned for a moment, warring emotions flitting across his face.

'It's not compulsory,' I put in mildly. 'She may not even be awake enough to talk to.'

'No, no, I'll come,' he said quickly. He nodded towards the kitchen window where we could just see his Honda outside and gave me a smirk. 'If you're feeling brave enough I can give you a lift on the back of my bike.'

'Yeah, I can well imagine that getting on the back of your bike would be a pretty quick way to a hospital,' I returned with an answering smile. 'But no thanks – I prefer to ride my own.'

Jamie watched rather anxiously as I wheeled the Suzuki out of the coach house. He only relaxed when he recognised the bike for what it was and worked out how much smaller it was than his own four hundred. Size matters – it's a guy thing.

Like my two-fifty, Jamie's bike was no longer a current model but it was in good nick, with a titanium exhaust can and an after-market steering damper.

Jamie already had his helmet on and the Honda revving as I locked up. I kicked my bike's engine over and, just to give it half a chance to warm through, took my time shrugging my way into the borrowed backpack containing the nightie and washbag full of bits and pieces that I'd thought Clare might appreciate. As it was, Jamie barely let me get my gloves on before he was away up the drive.

'Prat,' I muttered under my breath. I had no intention of

racing him. Not when it meant going hand-to-hand with a load of dopey car drivers in the Monday morning rush-hour, that's for sure. By the time I reached the top of the drive and pulled out into the stream of traffic on the main road, he was nowhere to be seen.

Maybe it was with the realities of the accident well forward in my mind, but I found myself riding more defensively than usual. A couple of vehicles behind me was a Ford Transit van with two men inside. Nothing sinister in itself, but Clare's words in the hospital came back and made me twitchy. At the next opportunity I toed the Suzuki down a gear, hit the narrow power band, and hopped three cars further up the line.

I'd just pulled back in when there was a flash of high-beam headlights in my right-hand mirror. Three big bikes came thrashing past a rake of traffic to slot in alongside me with the neatness and precision of jet fighters.

I glanced over automatically. The lead bike was an Aprilia RSV 1000, all dressed up in race replica paintwork that made it look like a cigarette packet on wheels.

Behind that was a two-year-old special edition Ducati 996, with carbon trim on the exhaust can and the fairing.

Bringing up the rear of the tight formation was a sleek Kawasaki ZX-9R in lurid green. The riders were all wearing leathers to suit the bikes and they had their heads turned in my direction but the iridium coating on their visors gave them a completely blank stare. All I could see was my own reflection.

I nodded, the usual friendly acknowledgement of one member of the fraternity to another. They totally ignored the greeting, staring at me for a moment longer. Then, as if at some signal, the trio blasted away down the white line like they were overtaking a slow-moving mule train, leaving me feeling small and pedestrian and ever so slightly insulted in their wake.

If I'd bothered to wonder where the three bikers were

heading, it didn't take long for me to find out. About two of them, at least.

When I got to the hospital I found the Ducati and the Kawasaki both in the car park. They had pulled up on either side of Jamie's machine, dwarfing the little four hundred like schoolground bullies. The Kawasaki rider was still on board. He was big enough for the bike to look small under him. Through the partly open visor I recognised William's features, cheeks squeezed by the foam padding inside his helmet.

The Ducati rider had dismounted, leaving his own lid perched on top of the tank. There was so much carbon fibre covering the body of the bike it looked like it was covered in tweed.

The rider was small and dapper, in one-piece leathers that were obviously made-to-measure rather than off the peg. He had a thin pencil moustache that circled his chin, and dark hair that was spiked into a blond mini mohican along his crown. I wondered how on earth he kept his hair-style intact under a helmet when I could never preserve mine.

He was currently standing nose-to-nose with Jamie. He had to rise up on his toes to do so. His back was towards me but their discussion didn't exactly look friendly.

I ran the Suzuki in alongside them and cut the engine but they hardly seemed to notice me. There was no sign of the guy who'd been on the cigarette packet Aprilia.

'You're in or you're out, mate – now more than ever,' the Ducati rider was saying, pointing an accusing finger. His voice sounded tight but it was difficult to tell just how wound he was without being able to see his face.

'I'm in, Paxo, believe me!' Jamie protested. He was trying not to sound desperate and not quite succeeding. He flicked his eyes nervously in my direction and lowered the volume a touch. 'I just can't believe you're still going ahead after what's happened.'

'We're too far along to back out now,' William said, his

tone placid, almost lazy. 'Life's a risk. You either take it or you may as well just give up now.'

Life's a risk. I remembered my defence of idiots like him to MacMillan and felt my anger climb. So it seemed that Slick had been road racing when he'd had his final crash, despite having a passenger on board. I got off the bike and yanked my helmet off, glaring at Jamie. He wouldn't meet my gaze.

'Does it mean nothing to you that your mate Slick's dead because of what you lot have been up to?' I demanded bitterly. 'Not to mention the fact that Clare might still lose her legs?

'Now look—' Jamie began earnestly.

All I did was turn my head slightly in his direction. He shut up.

'When I spoke to Clare yesterday she reckoned they were deliberately brought down,' I went on, my attention back on William and the Ducati rider Jamie had called Paxo. 'Who have you been annoying enough that they want you dead?' It was overly melodramatic, but I was aiming for shock value.

'We don't know what you're on about, Charlie,' William said evenly, but I hadn't missed the little anxious glances they'd shared.

My patience didn't so much run out then as it petered to a stop. I hadn't expected to be taken into anyone's confidence but being treated like I was stupid was always going to sting.

'OK,' I said wearily, shrugging. 'Whatever.' I began to turn away towards the entrance.

'Hey Charlie, hold up there, will you?' Jamie called after me. I stopped and looked back. 'Just give me ten minutes,' he said to Paxo, his tone close to pleading. 'Wait here, yeah? I'll be right back.'

Paxo cocked his head towards William. The big guy lifted one shoulder in lacklustre assent.

'Ten minutes,' Paxo warned, making a big show of

45

checking his watch. 'Then we're out of here. With or without you.'

Jamie gave them an anxious nod and hurried after me.

'Funny how you never mentioned last night that you run with the same crowd as Slick,' I said as we walked into the hospital reception area.

'You never asked,' he said.

I eyed him for a moment. That much was true. But the very fact that he hadn't volunteered the information as soon as I'd mentioned Slick's name was suspicious in itself.

'I'm asking now,' I said. 'Bit off your home ground, aren't you?'

'William works for one of the ferry companies and they come over to Ireland a lot,' Jamie said after a moment's pause. 'That's where I met them. They're a fun bunch to ride with, that's all.'

'Oh, a laugh a minute, by the looks of it,' I said. 'So, what the hell was that all about?'

He shrugged like he was trying to shake off a hand on his shoulder. 'Oh, nothing,' he said lightly.

'It didn't look like nothing,' I said. 'You want to end up like Slick? You carry on using the roads for a racetrack you're heading the right way. It will catch up with you in the end – just like it did with Slick.'

Just for a moment there was a flicker across Jamie's good-looking face.

'You don't know what the fuck you're talking about, Charlie,' he said, the smile belying the words. 'Until you do, why don't you keep your nose out of it, OK?'

It was my turn to shrug. 'It's your funeral.'

Being inside the hospital had the same tightening effect on my nerves that it had the night before. I couldn't quite pin down what it was about the place that made me so jumpy. Maybe it was just the total loss of control I had difficulty coping with.

I knew from bitter experience that if you came in here as

anything other than a visitor suddenly any personal freedom was stripped away. Complete strangers could come and rob you of your dignity any time they felt like it. They governed your sleep, your food and water, and your pain.

Making a conscious effort to relax, I led Jamie on towards the waiting area I'd occupied the night before. From there a nurse directed us to the female orthopaedic ward.

The male nurse at the ward entrance looked surprised when I mentioned her name. 'She's a popular lass today,' he remarked. And when we neared her bedside I found out what he meant.

Sean Meyer was sitting in a plastic visitor's chair next to Clare's bed and was chatting to her like it was the most natural thing in the world that he should be there.

I stopped dead and they both looked up at us. Clare was marginally less pale than she had been the night before, but it was a close-run thing.

They'd erected a framework around her bed like a minimalist four-poster. Wires stretched from it to pins that appeared, from this angle, to actually go right through her legs, like she was some kind of suspended executive toy. The equipment seemed medieval in its crudeness. I could almost believe that the pins I could see sticking out of her torso were penetrating her body completely, impaling her to the bed.

Jamie was silent next to me. When I glanced at him he was staring fixedly at Clare. He seemed to sense my gaze and looked away quickly. But for that unguarded moment his expression had been on full view and there was no mistaking its stricken quality. So he wasn't quite as hard-faced about all this as his mates had been.

Then Sean stood up and I'm ashamed to admit that my attention was entirely diverted. He looked exactly the same as he had the last time I'd seen him. Tall and wide without ever being bulky, he nevertheless filled the narrow space between the bed and the window, exceeded it, even.

47

He was wearing black jeans and a black v-necked T-shirt that emphasised the shifting layers of muscle across his chest and shoulders but I knew it wasn't intentional. He dressed more for comfort and necessity. There was no vanity to Sean.

'Hi,' I said, uncertain and a little defensive when I should have been nothing but grateful. 'I didn't expect you to come.'

I found I was clutching my Arai helmet against my body like a shield. My legs had started to tremble and I had the horrible feeling I was just about to burst into tears but I couldn't understand why.

'I know you didn't,' he said, eyeing me closely. He turned back to Clare with one of those slow smiles of his. 'Would you excuse us for a moment?'

'Of course,' Clare said, her cheeks dimpling.

Sean just gave me time to dump my stuff down on an empty chair before he took my arm.

Jamie, meanwhile, had kept his head down during the exchange. Now, he edged round the pair of us and sat down quickly in the chair Sean had just vacated. I wasn't sure if I needed to introduce Jacob's son to Clare, but Sean was already ushering me towards the door and I didn't get the chance.

We got as far as the waiting area where I'd spent so much time the previous day before he stopped and put both hands on my upper arms, turning me to face him.

'Are you OK?' he said, those near-black eyes skimming over my face like a laser targeting system.

'Yes, no – I don't know,' I said helplessly and my eyes began to fill. I shook my head, annoyed with myself. 'Sorry, I've been fine until now.'

'It's OK,' he said gently. 'It's not the first time you've been told someone you care for is dead. It was bound to be a shock.'

That was enough to set me off. I swallowed a couple of times, fighting it, but when he pulled me towards him I

48

barely resisted, allowing him to gather me up and hold me close. Sean was too angular to cuddle up to, but being in his arms made me lightheaded with both tension and relief.

Those clever hands began to smooth up and down my spine, one of his habitual gestures. He traced the indentations of my vertebrae with his fingertips through the thin cotton of my shirt, like he was reading the signs of my body by Braille.

It was supposed to comfort, but it was making me only too aware of the length of time since we'd last done this, and how much I wanted to do it again.

Maybe it was recognition of that need, of the temptation to give in to it that made me stiffen. Footsteps sounded loud in the corridor behind me and poured a further mental bucket of cold water on my thoughts. I pulled back a little so I could see his face.

'When did you get here?' I said, striving for the mundane. 'Have they told you anything about how she is?'

He smiled as though he knew exactly what had been going through my mind. 'I set off early this morning. I only got here about ten minutes ago,' he said. 'Clare said there's been quite a bit of nerve damage in her legs. They've been pretty candid with her about the fact that it might or might not all come back. They haven't told me anything but then,' he added with a wry smile, 'bearing in mind who one of her consultants is, I don't think he'd be inclined to take me into his confidence, do you?'

I frowned. My father and Sean had never been on the best of terms. Not least because the uncovering of our clandestine affair had been part of my abrupt and ignominious exit from the military. I could have pointed out any of this to Sean, but instead I felt the need to defend my father.

'Yesterday they were talking about the possibility of Clare losing her legs,' I said flatly. 'Whatever other failings he might have, my father is a bloody good surgeon.'

Sean pulled a face that could have been smile or grimace, take your pick. 'I have cause to know that,' he said wryly, rotating his shoulder a fraction, 'better than anyone.'

The silence beyond that stretched a moment too long and I rushed to fill it.

'Any news of Jacob?'

'One of the guys you found a number for is based in Wicklow, right down in the southeast corner,' he said, not commenting on my abrupt swerve of subject. 'He reckons he'll probably see Jacob later this week at an auction – if we haven't managed to get in touch with him before then.'

I nodded, jamming my hands into the pockets of my leather jeans so they wouldn't be lured into reaching for him again. 'How long do you plan to stay?' I asked.

He almost smiled, his body suddenly very still. 'As long as you need me.'

Release nearly had my eyes closing. 'Thank you,' I said, awkward but sincere. 'I really didn't expect you to drop everything and come rushing up here.' *But I wanted you to.*

'It's OK, Charlie,' he said. 'It's not a sign of weakness to need a shoulder to cry on every now and again.'

Sean had been through hell and back more times than I could count. The last time, in the States, he'd come within a whisker of execution and yet he would not – could not – talk about it, let alone cry. I turned and looked at him, dubious.

'Isn't it?' I said.

Chapter Four

When we got back to the ward Jamie had pulled his chair up close to the bedside and was sitting leaning forwards intently and holding Clare's hand. He jumped up looking flustered when he saw us.

'So who's the kid?' Sean asked quietly while we were still too far away for him to overhear.

'Jacob's son, apparently.'

He raised his eyebrows and I shrugged. 'Don't look at me,' I muttered. 'Until I caught him breaking in at some ungodly hour this morning, I didn't know Jacob had a son, either.'

Clare smiled warmly at us as we drew nearer and held out her hand to me.

'Charlie,' she said, giving my fingers a fierce, heartfelt squeeze. 'Thank you. For everything.'

'No problem,' I said, taking the chair Sean unstacked for me, alongside another for himself. We sat on the other side of the bed, facing Jamie across Clare's wired limbs. 'You were right about Bonny, by the way.'

She frowned. 'What about her?'

'Last night,' I said. 'You asked me to go and look after the dogs because they'd been stuck in all day. Don't you remember?'

She shook her head. 'Wow,' she said, looking round at us, 'I must have been completely out of it.'

'But you remember telling me about the van?' I said.

'Van?'

'You talked about the Transit van that hit you,' I persisted. 'You called him a determined sod.'

Sean glanced at me sharply but my eyes were on Clare's confused face.

'I-I can't remember,' she said, fretful. Her colour had begun to rise.

'Leave her alone,' Jamie said, tense. 'It'll come back to her when she's ready.'

I sat back and looked from Jamie's set expression to Clare's embarrassed one. Not the right time to push it.

'OK, OK,' I said, contrite. 'You're right. I'm sorry. I just want to get to the bottom of what happened.' Even then I couldn't entirely let it go, but I smiled to soften the question down. 'I thought you hated being a pillion passenger.'

'I do, but what I *do* remember is that the bloody Ducati wouldn't start and I'd promised to go up to Devil's Bridge,' Clare said, smiling back at me now, although a little faintly. 'Slick arrived – to see Jacob about some parts, I think – just as I was struggling with it and he offered me a lift.' She shrugged and lay back carefully against the pillows. 'Just bad timing, I suppose.'

It was more than bad timing, but even though I didn't voice the comment she regarded me anxiously. 'There are going to be all sorts of rumours flying round about this, aren't there?'

There already are, I thought, but what I actually said was: 'I expect so.'

She reached out and put her hand on my arm. 'Sean's told me you're looking for Jacob,' she said. 'When you find him, please don't say anything to him about Slick. I-I'd rather explain things to him myself.'

It was the note of desperation in her voice that rocked me and for a moment I didn't speak, straightening in my chair.

'Clare – what is there to tell him?' I demanded. *And what is there that you're not telling me?*

She seemed to realise she'd said too much. Her lips thinned and the lower one began to tremble. As if on cue, a nurse came bustling up and swept us all with an accusing glare.

'Are you all right, Clare?' she asked. 'Can I get you something for the pain?' And when Clare nodded she rounded on the rest of us, her tone ominous. 'I think it might be best if you all left now,' she said. 'I don't think you appreciate that Clare's been through major surgery and she needs to rest.'

We rose obediently. Sean bent to kiss her cheek and she gave him a quick hug. Jamie just offered a cross between a wave and salute. I reached down to squeeze Clare's hand but she gripped it, hard, and held on.

'I just need to speak to Charlie for a moment longer,' she said pleadingly to the nurse, not letting go of my hand. 'Just a moment. I promise.'

The nurse scowled a little more, but the heat went right out of it when the force of Clare's smile hit her. Clare could do that to people.

'All right then,' she said with a grudging indulgence. And to me, more sharply: 'Then you're out, yes?'

'OK,' I agreed meekly and sat down again.

Sean met my eyes fleetingly as he began to shepherd Jamie towards the doorway. There was everything and nothing in that brief glance.

Clare waited until they were well out of earshot before she spoke again, tracking them anxiously.

'Charlie, I need you to do something for me. For us, really,' she said, keeping her voice low so I had to lean towards her to hear it properly.

'Name it,' I said, without hesitation.

Clare hesitated a moment. She let go of me and toyed with her nightie instead. She was wearing an elderly sack in faded cotton with the words 'hospital garment' running through it in red and blue letters so that from a distance it looked like a pattern. Stops people stealing them, I suppose. I was suddenly glad I'd brought her her own stuff.

'I need you to look after Jamie for me,' she said in a rush.

'What?' It wasn't quite what I was expecting. I sat up, my face blank. 'Why?' I said.

She flushed a little. 'He's going to Ireland with a group of bikers at the end of this week,' she said. 'Some trip Slick was organising, I think. I-I don't want him to go.'

I frowned, remembering the conversation I'd had with Jamie last night. 'But he's *from* Ireland,' I said. 'I can't stop him going home.'

'It's not that,' Clare said, her face miserable. 'It's the people he's going with. They're, well, they're like Slick. They ride like a bunch of total idiots and they're going to get him killed. Jamie hasn't had his licence for that long. He's on a bike half their size and he won't admit he can't really keep up.' She gave me a wan smile. 'You know what these fellers are like.'

I did. Clare was ferociously quick. She'd left more than one bike wreck behind her as a testament to the foolish assumption of less experienced – and usually male – riders that any corner she could take, they could take faster.

'Why don't you ask him yourself?' I said. I nodded to the mechanical construction that was holding her bones together. 'At the moment, he might just listen to you.'

She shook her head. 'I've always been something of the wicked stepmother to Jamie,' she said with candour. She was folding the edge of the starched sheet over and over, her eyes fixed on her fingers. The knuckles of her right hand were bruised solid purple like she'd been in a fight. 'I mean, Jacob and Isobel's marriage was history long before I came on the scene but when I did I suppose Jamie knew they weren't ever going to get back together again. He's always resented me a little for that, I think.'

'So what do you want me to do?'

She stilled a moment, like she hadn't thought it through that far, then shrugged, looking close to tears again. 'I

54

don't know,' she said, back to restless. 'I suppose I was hoping that, if you can't stop him going with them, you could, maybe, even go with him?'

It was said hesitantly enough to turn it into a question, with a little wince at the end as though she was expecting me to shout her down.

I didn't shout. I sat still for probably five full seconds wondering how to ask when my friend had developed this massive maternal instinct for someone else's child. And why.

Clare took my silence for refusal. 'Please, Charlie,' she said, reaching to grab my hand again. 'Look, you're a bodyguard now, aren't you? So – I'll hire you! Name your price.'

She said the words with a big smile but there was panic in her voice and cowering behind her eyes. Across the other side of the ward the nurse's head snapped up like she could sniff the patient distress in the air. She started to move purposefully in our direction.

'Charlie, please!' Clare said quickly, sounding desperate now. The panic had climbed out of the background and was in full flight across her face. Her fingers gripped tight. They were unnaturally cold.

'I want you out, now!' the nurse snapped with thunderous restraint. 'I will not have you upsetting my patients.'

I stood up, ignoring her, and summoned up my best reassuring smile for Clare.

'It's OK,' I told her. 'I'll look after him.'

It wasn't until I was heading for the ward doorway that I wondered how on earth I was going to make good on that promise.

Sean was waiting for me, leaning against the wall in the corridor. Of Jamie there was no sign.

'She OK?' Sean asked, falling into step beside me.

'Mm,' I said, still distracted. 'She's just hired me to act as Jamie's bodyguard.'

Sean didn't scoff, as anyone else might have done. A

dent of concentration appeared between his eyebrows. 'What's the threat?'

I smiled. 'Himself, I think.'

He stopped. 'But you said no,' he said and it wasn't a question.

I stopped, too. 'I said yes,' I said, surprised. 'You saw her back there, Sean. How could I say no?'

'Because how can you protect him when you've no idea what the threat is and he'd probably run a mile rather than agree to submit to being under your protection anyway?'

'Thanks very much,' I said tartly.

He made a brief frustrated gesture. 'You know what I mean,' he said. 'It's like going on a lads' night out and taking your mum with you.'

I put my fists on my hips and tried to keep my face under control. 'You are *so* not helping.'

His frustration flashed over into humour. His face relaxed a little and he smiled ruefully. 'Sorry,' he said. He raised his hands in surrender. 'OK, let's go put it to him that you're going to be his bodyguard and see what happens.'

'After all,' I said, wry, as we started moving for the exit again, 'it won't be the first time I've had to babysit an arsy kid, now will it?'

When we got outside, though, breaking the news to Jamie about my new role in his life suddenly became a side issue.

William and Paxo were still there. In fact, William was still sitting on his Kawasaki not looking like he'd moved at all apart from removing his helmet. The padding had left two matching imprints in the flesh of his cheeks. The helmet was resting on the tank and he had his arms folded across the dome of it.

Paxo was still standing by his Ducati like a terrier – stiff and bristling and looking ready to bite someone at any moment. Jamie was next to William, as though for protection, but this time he wasn't the one who had Paxo's baleful attention.

The big biker who'd accompanied Tess to the hospital the day before was standing up close to the front of Paxo's bike. He had three carrier bags in one massive hand, and two bike helmets in the other, dangling from their straps.

One helmet was open face and matt black in colour – clearly his own. The other was an expensive custom-painted Shoei. It wasn't until we got closer I realised from the damage that it must have been Slick's. There was a nasty scrape across the front of the tinted visor and a size-able gouge out of the gelcoat on one side that allowed the white inner shell to show through like bone.

Poking out of the top of one of the bags I could see the zipped sleeve of a distinctive black leather bike jacket. He must have just been in to collect Slick's effects. All his worldly goods distilled into a few plastic bags.

The big man's eyes skated over Sean and me once, lingered on Sean for a moment longer, then he turned back to Paxo and carried on his conversation with hardly a break in stride.

Not that 'conversation' quite summed it up. Both of them looked just about ready to come to the boil.

'I'm tellin' you, you can't go without Tess,' the big guy said now, his jaw set stubbornly.

'Why not?' Paxo tossed back.

The biker's eyes slid pointedly in our direction for a second, then skipped back. 'We already been over that,' he said. 'You owe her, all of you. Big time.'

Paxo threw up his hands and clenched his fists, as though he would have liked nothing better than to feel them close round the other man's throat. He would have needed a stepladder.

It was left to William to say calmly, 'Look, Gleet, we know it was Slick's idea and we won't forget that, but we're on with it now. It's nothing to do with Tess any more. She's got to let it go.'

'*Let it go*,' Gleet, the big biker, echoed bitterly. 'What about the money?'

57

'She'll get her money back, don't worry,' William said, his voice soothing. 'We won't see her short.'

'That's not the point,' Gleet persisted, scowling. 'You need her.'

'I don't think so, mate,' Paxo said. He fished into the inside pocket of his leathers and came out with a packet of cigarettes that had all the corners bent, and a Zippo lighter. He lit up, cupping his hand round the flame and eyeing Gleet through the smoke. 'This is going to be a fast trip – you know that,' he said as he exhaled. 'We don't have room for passengers.'

As he spoke his gaze flicked to Jamie and it seemed the comment worked on more than one level. Jamie managed a defiant stare in return. *He's on a bike half their size and he won't admit he can't really keep up.*

'Tell 'em, Gnasher,' Gleet said, and it took me a moment to work out who he was talking to. 'You were Slick's mate. He stood up for you. You tell 'em.'

Jamie smiled blandly. 'It's not up to me, is it?'

'Oh right. Gone and fuckin' forgotten already, huh?' Gleet let his breath out fast down his nose, flaring his nostrils like a cart horse. It wasn't a good look for him. His arm came up and he stabbed out an accusing finger. The carrier bags swung wildly. 'Some mates of his you lot are!'

I felt my stomach tighten as the heat rose one notch closer to outright ignition but Sean was already moving in. He angled his body so Gleet was forced to turn away from the others, opening up a gap, giving the steam somewhere to go. I moved in, too, reinforcing the stance Sean had taken.

'I think that's enough,' Sean said quietly. 'You've said your piece. Don't take this further here than it needs to go.'

Gleet glared at him. He held his ground a few moments longer, his face belligerent, still hoping that his undoubted reputation would do the job for him. But when he realised at last that his bad name wasn't going to carry the fight alone, he weighed the odds and wisely threw in his hand.

Gleet stepped back and glared at each of the faces in front of him, ours included, as though he was committing them to memory.

'You bunch of losers have no idea,' he said with quiet venom, shaking his head, 'what you're gettin' yourselves into.'

And with that he turned on his heel and stalked away.

Sean and I were very restrained. We waited until we were away from the others before we backed Jamie up against a wall. At least, I backed him there with my fists wrapped deep in the weave of his T-shirt.

Gleet was long gone. William and Paxo had lidded up and hit the starters to fire up those loud pipes and swept out of the car park. I hadn't much cared about that one way or the other. I'd much more pressing matters on my mind. I wanted answers out of Jacob's son and I wasn't too fussy how I got them.

Sean let me lead it, just closing in on my left, standing apparently casual but in exactly the right place to block anyone's view. He had his head tilted slightly and a mildly interested expression on his face, like he was waiting to see how badly I was prepared to hurt Jamie, but he wasn't planning on interfering.

We were just outside the entrance to the wing that housed the Accident and Emergency unit. The planners had left nooks and crannies in the exterior design that I imagine were normally a refuge for the nicotine-addicted. It was certainly private enough for what I had in mind.

'Hey!' Jamie protested now as I bumped him back against the brickwork. He was smiling, as though he still believed he could laugh his way out of this. It was only when he took a proper look at my face that he fully realised the error he'd made in allowing me to get hold of him. His attempt at amusement began to slip as his eyes flicked from my face to Sean's and he found no comfort there either. His bravado surfaced.

59

'What is this?' he demanded. He brought his hands up angrily and swatted at my fists. That the action failed to break my grip clearly startled him. His head came up but the brickwork behind him gave him nowhere to go. I saw the first trace of unease. Not fear – not yet – but it wasn't far away.

'What is this?' he said again but there was less attitude this time.

'What this is,' I said, 'is the time that you stop bullshitting us and tell us exactly what's going on here.'

His eyes slid to Sean's face again. Mine followed and just for a second I saw what he saw. Without animation Sean's face was hard, even cold, the slanted cheekbones like the angles of a mask, studded with that black wintry gaze. An arresting yet deadly set of features, capable of showing no mercy.

As I knew only too well.

Jamie swallowed and whatever snappy comeback he'd been about to make died on his lips. But he wasn't quite out of courage yet.

'I don't know what you mean,' he said. He heard the nerves tightening his vocal cords and swallowed again, forcing himself to relax.

'Come on, Jamie,' I said. 'What was all that about with Gleet? Why is he getting so bent out of shape about this Irish trip? What's the big deal with Tess not being allowed to go with you?'

'Slick paid up front,' Jamie said. 'Gleet just wants to make sure she gets her money back.'

'How much are we talking about?'

He shrugged, as far as he could with me hanging onto the front of his shirt. 'I dunno. There's the ferry, hotels, that kind of thing. A fair amount.'

'Come on,' I said again. 'That's not enough to get so excited about.'

'It might not be for you, but Tess is on her own now and she's got a kid to look after,' Jamie said, reproachful.

'Slick wasn't exactly the kind of guy to have life insurance, now was he?'

He was right there. The Slick Grannells of this world were too convinced of their own immortality to bother with anything so mundane. There was more, but I had a sense that Jamie wasn't going to volunteer it.

'Clare's asked me to go with you to Ireland and watch your back,' I said instead.

'*You*?' The single word burst scornful from his lips, propelled by surprise and a fine touch of resentment. Then I watched the memory of getting beaten to the floor with a rolled-up magazine in his father's hallway come back to him. He flushed, a deep rosy colour that flooded up from the open neck of his leathers and finished in the roots of his hair. 'How?'

'Charlie's job is close protection, did nobody tell you that?' Sean said, his voice mild. His eyes made a lazy pass over me. 'She's very good at it.'

Jamie's own eyes shifted back to me and there was something else in them now. It was fleeting enough to be almost subliminal, but there might just have been a hint of relief. Then it was gone.

'No dice,' he said. 'This isn't some kind of grannies' outing. You can't just put your name down and turn up at the docks. It's members only. You've got to earn the right to be there.'

I chose to ignore the granny gibe. I was only twenty-six – a year younger than Clare – but I suppose she was, technically, almost his stepmother. 'Members of what?'

Jamie went silent, realising he'd probably said more than he'd set out to. Again the little flick of the eyes to Sean. Sean didn't speak, didn't change his expression, he just moved forwards maybe half an inch, barely more than a shifting of his weight. It was enough for Jamie. More than enough.

His gaze snapped back to meet mine, caught and held it like he was afraid to let it go. Like if he didn't look at Sean the danger he represented might go away.

61

'The Devil's Bridge Club,' he said quickly. 'It's just a group of bikers who've got together for a bit of a laugh, you know.'

'So how do I join?'

I felt his shoulders drop a fraction under my hands and he grinned at me unexpectedly. There was the sharp reminder of Jacob's bones under his skin. It served to make me ease off a little. But not that much.

'Simple,' he said. 'All you've got to do is qualify. There's a meet on Wednesday up in the Lakes. You ride the route quick enough, you're in.'

I got the impression from his sudden change of heart that the procedure was actually far more complicated than it sounded.

'Is that why William and Paxo are so set against Tess coming with you?' I asked. 'Is she not quick enough?'

'She doesn't even have a licence,' Jamie said, dismissive. 'Slick was going to take her on the back of his. He reckoned he was just as quick two up.'

Two up.

'Was that what he was doing when he crashed?' I demanded. 'Proving it – with someone who didn't matter on the back?'

I felt him flinch under my hands. I gave him a shake.

'Come on, Jamie,' I said. 'It doesn't end there. What were you really after when you broke in last night? And even without the drive alarm, why didn't the dogs go crazy?'

He huffed out a breath. 'Maybe they've got good memories. Look, you're making way too much of this, Charlie.' He paused, then hit me with that brilliant smile again. 'And I told you, I was just after a place to stay. Fuck me, I used to live there, remember? It used to be my home,' he said and the smile turned bright and brittle. 'I've more of a right to be there than you have, so back off or clear out, OK?'

And with that he jerked himself free of my loosened grasp, stepped round me and walked away, twitching one shoulder like a cat that's had its fur thoroughly ruffled. We watched him go.

'Well that was fun,' Sean said dryly. He leaned against the wall and folded his arms. 'What's next?'

'Shit, I don't know,' I said. My eyes were still on Jamie's departing figure until he turned a corner and disappeared from view. My tone was gloomy. 'You're the ideas' man.'

Sean smiled. 'I thought I was just providing the muscle.'

We walked back to where I'd left my bike. Although I hadn't known it, it was only three spaces away from Sean's vehicle. His company had a pool of big four-by-fours and this time he was driving a black Mitsubishi Shogun. We stood next to it, awkward, Sean holding his keys. I stuffed my hands into the pockets of my leather jeans.

'So, do you want to stay at Jacob and Clare's place?' I offered, trying to be casual.

'That would be good,' he said gravely. There was nothing in his face but I couldn't help the feeling that he might be laughing at me.

He checked his watch. It was a big multi-dial Breitling on a stainless steel strap, a new model that even had a built-in distress beacon. He'd only recently bought it to replace his old Breitling and seeing it made me shiver. I'd once had to identify what I'd believed was his body by his last watch.

'I ought to nip over and say hello to my dear old ma first,' he said. 'The bush telegraph will probably have told her I'm in town by now and if I don't report in within a couple of hours she'll never let me forget it.'

'You're brave,' I said, nodding to the shiny new Shogun. Despite his best efforts to relocate her, Sean's mother still lived on the notorious Copthorne estate on the other side of the river. Strange cars left round there unattended for longer than half an hour tended to come out minus various bits of their anatomy, like wheels and glass and stereo systems. 'You sure it will still be there when you come out?'

'Don't worry about me,' he said with a grim little smile. 'Are you going to go back to the house and keep an eye on Jamie?'

63

'Yeah,' I said. 'But first there's someone I've got to see as well.'

Sean didn't ask questions and I didn't fill him in on what I had planned. Instead I threaded the Suzuki through the traffic and cut through one of the side streets to bring me out close to the main police station. I parked the bike up in an inconspicuous alley nearby and walked in through the front door.

The officer on the desk took one look at my helmet and bike jacket and already had his hand out for my documents when I brought him up short with a demand to see one of his superiors. We had a brief stare-out competition while he decided whether to take me seriously or not. I won.

'Well, Charlie, this is an unexpected surprise,' Superintendent MacMillan said, rising from his chair a few minutes later as I was shown into his office. We were on a high floor with what amounted to a view, further away from the machine-gun chatter of a road drill breaking up part of Great John Street below.

He offered me his hand to shake, something he hadn't done when he'd come to see me at the cottage. There he'd been on my terms. Here I was most definitely on his.

I hovered for a moment, came within a fraction of turning round and walking out again. Then I remembered Clare's spiked figure and sat down abruptly. When I looked I found MacMillan watching me with that coolly calculating gaze of his, waiting for me to find my starting point.

That was another thing about MacMillan. Silences didn't make him uncomfortable, however awkward others might find them. He would have sat there until doomsday and waited for me to speak if he thought it might be to his advantage.

'You remember Clare Elliot?' I asked but it was a rhetorical question.

'Of course.'

How could he not? Clare had been in the wrong place at the wrong time – my time, my place – and had nearly died

64

for it. To my unending surprise both she and Jacob seemed to have forgiven me for that, even though I had yet to forgive myself.

'She was nearly killed yesterday,' I said. 'On the back of Slick Grannell's bike, on the road to Devil's Bridge.'

'Ah.' MacMillan stood up. 'Wait there,' he said and went out, not quite closing the door behind him.

I sat alone in the policeman's office, staring at the wall behind the desk but not seeing it. I was seeing Clare and Jacob as I'd last seen them, on the terrace at the back of their house after a relaxed supper.

We'd sat and watched the local bat population scything through the midge swarms by the edge of the wood as the sun had gone down. My friends, happy and whole. And I saw how, whatever happened next, nothing was going to be the same again after this.

The door was pushed wider and I heard MacMillan come back in. He walked back round to his side of the desk, reading a typed report and frowning as he regained his seat and put the report down in front of him.

I cleared my throat. 'Do you still need someone to infiltrate this road race gang?' I asked. 'Because if so, I'm in.'

He leaned forwards and placed his elbows on the desktop, steepling his fingers together very precisely. He regarded me for a few long moments. I stared back at him and tried not to fidget.

'When I asked you to get involved in this, Charlie, it was solely because you were completely *un*involved,' he said. 'Now you're not. Now, I fear, it's become personal.'

'Dead right it's personal,' I said evenly. 'Why else would I agree to this?'

'You do realise that there can't be any favouritism here?'

'Favouritism?'

'If this Grannell character was indeed taking part in an illegal road race at the time of his death, then anyone connected to organising or taking part in these races is open to prosecution as an accessory,' he said.

I held his gaze steady and didn't reply.

'At the moment,' he went on, tapping the report, 'we can't be certain exactly what happened. There was too much contamination of the scene by the other motorcyclists who arrived there before we did. Grannell and Miss Elliot were certainly hit by another vehicle, but as yet we don't know if that actually caused the accident. We were hoping,' he added mildly, 'that Miss Elliot herself might be able to help us.'

I thought of Clare's confusion of this morning, compared to her apparent clarity of last night, and shook my head. 'I doubt you'll get much out of her,' I said carefully.

MacMillan was too self-contained to snort, but he let his breath out faster than normal through his nose. 'Now there's a surprise,' he murmured, 'considering that, if she was a willing participant, she might also be liable.'

I felt my body stiffen, however much I tried to control it, and knew that MacMillan had seen it too.

'Whatever other game Slick was playing, he was just giving Clare a lift to Devil's Bridge,' I bit out, ignoring the clamour of doubt at the back of my mind. 'Nothing more than that.'

The policeman regarded me with a fraction of a smile. 'You see?' he said gently, shaking his head. 'You're much too close to this to be objective, Charlie. I can't use you.'

I stuck my open hands up in front of me to indicate surrender, stood abruptly and turned on my heel. I was halfway through the doorway when MacMillan's voice halted me.

'We haven't always seen eye-to-eye in the past, Charlie, but I hope you have enough respect for me to listen to some advice,' he said quietly. 'Stay out of this.'

There was finality in his tone. No second chances. I ducked my head back round the door and gave him a tight little smile.

'That's always been my trouble, Superintendent,' I said. 'I'm really bad at taking advice.'

66

Chapter Five

I rode straight from my abortive interview with MacMillan back to Jacob and Clare's. All the way I ran my conversation with the policeman over in my head. I didn't like it any better the fourth or fifth time than I had the first.

Bearing in mind Jamie's comment about digging in the alarm sensor, I made particular attempts to ride round anything on the driveway that I thought might be a likely candidate. I'm not entirely sure why. Maybe I wanted to check the dogs' reaction, or maybe I wanted to catch Jamie doing something he shouldn't when he thought he had the place to himself.

In the event, it wasn't Jamie I had to worry about.

His Honda was parked up at a rakish angle outside the house. No surprise there. But what I wasn't expecting was a big square Mercedes saloon to be lying alongside it.

The front door was open and as soon as I shut off the Suzuki's engine I could hear the racket the dogs were making. Just for a moment I hesitated over what I might be walking into, then anger got the better of my judgement.

I left my helmet hooked over one of the Suzuki's mirrors and went straight into the house with no further hesitation. I ignored the dogs who were going ballistic behind the closed kitchen door and headed straight for the study, where the noise was of a different and more human nature.

I nudged the door open and found a middle-aged woman

67

was just in the middle of sweeping piles of paperwork off Jacob's desk onto the floor and looking like she was enjoying her work.

Jamie was standing near the fireplace, looking unusually defensive, with his hands rammed in his pockets like he'd been told not to touch anything. I shot him a vicious look. When he saw me his face went into a kind of shameful spasm. He was not, I realised at that moment, an entirely willing participant in this enterprise.

'Charlie!' he said quickly. 'Look, I'm sorry. I didn't—'

The woman's head snapped up, her eyes glittering.

'And who in hell's name are you?' she demanded and, not waiting for an answer, 'Get the hell out of my house!'

She had a deep slightly husky voice that might have been attractive without the harsh note now flattening it. Her face was strong, full of character, mapped by fine thread veins under the surface of her skin.

'*Your* house?' I said mildly, not moving. I'd never met Jacob's ex-wife but in this case I didn't think I needed a formal introduction. 'I don't think so.'

For a moment Isobel Nash glared at me. Her gaze had turned calculating now, flicking from me to her son and back again. She might have been weighing up the possibilities of forcibly ejecting me and realising that Jamie probably wasn't going to be any help in the matter. She looked physically strong enough to consider doing the job herself but, if nothing else, she could see I had the best part of thirty years on her. Common sense prevailed.

After a moment she gave a slight nod, almost to herself, and seemed to relax. She dragged a battered pack of Dorchesters out of her pocket and shook one out before offering it halfheartedly in my direction. I shook my head. She shrugged as though I'd deliberately slighted her and lit up.

'Well now, there's no reason we can't be civilised about this,' she said as she exhaled her first deep drag. For someone who was pretending to be civilised she seemed to have been the cause of a lot of wanton destruction. I eyed it without comment as she perched on the corner of the desk, watching me intently through the smoke.

'Civilised about what?'

'Well, we're both after the same thing,' she said carefully. She had suddenly dropped her voice and seemed to be making an effort to keep impatience at bay, as though I was being unutterably dense. 'I expect we can come to some kind of arrangement.'

I had no idea what she was on about but Jamie's face was a picture of horrified embarrassment. His eyes slid away over my shoulder like they wouldn't stick.

'I expect we can,' I said evenly. 'How about you leave right now and I don't call the police. That civilised enough for you?'

She made a snorting sound that might have signified amusement. Jamie stood silent between us, equally ignored. I kept my eyes on Isobel's face and her hands and paid him no attention.

'If it came to it I do have a right to be here,' she pointed out at last. 'Legally I am, after all, still Jacob's wife.'

That was news to me. I knew Jacob and Isobel had been separated since before I'd moved to Lancaster to begin with, but that didn't mean they had ever actually jumped through the hoops and made it official. I tried to remember if he'd ever mentioned it but couldn't bring it to mind. She still could be lying, though. Isobel struck me as the kind who would try to brazen out being caught in the wrong.

I inclined my head, mentally crossing my fingers.

'Technically, yes,' I agreed with just enough of a drawl to be insulting. 'As far as the laws on trespass go, probably not. Would you care to put it to the test?'

Her eyes narrowed again at that. Her hair was dark and glossy, the colour younger than her face. She pursed her lips and let out a long stream of smoke towards the ceiling. 'So Jacob's left you to play guard dog, has he?' she said sharply. 'Where is the old bastard, by the way?'

69

'Away,' I said. 'In Ireland, as a matter of fact.'

She cast a glance towards Jamie but he didn't catch it. I saw something flicker behind her eyes, fast as a flame, then it was gone and I was left wondering if I'd seen it at all.

'Well, that's all right then.' She stood up and stubbed the last half of her cigarette out in a saucer containing foreign coins on the mantelpiece. 'Last chance. Are you going to play ball or not?'

I shook my head.

She hid the faintest flicker of a smile and shrugged. 'Well, if that's your attitude, I can't help you,' she said, then raised her voice and barked, 'Eamonn!'

I heard a door open behind me and footsteps moving quickly down the flagged passageway from the living room. I'd time to turn as a slim man in a pale grey suit came bowling across the hallway and scooped me up as he came by with an ease that took me by surprise.

'Get rid of her,' Isobel instructed, her tone indifferent.

I heard Jamie begin to protest as I was borne away down the hall towards the front door. His mother told him to shut up in the same crushing kind of voice she must have been using since he was six.

I cursed myself for not expecting that Jacob's wife might have brought some extra muscle. The man wasn't a traditional heavy but he was deft and professional, nonetheless. He'd undoubtedly done this kind of thing before and the confines of the hallway was not where I wanted to find out how much. I went limp in his arms and waited for the space to make a stand.

When we reached the forecourt Eamonn let go with a jerk, so I was abruptly sent scattering across the mossy cobbles on my hands and knees. Thankful I was in my bike leathers, I rolled through the fall without injury and came back up on my feet.

I found myself facing a pale man with narrow pointed features and dark reddish hair parted at the side. He wasn't wearing a tie and his shirt collar was open. The jacket of his suit had been intended for someone with wider shoulders, so the front bagged. Maybe he just liked to have plenty of room to manoeuvre, which was probably not a good sign.

He'd also been expecting the surprise manhandling to have thoroughly unnerved me. That it had clearly failed to do so must, I suspected, have been something of a disappointment to him. But there was a gleam of speculation and interest there, too, and that I did find disturbing.

As I watched, his tongue flipped out to wet his thin lips like he was trying to scent the faintest trace of my fear.

'Who sent you?' he demanded. He had a Northern Irish accent and his voice was all the more deadly for being so soft.

I thought of Clare. 'None of your damned business,' I said.

'Oh but it *is* my business,' he said. 'It is very much my business.' He smiled unpleasantly at me and moved in, putting his feet down with careful delicacy, I backed as he came on. 'I want you to take a message back to your boss man – whoever he is,' he went on, still smiling. 'You can tell them it was a nice try, but if they think that's going to stop me, they can think again.'

Before I had time to ask what the hell he was on about, Eamonn had reached into his jacket and pulled a black cylinder out of his inside pocket. I recognised it instantly and all the hairs stood up on the back of my neck.

As he brought it out he flicked the cylinder downwards with enough force to deploy the two inner segments. They telescoped outwards with a smooth mechanical click and locked into place making a solid baton about a foot and a half long.

The baton was similar to the asps the police use, the kind I'd been trained on for crowd control when firearms were not an option. The kind that, if wielded skilfully, could inflict all manner of nasty damage on the human body. And Eamonn struck me as someone who would practise with an unbecoming zeal.

71

His smile grew broader but my eyes were drawn to the baton which he was lazily swinging in front of me. I flicked my glance outwards, trying not to become blinded to other threats but there weren't any. It was just Eamonn and me.

'Now don't you be worrying too much,' he said. 'I'm only planning on breaking the one ankle, so you'll still be able to ride away on that little bike of yours.'

When outnumbered or outgunned and retreat is not an option, the only thing left to do is attack. And the best defence against a long weapon like a baton is to get in close, to negate the effect and hamper them with the one thing they thought was going to put them ahead.

I launched straight in, timing it between the swipes like the kind of skipping game we used to play as kids. I knew I had to get under Eamonn's guard and disable the arm holding the baton as fast as possible. Before it disabled me. But getting from safe distance to engagement meant passing through Eamonn's kill zone and that was never going to be easy.

I feinted a short right to his throat. He jerked his head back automatically and I grabbed the arm holding the baton with my left hand. I ignored the baton itself, aiming to get my thumb jabbed in hard to the radial nerve that sits on top of the forearm, a couple of inches below the elbow. I nearly made it, too.

Eamonn hadn't been expecting me to go for him there and it took him a fraction longer to react than it might have done otherwise. But not long enough. He wrenched his arm free and danced back. The baton swept round in a slashing arc and cracked against the outside of my left knee.

If I hadn't loosened his grip slightly, or been dressed for the possibility of falling off a motorbike, at speed onto tarmac, the blow would have put me on the ground and probably in the hospital. As it was, the lessened impact was partially absorbed by the closed-cell foam padding in my leathers. It stung like hell but it didn't do anything permanent and I didn't go down. With barely a break in stride I slapped Eamonn's wrist out sideways and brought the outside of my right forearm round and up hard into the side of his face.

Instinctively, he threw his head back again so I caught him on his cheekbone rather than his temple. Nevertheless, I'd put plenty into it, enough to stagger him back a pace or two. But he was tough and he'd done this kind of work before. He shook his head to clear it. His smile grew colder and wider.

'Oh ho, so you've got some fire in your belly, have you?' he murmured. 'Well, OK then, if you insist. Both ankles . . .'

He darted forwards then, letting off another whistling blow towards my upper body this time. I went forwards to meet him, blocking so the baton cannoned off the protective padding in the sleeve of my jacket. It jarred me to the bone without severe damage, but I was on the defensive and I knew it was only a matter of time before he got lucky.

And then the drive alarm went off. Jacob had an old fire alarm bell attached to the outside of the house so he could hear it if he was in the workshop and it was loud enough to make both of us jump.

We whipped round. Eamonn reversed the baton and twisted it shut in one flowing move. He dropped the weapon back into his inside pocket like a magician's sleight of hand. He was barely out of breath.

A black Mitsubishi Shogun rumbled quickly onto the forecourt and pulled up facing us, sharply enough to set its soft suspension rocking.

Isobel hurried out of the house with Jamie tailing along behind her. She glanced at me briefly, her eyebrows raised as though she was surprised to see me still on my feet.

Sean Meyer came out of the Shogun without seeming in any particular rush but that cool flat gaze was everywhere. He took in Eamonn's apparently relaxed stance and wasn't fooled for a moment by the thin veneer of civility he presented. His eyes swept over me and narrowed in much the same way that Isobel's had done. Except when she did it I wasn't quite so afraid of what she had in mind.

'You OK?' he asked.

I shrugged, feeling the protest in my muscles where the baton had bitten me. 'More or less,' I said.

He turned slowly towards Eamonn and made a slight sideways movement with his head, loosening the muscles in his neck. Eamonn smiled at him, reaching into his coat and bringing the baton back out into view.

'Knight in shining fucking armour, are we?' he said, extending the weapon again with a practised flick of his hand.

Suddenly he sniffed loudly, pulled a face of almost delicate distaste. 'Now that wouldn't be a bastard squaddie I can smell, would it? Seen plenty of your type. Think you're a hard man, do you? Think you can take me on?'

He made a couple of showy slashes with the baton, making the air whine as it sliced through.

'Maybe not,' Sean said calmly. He inclined his head in my direction. 'But between us we can.'

Just for a second Eamonn faltered, then he grinned fiercely. 'Oh, you think so?' And he beckoned us on.

Sean didn't respond to that, but something had died behind his eyes, like a light had gone out. He began to circle, clockwise, moving slowly. I circled in the opposite direction. Whether Eamonn liked it or not, we were moving in and out of his blind spots. He couldn't cover us both at once.

But the Irishman continued to smile. He knew that two against one were not good odds in his favour. He also knew, as we did, that if he could get a couple of decent blows in with the baton, he might yet stand a chance of coming out on top.

His eyes went to Sean's unprotected arms, then to my leather jacket and I saw he'd picked his first target. I wasn't about to give him a chance to act on that decision. And I wasn't about to let Sean take a hit to protect me, either.

74

We continued to circle. I waited until Eamonn had flicked his eyes away from me again, then jumped him. He caught the flash of my attack and spun round, uncoiling the baton at shoulder height, aiming for my head. A killing blow. I ducked underneath it and crashed through his defence, getting in close to his body.

I managed to snake my left hand round and get my fingers pinched hard into the pressure points at the back of his neck, controlling his upper body as I brought my knee up hard, once, twice, into his gut.

Sean moved in smooth and fast, landing a massive uppercut to the other man's face as he began to fold. The stinging blow broke Eamonn's nose and sent blood flying.

I let go and jumped back, getting out of Sean's way. He twisted the baton out of the Irishman's hand and into his own with almost negligent ease, turning the tables. His first slash took Eamonn's legs out from under him, then he went for his upper arms just above each elbow. Hit the nerves there hard enough and they shut down like circuit breakers, disconnecting each limb.

Sean hit him with a coldly scientific precision, throttling back to inflict pain rather than outright injury. Enough to put Eamonn down and make sure he wasn't going to get up in a hurry, nothing more. Then he stepped back and watched the Irishman as he lay writhing and groaning on the dusty ground.

It was too much for Isobel. She gave an outraged howl and launched herself at Sean, clawing for his face. He shook her off, sending the woman reeling.

Jamie jumped automatically to his mother's defence. I saw him start to sprint and turned to face him, taking half a step into his path to hook my right arm up inside his as it swung past me. His own momentum ensured that as he went on I jerked his arm up and back behind him. I twisted on the balls of my feet and locked his wrist up hard behind his own shoulder blade, a classic police restraint technique.

He struggled against me for a moment longer but I grabbed the point of his shoulder with my other hand and carefully applied a touch more force. It was only as he felt the joint start to tear apart that he gave up. I relaxed the pressure a little but didn't let go.

Eamonn meanwhile, despite making noise like he was mortally wounded, took advantage of the distraction to rear up far enough to take a swing at Sean. He caught the baton, sending it flying. It clattered away across the forecourt and disappeared under Isobel's Mercedes. If Eamonn thought that Sean would be easier to tackle without a weapon, however, he was to be severely disappointed.

Sean never blinked. He reached down and roughly picked Eamonn up by the lapels of his jacket, throwing him about like a dog worrying a lamb. Eamonn came down sprawled on his knees, facing away from Sean, who stepped over his legs and took hold of a big handful of the other man's shirt collar, using it as a tourniquet on his throat.

Eamonn's colour rose as he started to choke, his fingers scrabbling at his own clothing. Sean immediately shifted his grip so his forearms were clamped on either side of the man's neck, just below the jawbone, and started to pile on the pressure.

Restricting the blood flow through the carotid artery that feeds the brain will cause loss of consciousness in around ten seconds. It was a method I'd been taught a long time ago – by Sean as I seem to recall – for silently and effectively dealing with an enemy, but it was not something I'd ever shown to my self-defence students. Because when you're scared and under pressure, it's easy to misjudge the time and hold on too long. Somewhere around forty seconds, the starvation of oxygen to the brain starts to have permanent effects.

But already Sean had held onto Eamonn for more than ten seconds. The other man had ceased to struggle but I could see Sean's arms bunched with the effort of keeping the lock in place. And I knew full well that he wasn't under pressure and he certainly wasn't scared.

'Sean,' I said sharply. He looked over at me but his eyes were blank and empty.

'*Sean!*' I said again, and this time the anguish and the pleading in my voice seemed to reach him where anger had not. He abruptly relaxed his grip and Eamonn slid limply to the ground at his feet.

Isobel gave a fearful cry and knelt alongside the Irishman, cradling his head. I let go of Jamie. He wrenched himself away from me, rubbing his shoulder reproachfully, but didn't make any moves to continue his attack on Sean, nor to help his mother.

Isobel gave Eamonn a couple of businesslike slaps across his cheek. He started to come out of it, limbs spasming as life and control returned. He knocked her hands away angrily and instinctively tried to get to his feet, but his co-ordination was shot.

'You bastard,' Isobel spat at Sean.

He shrugged. 'He brought it on himself,' he said, indifferent. He took a step forward as Isobel started to hoist Eamonn to his feet. 'Wait, I'm not done with him yet.'

'Oh yes, I think you are. We're leaving – unless you plan to keep us here by force,' she said, with surprising dignity. 'Help me get him into the car,' she ordered her son in a peremptory voice. Jamie did as he was told without making eye contact with anyone.

Eamonn allowed himself to be shovelled into the passenger side of the Mercedes with ill grace. Isobel slammed the door on him and went round to the driver's side, starting up the engine with her foot heavy on the accelerator. She stuck the big car in reverse and it shot backwards across the forecourt, sweeping round to head off up the drive, sending up a cloud of dust. The baton must have been lying close to one of the tyres. As she set off it was sent skittering away across the mossy stone cobbles.

And all the while Eamonn stared at us through the glass,

blood covering his nose and mouth like he'd taken a bite out of something not yet dead. There was an evil intent in that gaze. Humiliation was not something he'd suffered much and he didn't like it. He would not easily forget this.

I glanced across at Jamie. 'Your mother should watch the company she keeps,' I said.

His eyes flicked to Sean, then back to me.

'Yeah,' he said. 'And so should you.'

Chapter Six

Though I did my best to get answers out of him, Jamie was saying nothing. He left soon after his mother, collecting his helmet and his rucksack from inside the house as though he wasn't planning on coming back. I didn't try and persuade him to stay. My mind was on Sean and the actions he'd taken.

'Don't you think you went in a bit hard on Eamonn?' I demanded as we walked back into the house with the Honda's exhaust note still fading up the drive.

Sean had collected the fallen baton and was turning it over in his hands. He held it up towards me. 'This is an older baton,' he said, not answering my question. 'The police-issue ones have a plastic end – this one's steel. You know why they don't let the police use ones like these any more?'

I shook my head.

'Because you have an unfortunate tendency to split people's skulls wide open with them,' he said, his voice like stone. 'If Eamonn had caught you a good one with this he could have killed you. And he was certainly trying.'

I swallowed. 'The rules on self defence don't allow you to kill someone if you can disarm them another way,' I said sharply, even though I knew he was right. 'We're not in the jungle now.'

For a moment there was a silent gulf between us. Yes,

I'd seen the violence and the cruelty running through Eamonn. But that didn't mean I was prepared to dispense instant justice to deal with him.

Sean gave me a humourless smile and twisted the baton shut with the same kind of practised ease that Eamonn had shown. 'A snake is still a snake, Charlie, regardless of where you find it.'

'Yeah? So what does that make you?'

I'd thrown it at him without thinking and regretted the words as soon as they were off and running.

Sean's head came up and he turned towards me, moving very deliberately, making the hair prickle at the base of my neck. Suddenly I was reminded of a big dog you've always been wary of and who's now decided he doesn't want to obey your commands any longer. Instinctively, I flinched, took a step back.

A mistake.

I saw the flare in Sean's eyes as he came for me. We were still in the hallway and I went back until the study wall brought me up short with a gasp. My heart was a leaden weight in my chest, the staccato beat echoing fiercely in my ears.

'Sean,' I said. 'Don't.' A breathless protest. Ignored.

He followed me back, crowded in on me. With my elbows against the wall behind me, I locked my wrists and wedged my fists into the tensed muscles of his stomach to keep him back. He leaned his weight against them, trapping me, and brought his head down until his mouth was within a whisper of mine. I could feel his breath fanning my cheek.

'You know what I am, Charlie,' he said in my ear, very quietly, mocking. 'And we both know you're out of the same mould, however much your damned parents have tried to have it psychoanalysed out of you.'

Anger pushed fear aside. I abruptly relaxed my wrists so I could squirm my right hand down the front of his jeans to grab a handful of his belt. Then I shoved the heel of my left hand up under his chin and pushed back, hard.

Sean's spine arched as his head was forced back. I kept a tight hold of his belt to unbalance him, using the leverage to run him back a couple of strides, giving me room. Then I let go, breathing harder than I should have needed to.

Sean recovered his poise like a falling cat and smiled coldly at me.

'Face it, Charlie, you've got the reflexes and the moves and you've got the killer instinct,' he said. 'Either you learn to master them or they'll master you.'

'And you're always so in control, are you?' I shot back. Another jibe I shouldn't have voiced aloud.

'Half the secret of being in control is knowing when to let go,' he said. He fixed me with a bleak stare. 'When we were in Germany you told me to accept you as you were or to get out of your life and leave you alone,' he went on, relentless, tearing me with my own bitter words. 'That I should make a choice because you wouldn't settle for half measures. Well maybe it's time you made that same choice about me.'

I looked up, ripped inside, feeling my eyes begin to burn. I opened my mouth but he reached out and put a finger to my lips, shushing me.

'Don't say anything now,' he said, gently, 'but soon. Think about it and give me your answer soon. Because I need to know one way or another where I stand with you, Charlie.'

He took his finger away again and I could still feel the imprint of his skin on mine. The noises of the house intruded, grown suddenly louder. The ticking of the clock, the whining of one of the dogs behind the kitchen door. It was like they'd gone away and only just returned.

Sean stepped back, shrugged into a different day.

'So, who were they, that pair?' he asked, suddenly practical, level.

I shrugged too, trying to match him. 'Isobel is Jacob's ex-wife – or his estranged wife, at least,' I said. There was

81

a wobble in my voice and I cleared my throat to get rid of it. 'Um, she wanted to make a deal over something. We didn't quite get down to the details of what. I'm afraid I turned her down. Maybe,' I added ruefully, 'I should have played her along a bit more.'

'Hm, it didn't take her long to find out the place was empty, did it?' he said. He gave me a tired smile, recognising the effort we were both making to strive for normality. 'Did Jamie tip her off, d'you reckon?'

'She must have moved fast, if he did,' I said. 'She lives in Northern Ireland. How long does the ferry take from Belfast? Four hours if you catch the fast cat to Heysham?' I shook my head. 'She would have had to be on starting blocks.'

'So,' Sean said, 'was she here already, or did they know in advance that Clare was going to be out of action?'

'I don't know,' I said, frowning. 'Eamonn made a weird comment, though. Before he had a go at me he wanted to know who sent me, then told me to tell my boss man it was a nice try, but if they thought that was going to stop him they could think again. Whatever that means.'

Sean's expression had gone blank while he was thinking, the mental equivalent of an hourglass on a computer screen.

'So, what were they looking for here?' he asked. 'And, more to the point, did they find it?'

'I don't know where Eamonn was when I arrived, but Isobel was ransacking the study.'

'OK,' he said. 'Let's start there then, shall we?'

It took Sean less than five minutes to discover the safe I never knew existed. It was set into the study wall, hidden behind a loose section of the wooden panelling that lined the room from floor to ceiling, which was in turn behind a large limited edition print of the Isle of Man TT.

The safe itself was a small steel door, painted dark grey, with a handle and a combination dial. Sean tried the handle. It was locked.

'Do we assume Jacob would have changed the combination after his ex moved out?' he said.

82

I thought of Jamie's comment the night before about his father being a creature of habit and shook my head. 'Somehow I doubt it.'

'So, either Isobel's been into the safe and re-locked the door behind her,' he said, 'or she didn't have time to get into it in the first place. What's your guess?'

I frowned. 'When I arrived she was throwing stuff all over the floor and not being too careful about it,' I said. 'She didn't strike me as the type who would have even shut the safe door, never mind put the panelling and the picture back.'

Sean shook his head. 'The art of distraction,' he said. 'What better way to make us think she hadn't touched it?'

Something about Jamie nudged at my memory. When I'd entered the room I'd stood with my back to the wall where the doorway was – the same wall which housed the safe – and Jamie's gaze had slid past me. 'When Isobel said we were after the same thing, I thought Jamie couldn't look at me, but he could just as easily have been looking at the safe behind me,' I said.

'One way to find out,' Sean said. He sighed. 'OK,' he said. 'I haven't had to sneak my way into one of these for a while but it's an old model so I might get lucky.' He shifted a small table away from the wall so he could get up close to the safe. 'Why don't you make yourself useful,' he said, smiling over his shoulder, 'and go and put some coffee on?'

'Yes sir,' I said, sarky. But I went back to the kitchen and fed the dogs and messed about with the cafetière as I was told. As I waited for the water to heat I leaned against the sink and absently rubbed at the bruise on the side of my arm where Eamonn had hit me, and tried not to think about Sean's ultimatum.

That I loved him wasn't in doubt. I'd admitted as much to myself when I thought I'd lost him for good in America. But the reality of Sean was more complicated than the idea. He brought out the best and the worst in me and confirmed my darkest fears about what I was capable of. In the end, it wasn't Sean I was scared of.

It was me.

When I took the filled cafetière through to the study, Sean was still up against the wall in a half crouch with his ear pressed against the safe door, inching the lock dial to the right with those long agile fingers of his. His movements slowed and finally stopped. He reached for the handle and I was aware of holding my breath.

It opened.

'*Et voila!*' He turned and grinned up at me, one of those breathtaking smiles that made him look young and carefree. One that made my heart flop over in my chest.

I grinned back. It was hard not to.

The safe turned out to be much smaller on the inside that it had first appeared.

'Data safe,' Sean said, as though I'd voiced the question. 'There's a canister of coolant in here that goes off if the temperature rises too high. Stops your computer disks getting corrupted if you have a fire.'

Sure enough, there were two boxes of floppy disks and several recordable CDs inside, together with a bundle of papers. He slid the whole lot out onto the nearest chair and started leafing through it.

'Sean,' I said, uncomfortable. 'Are you sure we should be doing this? I mean, we don't know Isobel knew the combination to—'

By way of answer Sean passed across a single sheet of paper. I took it reluctantly. It was a withdrawal slip from the local branch of a bank in Lancaster, for the sum of ten thousand pounds.

'Ten grand?' I echoed blankly. 'Jacob might have taken it with him to Ireland. Supposing he wanted to pay cash at an auction—'

'He would have taken euros,' Sean interrupted. 'And look at the date.'

I found the stamp and checked it. The slip was dated

three days previously. Friday. The day Jacob had caught the ferry to Dublin. Even if he'd had time to get to the bank before he set off, why would he have taken the wrong currency with him?

'I don't suppose there's any sign of the money?'

Sean moved to run his hand round the inside of the safe, just to be certain, then shook his head. 'Nothing,' he said. 'So either Clare went on a serious shopping bender on Saturday, or she had it with her on Sunday when she and Slick crashed.'

'Or someone's been in here since and taken it,' I finished for him. I sat down heavily on the edge of the desk. 'Shit,' I muttered. 'How the hell am I going to explain this one to Clare?'

He put the disks and papers back into the safe and shut the door again. Gloomy, I pressed the plunger on the cafetière and poured two coffees. As I handed one across I saw Sean's face go tense, like he'd been steamrollered by a sudden thought.

'What is it?' I said.

'Come with me.'

I almost had to run to keep up with his long stride down the hallway. He paused only to duck into the kitchen, quickly scanning the keys hanging on the rack behind the door and selecting a set.

'Sean?' I said. 'Come on, talk to me!'

But he was already outside and halfway across the fore-court towards the coach house. I caught him up again as he was unlocking the door.

'Why did Clare say she accepted a lift with Slick Grannell in the first place?' he asked then.

'Because,' I said slowly, as it dawned on me what line he was taking, 'she said the Ducati wouldn't start.'

I glanced past him to where Clare's beautiful scarlet 851 Strada sat on its paddock stand, looking like a refugee from a racetrack. Clare loved that bike and Jacob maintained it regardless of expense. Without another word I took the

85

keys out of Sean's hand and stuck one into the ignition, twisting it to run and turning on the fuel tap. I pulled the choke out a notch, flicking my eyes to Sean's. He was watching me without expression. I hit the starter button.

The Ducati fired on the first spin and revved up without any hesitation. The exhaust note reverberated gruff and loud inside the old stone building.

I let it run for a moment or two, then cut the motor and pulled the key out again. I handed it back to him with a deep frown.

'You might want to look at it this way instead,' Sean said. 'How the hell is Clare going to explain this one to *you*?'

An hour later, completely unexpectedly, the police turned up. Superintendent MacMillan in his usual unmarked Rover, plus two pairs of uniforms in a couple of full-dress squad cars.

Sean and I were back in the study, trying to make some sense out of the disorder and clearing up after Isobel's destructive intervention.

We heard the drive alarm go off three times in quick succession. The first thought that went through both our minds was that Eamonn was back and he'd brought re-inforcements. After that, MacMillan's arrival came almost as a relief.

We met them on the forecourt just as they were getting out of their cars. MacMillan nodded gravely to me, then he and Sean locked gazes like a pair of rutting stags.

The two of them had run up against each other before and the collision had caused more sparks than a foundry. MacMillan had wanted Sean for murder and it had taken some fast talking to persuade the policeman to let us go after the real killer. The fact that we'd achieved our purpose had done little to inspire friendly feelings on either side.

'We'd like to do a search of these premises, Charlie, if

you have no objections,' he said coolly, not breaking eye contact with Sean while he spoke.

'Do you have a warrant?' Sean asked.

'Do I need one?'

'Not necessarily,' I said carefully, moving between them and passing Sean a warning glance. 'Not if you tell me what you're looking for.'

MacMillan turned and rested his gaze on me, murky like canal water and just as difficult to see the bottom of. 'A motorbike,' he said at last.

'Well, considering Jacob deals in the things, it won't come as any surprise to you to find lots of those here,' I said acidly. 'Try being more specific.'

MacMillan stilled for a moment, the only outward sign of his disapproval at my attitude. I was struck then by the similarities between the policeman and my father. And both of them made me nervous.

'Oh, we're looking for something very specific,' he said then, moving over to join us. 'We're after a customised machine based, so I'm told, on Suzuki mechanicals and, I believe, a Harris frame,' he went on. He raised an eyebrow as he spoke, as though he was trying out words from a foreign language and was surprised that they were understood.

'A streetfighter,' I said blankly. 'You're looking for Slick's bike. Why? I thought you already had it.'

'We did,' he said, emphasising the past tense.

'Careless.' Sean was back to the gently mocking tone he'd used on me earlier. The Superintendent didn't appear to like it any more than I had.

'What happened?' I said quickly, as much to distract MacMillan as anything else.

He paused, as though reluctant to admit to any mistakes in front of an outsider. And particularly not in front of an outsider like Sean.

'The wreckage was transported to a nearby garage to await collection by our accident investigation lads,' he said

87

at last. 'When they came to pick it up today, it had already gone.'

'And what makes you think I might have had anything to do with that?' I asked softly.

'Someone was making off with Grannell's bike at just about the same time you were sitting in my office this morning, thus providing you with a fairly unassailable alibi,' he said with a fraction of a smile. 'Which could, naturally, be taken as a coincidence but I've never liked them much. Besides,' he added crisply, 'even you must admit that you do have a bit of a reputation for taking matters into your own hands, Charlie.' His eyes went to Sean again. 'And you could have had help.'

'Well, since I know I didn't – search away,' I said, reckless. 'Just tell them to wipe their feet and don't break anything.'

We sat in the sun by the front door and watched them poke their way through every nook and cranny for the best part of the next hour, MacMillan supervising proceedings without actually getting his hands dirty. I wondered how I was going to explain to Jacob that I'd let the cops search his place. Still, on top of everything else it seemed a minor additional transgression.

Just as the searchers began to lose their initial fervour in the face of disappointment, one of the uniforms sidled up to announce that they couldn't get into the locked coach house.

MacMillan looked at me enquiringly. I stood up but it was Sean who said, 'I'll do it,' and put his glass of iced water down, getting to his feet and heading for the front door.

MacMillan moved beside me and watched him go. 'I can't pretend I'm happy to see you renewing your association with Meyer,' he said quietly.

'That's my business,' I snapped, my own earlier doubts making my voice sharper than I'd intended. I shoved my hands into the pockets of my leather jeans. 'I know what I'm doing.'

88

'I'm sure you believe that to be so,' he murmured, solemn. 'Just be careful, Charlie.'

Sean reappeared with Clare's keys and dutifully unlocked the coach house before rejoining us. Two policemen disappeared eagerly inside, only to return a few minutes later, shaking their heads, disappointed.'

'Nothing, sir,' one of them reported. He jerked a thumb back towards the coach house door. 'He's got a lovely old Laverda Jota in there, though. Looks like new. I wouldn't mind making him a bid at that.'

'That's Jacob's own bike,' I said, my voice cool. 'He'd bite his own leg off rather than part with it.'

MacMillan glanced at me. 'Everyone has their price,' he said, cryptic. He nodded to his men again and they made for their cars, then he inclined his head to me. 'Thank you for your co-operation, Charlie. No doubt we'll be in touch again soon.'

And with that slightly ominous promise, the police climbed back into their vehicles and departed up the dusty driveway. I turned and found Sean at my shoulder.

'So, if *we* haven't nicked Slick's bike,' I said lightly, 'who has?'

'His friends?' Sean suggested. 'Or his enemies?'

'I'm not sure who his enemies are,' I said, 'but I do know how to get hold of one of his friends.'

I dug the number William had given me out of my jacket pocket, together with my mobile phone and dialled one into the other. William's phone clicked straight onto voice mail and I didn't think it was worth leaving him a message. I ended the call, muttering curses under my breath.

'Annoying, isn't it?' Sean said, his voice suddenly cheerful. 'When someone doesn't leave their mobile phone switched on.'

The only person I could think of who might know something about Slick's enemies was Clare. The only person I knew where to find, at any rate. I didn't believe the remains of his bike had disappeared without good reason. Was it to protect Slick, or to hide the evidence of whatever had hit him? The only trouble was, I was increasingly unsure how much Clare would be prepared to tell us.

I wavered over calling the hospital first, to check it was OK to visit her again, but decided against it. Ask permission and you stand a chance of being refused – especially if the same nurse who'd chucked us out this morning was the one who answered the phone.

Sean offered to drive me into town and the prospect of being able to get out of my bike leathers in this weather was tempting enough to make me say yes.

I went upstairs and changed into the shirt and jeans I'd packed at the cottage. The skin round my knee was already starting to yellow where Eamonn had clouted it and a painful lump had come up on the outside of the joint. I prodded at it experimentally and was thankful I hadn't taken the blow completely unprotected.

Sean was already in the Shogun with the motor running when I came downstairs and locked the front door. I hopped up into the passenger seat and we headed out along the drive.

Sean drove the same way he did everything, self-contained, with a relaxed casual competence. I found myself watching the way the definition formed and shifted in the muscles of his left forearm as he changed gear. Then I remembered those same muscles clenched around Eamonn's neck, starving his brain. I looked away.

I sat in silence as we turned out onto the main road and travelled towards town. Even on a Monday a couple of big bikes passed us, heading in the opposite direction. The Shogun had air conditioning, which made the plush interior cool and bearable in the summer heat, but I was aware of being one step removed from the road and the conditions. Removed from the facts of what had brought Slick down.

The prospect of interrogating my friend as she lay helpless and injured in her hospital bed was not a pleasant one. That she'd lied to me and I knew it, only made it worse. Elderly Ducatis could be temperamental, but I couldn't believe her bike had completely failed to start one day, and fired up first time the next. So what was she really doing out with Slick?

We pulled up at the traffic lights leading onto the motorway junction. There must have been another ferry into the port at Heysham from the Isle of Man or Belfast because a rake of bikes were waiting for the lights to change in their favour. Sports bikes rather than cruisers, but piled high with luggage like racehorses wearing donkey panniers.

'How do I handle this?' I asked suddenly. Sean hadn't been privy to my thoughts but he seemed to know instantly what I meant, even so.

'It depends what you want to get out of it.'

I thought for a moment. 'The truth?' I said. It should have been a decisive statement but it came out a lot more uncertain than that.

'About what, exactly?' The lights went green for the bikers and they flowed across the front of us like running deer. I watched them go, feeling the tug of not being on my Suzuki.

'About what Clare was really doing on the back of Slick's bike,' I said, turning back to him. 'About what really brought them off and why she won't tell me what it was. And about what she was doing with ten grand in cash.'

'Come on, Charlie,' Sean said, mildly reproving as we moved forwards again. 'You don't know if she can remember the accident or not – anaesthetics can take you that way. And as for the ten thousand, we don't know what's happened to that. Not yet, anyway. The real question,' he went on, 'is what are you prepared to sacrifice to find these things out?'

'Sacrifice?'

He smiled, although his voice remained cool and neutral.

91

'Every victory is a compromise of gains and loses. You need to think about what you might lose in order to win the battle. What you can afford to lose.'

Why do I get the feeling you're talking about me and you as much as about Clare, Sean? And what will I lose?

When I didn't speak right away he added, 'If you come right out with an accusation you might irrevocably harm or even lose your friendship with Clare. Is that a sacrifice you're prepared to make?'

My mind gave a stark and immediate, 'No!' But my mouth was contrary. 'She lied to me,' I muttered, aware of the pain that fact caused me. 'After everything . . .'

I fell silent as we rolled up through the centre of Lancaster, past Dalton Square with its immense green-tinged statue of Queen Victoria.

What could I say? Clare and I had been through a lot together, had come close to dying because of each other. Enough that I had thought she would trust me completely with any dark secret. I wasn't just upset that she evidently did not but, I also recognised with a touch of shame, that my pride was wounded. It was an admission that made me feel rather small.

A few minutes later Sean braked to a halt in the hospital car park again. He unclipped his seatbelt and twisted to face me.

'Well?' he said.

'No.' I shook my head, took a breath. 'I'm not prepared to lose Clare as a friend. If that means finding out what's going on another way, well—' I broke off with a shrug.

'OK,' he said evenly. 'Then that's how you handle it.'

Chapter Seven

Even if I hadn't come to my decision about Clare on the drive in, one look at her face when we reached the hospital would have convinced me not to push her.

Not that we got to see her right away. When we arrived on the ward the curtains surrounding her bed were closed and we could hear the murmur of voices beyond.

Sean and I waited by the doorway. Much as I wanted to know what was going on, I didn't want to be caught eavesdropping when those curtains went back. Particularly not by Clare. Or my father, come to that.

In the event, when the fiercely protective nurse I'd crossed swords with earlier swished the curtains aside, the man closeted with Clare was nobody I recognised. He was Asian, of medium height and rather portly, with a magnificent moustache that was waxed into needle points at either side.

He was just rising from the chair next to Clare's bed, bending to speak to her in low tones and patting her hand. He was wearing a beautiful dark pinstripe suit. A box of tissues was sitting on the blanket next to my friend, half its contents having been used and scattered around her. She was still very red around her nose and eyes.

I hurried forwards just as the man was moving away from the bed. Both Sean and I fixed him with a hard stare as he came past us, but he swept on oblivious to us lesser mortals. He could only have been a consultant.

'Clare!' I said. 'Are you OK?'

She made the effort of a big brave smile that just managed to break the surface then sank like a rock. 'Oh, hello Charlie,' she said, her voice a little wavery. 'Yes, I think so.'

'Who was that?' I demanded, jerking my head in the direction of the departing Asian doctor. 'What's he said to upset you?'

For a moment she looked confused. 'Oh, no, Mr Chandry's been lovely,' she said vaguely, picking up the tissues and dropping them into a carrier bag that was hooked onto the door of her cabinet. 'I s'pose I'm just not having a good day, that's all.'

'Do you want us to go?' I asked, uncertain.

'No, no, please, sit down. I'm glad you're here. I wanted to talk to you anyway.'

I sank onto the chair the consultant had occupied. Sean was still standing by the foot of the bed. He glanced from one of us to the other.

'I think I'll raid the coffee machine,' he said.

'No, Sean, don't go.' Clare gave him a watery smile. 'I know you're just being tactful, but I wanted to talk to you, too.'

She waited until he'd pulled up his own chair on the opposite side of the bed. She was looking down at a tissue in her bruised hands, concentrating on teasing the edges apart so it split into gossamer-thin layers. There was a drip plugged into the back of her left hand and a bag of clear fluid suspended from the bed frame.

'I don't really know where to start,' she said.

I glanced across at Sean briefly. Maybe now we were going to get the whole story.

Then Clare looked up suddenly, straight into my face, and said, 'How do you cope with causing someone's death?'

I opened my mouth and shut it again.

94

Sean came to my rescue. 'In what way "causing",
Clare?' he asked gently.

She shrugged awkwardly, pushing both fists into the
mattress to ease her body into a more comfortable position.
The pins moved too, like porcupine quills. The whole of the
frame creaked slightly as it tracked with her and readjusted.

'Yesterday Slick was alive and now he's dead,' she said,
her voice miserable. 'I keep thinking suppose there was
something I should have done differently, you know?
Suppose by one action, somewhere back down the line – a
day ago, a week ago – I could have averted this. And I
didn't do it. How do you cope with that?'

'Time,' Sean said. He was leaning forwards with his
elbows resting on his knees and his eyes fixed intently on
Clare. 'There's an old saying – this too will pass. Sounds
corny, but it's true. The memory fades and things will get
better. You just have to let it go.'

Clare looked wholly unconvinced. I desperately wanted
to ask why she thought it might have been down to her, but
I knew I couldn't do it. To introduce an element of doubt
now would be devastating. Besides, her eyes had already
started to fill again.

'I just feel so guilty,' she gulped, pulling another tissue
from the box. It snagged and tore and she let her hand
drop, defeated. 'I've made such a mess of things.'

'Come on, Clare,' I said, desperately searching for
something to encourage her. 'Madeleine will track down
Jacob soon and he'll be home before you know it—'

If I was hoping to hearten her, I had the opposite effect.
The tears spilled over and trickled down her white cheeks.
She scrubbed at them angrily.

'I've caused so much disruption to everyone,' she said,
forlorn. 'Jacob was so excited about this trip. There are
some classic bikes coming up for grabs this week that he's
been trying to get hold of for years. And now I've messed
it up for him.'

'How can you say that?' I asked quietly. 'If it was Jacob

lying here and you were away you'd drop everything to be back with him, in a heartbeat. You know you would.'

'Jacob wouldn't have got himself into this in the first place,' she said, sobbing now. 'Jacob's too s-sensible to have made such a stupid decision on the s-spur of the moment.'

'We all make them,' Sean said. 'The big decisions are never the ones that trip you.'

Clare looked at him and tried for a smile that was only partially successful. 'Even you, huh?'

'Especially me,' he said, giving her one of his smiles that usually made my knees buckle. But despite his light tone I knew it was no easy responsibility for Sean. When he made the wrong decisions, people died. He'd so nearly become the victim of his own error of judgement.

'So how do you do it?' she asked. 'How do you go on like nothing has happened, day after day?'

She was talking personally now. Clare knew I'd been driven far enough to kill. Hell, she ought to know. Death wasn't an abstract concept to me. It was a reality. Maybe that was precisely why she was asking.

I glanced at Sean, sitting calmly on the other side of the bed, that sometimes cold face creased with concern over my friend's tears. In a twisted way I took comfort from the fact that her anguish disturbed him. It seemed to indicate a measure of humanity that, watching him dealing Eamonn, I'd been deeply afraid he'd lost.

'You just—' I broke off, helpless. *Just what? Got over it? Moved on?* 'I don't know,' I said at last. 'You just do.'

There were people moving around the ward all the time, so I'd ignored the footsteps behind me until they stopped close by.

'Charlotte,' said my father's voice, quietly reproachful.

I turned in my seat and found him eyeing Clare's distressed face. He was wearing surgical garb. The top of his head was covered by a bandana that seemed absurdly jaunty, given his position.

96

'I'd like a word with you before you leave.' His tone made it clear that departure was going to happen sooner rather than later. We rose obediently and said our goodbyes to Clare.

'We'll call back this evening,' I promised.

'Clare is scheduled to go back down to theatre this afternoon,' my father said as we walked away. 'I would suggest you leave any further visits until tomorrow.' From him it was an order.

He waited until he'd got us outside the entrance to the ward before he delivered his next punch.

'Please do not harass my patients,' he said coldly, once he'd got my attention, 'or I will ask for you to be excluded.'

I couldn't suppress a gasp at that. Sean was standing behind me and I felt his hands close on my upper arms. I wasn't sure if it was to stop me hitting my father, or to stop himself. I swallowed.

'It was one of the consultants who was harassing her, not us,' I snapped. I took a breath and said, more calmly, 'Why's she going back into theatre? Is she all right?'

My father regarded me for a moment. 'The damage to your friend's limbs may well require a number of surgical procedures over the coming weeks,' he said, icily mild. 'I trust I do not need to consult you about each of them?'

'No,' I muttered. 'Of course not.'

His gaze remained on me a moment longer, then shifted to take in Sean. His curt nod of recognition was the only greeting he imparted.

'Sir,' Sean said, the same noncommittal response he'd given to officers in the army who had yet to earn his respect. He let his hands drop away and I saw my father's eyes narrow, as though he didn't like Sean touching his daughter. I stepped forwards.

'I'm sorry,' I said, making peace. 'Clare was crying when we arrived. I was worried about her.'

97

'I understand,' he said stiffly. He transferred his scrutiny from Sean back to me. 'Why are you limping?'

'I'm not,' I said automatically, surprised.

'You have a problem with your knee.'

I shrugged. I knew exactly what was the matter with that knee but I wasn't about to tell my father. 'Then I suppose I must have banged it,' I said.

He was silent for a moment, as though he sensed I wasn't telling him the whole truth. Another figure appeared, wearing the same kind of pale blue outfit, and hovered just inside his line of sight. He nodded to them.

'As I mentioned, Clare won't be up to visitors again today,' he said to me, with a touch of impatience. 'I have your number, Charlotte. I'll call you when there's any progress to report.'

I nodded, feeling dismissed.

'Put some ice on that knee,' he said as he moved for the door, his parting shot. And to Sean: 'You should take better care of her.'

I felt Sean stiffen as the comment hit home on all kinds of levels.

'Yes sir,' he said, his face expressionless. He waited until my father had turned his back and was three paces away. 'And so should you.'

My father's hearing was excellent, always had been. But he carried on walking without a break in stride, as though Sean had never spoken.

I waited until we were nearly back to the Shogun before I asked the question that had been in my mind ever since Clare put the subject there.

'So how *do* you cope with it?'

Sean was in the middle of fishing his car keys out of his jacket pocket. He stopped and half-turned towards me. 'With what?'

'With having blood on your hands,' I said.

He went still again but his answer came fast enough that I knew it was something he'd either been asked before, or had asked himself.

'I concentrate on what isn't there,' he said. 'On the blood that never got spilt because I did my job and I was good at it.'

'So it doesn't bother you?'

He shrugged. 'Not as much as it probably should. But I've never lost a principal I was guarding and I never killed anyone I didn't intend to,' he said, his words cool and totally matter-of-fact. 'There's not many people in our line of business who can say the same.'

I was still thinking about a response to that when Sam's Norton Commando came burbling into the car park. Sam spotted me and pulled up alongside. He cut the engine and fumbled with the strap on his helmet.

'Hi, Charlie!' he said, flicking wary little glances in Sean's direction. 'How's Clare?'

'Not so good,' I said. 'They're operating on her legs again this afternoon. No visitors for a while.'

He looked disappointed and relieved at the same time. 'Any sign of Jacob?'

Sean shook his head. 'Not yet,' he said.

Sam looked at him fully then. 'You must be Sean,' he said in a hearty tone, holding his hand out. 'I'm Sam Pickering. Charlie and I are old mates, aren't we, Charlie?'

Sean raised an eyebrow but shook Sam's proffered hand easily enough. Sam was wearing his habitual old jeans and battered black leather jacket and when he took his helmet off his hair reached down to his shoulder blades. I watched them sizing each other up. The ex-squaddie and the modern hippie. What a combination.

'Really?' he said, pleasantly. 'Well, thank you for coming and telling her about Clare's accident. We appreciate it.'

'Er, no problem,' Sam said, frowning as he realised he'd just been firmly sidelined and scrambling to regain lost ground. 'So, you going tonight then, Charlie?'

'Going where?'

'Slick's wake,' he said. He'd turned slightly further

99

round to face me, as though he was trying to exclude Sean from the conversation altogether.

'Wake?' I said. I glanced at Sean to see how he was taking this behaviour but his face was shuttered. 'That might not be a bad idea. See what rumours are flying around.'

I turned back to Sam. 'OK,' I said. 'We'll come. When and where?'

'Kicks off about seven. It's up at Gleet's place – he's got a workshop on a farm somewhere out towards Wray. I can probably get you in but—' He cast Sean a dubious look. 'Look, don't take this the wrong way, mate, but I'm not sure you'll blend in too well. You've gotta be on a bike, for a kickoff.'

'I'll take it the way it was meant,' Sean said dryly.

My mind skated over the spare bikes at Jacob's, but there wasn't much beyond the Laverda and Clare's Ducati. Both of which were too well known not to cause comment. I thought of my own FireBlade, sitting down at my parents' place in Cheshire, but there wasn't the time to go and fetch it. Even if Sean had had a helmet or any leathers.

'OK,' I said. 'I'll go with you, Sam.'

Sam's grin flashed. I saw Sean gathering himself to object and put my hand on his arm. 'Don't worry, I'll be fine,' I said. 'I'm only going for a nosy. And Sam's right about needing to be on a bike.'

He saw the sense in that. Didn't like it, but saw the sense in it nevertheless.

'So, we going undercover, Charlie?' Sam kicked the Norton back into life and rammed his helmet on. He grinned at me again through his open visor. 'Just like old times then, eh?'

Sean stepped in close to him, moving suddenly enough to make Sam jerk back in the seat. 'Just make sure you look out for her,' he said with quiet intensity.

Sam swallowed and flipped his visor down so he didn't have to reply. He toed the bike into gear, circling out of the car park with a roar.

'Well, that was mildly embarrassing,' I said lightly, watching him go.

Sean smiled at me and there was a hint of smugness to it. 'Sometimes you've just got to reinforce who's top dog.'

'Top dog?' I repeated in disgust. 'You two were practically sniffing each other's bollocks. I expected one of you to start humping my leg at any moment.'

Sean's smile widened into a proper grin. 'Charlie,' he said, 'I'd hump your leg any time.'

'Try it,' I said sweetly, 'and I'll have you straight down to the vet's.'

'Damn, but you're a hard woman . . .'

The wake for Slick Grannell was held in a long sloping field behind the barn workshop belonging to Gleet, out in the wilds. When Sam explained the format I was expecting something rather cheesy. In the event it was a thoroughly pagan affair, heartfelt and strangely moving.

The field, cut and cleared for hay, was stubble under foot. Someone had gathered a huge stack of dead branches and old pallets for a bonfire at the top end to rival anything put together on Guy Fawkes' night. Perched on top, in a bizarre piece of symbolism, was Slick's disfigured Shoei helmet and his gloves.

The music was mainly rock ballads, played at volume through a pair of Marshall stacks that had been dragged just inside the gateway on extension leads from the barn. Lots of raw-throated songs about crashing and burning and dying young.

Gleet, so Sam informed us when he swung by to collect me, was big on the custom bike scene. His family had been farmers but Gleet left the running of the farm to his sister, a sour big-boned woman who trudged silently round the place like a resentful ghost. Gleet turned his back on the day-to-day drudgery and instead, in the barn behind the house, he devoted his time to building show-winning creations that were masterpieces of steel and paint.

101

It was probably as much out of respect for Gleet as for Slick that the attendance for the wake was so high. There must have been over a hundred bikers turned up. Their machines clogged the yard outside the barn and ended up slotted in rows across the end of the field. Everything from the latest MV Agustas to tatty old rat bikes. My Suzuki and Sam's Norton were safely swallowed up in the crowd. We grabbed bottles of beer from one of the overflowing barrels next to the hedge and did our best to mingle with the others.

The hot sultry weather had taken on a sudden glowering edge, like it was spoiling for a fight. The shock of the early evening sunlight on the brilliant greens of the far tree-line was startling against a gunmetal gathering sky. It was heavy enough for thunder and I began to wish I'd remembered to pick up my waterproofs when I was at the cottage.

They lit the bonfire just after eight. Gleet himself walked up the hill from the barn carrying a flaming torch, with Tess by his side. She had forsaken the scrunchie and had her thin flat hair down around her face. Over a shapeless black dress she was wearing a scuffed leather bike jacket that was much too big for her. I recognised it as Slick's.

Trotting by her side, stumbling over the stubbly ground, was an extraordinarily beautiful blonde-haired child of about four. She clutched tight to Tess's hand and stared at the apparitions around her with her eyes big and wide and her thumb in her mouth.

'Slick's daughter,' Sam muttered to me.

I remembered Jamie saying Tess had a kid. My only brief recollections of Slick were of a cocky womaniser, not a family man. I wondered how Tess felt, sitting at home with the baby while he was out on the prowl. And suddenly I could understand her bitter anger towards Clare. Whether there'd been anything actually going on between her and Slick was beside the point. It was enough that Clare had been the one who was with him at the time of the accident.

The bonfire grabbed instantly at the flames when Gleet

102

dipped the torch against the dry timbers. He walked right round the stack so it caught evenly from all sides and went up with artificially accelerated momentum.

Within a few minutes the flames were dancing round the helmet on the top of the pile. I moved in a little closer and watched the visor twist and buckle and blacken in the heat. Someone turned off the music mid-chord and then all you could hear was the crackle of the fire.

'You all know why we're here,' Gleet said then, his deep voice loud enough to boom and carry across the field. 'We all knew Slick. Some of us are probably going to his funeral next week.' He nodded to Tess and took a swig from the bottle of beer he was holding. 'But some bloody vicar who never knew him, mouthing a few meaningless phrases, don't mean jack shit to us, his mates. So we're here to give him a proper send off and to tell it like it is!'

He glared at the people who'd bunched up close around the fire. They stared back in silence. The little girl was now clinging to Tess's leg, hiding her face from the heat of the flames. Tess reached down and hoisted the child onto her hip, never taking her eyes off Gleet.

'Me, I knew Slick for ten years. Since he built his first bike and came begging a welding rig he'd no idea how to use,' Gleet said. He shook his head sadly and smiled. 'The daft bastard. Blew so many holes in the frame he was trying to repair, it was fit for scrap by the time he was done.'

The crowd let out its collective breath, almost a sigh, the surface tension broken.

Gleet raised his beer bottle and took another gulp. 'He was loud and flash and he was mouthy, but if you needed a lift with something, Slick was the first to volunteer. He was a good mate to me.' He glanced at Tess for the first time, meeting and holding her gaze. 'And I know he thought the world of you, Tess, and little Ashley,' he went on, gruff. 'And if there's anything I can ever do to help you, you know you've only got to shout.'

There was a general murmur at this sentiment. Gleet

103

necked the rest of his drink in one long swallow and turned away before she had time to react to that one. Telling. Either he didn't really mean it, or he meant it too much for his own comfort.

'To Slick!' he shouted. 'Wherever he is now, I hope he's giving 'em hell!'

And amid the murmuring of assent he turned and threw the empty bottle into the fire hard enough to smash the glass against the burning timber.

While he'd been speaking, I noticed Jamie had moved up to talk to Tess. I hadn't spotted his bike when we arrived, but one little Irish-registered four hundred would have been easily swallowed up in the crowd.

He and Tess were too far away for me to hear anything that passed between them but I could follow the body language without needing much of a phrase book.

At first she shook him off but he persisted, speaking urgently. Gradually I saw Tess's hostility turn to disbelief, then a saddened anger. By the time Gleet had finished his eulogy, she looked close to tears. What the hell had Jamie said to her?

I saw her throw him a brief smile, then she stepped forward and raised her own bottle. The silver and glass rings on her fingers flashed in the light.

'I know Slick could be a bit of an arsehole when he was pissed. And I know he wasn't always faithful to me,' she said, her voice thin and reedy, 'but he was always trying to get the best for me and Ashley, and he always came back in the end. He would have done this time, too,' she added. 'And I'd've kicked him down the bloody stairs before I'd have let him explain, but I'd have taken him back ...'

Her voice tailed off and she gave the little girl she was holding a fierce hug. She, too, threw her empty bottle at the feet of the flames and turned away.

Interesting choice of words. I went over them in my head while I took another minute sip of the beer I'd been nursing all evening. Had whatever Jamie had told her only moments before made any difference to what she'd just said?

Other people came forwards and over the next half an hour or so I discovered that Slick was both generous and mean, short-tempered and immensely humorous. He also seemed to owe money all over the place. Enough that someone might have gone after his bike to cover his debts?

Then Jamie stepped up to the fire to have his say. 'Slick gave me a chance to prove myself when others wouldn't,' he said, that handsome face sober. 'He trusted me. I won't forget that.'

As he spoke he glanced across to where I could just see William standing near the front of the crowd, with Paxo to the left of him.

I realised, too, that there was a third figure involved. He was too close to be just a bystander, his head tilted with too much obvious interest in the proceedings. As I watched, he leaned a casual arm on William's broad shoulder, swinging a beer bottle by the neck between his forefinger and thumb. A tall, almost slender guy, not far into his twenties if I was any judge, with short-cropped dark hair and wearing race-replica leathers that made him look like a walking cigarette packet.

Cigarette packet.

I knew there was something familiar about that colour scheme and then it clicked. I remembered the bikers who'd buzzed past me on the way to the hospital. Two of them had clearly been William on his Kawasaki and Paxo on his Ducati. It was too much of a coincidence that those same matching leathers of the Aprilia rider who'd been with him didn't belong to the man now regarding Jamie with a mixture of irritation and amusement on his face.

Jamie started to move towards the group and I was keen to see what happened but at that moment I felt a tug on my own sleeve. I turned to find Sam beckoning me over to one side.

'Did you know Slick was supposed to be organising a

105

trip to Ireland at the end of this week?' he said when we'd moved far enough away not to be overheard ourselves.

'Yes,' I said, frowning, even a little annoyed that Sam had dragged me away from witnessing a much more interesting exchange. 'It's a Devil's Bridge Club thing, isn't it? Why?'

Sam looked slightly crestfallen at my reaction. 'Oh,' he said. 'Well, there were rumours that it would all be off, what with Slick kicking the bucket an' all.'

'You're all heart, Sam,' I said, glancing round to check none of the dead man's mates were standing close enough to take offence.

'Yeah, but that's not all,' Sam went on, grinning at me through his beard. 'When someone said the trip was probably going to be cancelled, someone else said they thought there was too much at stake for the rest of them not to go.'

'Too much at stake?' I queried. 'What the hell does that mean?'

He shrugged, looking pleased with himself. 'Hey, I'm just the oily rag, not the engine driver,' he said. 'I just thought you ought to know.'

'Yeah,' I said, distracted. 'Thanks, Sam. Keep your ears open.'

Why did I get the feeling this Irish trip was more than just a bikers' outing? Jamie was from Ireland. So was Isobel – and Eamonn. Jacob was there now. Coincidence, or design? I couldn't help wondering what Jamie had just told Tess that seemed to have put her mind at rest. And what was this chance that Slick had given him? Was it as simple as proving he could ride fast, or was there more to it than that?

I turned away, so caught up in my tumbling thoughts that when someone moved deliberately in front of me I came to an abrupt halt and only just avoided bumping into them. I looked up and found William's stony face staring down at me. Such was the intensity in his expression that I took a half-step back away from him.

My focus expanded rapidly and I realised that Paxo was

just behind William's left shoulder, Gleet behind his right. None of them looked what you might call friendly, except with each other, which – after their run-in outside the hospital – did surprise me. I glanced casually over my own shoulder in case the Aprilia rider was closing in on me from behind but he was nowhere to be seen. Sam had melted away into the background.

'This is a private party for Slick's mates,' Paxo said meaningfully. 'What the fuck made you think you were invited?'

'I didn't hear anybody tell me I wasn't,' I said, keeping my voice calm and level. I mentally traced my escape route. Too far to get to the Suzuki in a hurry. Better hope I didn't need to.

'Well, Charlie, you're hearing it now,' William said evenly.

'Oh really?' I shifted my gaze briefly between the three of them. 'I've had to put up with the cops raiding Jacob's place this afternoon looking for the carcass of Slick's bike,' I said, wondering if MacMillan's polite search quite qualified as a raid. 'I told them jack shit – to borrow a phrase – about what he might have been up to and where else they might care to look. And you tell me that's not the action of a mate?'

Gleet raised his eyebrows. 'She's got a point,' he allowed. 'If she's come to pay her respects, why not let her stay?'

'No!' Paxo said, vehement. 'She's just come to snoop.'

Gleet regarded me solemnly for a moment although there might have been more than that going on under the surface. 'Well at least she's not brought that tame thug of hers with her,' he said. 'Who is he, by the way?'

'His name's Sean Meyer and he's a real nasty piece of work,' said a new voice from my left. Jamie stepped into view and faced me with barely concealed glee at this unexpected opportunity to put the boot in.

'Sean Meyer?' William repeated slowly. 'I remember

107

that name now – from years back. Racist bastard, wasn't he? Went down for it.'

'No,' I said flatly. 'He wasn't. And he didn't.'

'I know Mum was down at Dad's place this morning and Sean beat the shit out of her boyfriend,' Jamie said. 'Splatted his nose all over his face.'

'Considering Eamonn was attempting to break both my ankles at the time,' I snapped, 'I'd say he had it coming, wouldn't you?'

I glanced back at the others. Gleet's heavy features might even have been looking amused. William and Paxo exchanged silent glances I didn't catch the meaning of.

'I think you should leave now,' William said then, his voice almost indifferent. 'Either of your own accord or not. Makes no odds to us.'

I shrugged, tossed my three-quarter empty bottle of beer into the fire and turned away, starting to walk down the hill towards where the bikes were parked. Gleet and the others walked with me in silence. I could feel them behind me all the way and it was tempting to break into a run but I kept my pace steady. By the time I reached the Suzuki my shoulder blades were twitching with the effort.

They watched me retrieve my helmet from the bar end, kick the RGV into life and wheel it out of the line. All the while I was expecting one of them to reinforce the threat with something more physical. I knew I didn't stand a chance if they decided to make their displeasure more actively felt and I concentrated on keeping my face blank, my stance passive. But they said nothing. Did nothing. Just standing there glaring was more than enough.

As I rode away carefully along the potholed farm track leading to the main road I could feel the nervous sweat sticking my shirt to my back under my leathers. I hadn't learned much, that was true, but at least I'd escaped unscathed from the encounter.

I only hoped that Sam would be able to do the same.

108

Chapter Eight

The first spots of rain began to fall just as I hit the main road and turned the Suzuki's head back towards Lancaster.

I cursed under my breath as I felt the rain splash onto my visor. It wouldn't be long before the water was down the back of my neck. I reached up and pulled the collar of my jacket tighter, like that was really going to make a difference.

We hadn't had any significant rain for weeks and the Wray road was out in farm country, bordered by tall hedges and dry stone walls. Constant agricultural traffic meant the tarmac was coated with dust and muck and diesel. Just add water and it quickly turned to a lethally slippery film on the surface. Until the rainfall was heavy enough to wash the road clean, it was like riding on black ice.

The light was dropping, too. That halfway stage between day and evening when you need your headlights on but they don't actually seem to do much. I slowed right down.

Which was how they managed to catch me quite so easily.

I don't know precisely where they came from. One moment my mirrors were empty, and the next there was the sudden flare of main beam headlights behind me.

My first thought was that some stupid car driver had only just cottoned on to the fact that the approaching gloom meant it might be a good idea to put his lights on.

As soon as I'd finished that thought, the suspicious part of my mind took over. When I first took to two wheels I learned very quickly how vulnerable you are to other road users. I was knocked off the first time before I'd even passed my test.

Looks like someone was aiming for a rematch.

The lights had closed up fast on my rear end, blazing. I edged slightly over to the left, hoping the driver would take the hint and just go past me.

The lights moved up closer still. I couldn't see anything of the vehicle or the driver because of the glare of them. I held my position and speed. As I approached a left-hander the driver following me put on a burst of speed and swung out to the right. As he drew level with my knee I realised that the lights were too big and too widely spaced to belong to a car. More like a van.

Transit van, Clare had said when I'd asked what had hit her. *Determined sod*.

Instinctively, I whacked the throttle wide open just as the van lurched sideways into my airspace.

The bike's engine screamed as the tacho needle bounced into the red line at 12,000rpm. I backed off before the rev limiter cut in, just long enough to kick a fast clutchless change, and threw my weight over the forks to try to keep the front wheel on the ground.

I wasn't fast enough. The van hit the back end of the Suzuki, jolting it sideways and nearly bucking me head first into the dry stone wall by the edge of the road. That was probably the idea. I swear I heard the crack of splintering plastic as my back mudguard and numberplate shattered.

The van's headlights shrank abruptly as I pulled away from him. The needle on the bike's speedo rushed upwards as the outskirts of the little village of Wray leapt towards me. Just before the speed restriction signs the road curved sharp left. To remind you to slow down the planners had helpfully placed a series of vicious ridges in the tarmac which were right across the apex to the bend. Maybe the

110

van driver was just hanging back waiting for me to crash. I tried hard to disappoint him.

I held my breath as I chucked the Suzuki into the turn faster than I normally would have dared if it had been smooth, and daylight, and dry.

The tyres, already scrabbling for grip on the slick surface, hit the ridges and let go altogether. The bike leapt and twisted like a terrified horse. All I could do was sit tight and try to control it when we came down again.

Any moment I expected the front end to wash out completely and send me barrelling into the far kerb. Not good at the best of times. Particularly not good when I had a Transit van on my tail who had no chance of stopping before he ran me down.

Even if he'd wanted to.

I had a horrifying flash vision of the pins holding Clare's bones together. *If whatever vehicle that hit them had run over her torso instead of her legs,* the young doctor had told me, *she'd be dead right now.*

I was still completely out of shape when the left-hander snapped into a right-hander. Praying, I flung my body-weight across the bike to flick it into the next corner and hit the gas, feeling the back end start to shimmy as the rear wheel spun up. In the dry the Suzuki didn't have enough brute horsepower to rip the fat back tyre loose, but in these greasy conditions it let go in a heartbeat.

And all at once, everything slowed around me. Peripherally, I could see the continuous splatter of the rain hitting my visor, the water beading up and being instantly shed by the Rain-X dispersant I always used.

But most of all I could feel the tenuous contact between the two palm-sized areas of rubber and the glassy tarmac under them. The front end was still clinging on, teetering on the limit of adhesion so that every trembling vibration was transmitted up through the forks and into my hands.

The back end had let go like it was slowly tearing, the revs ripping up as the engine gouted power through the broken grip like blood. The bike was starting to skate and I had fractions of a second to do something about it or become another one of Superintendent MacMillan's much-vaunted statistics.

I rolled the throttle off just a fraction, an infinitesimal amount. Enough to control the slide and use the rear-wheel-steer effect to get me through the bend.

I catapulted out the other side, amazed to find myself still attached to the bike, and the bike still attached to the road. Reality righted itself and resumed its pace. I snapped upright and sent the Suzuki hurtling into the village main street, the exhaust howling its triumph and rage in equal measure.

Behind me, the Transit's lights suddenly began to thrash wildly from side to side. It took me a moment to work out that the erratic movement was caused by a monumental slide of its own. The driver had pushed too far in his efforts to pursue me and the van responded violently to the abuse.

The fact that the driver was prepared to try so hard scared me badly. Not that I wasn't fairly well scared already. The rain was falling more strongly now and I knew I hadn't a hope in hell of outrunning him in this.

A side turning opened up seemingly almost alongside me. I grabbed for the brakes, locking up the rear wheel, and just made the turn in. The side street was lined with semi-detached houses, mostly with cars in the driveway. I picked the first one that looked empty and threw the bike up onto the pavement, diving down the side of the house right up to the gate into the back garden. I'd flicked the lights off and killed the engine before I'd even come to a stop.

I struggled to turn the bike round so it was facing outwards again, just in case they spotted the damaged back end, and jumped off, crouching down in its shadow. My breath was a harsh rasp in my throat. I was hard up against the fence, my feet in a flower border. All I could smell was creosote and honeysuckle and hot rubber and rain.

The Suzuki nearly rolled on top of me and I realised belatedly that I hadn't put the side-stand down. I shoved it down and wedged it in place with my fist, aware of the blood pounding in my ears and beating against the inside of my ribs until I thought they'd crack.

The van wasn't far behind me. It fishtailed into the end of the road, engine wailing, and slowed to a crawl. I peered round the Suzuki's fairing and saw it creep past the end of the driveway, the slanting rain coming and going in the headlights.

There were at least two people inside. I caught outlines but no detail as they passed in front of the light from the house opposite. They were both leaning forwards, hunting, and despite the cloudburst they had the windows wound down to catch the slightest trace of me. Professionals.

The van seemed to pause for a long time in front of the driveway where I was hiding but it could only have been a second or two, then they were moving on to the next one. I shut my eyes briefly, sagging against the bike.

I should have known it wouldn't last.

A bright light flared in my eyes, making me jerk back, blinded. The light over the back door to the house had come on. There was the rattle of a key turning in a lock and the door opened. An elderly woman ventured out onto the step. She was in her slippers, with a fire iron gripped in her bony fist.

'Oy,' she yelled. 'What d'you think you're doing in my bloody garden?'

My eyes skated to the van. All I could see of it over the front hedge was the roof but that was enough. It jerked to a stop fiercely enough to make the nose dip.

I glanced back. Persuading the old lady to let me in to her house was going to take too long. Besides, the men who were after me seemed determined enough that they might choose to follow regardless. I couldn't take the risk.

Ignoring the irate householder, I vaulted back onto the bike, hitting the run switch and the kick start at the same

113

time. The Suzuki, bless it, fired up first time. Out on the street came the graunch of gears and the harsh whine of the van's differential spinning up in reverse.

I rammed the bike into gear and launched along the drive, feet trailing. The van reached the mouth of the driveway at almost the same moment I did and I had to swerve across the pavement to evade him. I thumped down off the kerb, taking the wing mirror off a parked car with my elbow as I went. Its alarm started shrieking.

The back of the Transit bore down like a wall as it came storming after me, still locked in reverse. There were cars approaching on the main road and I dived fleetingly on the brakes at the junction. My choice of direction was made entirely on the first gap in traffic that presented itself. Unfortunately, it meant I turned back the way I'd come, away from the safety of home.

As it was, I just made it out in front of a car that had to veer violently to avoid me, braking hard enough to skid. Shit! I ducked my head and risked a quick look in my mirrors as I caned the bike away, thinking at least that should slow the van down a bit.

It didn't.

The Transit driver never even hesitated. He punched straight out across the main street, T-boning the car that had nearly collided with me and sending it spinning across the road. It bounced up the kerb and into a low garden wall, scattering debris.

By the time I hit that nasty S-bend again on the way out of the village, the van was less than a hundred and fifty metres behind and closing faster than was healthy for me. The road was still slick and the rain had become a steady downpour.

I knew then that I needed a particular kind of help and I needed it fast. And there was only one immediate place I stood a chance of getting it.

When I'd ridden the lane up to Gleet's place with Sam earlier in the evening, I'd done so slowly and with great care, skirting round the larger craters rather than risk buckling a wheel by riding into them. Now the puny beam from the Suzuki's headlight meant I couldn't see them in time, in any case.

I stood up on the footpegs to lessen the jarring on my back and kept the throttle hard on, gripping tight with my knees. Even in very low light the Suzuki couldn't be mistaken for a trail bike but it scrambled gamely over the rough ground. The only protest was the intermittent squealing of the engine as the back wheel bounced, slithered and bit on the loose surface.

As I reached the pair of stone gateposts leading into the farmyard the Transit was around sixty metres behind me. It suddenly occurred to me that I could have made a fatally stupid error of judgement. If Gleet and the rest of the Devil's Bridge Club decided not to step in, the yard would turn into a dead-end rat trap. My attackers must have thought they couldn't have planned for a better place to finish what they'd started.

I flicked my eyes away from the mirrors and realised that I was aiming for the side of a barn at a speed not best suited to good health and long life. I hauled on the brake lever and prayed the Suzuki would stay upright on the gravelly surface. The bike skidded slightly, wriggling its body in disgust, but it didn't let go on me.

There were two sodium lights on, their orange beams crossing in the centre of the yard, misting the rain. It looked different in the dark and I realised I'd missed the gateway to the field where Slick's wake was being held. I started to swear inside my helmet.

The yard was too small and too overcrowded to play dodgems and hope to get away with it for long. There were half a dozen partly dismantled bikes of various descriptions parked up along the front wall of the barn, next to a rusting Bedford van and a collection of other vehicles that looked as if they might or might not still crank.

But, more importantly, there were no signs of any people.

115

I knew from experience that the horn on the RGV was a pathetic toot that didn't even make errant cyclists look round. The only thing I could think of doing was yanking the clutch in and whacking the throttle wide open.

The Suzuki's two-stroke motor surged round to the redline and sat there, screaming. It was the mechanical equivalent of Faye Wray stuck fast in King Kong's fist, and just as good at attracting male attention. I winced at the sound and prayed the rev limiter would hold the engine intact.

Faces appeared in the gateway and I shut off instantly. The door to the workshop swung open, spilling light out across the yard, and I saw Gleet's head appear round it. He made fleeting eye contact, turning to inspect the Transit, which had scraped to a halt just through the gateway. My adversaries sat it there, blocking my escape route. The only sound was our combined engines ticking over and the slap of the van's wipers across the glass.

Gleet glanced back at me calmly, then disappeared back inside the workshop, letting the door bang shut behind him.

'You bastard!' I muttered under my breath, a bitter taste in my mouth. I would have expanded further on this theme, but at that moment the Transit leapt forwards.

As he came at me I tried to duck round him and head back for the gateway, but the Suzuki's steering lock at low speed was awful. Unless I got lucky, I knew I wasn't going to make it back out onto the open road again. And then where did I go?

Instead, I ran the bike down the narrow gap between the old Bedford and the stone wall that bordered the yard, and jumped off onto the top of the wall. Without the stand down, the bike toppled sideways and scraped against the stone, gouging the end of the handlebar and mirror as it did so, and then stalled. On top of the abuse I'd already heaped on the poor thing, I didn't think a bit more would make much difference one way or the other but it grieved me to let it happen, all the same.

The Transit driver obviously thought seriously about ramming the bulky Bedford to get to me, but even he must have realised that he'd be on to a loser if he tried it.

Instead, he lurched the front corner of his vehicle into part of the dry stone wall further down. The ripple effect caused the whole thing to buckle. A section about five metres long, including the part I was standing on, collapsed as neatly as if the Royal Engineers had laid the charges.

I felt it start to cave under me and half-fell, half-jumped, clear. If I'd been given a free choice, I would have gone for the other side of the wall, into the comparative safety of the field beyond, but luck and the laws of physics weren't on my side.

Instead, I cannoned off the front of the Bedford's bodywork and landed sprawled on my hands and knees in the yard, only a couple of metres away from the van. Even as I started scrambling to my feet, he was backing out of the debris and swinging the vehicle towards me. God, that front grille looked like a truck from down there.

Then, just when I thought it was all over, we went into unexpected injury time.

The door to the workshop swung open again, and people started pouring out. Not just any people, but big, pissed-off looking bikers, wearing greased down denim and leather. They were brandishing a collection of improvised armaments and they advanced as one body, ominous.

It was enough to take the Transit driver's mind off grinding me into the dirt under his wheels. He paused, uncertain. But that wasn't what made my assailants decide to cut and run.

Gleet himself reappeared, stepping neatly to one side like a showman introducing his star turn. Behind him stumped a bulky woman in a grubby dress and Wellington boots who could only have been his sullen sister.

In her hands she was holding a wicked-looking crossbow with the string drawn taut, an arrow already in the groove. When she brought the weapon up to her shoulder it was

117

with a practised grace, like the steps of a formal dance. She was leaning in to it, with her feet planted wide to steady her aim.

By this time the Transit had gone into full retreat. It shot backwards, transmission howling, then swung into a wild reverse flip and made a dash for the gateway. He was nearly out of the yard when Gleet's sister delicately squeezed the trigger and let fly. The string snapped forwards with a crack, and the stubby arrow whirred through the air on a surprisingly level flight.

The woman must have put in a few hours of practice with that thing, because her first shot ran true. The bolt punched a hole the size of a closed fist in the glass of one of the van's rear doors, instantly shattering it into fragments. The vehicle flinched wildly, colliding with one of the gateposts as it was caned away down the drive.

The lump of stone he'd hit suddenly grew a diagonal split about two-thirds of the way up. Very slowly, the top half of it canted over and then fell off, bringing up a splash of mud as it landed with a dull wet thud.

Gleet had been watching the van retreat with a certain amount of satisfaction. Now he scowled as he eyed his ruined stonework. He turned to me. His entourage did the same. By the darkly glowering looks on their faces I wasn't sure if I'd just found a refuge, or a new fire to jump into.

I got unsteadily to my feet, undoing the strap on my helmet and pulling it off slowly with hands that I couldn't stop from shaking. My hair was plastered wet to my head but it was a relief to be out in the rain.

Gleet walked over to me and I forced myself not to back away from him.

'Well, Charlie, I gotta hand it to you,' he rumbled. 'You certainly know how to make a fucking entrance.'

Chapter Nine

I sat on a paint-splattered chair in the middle of Gleet's workshop, shaky hands wrapped round a mug of tea so sweet I could feel my teeth loosening with every mouthful.

'Get that down yer neck,' Gleet's sister said with gruff approval. 'Do you the world of good.' Close to she was a hulking woman, so near a match in build to her brother that if I hadn't seen them both together at the same time I'd suspect it was one person in drag. She'd put on a dirty green waterproof jacket in deference to the rain. It was ripped in places and tied round the middle with bailer twine.

I smiled at her, though it had no obvious effect. 'Thank you,' I said, heartfelt, and meant not just for the tea.

I didn't need to say anything else. I got the impression words embarrassed her and, just in case I was planning on coming out with any more, she nodded sharply and stamped out of the workshop, rolling her gait to compensate for her knackered knees.

She'd hustled me inside the moment the Transit had gone, with an angry instruction to her brother and the others to stop gawping and do something useful. I'd spotted Sam hovering anxiously on the outskirts of the crowd and fractionally shaken my head. He'd hesitated, torn, then nodded his agreement and withdrawn. No point in him revealing his allegiances and getting chucked out, too.

Particularly not when that van was still on the loose.

For a moment I sat alone in silence, waiting for my system to reboot. The realisation of what had so nearly happened, coupled with the memory of what *had* actually happened to Clare and Slick, was stark in my mind. The adrenaline was dissipating, leaving me trembly and light-headed.

I'd got away with it. But only just.

I concentrated on my surroundings. The workshop was in half of the big barn, partitioned off with slatted planks at one side. There was probably a hayloft above and someone had lined the ceiling with pegboard that was sagging in places and had come down altogether in others. Above it were layers of black plastic and what looked like sheep fleeces. Insulation, I guessed. Even allowing for the stone barn's natural thermal qualities, it must be bitter working out here in the winter.

The place was full of bikes and bits of bikes. It smelt of oil and paint and thinners and, very faintly, of sweet meadow hay. A partially completed bike frame stood on a low bench in the centre, surrounded by off-cuts of tubing. A TIG welder was nearby. In the corner a small area had been closed off with sheets of heavy clear plastic to make a paint spray booth. It might all look a bit scruffy but the tools on show were good quality and Gleet clearly knew what he was doing with them.

I got to my feet and did a quick circuit while I finished my tea, walking the wobbles out of my legs. At the back, behind a huge Snap-On tool chest, were piles of dead bikes and engines, stacked one on top of another. Either discarded parts of Gleet's old projects, or future ones he hadn't got around to starting yet.

It was darker back there, the light from the bank of fluoro tubes strung across the ceiling hardly penetrating. I stuck my head round the tool box and peered into the gloom, reluctant to venture much further in case of rats. I shuddered. Why did I have to go thinking about rats?

120

Then something caught my eye. A little flash of colour among the oil stains and the grime. I glanced behind me but the door to the workshop was still closed, so I dumped my empty mug on top of the tool box and stepped over a cracked crankcase, bending to pick up what I'd seen.

It was a small piece of broken fairing, not quite the size of my hand and jagged at the edges. It was dull white on one side but sprayed partly metallic blue, partly gold on the other. Distinctive colours that were instantly recognisable.

Slick's bike.

I was so caught up in my discovery that I didn't immediately hear the growling.

It started low and quiet over to my right, building until it sounded like a diesel engine running. A big diesel engine at that. I slipped the piece of broken fairing inside my jacket but kept the rest of my body very still, turning my head slowly to find a pair of wide-spaced eyes glowing at me from the dark, less than a couple of metres away.

The dog was massive. I didn't realise just how big until it stood up. Up until that point I'd thought it was already on its feet. I began to back away, moving carefully, not straightening up in case the animal took me as more of a threat than it did already.

I kept moving backwards until I was just about in the centre of the workshop. The dog followed me out, head low, hackles up, still growling. As it came out into the light I could see it was a Rottweiler bitch wearing a chain collar around its enormous neck. She moved with amazing delicacy for her bulk, hinting at speed and agility as well as sheer muscle. The eyes gleamed with a shifty intelligence.

I backed past the partly constructed frame and snatched up a section of tubing, just in case. The dog shook its head just once, jangling the collar, as if to tell me that such a puny weapon wasn't going to do me much good.

Behind me, the main door opened suddenly. I half turned so I could still keep my eye on the Rottweiler as Gleet stepped through. He stopped, saw me poised to take on his

121

guard dog and almost smiled. Just for a moment it crossed my mind that he wasn't going to call her off, then he clicked his fingers.

It was like he'd flicked a switch. The dog forgot all about me and trotted over to his side, butting against his thigh with her mammoth flat skull.

'I see you've met my Queenie,' he said, leaning down to ruffle her ears. The dog squeezed her eyes shut and yawned in pleasure, leaning against him. Even Gleet had to brace himself to take her weight.

I slowly put down the tubing and allowed myself to uncoil.

'We were just getting acquainted.'

'There's no harm in her,' Gleet said, 'if you don't cause no trouble, like.'

'I'm sure you're right,' I said dryly.

Gleet gave a grunt in reply and pushed the door all the way open. The dog sat down where she was and watched me carefully, just in case, barely turning her head as William and the tall Aprilia rider in the race-replica leathers half-pushed, half-dragged the remains of my bike into the workshop.

The gallant little Suzuki was looking pretty sorry for itself. Ignoring Queenie I hurried across for a closer look. The left-hand side of the fairing was wrecked, half of the clutch lever was broken off and one mirror was dangling. The whole of the plastic bodywork around the rear lights was smashed away, too. But that hadn't happened out in the yard.

'It's stuck in gear,' William said, waving a hand towards the locked-up rear wheel. 'The gear-lever must have snapped off when you hit the wall.'

'Shit,' I muttered. Until then I'd fostered the vain hope that the Suzuki might still be rideable.

Gleet leaned across the seat and had a look. 'Give me five minutes and I'll cobble you something together,' he said, brusque. 'It'll get you home, if nothing else.'

122

'Thank you,' I said, surprised. Expressing my gratitude to his family was getting to be a habit, so while I was at it I added, 'Your sister's a bit handy with that crossbow.'

Gleet shrugged as he wheeled the welder over. 'Yeah, well. They took away her shotgun licence,' he said, like that explained it.

He moved around the workshop, rooting through a box of spare bits for some square-section tubing he could graft on, then choosing clamps to hold it in place while he tacked it all together.

Meantime, I was aware of the scrutiny from the tall biker I'd seen with William and Paxo earlier.

'So you're Charlie Fox,' he said. He had a soft voice that seemed given easily to mockery.

I didn't reply to that one. There wasn't much I could say other than to agree with him.

He flicked his eyes to the bike, then back to me. They were very blue, and intense with it. 'Somebody doesn't like you, Charlie,' he said.

'Hm,' I said, thinking of my earlier ejection, 'I get a lot of that.'

He almost smiled. 'So who have you been upsetting?' he asked. 'Or do you just have a confrontational personality?'

'Well, look on the bright side,' I threw back, reckless. 'I haven't hit you yet.'

William's face creased into a big smile. 'I *like* this girl,' he said.

The other biker glanced across at him, frowning. 'Yes, but that's no reason,' he said, cryptic.

'True,' William agreed gravely.

I didn't ask what they were discussing and they didn't seem inclined to expand. At that moment the workshop door opened again and Paxo walked in. He took his helmet off and shook himself like a dog, scattering water off his leathers in all directions. Even his normally spiky hair looked bedraggled.

'Pigging weather! There's no sign of him, Daz,' he said

123

to the tall biker. 'We've been a few miles in every direction but he's long gone.'

'Never mind,' Daz said. 'Perhaps it's just as well.'

'Considering it's probably the same van that went after your mate Slick, I don't think chasing after it on bikes was a good idea to start with, do you?' I said mildly. 'What were you planning on doing if you caught up with it, anyway?'

Paxo scowled at me, but Daz silenced whatever snappy comment he'd been about to make with a single look.

'We don't know who was chasing you,' he said carefully, 'and we don't know what hit Slick, either – or why. It could just be one of those freak accidents and freak coincidences.'

'Come off it,' I said, letting the frustration show through. 'What was Slick up to the day he died, Daz? If he was racing then why the hell was he doing it with a pillion passenger? You running a handicap system all of a sudden?'

'Of course not.' Daz's eyes flicked in the direction of the others as he hurried to cover the slip. 'I don't know what you're on about.'

'Of course you don't,' I agreed tiredly. 'Funny that, when it's not exactly a secret that the Devil's Bridge Club have been road racing up and down the Lune valley all year. Are you planning on disbanding now that Slick's dead, or are you just going to wait until the cops catch up with you?'

Daz looked startled for a moment, then he took a deep breath, letting it out down his nose. The silence was broken by Gleet belting something with a lump hammer on the far side of my bike. I thought of the Suzuki's delicate aluminium alloy engine and tried not to wince.

'Slick wasn't supposed to be doing anything on Sunday,' Daz said when Gleet stopped hammering. He spoke with low precision, like he was speaking through tightly clenched teeth. 'He was just picking up your friend and bringing her along to Devil's Bridge, that's all.'

124

'Why?'

Daz opened his mouth, frowned sharply and closed it again. 'I don't know,' he said, too quickly. He gave me a slightly cold-edged smile. 'Maybe he got lucky.'

I mentally ducked under the jibe and kept coming. 'I don't think so. Why was he knocked off?'

'Hell, I don't know!' he tossed back. 'That's what William and Paxo were trying to find out when they came to the hospital, wasn't it? And it could just have been an accident. Who says it was deliberate?'

'I would have thought tonight proves it wasn't.' I nodded to where Gleet was fiddling with my bike. 'Besides, I spoke to Clare just before she went into theatre,' I said, not adding that she'd since changed her mind. 'It wouldn't have anything to do with this Irish trip Slick was running, would it?'

Gleet chose that moment to strike an arc on the other side of the Suzuki. The workshop was abruptly bathed in an intense blue-white light. So it might have been my imagination or something bright and quick might really have flashed across behind Daz's eyes.

He and William and Paxo had tensed, I saw, and that had nothing to do with the welding process going on nearby. Daz's face closed down. He moved in, got right in my face and loomed over me.

'You want to back up a little, Charlie, and look at this from another direction,' he said tightly. 'What makes you think that Slick was the target, huh? It could have been *your* mate who was the one they were after and Slick just got in the way.' He stepped back and delivered his parting shot. 'And I'd watch my step if I were you, Charlie, because it looks like you're next.'

Chapter Ten

As soon as Gleet had finished his makeshift repairs he wheeled the Suzuki back out into the yard for me to leave. It was clear that none of them wanted me to hang around and I wasn't keen on the idea myself.

'Looks like a dog's breakfast, but it should get you home, like,' Gleet said shortly, nodding to his handiwork. 'Just don't tell anyone who done it, OK? I got a reputation to think of.'

I agreed solemnly not to say a word and he almost smiled at me. Almost.

The gear lever now consisted of one piece of tubing rammed onto the broken shaft and another shorter piece welded on at right-angles to form a foot peg. It wasn't exactly pretty but it would do the job.

It was very dark outside now but the rain had eased off to a persistent drizzle. Behind the barn the sky glowed orange from the bonfire that burned on, undeterred by the weather. Most of the onlookers who'd gathered to watch my arrival had gone back to stand around it. Only a few of the nosier ones still remained and I was surprised to see that Tess was among them.

She had abandoned her little girl to someone else's care and, as I swung my leg over the Suzuki, she came forwards to speak to me. I waited to hear what she had to say before I tried kicking the bike into life. I wasn't sure the engine would still turn over after all it had been through and the fewer witnesses to my struggles the better.

As it was, she glared at Gleet and the others until they reluctantly moved away. She waited until they had all disappeared through the gate out of the yard before she turned her attention back to me.

'Why did you come?' she asked then, abrupt. Her mouth twisted into a sneer. 'Don't tell me you were another of Slick's bits on the side?'

I tried to remind myself that grief can make you say things you might otherwise regret.

'Of course I wasn't, Tess,' I said, keeping my voice reasonable. 'I just came to find out what he was up to.'

She eyed me for a moment. 'So you don't believe that he was knocking off that blonde tart?' she asked, her voice suddenly more uncertain.

I bit my tongue and shook my head, reasoning that a smack in the mouth was not designed to make Tess more forthcoming.

'Not for a moment,' I said. She looked so relieved I didn't add that my certainty was more down to belief in Clare's good taste than in the morals of a man who made an alley cat look positively choosy.

'You're about the only one here who don't believe it,' Tess said gloomily, twisting at the rings she was wearing. She had them just about to the first joint on every finger. 'God knows what I'm goin' to tell Ashley.'

The daughter, I remembered belatedly. Well, if she hadn't wanted the little girl exposed to malicious gossip, I considered, she should have left her with a baby-sitter or a grandparent rather than bringing her to a biker's wake.

'And now I know,' Tess said, her breath gushing out on a long sigh, 'I can't tell 'em.'

'What do you mean?'

She glanced at me, still looking miserable. 'I found out tonight that Slick *was* just giving your mate a lift up to Devil's Bridge. *He* wasn't the one she was—'

127

She broke off, uncomfortable, giving me a sideways flicker of her eyes.

'What?'

'Nothing.'

It was my turn to sigh. 'Just spit it out, Tess,' I said tiredly. 'I don't believe Clare would ever cheat on Jacob, so just say your piece and get it over with.'

Her chin came up, defiant, like I'd asked for it. 'Don't think of it as cheatin', so much,' she said and there was something a little sly about her now. 'Think of it as tradin' him in for a younger model . . .'

It took a beat before that one went in but it rocked me when it did.

'*Jamie*? You've got to be joking!' I managed. 'Who the hell told you that?'

Tess didn't reply directly but her eyes slid over towards the field where the wake had been held and I knew instantly who she meant.

Jamie himself.

I remembered her anger, which had turned to relief when he'd come over to speak to her earlier. Had he admitted that Slick was just playing taxi driver on his behalf?

Other smaller facts crowded in on me, jostling for position. Jamie's familiarity with a house he hadn't lived in for more than five years. The way the dogs hadn't barked at him when he'd broken in in the middle of the night, like he was still a regular visitor despite his denials. Clare's desperation for me to protect him in Ireland. Her lies about the day of the accident.

I saw again a picture of Jamie standing by the fire, toasting Slick as a friend and looking very like Jacob must have done when he was a young man. And I could well believe that anyone, even Clare, might have fallen for those good looks and that easygoing charm.

I glanced back at Tess and found her watching me speculatively.

'Why are you telling me this?'

128

'I asked around about you,' she said. 'You've got a name for gettin' your teeth into something and not lettin' go.' She moved in, put a hand on the sleeve of my jacket. 'I'm just warnin' you, friendly like, that you do that this time and you might not like what you find . . .'

I was tired enough not to bother trying to avoid the driveway alarm when I got back to Jacob and Clare's place. The Suzuki had run like it was on its last legs, but it got me there. As I rolled down the driveway I leaned down and patted the crumpled side of its tank. Even if it died on me now, I could still coast into the yard.

When I put my feet down on the forecourt and cut the engine I half-expected Sean to have heard it and be waiting for me, but only silence greeted my arrival. Not even the usual frantic barking of the dogs. The house seemed to be in shadowed solitude and for a moment I was assailed by unformed fears.

Sean hadn't been happy that I was intending to go to the wake with Sam, and Sam hadn't helped by his gloating attitude when he'd turned up earlier. Sean had retreated into the cool, icily civil shell in the face of it. It was either that or deck him. Sam might not have crowed about it quite so much if he'd realised the fact.

I'd hurried Sam out of the house and tried not to worry about what I'd have to deal with when I got back. If it wasn't for the Shogun still parked outside, I might almost have wondered if Sean had packed his bags and headed back down to King's Langley. Almost. But Sean didn't like quitting.

Even when the army had tried to lever him out of his career after the scandal of our affair had surfaced, he'd clung on with a tenacity that must have surprised them. It had taken a couple of years of shitty postings and near-suicidal operations before he'd finally bowed to the inevitable and got out while he could still do it on his feet.

And even then, he hadn't let them beat him. Driven to succeed, he'd built up the close protection agency to its current level just by being better than the competition. I knew Sean hadn't offered me a job for any other reason than because he believed I could meet his standards. I suppose events in Florida – however much a baptism of fire that had turned out to be – had proved I was up to it.

Now, as I put the bike away in the coach house and went inside, I was aware of a tightening in my shoulders. And it had very little to do with the prospect of explaining what had happened at the wake.

I found Sean slouched on the sofa in the living room, watching one of the satellite news channels. The reason for the lack of noise from the dogs became immediately apparent. The terrier was asleep on his lap and Bonneville, not to be outdone, was stretched out alongside him on the cushions with her head resting on his thigh. She was too old and arthritic to jump onto the sofa any more, so I knew Sean must have lifted her up there.

'Hi. I'm back,' I said unnecessarily.

There was a bottle of Jim Beam and a glass on the low table in front of him. The cap was off and the bottle was half empty. I eyed it warily. I'd seen Sean drink before but I'd never seen it have any particular effect on him. I hoped this wasn't going to be a first time.

He took one look at me and sat up suddenly, muting the sound on the TV.

'What happened?'

I gave him a tired smile. 'Long story,' I said. I gestured to my leathers. 'Just let me go and get changed first. I'm filthy and I'm soaked and—'

He stood up fast, tipping the terrier onto the floor. Before I knew it he'd grabbed my shoulders and turned my face into the light.

'What did they do to you?' he demanded.

'It's nothing.' I tried to pull my arms away and his fingers bit in, holding me still. I could have struggled further but I was too tired to try.

130

'You've been off the bike.' It was a statement, not a question.

For a moment I shied away from telling him the truth. Pointless, when he would have sniffed it out anyway. 'Yes,' I admitted finally, 'but I'm OK.'

He let his breath out in a controlled hiss. 'Where the hell was Pickering while all this was going on?'

'Doing the sensible thing and keeping a low profile.'

'Hm. Good back-up for going undercover, isn't he?'

'It wasn't like that,' I said, trying not to rise to his studied insolence. A burst of temper escaped anyway and took flight. 'What was it you told me once about Madeleine? That I should go easy on her because she wasn't a field agent? Well, Sam's not a field agent either so why can't you just cut him some slack, Sean? He does what he can.'

Sean was utterly still for a moment, then he shifted a fraction and I felt some of the tautness loosen out of him. 'I'm sorry. You're right, of course,' he said lightly. He gave me one of those lazy smoky smiles. 'Put it down to the fact that I don't like leaving anyone else to watch your back for you.'

'My back is fine,' I said stiffly.

The silence stretched between us.

'Go have your shower,' he said at last, his voice unreadable. 'You can tell me all about it when you come back down.'

I went upstairs and did as I was ordered, standing under water as hot as I could take it to ease the tension out of the back of my neck. It was only partially successful. Afterwards I climbed into my jeans and a clean shirt and all the while a set of invidious thoughts were circling inside my head.

If Sean had been with me at Slick's wake, I realised, the violence I'd sensed lurking under the surface when I got thrown out would not have stayed there. Quite apart from William's comments, Sean would have instinctively jumped to my defence and the whole confrontation might have escalated rapidly beyond all control, like a riot.

131

Sean might view Sam's actions as those of a coward but, as it was, he'd left me to my own resources and allowed me to extricate myself from the situation without a mess. Without a fight.

After the wake, out on the road, what could Sean have done to help me there? How do you take on a van when you're on a motorbike, without being splattered into the middle of next week? Besides, if things had gone badly earlier my bridges would have been burned and I wouldn't have been able to go back to Gleet's place for sanctuary.

I would have been on my own . . .

When I walked back into the living room the dogs were gone and the TV screen was blank. Sean had fetched another glass and was pouring generous slugs of Jim Beam for us both. As I sat he handed one across and raised an enquiring eyebrow.

'So, what did they do to you?' he asked again.

'They didn't do anything,' I said. 'I got spotted and chucked out – not physically, it didn't come to that,' I added quickly, catching the fire rising in his eyes. 'But then someone had a go at running me off the road on the way back.'

'Tell me.'

Briefly, I filled him in on the night's events, from my discovery and eviction from the wake to an edited version of the run-in with the Transit van and the discovery I'd made in the workshop. I'd brought the remnant of Slick's bike that I'd hidden in my jacket back downstairs with me and I handed it across as I spoke.

Sean took it, turning the piece of fairing over in his hands like he was reading sign.

'You're sure it's Slick's?'

I shrugged. 'It's the right colour scheme and his bike was pretty distinctive,' I said. 'Mind you, if Gleet built and sprayed it for him in the first place, that could be an old piece.'

'Or Gleet could have done one the same for someone else.'

'No, I don't think so.' I shook my head. 'Gleet's a bit of an

132

artist, so I'm told. He does one-offs, not a production line. He might do something similar, but I don't think he'd copy.'

'So does this mean Gleet's got Slick's bike?' Sean mused. 'And if so, why?'

'Good question. The police would have impounded it, I suppose. Maybe used it to prove how fast he was going at the time of the accident.'

Sean shook his head. 'They can do that better from the skidmarks and what was left at the scene,' he said. 'There has to be another reason.'

'Yeah,' I said, raising an excuse for a smile. 'Damned if I know what it is, though.'

Sean had slanted back into the corner of the sofa and turned half to face me while I spoke. When he leaned forwards and reached for his drink my eyes automatically followed the movement, then skittered guiltily away. I took a gulp of my own whiskey and nearly choked as the spirit responded to this blatant lack of respect by biting me in the throat.

I felt Sean's hand smoothing my back while I coughed and spluttered and that only made things worse. It drove all the reservations I'd ever had about him clean out of my mind and replaced them with vivid recollections of what we'd shared.

Just keep touching me for a few moments longer, I thought desperately, *then I'll make you stop. Just not quite yet ...*

The coughing fit eased at last and I found I could draw in breath again without drowning. Only now I was drowning in a different way. Drowning in sensation and need. His fingers feathered at the back of my neck, drifting up into my hairline. An infinitely gentle caress designed to soothe rather than inflame.

It made no difference. I wanted him with a howling, raging intensity that was threatening to launch itself out of my chest and devour us both.

I turned my head slightly to meet Sean's gaze, almost afraid of what I might see there. If there'd been nothing

133

then I might have been able to get a grip on my emotions. As it was, I saw only my own ferocious hunger reflected in his face, in his eyes.

'Sean . . .' I murmured a warning. Unheeded.

Slowly he reeled me in, keeping our eyes locked, totally single-minded in his pursuit. It still seemed to take forever to close the gap between us.

Then, when I was too close to escape, his mouth came down hard on mine and my mind and body exploded simultaneously, triumphant, ecstatic.

Before I knew it, Sean shifted his balance and bore me back against the cushions of the sofa. His hand was under my shirt, sliding up my ribcage to close possessively over my breast. My temperature rocketed as my pulse soared, senses screaming. I tore my mouth free.

'Jesus!' I gasped.

My sight was gone, focus blurring, vision tunnelling out until all I could see was Sean's face above me. And all I could feel was the glide of his hands and the beat and the weight of his body over mine.

I don't know precisely when it all changed. One moment I was oblivious to everything except Sean and the effect he was having. The next there was only a gaping black hole of panic.

The taste of the whiskey on his tongue was the start of it, sending uneasy ripples through my mind. Then one of his hands moved back to the nape of my neck and his fingers must have flexed slightly, little more than a muscle spasm. The sudden tightening of his grip sparked a memory that shattered through the haze of lust like a fist through glass.

Donalson, Hackett, Morton and Clay.

Passion decompressed, whipping out through the cracks to leave me icy and shivering. It was suddenly dark and cold enough to see their breath grunting out like cattle as the four of them brutally set about softening me up for what was to come. They'd been drinking, too, and I could still remember the taint of it on their voices. I could feel the wet gravel grating beneath my back, rough hands snatching at my body, ripping at my clothes, lifting me ...

Eyes wild and totally blind, I began to thrash, twisting and bucking in a pure visceral response. I was dimly aware of a gap opening up and I lunged for it. Everything I'd ever learned kaleidoscoped through my mind and bypassed logical thought to translate straight into action, so fast that afterwards I had no idea of exactly what I'd done.

'Charlie!'

The voice was urgent but calm, if a little croaky.

I blinked a couple of times. The bitter cold receded, leaching away the pain and the fear, sliding them off into my subconscious.

I came back to myself and found Sean was lying flat on the living room floor with me kneeling over him. My fists were bunched in his shirt, forearms crossed so I had one elbow wedged onto his throat. The low table was knocked on its side next to us and what was left of the bottle of Jim Beam was emptying steadily into the pattern on the carpet, making quiet glugging noises. Away in the kitchen, the dogs were barking like crazy.

'Charlie,' Sean said again, his voice soft. Not easy to speak when someone's half-throttling you. He had his hands open at shoulder height, submissive, not making any attempt to touch or provoke me. 'It's OK,' he murmured, like he was talking down someone on a high ledge. 'It's all OK. Come on, talk to me, Charlie. Who am I?'

Utterly mortified, I released my grip without speaking, tried to rise and discovered that my legs wouldn't support me. I managed it on the second attempt and staggered to the sofa, sinking down onto it with my head in my hands.

'Oh God,' I said, shaken and ashamed. 'I am so sorry. I don't know what—'

'I do.'

I looked up at him then. A mouse was forming on his cheekbone. There would be a bruise there tomorrow that I didn't remember causing. But I knew I had.

Sean sat up and leaned over to right the leaking whiskey bottle and put it out of harm's way. One of the glasses had smashed, too, leaving gleefully glittering shards across the floor.

'You're afraid of me,' he said quietly.

'No!' The denial was instant, but even as I said it I realised the futility of such an argument in the face of over-whelming evidence to the contrary. Hadn't I just proved my fear in a moment of adrenaline-fuelled rage and terror? 'It's not like that. I mean, I didn't react like this the last time we ... in Florida.' I broke off, embarrassed, totally muddled. 'Well, it was fine.'

'Only "fine"?' Sean's voice was lightly mocking. 'Oh Charlie, you flatter me.'

But despite his attempt at humour I'd caught the flash of pain on his face. One that had nothing to do with the minor physical injuries I'd inflicted on him. I watched in anguish as he gathered back into himself, mentally bringing down the shutters.

I reached out an unsteady hand. 'Sean—'

The drive alarm buzzer sounded so loudly in the hallway that it made both of us jump. The dogs kicked off again and Sean swore under his breath. He got to his feet and moved for the door, pausing to look down at me briefly as he passed.

'If we're having visitors you might want to tidy up some,' he said, impassive, and went out.

I flushed, realising that my shirt was gaping open all the way down the front. My fingers fumbled with the buttons, then I hastily picked up the low table and set it back on its feet. When Sean returned I was on my hands and knees collecting bits of broken glass together.

'For you, I think,' Scan said blandly.

I looked up and found Sam hovering uncomfortably in the doorway. His eyes flicked nervously from my miserable face to Sean's set and impenetrable features.

He cleared his throat. 'Er, have I come at a bad time?'

Chapter Eleven

'Of course not,' I said, determinedly bright. 'Come on in, Sam. Can I get you some coffee?'

Sam gave Sean another anxious skim, wavered and almost fled. But he'd come for a purpose and that was enough to make him stand his ground, however hesitantly. He sidled further into the room. 'Well, I know it's late and I don't want to put you out or—'

'Just sit down and have a bloody drink,' Sean said tiredly.

Sam's knees gave way at the deadly quiet in his voice. It was lucky there was an armchair behind him at the time.

'Oh, er, yeah, OK,' he said, with a fearful little smile. His eyes were big and brown and pleading above his beard. 'Thanks.'

'Good. I'll make a fresh pot,' I said. I headed for the door, pausing only to throw Sean a warning glance. 'Don't bully him while I'm gone.'

That almost raised a smile. 'I'll try not to.'

In fact, when I got back I found Sean had shaken off his black mood and somehow drawn Sam far enough out of his shell to recount the tale of my spectacular reappearance at Gleet's place. I think I preferred it when Sam was terrified and silent.

'So she comes screaming into the yard with this guy right on her tail,' he was saying, drawing air diagrams with those long skinny hands of his. 'Charlie, she doesn't turn a hair. She just heads for this dry stone wall and bails out at the last minute and bang! The guy slams the wall and down it all goes, with her still on top. House of cards. Didn't she tell you?'

I put the tray I was carrying down onto the table with more of a clatter than I'd been intending.

'No,' Sean said softly, his eyes on my face as I handed him his coffee. 'Funnily enough, she didn't quite get round to mentioning that part.'

I looked away. 'What happened after I got chucked out the first time, anyway?'

'Well, there were some nasty rumours floating around about Tess,' Sam said, nodding his thanks as he took a swig of his brew. He sat hunched forwards with his hands wrapped round his mug like the effort of recall made him cold. 'There were a few people there who reckoned she wasn't quite as sorry to see the back of Slick as she made out. They reckon she and Gleet have had a bit of a thing going, on the quiet.'

'Tess and Gleet?' I repeated, almost to myself. I remembered the way Gleet had behaved around Tess at the wake and realised that the suggestion didn't surprise me. In fact, it didn't surprise me at all.

'Well that would be a reason, I suppose,' Sean said, as though he'd read my mind.

Sam looked from one of us to the other. 'A reason for what?'

I reached for the piece of broken fairing and handed it over. Sam put his mug down on the table and turned the brightly-coloured plastic over in his hands, frowning.

'This is from Slick's bike, isn't it?' he said at last. 'Where did you get it?'

'Gleet's workshop. Hidden away just about underneath that damned great dog of his.'

Sam snorted into his coffee. 'So you've met the infamous Queenie and lived to tell the tale.' he said. 'Puts you in the minority, by all accounts.'

'Yeah,' Sean said, wry. 'Between that dog and his sister, sounds like Gleet is surrounded by tough bitches.'

That gained him a grin from Sam that came close to being relaxed, friendly. Sam held up the bit of fairing, twirled it in his nimble fingers. 'So what does this mean, exactly?'

'Slick's bike has gone AWOL,' Sean told him. 'The police were supposed to pick it up from some garage near the crash site this morning but it had already been lifted.' He nodded to the fairing. 'This would seem to indicate that Gleet might have it. What we've been trying to work out is why.'

'Supposing the rumours are right and he *did* have his eye on Tess,' I put in. 'What better way for him to get rid of the competition than a nice convenient road accident? Everybody knew Slick rode like he'd left his brains in a box under the bed. Right on the edge. Gleet could have sabotaged the bike easily enough – hell, he built it. It wouldn't have taken much.'

'So now he's nicked it back to stop the police finding whatever it is he'd done,' Sam murmured. 'Bit risky, isn't it? What if Slick had spotted it? And what if the cops had carted the wreckage straight to their own impound yard?'

'On a Sunday?' I shook my head. 'It would have been a good guess that they wouldn't come for it until today.'

'OK,' Sean said slowly. 'Let's run with that for a moment. If Gleet fixed Slick's bike in some way, why was Clare so convinced that someone in a Transit van had run them off the road?'

I shrugged. 'Like you said, she might not have been thinking clearly when she said it. Christ, she was in tremendous pain, doped up to the eyeballs—'

'That wasn't your gut feeling at the time, Charlie,' he cut in. 'She told you the van had come after them and you believed her. You've got good instincts – trust them.'

'Yeah, but she also told me the reason she was out with Slick in the first place was because the Ducati wouldn't start,' I said with just a touch of bitterness, 'and I believed her about that, too.'

I had a sudden painful recall of my conversation with Tess just before I'd left Gleet's. It would seem there were a lot of things Clare wasn't telling me the whole story on. Even so, something stopped me from speaking out about her possible relationship with Jamie. I couldn't do it in front of Sam.

'Hang on,' Sam said now, sounding puzzled, 'if you're saying Slick's accident might have been down to Gleet, then who was after *you* tonight?'

'Good question.' Sean's face was grim. 'Here's another one for you, Charlie – will they try again?'

Our eyes clashed and locked. 'I'll be more careful.'

'And just how do you intend to do that on a bike?'

Sam cleared his throat nervously. 'Er, maybe someone's just trying to scare you off, you know?' he suggested, ducking his head. 'I mean, maybe not you personally, but there've been a lot of complaints about the road racing up and down that valley every weekend. Could be that someone's decided to take the law into their own hands, so to speak.'

'So why go after a bike on the Wray road, on a Monday?' I said, still looking at Sean.

Sam shrugged uncomfortably. 'Well, Slick's wake wasn't any secret,' he said. 'It would have been obvious that there were going to be loads of bikers up at Gleet's farm. Maybe you were just in the wrong place at the wrong time.'

I shook my head, still doubtful. 'I didn't get the impression that it was a random thing,' I said. 'Whoever the guy driving that van was, he was waiting for me.'

'Or somebody like you – small bike, on their own, going dark, just starting to rain,' Sam said, ticking off the points on his fingers. 'You were a perfect target.'

'Was Slick a perfect target, too?' I wondered. 'Big bike, two-up, on a dry road in broad daylight.'

'We don't know that it was the same van,' Sean said. 'I don't suppose you got the number, by any chance?'

140

I shut my eyes for a moment and a vision of the Transit sprang into my head, towering over me where I'd fallen in the yard. I remembered the black bull bars on the front end, the oval Ford badge on the bonnet, the blaze of the headlights. I saw again the way the van had slewed wildly out of the gateway, the rear door with the disintegrating window. But no registration number. Nothing. I opened my eyes again. 'He must have taken the plates off.'

'Serious boy,' Sean said.

'I, er, don't suppose this might have anything to do with, um, your work?' Sam asked.

'I'm not working at the moment,' I said automatically, then paused.

Clare had wanted to hire me as Jamie's bodyguard and I'd agreed to do it. At the time I'd thought it was misplaced maternal instinct that had motivated her. Now I wasn't so sure.

But even so, wanting me to stop the kid from riding himself into the ground – or the nearest telegraph pole – on this trip to Ireland was hardly the same as protecting him from a determined outside threat. And besides, there was no reason to assume the mysterious van driver had been after anybody but me. Unless he was following the basic rule of assault on a principal: first kill the bodyguard.

I looked up and saw from Sean's face that he was thinking about Clare's urgent request, too. I saw his eyebrow lift when I shook my head a fraction. *I'll tell you later.*

'What do you know about this trip to Ireland?' I asked.

Sam gave a short bark of laughter as he reached for his mug again. 'The Devil's Bridge Club outing?' he said. 'Biggest bunch of loonies going. Half of that lot will come back in body bags, the way they ride.'

As soon as the words were out of his mouth he realised what he'd said and shut up abruptly, taking a guilty gulp of coffee.

141

'I take it from that, you're not a member,' Sean said.

Sam shook his head. 'Oh no,' he said. 'On my old Norton? They wouldn't have me – even if I was quick enough.' His lips twisted in self-derision and he waved a hand at his battered black leather jacket and oil-stained jeans. 'I'm nowhere near trendy enough for that lot.'

I digested the information for a moment. Questionable style and elderly Brit bike notwithstanding, Sam was a rapid and tenacious rider. I'd chased him through the Trough of Bowland's narrow switchback country lanes often enough to know that for a fact.

'So who is a member?'

'Well Slick was, for a start. And your mates William and Paxo.'

'And the guy they were with tonight – Daz?'

'With the Aprilia?' Sam said, nodding. 'Oh yeah.'

'And Gleet?'

Sam looked surprised. 'No,' he said slowly. 'In fact, I would have said Gleet was dead against 'em. He was Slick's mate, of course, but until tonight I've never seen him have anything to do with the rest of them. Funny, that.'

'Well it would seem they've buried the hatchet,' Sean said with a glance at me, 'if what you've told me about tonight is anything to go by. Maybe they've relented about letting Tess go with them.'

'Mm,' I said. 'What about Jamie? That bike of his is only a four hundred. Would they let him join?'

'Who? Oh, the kid at the wake?' Sam asked. He frowned and tugged at his lower lip. 'I don't think I've seen him before, but he did say Slick had given him a chance to prove himself, didn't he? Maybe that's what he meant.'

'Jamie's from Ireland,' I murmured. 'I wonder if that has anything to do with it.'

'Might do,' Sean considered. 'Why are they going over there, anyway? What can they do there that they can't do here?'

'Drink better Guinness?' I suggested.

'Only in the south,' he said with a smile. 'The Guinness in Dublin is the best you'll get anywhere.' He glanced at Sam. 'Do you know where they're going?'

Sam shook his head. 'Search me. Why are you so interested?' he said, smiling a little weakly. 'Not thinking of joining 'em are you, Charlie?'

'Yes, as a matter of fact, I am.'

He nearly choked on the last of his drink. 'Hell fire!' he yelped when he could speak again. 'Have you lost your mind? Why the hell would you want to do something as stupid as that?'

It wasn't Sam's outburst that worried me. It was the fact that Sean had gone very quiet and very still. I risked a quick glance in his direction but his face was a veneer of polite indifference. A muscle jumped, just once, at the side of his jaw, the only outward sign of tension. Ah well, I'd deal with that later.

I turned back to Sam. He took in my measured stare and coloured up, dropping his gaze. 'Sorry,' he muttered. 'I didn't mean—'

'It's OK Sam, I know it looks crazy but I made a promise,' I said gently, talking as much to Sean as to him, thinking of Clare's desperation that I should protect Jacob's son. 'I'm doing this for Clare and Jacob, and ... what?'

Sam's flinch had been unmistakable. 'For Jacob?' he repeated.

'Yes,' I said. 'After all—'

'What else is there, Sam?' Sean cut in, his voice soft but dangerous. 'What have you been leaving out?'

Sam shifted uncomfortably in his seat. He opened his mouth to protest that Sean must be mistaken, but then he took one look at the other man's sudden alertness and clearly changed his mind.

'It was just something Tess said – after you'd left the first time,' he muttered, strangely reluctant to maintain eye contact with either of us. 'Look, Charlie, they'd turned the music up by this time and I couldn't get that close and I might not have—'

'Just spit it out,' Sean said quietly.

'All right, all right,' Sam said, miserable. 'Someone asked why didn't they just postpone this Irish trip. You know, leave it a bit, what with Slick ... Well, y'know. But Tess said they had to go. She was really insistent about it. She said it was too late to back out now, that the stuff was waiting for them.'

'Stuff?' I queried sharply. 'What stuff?'

Sean laughed without amusement. 'From Ireland?' he said. 'It could be anything. Quite apart from any terrorist connotations, there's been a hell of a lot of counterfeit currency being filtered into the UK from over there in the last few years. Or drugs.' He glanced at Sam and his eyes narrowed. 'But that's not all, is it?'

Sam was looking thoroughly wretched. 'She also said—' he hesitated again '—she said they'd got Jacob on board.'

'Jacob?' I repeated blankly. 'Are you sure?'

Sam squirmed again. 'I'm sorry, Charlie, but she definitely mentioned him. By name.'

'Jacob's in Ireland now,' I said, almost to myself. *Possibly with ten grand in cash on him. For what?*

'But he's on his way home,' Sean said grimly and, as if he'd heard my unvoiced question, he added, 'So you can ask him yourself.'

I straightened. 'You've heard from him,' I said, unable to suppress an accusing note. 'When?'

'He called while you were out. I was going to tell you as soon as you got back but we were, ah, distracted.'

I hoped the lights weren't up high enough for Sam to spot the way my colour rose but I wouldn't have liked to bet on it.

'What did he say?' I rushed on. 'Did you tell him anything about the accident? What—'

'Whoa.' Sean held up his hands. 'I told him no more than he needed to know, Charlie,' he said. 'Jacob's down in County Cork. He was going to head straight up to Dublin and pick up the first available ferry service to Holyhead. He'll be home sometime tomorrow.' He drained his coffee cup and regarded me with that unnerving calm of his. 'There'll be plenty of time to talk to him about what both he and Clare might – or might not – have been up to with Slick when he gets back.'

Sam left soon after that, slinking out like a dinner party guest who suddenly finds his hosts having a domestic over the soufflé. Not that Sean and I got to blows over the fact he hadn't told me about Jacob's call. I was just upset by the way he ducked out of answering any questions about it.

It wasn't until we were alone that I found out the reason he was being so evasive.

'Your friend Jacob is not exactly squeaky clean when it comes to the law,' he said, folding his arms and leaning his shoulder against the kitchen doorway. 'Did you know he's got form for handling stolen goods?'

I was feeding the dogs and froze right in the middle of putting their bowls down onto the flagged floor. It was as much at the emphasis on *your friend* as on anything else.

'No,' I admitted. I straightened and stuffed my hands in my pockets, feeling my chin come up almost of its own accord. 'How did you find that one out?'

He shrugged. 'Madeleine,' was all he said.

'Sometimes,' I muttered, 'that girl doesn't know when to stop digging.'

'Better to know what we're dealing with,' he said, his tone cool now. 'You told me yourself you don't think Clare's being entirely truthful with you. Maybe that's why.'

'Ah,' I said, aware of a sickly taste in my mouth, 'I heard something tonight that puts a bit of a different spin on things. According to Tess, Jamie told her the reason Slick was giving Clare a lift up to Devil's Bridge on Sunday was to meet him. She reckoned Clare and Jamie were . . . involved.'

'Ah,' Sean said, unconsciously echoing me. 'That does

alter things somewhat, doesn't it? And you believe her?'

'I don't know,' I said unhappily. 'I don't *want* to, but that's not the same thing. It does make a twisted kind of sense. I mean, it would explain a lot of things.'

'It would explain why Clare's been so cute with you, but it doesn't explain why Jacob would want to get himself involved with something dodgy going on in Ireland.'

'We don't know that he's involved with anything,' I said quickly.

'When Slick's bike disappeared, where was the first place MacMillan's lot came looking? Here. Why do you think that was, hm?' Sean fired back at me. 'And he has Irish connections – not least of which is his ex-wife.'

'They're not divorced,' I corrected automatically.

'Estranged then,' Sean dismissed. 'Whatever. We don't know what she was after here today, unless it was the ten grand, but if that was what they were after and they found it, why try and throw you out? Why not just leave peaceably, if they'd got what they came for?'

I thought about that one for a few moments, leaning my hip against the sink. The only sound in the kitchen was the scrape of the metal bowls being pursued across the floor as the dogs stuffed themselves.

'Do you think she knows about Jamie and Clare?' I asked then. 'Could she have demanded money to keep quiet about it? What if that's why Clare had the money in the safe, ready to pay her off? Then she has her accident with Slick and Isobel goes looking for the money because she knows it's there.'

Sean shook his head. 'You're clutching at straws, Charlie,' he said. 'It doesn't answer who knocked them off – or came after you for that matter. And anyway, if Clare was in that kind of trouble, don't you think she would have told you the truth?'

I thought of Jacob, who was just as much my friend as Clare was. 'I don't know.'

I wanted to cast Jacob's former wife into the role of

146

villain, I realised. With a boyfriend like Eamonn in tow, it wasn't difficult.

'Did Madeleine manage to dig up anything on Eamonn?'

Mention of his name did something dark to Sean's face, as though he was recalling the encounter with the Irishman and regretting something.

'She's on with it at the moment,' he said. He gave me a weary smile. 'The Merc was registered to Isobel, so all we've got to go on is Eamonn's first name. Even for Madeleine that's a tall order.'

'When were you going to tell me about this?' I asked quietly.

'I wasn't,' he said, making no bones about it, 'right up until Pickering mentioned that bit about the stuff waiting in Ireland and Jacob being in on it.'

'Just how long ago was Jacob done for receiving?' My own defensiveness made me snappy. 'Only, in all the time I've known them the only illegal thing they've done is broken the speed limit. Oh – and given *you* shelter when MacMillan was after you for murder.'

Sean ducked his head in wry acknowledgement. 'The conviction was a while ago,' he allowed. 'Eight years, I think. Nearly nine.'

'Before my time.' *Before Clare's time*, too. I remembered Jamie's comment about helping Jacob dig the driveway sensor in. How old did he say he'd been at the time? Ten. He was barely twenty now. 'I think he and Isobel were still together back then,' I said.

'So he could have learned to hide it better. Or he's been keeping his nose clean and something's come up that's got him involved again.'

'Like what?'

Sean shrugged again. 'You tell me?' he said. 'His girl-friend's just been knocked off another man's bike and damned near killed; his ex – sorry – *estranged* wife has turned up out of the blue, running around with a psycho who likes to burgle his house when he's not there and beat

147

up his friends; and his son's part of an illegal road racing gang who may be about to be prosecuted for their part in Slick's death. Oh and, to cap it all, his boy might just be knocking off his girlfriend. Face it, Charlie, Jacob Nash is in the shit – we're just trying to work out how deep.'

I sighed and rubbed a hand across my eyes, defeated. 'OK,' I said. 'I give in. You're right. The thing is, what the hell is he mixed up in, and how do we get him out of it?'

'He may not want to be got out of it, have you thought of that?'

I didn't answer that one right away, just met his gaze and held it. *What are you saying, Sean – that not everybody wants to be saved?*

'I know,' I said, 'but I have to try.'

It wasn't long before I dragged myself up to bed, hoping to catch up on some of the sleep I'd missed the night before, but it wasn't to be. Instead, I lay awake for a long time after I'd turned out the light. Maybe I should start drinking decaf, but that wasn't the only thing that kept me from sleeping.

Even after I'd talked it through with Sean, I still had no idea what Jacob and Clare might be caught up in. Again I berated myself for not seeing more of them lately. If there'd been something troubling either of them I should have been there to see it. Been there to offer my help.

Somewhere below me I could just hear Sean making phone calls in the study and I was washed with guilt that I'd dragged him away from his work.

And for what? He'd come because he'd heard the pain in my voice. He'd dropped everything and driven three hundred miles for no other reason than because I needed him. If there was one thing I didn't doubt, it was the strength of his feelings for me.

Then I remembered again the way he'd calmly prepared to dispatch Eamonn, like he was a rogue animal who simply needed putting down. It wasn't just the deadly skill he possessed, it was his apparent willingness to use it.

Not in a foreign country, hunted and on the run, in a desperate situation of kill or be killed. But in the middle of the English countryside, on a man who'd already been disarmed and who posed no immediate threat. The memory sent a cold fear clutching at my stomach, made me roll away and bury my face in the pillow.

Sean had been trained as a killer by the army, no two ways about it. That he'd found a legal use for that training and that instinct in civilian life was to his credit. But he'd been pushed to his very limit and beyond. What had he lost along the way?

I'd been frightened for Sean before. Of the danger he found himself in, of what it might do to him. But I'd never been personally frightened of him. My reaction tonight had shaken me more than I liked to admit. As if, by giving in to it, I was admitting he was out of control and dangerous. Even to me.

Perhaps *especially* to me.

I tossed and turned for over an hour. Eventually, I caught his soft footfall on the stairs. He didn't know the house well, but he still intuitively managed to avoid the creaky boards. He moved along the corridor and paused, seemingly right outside my unlocked bedroom door.

I held my breath, not that it would make any difference. He'd be able to hear my heart hammering against my ribs anyway.

There was the slightest rattle of the old brass door handle being turned, the movement of hinges. I raised my head and peered into the gloom, but my own door had remained firmly shut. I heard the slight click of another door closing. The one across the corridor. The spare room Jamie had used last night.

I dropped my head back onto the pillow not sure if it was relief or disappointment that flooded through me.

149

Chapter Twelve

I woke the next morning to the smell of fresh coffee. When I opened my eyes I found that someone – it could only be Sean – had been into my room and left a mug of it on the bedside table while I slept.

I sat up in bed fast, twisting round to stare at the door, but it was shut tight. I reached out to the mug and picked it up carefully. Still warm.

I'm a light sleeper. The slightest noise usually wakes me but Sean had always had the unnerving ability to creep up on you unawares. When I'd been training there were times when I would have sworn there was something paranormal about it. Now I knew for sure.

Feeling twitchy and vulnerable, I grabbed a quick shower, dressed and headed downstairs, only to find the house was empty. I ducked my head into all the rooms but there was nobody there, not even the dogs.

From outside came a distant yipping noise and when I looked out of the kitchen window I saw Sean heading up from the direction of the river. He was walking through the tall grass towards the back of the house with a long easy stride.

Behind him came Bonneville, holding her head up high out of the seeds like a nervous swimmer trying to keep water out of her eyes. The only sign of the terrier was an erratic swirling disturbance through the grass around Sean's feet and the occasional excited bark as she encountered something interesting and furry lurking there.

Sean was watching the swallows swooping and diving over his head and he was smiling. Every now and again he paused long enough to let the old Labrador catch him up, turning to scan the tree-line behind him while he waited. It was difficult to tell with Sean if he suspected there was something out there, or if he was just obeying long-ingrained habits.

When he walked back in I held up the mug, self-conscious. 'Hi,' I said. 'Thanks for the coffee.'

'You're welcome,' he said, giving me a slow smile that could have meant he'd done just about anything while he'd been in my room. Damn, the man made me nervous.

He was wearing black jeans and a ribbed T-shirt today and his hair was still damp from his own shower. So were the legs of his jeans where he'd walked through the dewed grass. He looked, not relaxed exactly, but a hell of a lot more composed than I felt. The dark smudge under his left eye was the only indication of what had happened between us last night.

He was carrying a white plastic bag, which he turned upside down next to the sink, emptying the contents onto the worktop.

'Mushrooms?' I said in surprise.

He flashed a quick smile. 'Why not?' he said. 'The field at the back there's full of them. Be just the thing with a bit of bacon.'

I didn't bother to ask him if they were safe to eat. Sean had been taught to survive on what he could pick, dig out, catch or steal by the best in the business.

'So,' he said as he began sorting through his harvest and wiping dirt from the stalks. 'Where do we go from here?'

For a moment I couldn't speak. I just stared at him, floundering.

'I meant,' he said gently, 'about the situation with Jacob and Clare.'

151

'Oh. Right,' I managed, trying and failing not to let the relief show. I hauled my brain back on track, forced it to concentrate. 'Well—'

That was as far as I got. The drive alarm squawked at that moment and the dogs, who'd slumped onto their blankets trying to pretend Sean had run them to the point of exhaustion, suddenly leapt up and started shouting.

'Oh, for God's sake, you two,' Sean muttered. 'All right, all right. We heard it.'

In fact, you couldn't fail to catch the heavy rattle of the diesel engine that arrived on the forecourt a minute or so later. We moved to the window and watched as a Citroën Relay van covered with local hire company stickers pulled up outside.

'It must be Jacob,' I said in surprise. 'I didn't expect him this early.'

'Neither did I,' Sean said. 'He must have driven through the night and caught an earlier boat.' There was a trace of suspicion in his voice, as though hurrying home faster than expected was a sign of guilt rather than devotion.

Outside, Jacob was climbing stiffly out of the cab. His long peppered dark hair was scraped back into a ponytail and the back of his shirt was soaked through with sweat. He looked utterly exhausted, stressed out, and every one of his fifty-two years. My heart went out to him.

'So,' Sean murmured, 'how much do you want to tell him?'

'All of it,' I said, on impulse, then caught his disbelieving glance and amended quickly, 'Most of it, anyway.'

When Jacob caught sight of us coming out to greet him his face creased into a desperately relieved smile. The desire to pour out everything to him was a strong and insistent one.

'Charlie!' he said, coming forward to give me a quick fierce hug. His wiry arms enfolded me so tight they dug in and actually hurt, but I held on just as hard. 'Sean! It's good to see you again, boy.'

'You too,' Sean said, shaking Jacob's hand once he'd released me. 'I'm just sorry it's in these circumstances.'

A shadow passed across the older man's face, carving a deep vee between his eyebrows. He had rich dark velvet eyes you could almost drown in.

'Well, you can say that again. I rang the hospital when I got off the motorway but they told me she's still sleeping so I thought I'd nip home and clean up before I go in.' He pulled a rueful face and scratched at the day's worth of greying stubble on his chin. 'I don't think it'd do the poor girl much good seeing me like this, do you?'

I thought of Clare's pallor. Anybody putting the two of them together at this moment would almost think that Jacob was her father. Perhaps it wasn't surprising that Jamie should seem so attractive . . .

I forced a smile. 'I think she'd be glad to see you any time.'

He smiled back at me and dragged a small overnight bag out of the passenger side of the van and slammed the door. Sean took it from him to carry inside. Hard to believe, watching them, that Sean had been the one so sceptical of Jacob's motives only a few moments before.

It was a sign of Jacob's fatigue that he was limping more heavily than usual, a harsh reminder that he knew exactly what Clare was going through because he'd been there himself. Too many times. Some of the tales he tells about the bike crashes he's been through, both on road and racetrack, make my bones itch in sympathy. The cobble-together he's walking around on now is the best the surgeons at the time could do with the bits he had left.

'Did you speak to any of Clare's doctors?' I asked as we passed along the hallway. 'Have they given you any idea how she's getting on?'

'I talked briefly to your father,' he said over his shoulder. 'He tells me she's making progress but the nerves grow back very slowly – barely a millimetre a day – so it'll be a while before we really know how much she's going to get back in her legs. I want to try and speak to him further when I go in today. He's going home this afternoon.'

'Is he?' That was news to me. Affront that he was leaving without telling me warred with a sense of relief. He wouldn't go if he didn't think his patient was out of danger.

We reached the bottom of the stairs and Jacob put a hand on the newel post. 'Anyway, I'll go and get cleaned up and then we can talk,' he said, dredging up a false brightness. 'I don't suppose there'd be the likelihood of any grub going, would there? I'm half starved.'

'Of course,' I said. 'We even have fresh mushrooms.'

He smiled at me again, pausing. 'Thank you, Charlie,' he said quietly, heartfelt. 'For being here for her. For us.'

With that he turned and trudged slowly up the staircase, his shoulders coming down a little more with each step, as though he'd made a superhuman effort to be upbeat in front of us and now he'd done his bit he could stop putting on the act.

I turned away, feeling his pain like my own.

'Be very careful here, Charlie,' Sean's soft tone stopped me dead. I looked over and found him watching me intently, a certain coldness to his features. 'Just remember – you can always tell him more later if you want to. But once it's out in the open you can't take it back . . .'

An hour later we sat at the scrubbed pine kitchen table, regarding the debris of a huge thrown-together breakfast. It's amazing what you can do when you've access to a well-stocked freezer and a microwave with a fast defrost setting. And, of course, someone who can tell a mushroom from a toadstool.

Sean had taken care of the cooking with his usual un-dramatic competence, leaving me to sit and fill Jacob in on events so far. Bearing in mind Sean's warning, it was an edited version I delivered.

He made shocked noises about the Transit van that had tried to run me down and had been responsible for my

154

trashed Suzuki but for the moment I glossed over its true significance. I'd skipped over quite a few other elements, too, including MacMillan's visit and all of what Tess had said at the wake about Clare's possible entanglement with Jamie.

When Jacob raised an eyebrow that she should have been on the back of anyone's bike, let alone a chancer like Slick, I'd just shrugged and repeated Clare's story about the Ducati, without adding that Sean and I had already torn holes in it.

Jacob seemed surprised when I told him about Jamie's arrival. But more by the fact he'd turned up at all, rather than by his unorthodox method of entry at some ungodly hour of the night. Jamie clearly wasn't a regular visitor – at least, not when his father was around.

Jacob was even more taken aback when I told him about Isobel's visit.

'She was in here turning the place over?' he queried, frowning. 'Well I can't imagine what she was hoping she'd find. Hell, I thought she took everything of value with her when she went.'

'We didn't spot anything obviously missing,' Sean said, starting to clear away the dirty plates and taking the opportunity to pass me a meaningful flicker as he did so. 'But you might want to have a check round yourself, just to make sure.'

Jacob nodded, distracted. 'Mm, I'll do that later,' he said wearily. 'Nothing like asking for a divorce to bring them out of the woodwork, is there?' he murmured, almost to himself.

He rescued a piece of crispy bacon rind off the plate Sean was collecting and dropped it towards the floor. I don't think it ever hit the tiles. There was some undignified scuffling under the table and a low growl before Beezer emerged the victor.

'Until she told me, I thought you two were already divorced,' I commented.

155

Jacob shook his head, eyes fixed on the terrier. 'Never had the need for it,' he said, sounding gruff. 'But I thought Clare might ...' He broke off, glanced up and smiled suddenly. 'I thought it was time I made an honest woman of her.'

'You don't know anything about the guy Isobel was with – Eamonn – do you?' I asked, remembering his venom and his speed. My knee still ached this morning and the skin on the outside had turned the colour of summer storm clouds. 'Seemed a bit of a nasty piece of work.'

'New one on me,' he said. 'But then, I never did keep track of her dalliances – before or after we separated.'

Sean finished filling the dishwasher and came and sat down, leaning his forearms on the table and linking his fingers together. When they weren't actually engaged in activity he'd always had the quietest hands.

'What do you know about a mob called the Devil's Bridge Club?' he asked Jacob.

Jacob reached for his mug, took a sip. 'Not much,' he said but there was something uneasy tugging at the back of his voice. He must have heard it, too, and he rushed to elaborate. 'I know of them, of course. Can't go to Devil's Bridge of a Sunday and not be aware of that bunch of idiots. Why?'

It was quite something, I thought, for a rider as fast and as fearless as Jacob to refer to them that way.

'So you don't know about Jamie being part of some jaunt to Ireland they've got planned?' Sean asked. He'd kept his voice absolutely level, but there was still a challenge there, even so, that wasn't lost on Jacob.

'Is he?' he said, his expression hardening fractionally. 'Well, I'd have hoped he'd have more sense, but the lad's old enough to make his own mistakes.'

'But you're not a member yourself?'

'Of course not,' Jacob said, more confidently now, with maybe a touch of defiance. 'Why would you think so?'

'Just something we heard,' Sean said with a shrug, and

156

suddenly I wished he hadn't included me in that statement.

As it was Jacob sat back in his chair and looked sharply from one of us to the other. 'I think,' he said grimly, 'you'd better tell me what else it is you've heard.'

'It seems that the Devil's Bridge mob have got something dodgy going on in Ireland at the end of this week, and we've heard that you're mixed up in it,' Sean said baldly. He'd gone very still again but I could almost feel the air quivering between them.

'And just why would you think I'd want to be involved in something "dodgy", as you so nicely put it?' Jacob said, his tone flat now.

'Because it wouldn't be the first time, Jacob, now would it?' Sean said softly.

A dull flush had crept up the sides of the older man's neck. I could feel the anger blossoming – on both sides. I jumped to my feet and slapped my hands down on the table top hard enough to make the coffee cups rattle. The dogs sidled nervously across the room and slunk into their beds.

'OK. Whoa. Time out,' I said. 'Now just hear me out, Jacob, before you go off on one. We don't know what's going on. I don't think Clare's telling us the whole story about what she was doing, or why, but this Devil's Bridge lot have got the police right on their tail.'

It wasn't the whole truth, but it was the best version of it I could come up with and I was too much of a coward to tell Jacob what Clare might really have been up to.

'If Slick was taking part in some kind of road race when he died,' I went on, only too aware of Jacob's doubtful stare, 'then MacMillan's going to go after everyone involved and that includes Clare. All we want to do is keep her out of it but we can't do that if we don't know what's going on.'

Jacob slid his eyes away but I could see him making an effort at calm.

'I can't tell you what's going on if I don't know what's going on,' he said at last. 'I don't know why Clare should

157

be trying to hide anything from you, Charlie – if she is. Until I've had the chance to talk to her myself, I can't answer that.'

He drained the last of his coffee and stood up, planting his knuckles on the table top to push himself stiffly out of his seat.

'As you're well aware,' he went on, 'I was in Ireland to buy motorbikes. Two Vincents and a Brough Superior that were due under the hammer this morning.' He jerked his head towards the hired Citroën outside. 'The only reason they're not in the back of the van right now is because I dropped everything when I got that phone call. I've already got a buyer lined up for one of the Vincents, who's going to be very fucking pissed off that I've come back empty-handed, I can tell you.'

I hardly ever heard Jacob swear seriously and now, despite the evenness of his tone, it gave the profanity an uncommon weight.

And still I had to have one last go.

'Clare's asked me to go to Ireland and keep an eye on Jamie,' I said. 'She said she's worried about him punching out of his weight, trying to keep up with the big boys. Can you think of any other reason why she might be worried for his safety?'

'I don't know. Jamie and I don't see as much of each other as we probably could – or should – have done,' Jacob said, candid. 'But if he's any sense he'll have given Slick and his bunch of nutcase mates a wide berth. I've certainly been doing nothing underhand with them and you either believe that or you don't,' he added with a quiet dignity. 'Now, if you'll excuse me, I think it's time I went to see my other half.'

He didn't even slam the kitchen door on his way out but the soft click it made when he pulled it shut behind him still made me flinch. He closed the front door on his way out with more force, though, and we watched him hurry across the forecourt to the Range Rover. I let out a long breath.

158

'Well, that went down well, I thought,' Sean said, heavy on the irony.

'Yeah, like a knackered lift.'

The elderly diesel Range Rover, ostensibly cream but long patinated with rust, started up in a cloud of black smoke. It swung round in a tight circle on the mossy cobbles, leaning precariously, and shot off up the driveway.

'So, do you believe him?' Sean asked then.

'About what?'

'That he's nothing to do with the Devil's Bridge brigade.'

'I'm not sure,' I said, aware of a low-level churning beneath my ribs that could have been anxiety. 'When you first mentioned them, I don't know, there was something in his face ...' I broke off, remembering the doubt. 'But when you mentioned Ireland he seemed a lot more ... emphatic, somehow.'

'And you don't fancy the idea of tying him to a chair and shining bright lights in his eyes until he cracks,' Sean said.

'No,' I said with a smile, 'I guess I don't.' I paused, let my breath out hard through my nose. 'Why is it that it's a hell of a lot easier asking questions of people when you don't give a shit about them?' I muttered.

'I always make it a rule never to interrogate people I like,' Sean agreed gravely, although there was a flicker of amusement at the corner of his mouth.

'So, where do we go from here?' I asked, repeating his earlier question.

'I think you just have to wait and see what story Jacob comes back with.'

I glanced up. '*I* have to wait?'

He nodded. 'Yeah. My gear's already packed. I'm afraid I have to go back to work,' he said, softening the blow with a smile of his own. 'There's a diamond courier flying in to Heathrow tomorrow afternoon from Amsterdam and they want me to head the team looking after him personally.'

159

'Why do they need you?' *Can't someone else do it?* 'I mean, why are they so jumpy?'

'The customer is always right.' Sean shrugged. 'And if you were walking round with a briefcase chained to your wrist with half a million in gems inside, you'd be jumpy, too.'

I didn't answer that. *He's going.* I felt a sudden tightness in my chest, the anxiety upgraded close to panic.

'I think it might be for the best, in any case,' he added.

'Oh. I see,' I said. Stupid, when clearly I didn't. 'Why?'

He shrugged again, little more than a restless lift of a shoulder. 'I need you to come to a decision about me – us, the future,' he said, turning away. 'I'm not sure you can do that when we're together.'

I opened my mouth to speak, realised I didn't have anything worthwhile to say, and shut it again. The silence stretched between us until it had become a chasm too wide to fill with mere words.

'OK,' I said at last. *Tell him,* an internal voice urged loudly in my ear. *Tell him not to go. Tell him how you feel.*

But I couldn't, and I didn't.

Chapter Thirteen

The motorway was quiet. Sean kept the Shogun at a steady eighty-five in the centre lane, overtaking a strung-out line of trucks. At the same time he was making arrangements for the Heathrow job on his mobile, which was plugged into a hands-free kit on the dash.

I sat in the passenger seat staring out at the country-side flowing past my window. I tuned out Sean going over the logistics of mapping the route they were going to take to the courier's destination, the possible bottle-necks and choke points, how many vehicles, how many men.

I knew he would have already pre-planned all this meticulously enough not to need to double-check it now. It was just Sean's inbuilt thoroughness.

That didn't make it any easier to bear.

With my stomach clenched tight, I was trying not to let my desperation show on my face. But I could feel my chances of getting across half of what I wanted to say to him slipping away with each passing mile.

It had seemed like an ideal opportunity at first. Sean was heading back down to King's Langley and I needed to collect my Honda FireBlade from my parents' place in Cheshire. It meant only a relatively minor detour off the M6 for Sean and I'd thought the hour-and-a-half journey would have given us plenty of time to talk. As it was, we were already passing the Blackpool turnoff and had barely exchanged a word.

Before we'd left Jacob and Clare's I'd had a thorough look at the damage to the Suzuki, just in case it could be patched together to last me a bit longer. It looked a lot worse in daylight than it had in Gleet's workshop the night before. The back end was a mess. It was pure luck, I considered, that the Transit driver hadn't wiped my rear wheel right out from under me. I patted the bike apologetically on its dented tank.

'What are you going to do with it?' Sean had asked. 'Claim on your insurance?'

'It's not worth it,' I'd said, shaking my head. 'They'd just write it off. No, I'll ring round some bike breakers and see what bits I can pick up secondhand. It might take me a while, but I'll get it back on the road eventually.'

'And in the meantime?'

I knew he already had the answer to that one. He just wanted to hear me say it.

'Well, it's a good job I've got the FireBlade,' I said, aiming for lightness.

Sean was well aware of the superbike I'd been given and, without us ever actually discussing the subject, I knew he wasn't particularly happy about it. He stared at me for a long time without speaking and I felt it have the usual effect on my chin, which was rising almost of its own accord. I suppose we were just as stubborn as each other. Maybe that was the problem.

'Are you trying to get yourself killed, Charlie?' he demanded and there was a raw note to his voice I hadn't heard for a long time. 'I know you're planning on trying out for this Devil's Bridge Club, despite what's happened. It was bad enough when you were planning to do it on the Suzuki, but on a 'Blade ...'

He let his voice trail off but I didn't need him to finish the sentence.

'Clare's my friend,' I said. 'Probably my best friend. I

know she's not telling me the whole story and that hurts, but I have to do this for her.'

Sean made a rare gesture of frustration. 'Friends don't ask you to do something for them that could get you killed.'

A microsecond image flashed into my head like a strobe light. A picture of a dark cold night with the looting fires burning, of Sean wounded and vulnerable, of a man with a gun. And of me, putting myself between them without a second thought. Sean would willingly have died rather than have asked me to do it, but it had never occurred to me not to.

'That's just it,' I said gently. 'Friends don't *have* to ask.'

My parents' house, on the outskirts of a little village near Alderley Edge, was a gracefully proportioned Georgian pile with a stiflingly manicured walled garden at the back and impressive circular gravel drive at the front.

They've lived there since they were married, before the area went stratospheric and all the celebrity Manchester United footballers moved in. My mother pretends to sneer but I suspect that she's secretly as smitten by their glamour as everyone else.

We arrived a little before eleven o'clock. Early enough that my mother's beautiful manners didn't oblige her to invite Sean to stay to lunch. Her barely concealed relief, when he apologised that he didn't even have the time to come in for a cup of tea, might have been funny if it hadn't been so pathetic.

Sean deposited the rucksack containing my bike gear on the old church pew in the tiled hallway and laid a hand on my arm.

'Take care of yourself, Charlie,' he murmured.

'Yeah, you too.'

'I'll try and get back up again before the weekend.' Undoubtedly aware that my mother was hovering in the doorway at the end of the hall, he bent his head and kissed me, no more than a fleeting brush of his lips. 'And remember what I said.'

163

'Which bit?' I asked, suddenly a little breathless and stupid from the effects of even so ephemeral a contact.

He smiled, a full-blown knock-you-off-your-feet kind of smile. One that had my heart turning somersaults and made me want to beg him either to stay, or to take me with him. Hell, or just to take me.

'All of it,' he said.

Then he walked out of the front door and climbed into the Shogun without looking back. I watched him turn out of the gateway at the end of the drive and disappear from view before I closed the door. I turned to find my mother had moved up into the hall, as though it was safe to venture closer now he'd gone. She was wearing pearls and a summer dress with an apron over the top of it, and wiping flour from her hands on a tea towel.

'*You'll* stay for lunch, Charlotte, won't you?' she said and although her voice was coolly gracious there was something a little despairing in her eyes.

In a moment of pity, I nodded. 'I have to get back up to Lancaster this afternoon, though,' I said quickly, forestalling her next question.

'Of course,' she said, more brightly. 'I'll just go and check how those rhubarb pies are doing. We've had so much of it this year I've been baking for the WI market but I'm sure I can spare one for dessert.' She waited until her back was towards me and she was halfway to the kitchen door before she delivered her killer punch. 'Your father will be so pleased to have caught you.'

I'd forgotten. I froze in the middle of picking up my rucksack and it bumped against my hip. 'Excuse me?'

She paused then, turned to give me an anxious smile. 'Oh, didn't I say?' she said, artfully casual. 'He rang earlier to let me know he's on his way home. If the traffic isn't too bad we should all be able to sit down together at one o'clock. Now, why don't you go and wash your face and get changed, darling?' She gave my jeans and rumpled shirt a slightly pained glance. 'I'm sure there

164

are still some lovely dresses in your wardrobe.'

My father rolled up on the dot of twelve-thirty, as though he'd been waiting in some lay-by down the road in order to arrive at such a neat and precise time.

I heard the crunch of tyres on gravel and crossed to my bedroom window. When I looked down, I could see the roof of his dark green Jaguar XK-8 just disappearing into the garage. After a few moments, the car door thunked shut and he walked out carrying a small overnight bag and a briefcase. The garage door slid smoothly down behind him.

He looked tired, I realised. From this angle I could see the slight drag to his shoulders. As I watched, he paused and seemed to take a deep breath before climbing the two low steps to the front door more briskly.

It was interesting, I thought, to learn that even my father had to brace himself before he could face my mother's company.

Not to put off the inevitable, I came downstairs straight away to greet him. I reached the half landing just as he was setting his luggage down on the pew in the hall. He heard my footsteps and looked up.

'Charlotte,' he greeted me distantly and his gaze skimmed over my clothing.

I had, as my mother suggested, washed my face and changed – into my bike leather jeans, ready to beat a hasty retreat as soon as lunch was over. Rather childishly, I'd been skulking upstairs until my father arrived, knowing she wouldn't make a big production about it in front of him.

Now, I thought I saw a fractional smile tug at the corner of his mouth, as though he knew exactly what my motives had been.

My mother appeared out of the kitchen at the end of the hallway and came forwards to welcome him. He put his hand on her arm, almost exactly the way Sean had done with me but, when he bent to kiss her, it was a sterile little peck on the cheek.

165

She stepped back and caught sight of me descending. Her face registered her disappointment but I didn't have time to feel ashamed of my petty behaviour.

'I'd like a word with you before lunch, Charlotte,' my father said. He inclined his head politely. 'If we have time?'

'Of course,' my mother said. But she would have said that even if she'd been keeping the food warm for an hour already.

My father smiled at her and led the way into his study. I followed. He closed the door behind us. I expected him to cross to the antique rosewood desk and take a position of authority behind it, but instead he moved to the silver tray of drink bottles on the sideboard.

I took one of the wingback leather armchairs standing at right angles to the desk.

'How's Clare?' I asked, before he had chance to get a shot in.

'Doing as well as can be expected,' he said, professionally neutral. 'The last procedure went well. I have one or two things to attend to here, then I'll be going back up on Thursday.' He caught my expression. 'It's all going to take time, Charlotte,' he went on, gently. 'The human body is a remarkable machine when it comes to repairing itself, but it isn't quick.'

'I know,' I said, 'and I'm very grateful for everything you've done for her. Without you ... well, they were talking about amputation.'

He nodded, a regal acceptance of his own brilliance. 'Sherry?' he offered.

I calculated the time until I was due to hit the road, and the fact that the mighty lunch my mother would undoubtedly serve would sop up the worst of the alcohol.

'I'd rather have a whisky,' I said, stretching my legs out in front of me, 'if you still have any of that rather good single malt?'

He raised an eyebrow but poured a finger of rich golden

166

liquid into a pair of crystal tumblers without comment. As he handed one across he clinked his with mine before perching on the edge of the desk beside me.

'So,' I said, inhaling the smoky earth tones in my glass, 'what have I done now?'

'Why should you think you've done anything?' he asked, his voice deceptively mild.

'Oh, habit,' I said, not to be deflected. 'Why else the cosy chat?'

He took a sip of his whisky, savoured the taste and side-stepped the question. 'Your mother said you've come to collect your other motorbike – the new one,' he said then. 'Can I ask why?'

I shrugged. 'The Suzuki got trashed last night,' I said shortly. 'I need transport.'

If I'd been hoping to shock him into a reaction, I was to be disappointed. Instead, his eyes tracked over my leathers and I realised, belatedly, that they still bore the scuffs and scars of my Transit encounter.

'I would ask if you are all right, but clearly you are,' he said. 'This was in addition to you banging your knee yesterday, I assume?' he added dryly. 'You were never so clumsy as a child, Charlotte.'

'Sometimes,' I said with a smile. 'But back then it was usually ponies I was falling off.'

'Hm. Strange that you should suddenly become so accident prone just as Sean Meyer makes a reappearance, don't you think?'

Ah, so that's *what this was all about.* I sat up straighter in my chair, the smile fading.

'No,' I said baldly. 'Sean came because I called him after Clare's accident, because I asked him to. Don't go blaming him for any of this.'

'Any of what?'

Damn. I glared at him, as though he'd set out to deliberately trick me. Silence was the best card I'd got and I played it with a flourish, taking another mouthful of whisky.

167

He set his own glass down carefully on the leather blotter, folding his hands together in front of him. 'I understand you've stopped seeing Dr Yates.'

'Oh, and what happened to patient confidentiality?' I threw back at him. 'Or doesn't that apply when it's one of your golfing cronies?'

His moment of stillness signified his irritation. 'That was unworthy of you, Charlotte,' he said. 'Dr Yates agreed to see you as a personal favour to me and he would no more discuss one of his patients with a third party than would I. But, since I've been footing the bill for his services, he thought I ought to be aware that your last session was six weeks ago and you have failed to make any further appointments. Would you care to tell me why?'

'I'm sorry,' I said quickly, flashed with genuine contrition for my lack of gratitude. 'Maybe I'm just not the type who responds well to psychotherapy. I didn't feel it was doing me much good.'

'Perhaps that is precisely why you should have continued.'

'Perhaps I will,' I said, noncommittal. 'But if you were hoping he'd talk me out of working in close protection – or working with Sean – you'll be sadly disappointed.'

He regarded me for a moment longer, then sighed and got to his feet. He went over to the tall sash window and seemed lost in contemplation of the garden. 'This wasn't quite the future we envisaged for you, you know,' he said, without turning round.

'It wasn't quite the future I had mapped out myself,' I agreed. 'But I'm here now and it would appear to be something I'm quite good at. It's not everyone who finds their niche.'

My flippancy was a mistake. He turned and the expression on his face held surprising bitterness. '*Good at?*' he repeated, his voice slipping uncharacteristically into harshness. 'At what? Killing people?'

My hands gave a quick convulsive clench. I set the glass down before I was tempted to throw it at him.

'No – at keeping them alive,' I said with quiet vehemence. 'By whatever means necessary.'

He moved to the other side of the desk, leaning forwards and resting his fists on the polished surface, staring at my face. 'Necessary in whose opinion? Yours? Meyer's?'

'Leave Sean out of this.'

He made a gesture of impatience with one hand. 'How can I, when you persist in connecting yourself to the man? He's dangerous and he's leading you down a very dark path. What happens when your judgement fails you and you take a life when it isn't *necessary*, hm? What happens then?'

Into the silence that followed his outburst, there came a quiet tapping at the door and my mother stuck her head into the room.

'I'm sorry to disturb your discussion,' she said, with enough emphasis on the last word to make me wonder how long she'd been eavesdropping, 'but lunch is ready.'

'Thank you, we'll be through directly.' My father nodded briefly in dismissal. He waited until she'd gone out and closed the door behind her before he launched his final warning.

'If you stay involved with Sean Meyer you *will* end up killing again,' he said, calm now but certain as stone. 'And next time, Charlotte, you might not get away with it.'

Lunch was a subdued affair. My mother chattered brightly into the vacuum, doing her best to play the perfect hostess even under the most difficult circumstances. By the time we reached the rhubarb pie, however, even she had lapsed into uncomfortable silence.

As soon as was decently possible afterwards, I gathered my kit together in the hallway and prepared to leave. Surprisingly, perhaps, both my parents came out onto the driveway as I unhooked the trickle-charger from the

169

FireBlade's battery. I wheeled the bike out of the garage and fired it up to let the engine warm through.

'Take care of yourself, Charlotte,' my father said gravely as I zipped up my jacket. 'I would rather not meet you in a professional capacity, if it can be avoided.'

I nodded briefly and swung my leg over the 'Blade, but hesitated before I slid my helmet into place.

Ah well, I thought. *In for a penny . . .*

'By the way, who's Mr Chandry?' I asked.

'He's the consultant gynaecologist at Lancaster, I believe,' my father said and I saw his eyes flicker over my mother's face, as though concerned about embarrassing her. 'Why do you ask?'

'When we went to see Clare yesterday he was with her and she was in floods of tears,' I explained.

'Clare has been through a good deal of physical and emotional trauma,' he said sharply. 'Under those circumstances it's hardly surprising that she will be subject to emotional outbursts. It's a normal reaction.'

I shrugged, diffident. 'I just wondered what he might have told her that would upset her so much.'

My father sighed. 'Your friend suffered severe damage to her pelvic area,' he said, spelling it out. 'Besides anything else, there's the possibility it may prevent her from having children in the future. She's a young woman. Naturally she would find that information very distressing, don't you think?'

Thrashing back up the motorway, dicing with the thickening traffic over the Thelwall Viaduct, I was concentrating too much on getting used to the bike again to ponder much over the discussion I'd had with my father in his study. Once I got onto the stretch north of Preston, however, things quietened down enough for it all to creep back into my mind, unwelcome as a thief.

I tried to tell myself that he was overstating Sean's effect on me and the dangers he represented, but my father had never been much prone to exaggeration. Besides, after the last few days I couldn't refute his allegations with a clear conscience.

That seemed almost as bad as agreeing with him completely.

It wasn't Sean's instinct to kill that troubled me, even though in the past I'd seen him give it free rein with results that had shocked me to the centre.

It was the fact that, given time, I knew I could be just like him. And, more than that, part of me wanted to be.

Maybe that was why I'd stopped going to see my father's tame psychotherapist. Just in case he managed to dig deep enough to uncover that shameful little secret.

Ahead of me a car abruptly pulled across into my path in the right-hand lane, oblivious despite the fact that you need a welder's mask to look at the FireBlade's black and yellow paintwork, and my headlight was on. I cursed under my breath as I dived on the brakes and hit the main beam switch.

When the car had drifted out of my way I drew level, with just enough time to glance sideways at the driver as I did so. A woman, I'm sorry to say, still too busy talking to her passenger to have noticed me. There was a young kid in the back who was paying more attention, though. As I came past his nose was pressed against the glass, his mouth open as he stared out at the bike. I gave him a tiny wave and snapped the power on hard, just for badness.

The FireBlade catapulted viciously forwards like a jet fighter leaving a carrier deck. I held on tight, crouching behind the screen to cut down the buffeting from the wind, and grinned fiercely under my visor. The Suzuki was a toy compared to this, I thought, with gross but triumphant disloyalty. This was the real thing.

I flicked my eyes down at the speedo and found I'd romped up to a hundred and thirty. Vehicles in the centre lane disappeared behind me like they were going backwards. Sooner or later one of them was going to step out

171

in front of me again. Either that or I was going to get nicked.

I rolled the throttle off until I was back down somewhere around the legal limit and sat up, still grinning. *Probably made that kid's day.* One thought sparked another and my smile withered.

Clare had never expressed any particular desire to have children, but maybe she always thought there'd be plenty of time for that later. Maybe being told she might not be able to have them at all had proved something of an epiphany for her.

Then I thought of Jacob, who'd done the family thing and moved on. Did he really want to start again with sleepless nights and nappies and baby buggies and all the rest of that stuff? Besides, by the time the kid was old enough to want to go play football in the park with Daddy, Jacob would be collecting his pension. That wasn't going to be fair on anybody.

Think of it as trading him in for a younger model ...

I shook my head to try and get Tess's sly words out of there but they were stuck fast. And once I'd thought about them, I couldn't seem to shut them out.

Because, there was always the possibility that it wasn't Jacob Clare was contemplating having children with, but someone who was much closer to her own age and in a much better position to start a family. Someone who was so similar to Jacob it was like he'd stepped into a time machine and gone back thirty years.

His son.

Chapter Fourteen

By the time I got back to Lancaster I'd blown the cobwebs out of my head, if not the doubts, and more or less relearned the rules of the FireBlade.

By comparison, the Suzuki was smaller and more nimble on its feet on the twisties. It had once represented the outer boundaries of my abilities, but now it seemed a less challenging and ultimately a less rewarding ride.

Now, I'd climbed aboard something with outrageous speed and power that just begged me to lean that little bit further, push that little bit harder. Something that coaxed and beguiled and seduced me to take another risk. And would kill me in a heartbeat if I let it get away from me.

I got off the motorway just after Forton services, intending to drop into the south side of Lancaster. Last night's downpour had washed all the diesel off the long curving slip road and the roundabout at the end of it, and I took full advantage of the fact.

I stooged along the A6 through Galgate village, the FireBlade shivering with compressed violence as I kept it down to thirty. It was hard to get it out of my mind that only a few minutes earlier I'd been going a hundred miles an hour faster than this.

I rode with my right fore- and index fingers hooked lightly over the front brake lever, just in case of any stupid moves from other traffic. And I suppose that a part of my mind was looking for any sign of a certain Transit van with a broken rear window. Or one that had been very recently repaired.

To keep the bike humming along all it took was the slightest pressure of my right hand on the throttle. It seemed that I barely had to increase the input to overtake a slow-moving caravan. The 'Blade just zipped past it, contemptuous.

When the lights opposite the sprawling urban mass of the university went red against me, I automatically filtered down the white line until I had my nose stuck out between the first two cars in the queue.

The driver to my left shot me a disdainful glance. I glared back. *You lookin' at me*? He ducked his head away quickly, suddenly intent on retuning his radio.

In a detached way I recognised that the FireBlade had altered not just my riding style but my whole personality, the way beautiful clothes can make you walk sexier. It had nothing to do with the mechanics. It was a state of mind.

Like now. I wasn't prepared to wait dutifully in a line of traffic any more, I wanted – no, I *deserved* – to be out there in front. Was I showing my assertiveness, I wondered, or just being plain arrogant?

Either way, was it going to be enough to enable me to take on the Devil's Bridge Club at their own game?

The RLI was home to its usual swirling population of the worried and the exhausted and the sick. And then there were the patients.

I wasn't quite sure why I'd come to see Clare as soon as I'd hit town. According to Jamie, the auditions for the Devil's Bridge Club weren't until tomorrow evening, but I suppose I just wanted to find out if she had changed her mind. Or was prepared to tell me what was really on it.

When I walked onto the ward the curtain between Clare's bed and the next was drawn halfway along to provide some privacy but I could just see Jacob sitting on the far side, near the window. My stride faltered a little. He already knew Clare had asked me to look out for Jamie but I wasn't sure how much else I could say without arousing his suspicions.

Jacob and Clare were both my friends and I hated the feeling that I was being sneaky with him. I'd already decided that if he asked me a direct question, I wasn't prepared to lie. But, at the same time, there was no point in prompting him to ask. And anyway, if he'd been here all day, how much had Clare told him?

It wasn't until I reached the foot of the bed and they looked up that I realised Clare had a second visitor who'd been hidden by the curtain. Not someone I would have expected to be sitting at the bedside of the girl who was living with her husband.

Isobel.

'Charlie!' Clare said, before I had time to do much more than stare. She gave me a smile that was strained and relieved at the same time, as though my arrival had put paid to a difficult conversation.

Jacob nodded to me, cordial, his anger of the morning seemingly forgotten or at least temporarily put aside.

'Hi,' I said.

'You and Isobel have met, I believe,' Jacob said without inflection.

Isobel shifted in her seat, juggling the handbag on her lap as though preparing to offer me a hand to shake. It seemed a ludicrous gesture given the circumstances of our previous encounter. I was carrying my helmet in one hand and I forestalled her by pointedly jamming the other into the pocket of my leathers.

'Yes,' I said, stony. And, with more of a challenge: 'Eamonn not with you today?'

Isobel hesitated a moment, something scuttering across her face too fast for me to latch on to, then she settled back with a carefully pained expression.

'No. Look, I wanted to apologise about that, Charlie,'

she said quickly, sounding for all the world sincere. 'Eamonn can be so over-protective and sometimes he gets a bit carried away.' Her voice might be placatory but there was something calculating in her eyes. 'I suppose he's very much like that young man of yours, in that respect.'

I ignored the jibe, if that's what it was. Hell, Isobel might have meant it as a compliment.

Jacob looked round. 'Where is Sean, by the way?'

'Away,' I said shortly.

Isobel looked smug at this news, as though she'd won a victory. She got to her feet and smiled, somewhat cloyingly I thought, at Clare.

'Right, I'll leave you to it,' she said, bracing, as though Clare was just about to nip out and do a little shopping.

'Don't forget to sign those papers,' Jacob said. He reached for Clare's hand, lying limply on the folded-back sheet, and gave it a squeeze. 'We want to get this sorted as soon as we can.'

'Of course.' Isobel's smile became even sicklier. 'Well, now I've found that certificate I can get on with it,' she said, her eyes locked on their entwined fingers. 'You'll be very happy together, I'm sure.'

The way she managed to inject just the faintest whiff of doubt into such otherwise hearty tones was a masterclass, all by itself.

After Isobel had gone I peeled off my leather jacket and took the chair she'd vacated. It was unbearably hot near the window and the two oscillating electric fans the staff had set up did little more than stir the warm air about a bit.

Clare looked tired and overheated, her normally lustrous long blonde hair hanging lank around her face.

'Are you OK?' I asked. Stupid question to ask anyone lying in a hospital bed, I know, but there are degrees of OK.

'Are *you* OK?' She smiled faintly. 'Jacob said you'd come off the RGV.'

I glanced at him sharply. Had he avoided telling her

about the van that had played a considerable part because it was too close to the bone?

He gave me the slightest nod, little more than a slow blink. *Yes*.

'I'm fine,' I said cheerfully, reaching up to push my hair out of my eyes. 'The bike's looking a bit worse for wear but it's a good excuse to get that wacky paint job I've always wanted, I suppose.'

She frowned, her face anxious. 'Are you sure you're all right? You've got a hell of a bruise on your arm.'

I followed her gaze and discovered a mottled deep aubergine-coloured blotch across the outside of my left forearm, fading to yellow at the edges like my skin was sucking the colours out of it one at a time. The bruise ran in a narrow diagonal line across my arm and it hadn't come from any accidental source. I dropped my arm quickly.

'That was Isobel's little playmate, yesterday afternoon,' I said. 'I don't suppose she happened to mention that part of it, did she?'

Jacob frowned. 'She said she was looking for a copy of our marriage certificate,' he said. 'I've been nagging her to get the paperwork for the divorce sorted at her end for the last couple of months. She'd told me it was all in hand and reckons she was too embarrassed to admit that she had lost her copy.'

'So why was she ransacking the study when I arrived?'

He gave a half-smile. 'Depends on your definition of ransacking,' he said. 'I remember, if she was looking for something in a kitchen drawer she'd be likely to pull the whole drawer out of the dresser and tip it upside down onto the floor. Isobel's just like that.'

'So if I'm exaggerating, why did she bring that tame psycho with her and set him onto me like a bloody attack dog?'

'According to her, Sean broke his nose.'

I sighed in frustration. 'Yes, but that was *after* Eamonn had already started in on me and threatened to break both my ankles,' I said, my voice low with anger. 'He went after me with an asp, for heaven's sake. You don't carry one of those for any other reason than to hit people, Jacob. It's a tool of the trade.'

Jacob didn't reply to that and I realised that I was probably reaping the rewards of having been so accusative with him this morning. Sean and I had gone in hard and lost his trust. Now it was payback time. I swallowed, trying to clear the bitter taste in my mouth.

'So what was Isobel doing here?' I asked, as calmly as I could.

'She'd come to see Clare,' Jacob said. I glanced at Clare and the look on her face told me what she thought about that. *Came to gloat, more like.* 'And,' he went on, 'she wanted to talk about Jamie.'

Because I was already watching Clare's face I saw the flash of fear cross it at the mention of Jamie's name. She disentangled her hand from Jacob's to push herself a little more upright in the bed. The whole of the framework attached to her legs creaked as it readjusted.

'What about him?' I said.

'She doesn't want him to go on this Devil's Bridge Club outing either,' Jacob said. 'She thinks that these lads he's fallen in with will get him into trouble.'

'I've already told Charlie about this,' Clare said quickly, as though trying to hurry him off the subject.

'If you're all so worried about him, why don't you just tell him not to go?' I said, looking at Jacob again.

He grunted. 'You've never had kids have you, Charlie?' he said and I thought I saw Clare flinch. 'When they get beyond about four years old you can't just *tell* them to do anything. You can suggest and persuade and that's about it.'

'And you've tried suggesting and persuading him?'

'Mm. Waste of breath. Like trying to get him to eat spinach when he was a little boy,' he said and he smiled a little sadly. 'Didn't matter how many Popeye stories we told him. Wouldn't touch the stuff.'

178

We lapsed into contemplative silence. Clare looked as though she was about to burst into tears at any moment. *Oh God, what a mess.*

'So,' I said, tentative, 'do you still want me to go to Ireland with him?'

'Yes!' Clare said. 'Charlie, I—'

'It's all right, love,' Jacob interrupted, his voice firm but gentle. 'Charlie will look after him, don't you worry.'

A young nurse appeared round the edge of the curtain. She was wearing a polythene pinny and gloves and carrying a bowl of antiseptic wipes and paper towel.

'Sorry to barge in on you,' she said, sounding a lot more cheery than the nurse who'd thrown me out previously, 'but we need to get those pins twiddled don't we, Clare?'

Whatever she was planning to do, it sounded nasty. Jacob and I obediently got to our feet.

'We'll go and grab a coffee, give you half an hour,' he said, bending to kiss Clare's cheek. She put her arms round him and gave him a big hug, close to tears.

We moved away. The nurse had whizzed the curtains fully shut around the bed before we'd reached the ward door.

'What on earth is she going to do?' I asked.

'They have to manipulate the skin round where the pins go in, otherwise they heal into your flesh,' Jacob said, matter-of-fact. 'First time they ever put me in an ex-fix they weren't too assiduous about doing it. Hurt like the very devil when they took it out, I can tell you.'

We found a vending machine and took our coffees outside into the sunshine where there was enough of a breeze to make it cooler.

'So, did Clare tell you anything about what happened?'

'There was a van,' he said. 'A white Transit with bull bars on the front of it. She said it seemed to swerve twice before it hit them, like it was a determined effort.'

'And never stopped,' I muttered. 'Bastard.'

'Oh he stopped all right,' Jacob said, his voice grim.

179

'Clare said she remembers lying in the middle of the road and seeing the brake lights come on, and hearing the transmission wind up as it went into reverse, like he was coming back for another go.'

'Jesus.'

'And then she heard more bikes approaching and the van just took off. For obvious reasons I didn't tell her about the van that chased you to Gleet's,' he added, his voice a little bitter now. 'She's got nothing to do but lie there and worry as it is.'

'Why didn't she tell me the truth?' I asked quietly. 'Why did she claim she couldn't remember, when it sounds like she remembers only too well?'

Jacob frowned. 'Jamie,' he said, and that churning feeling crept back into my stomach. 'She says when he came in to see her yesterday morning he begged her not to say anything.'

I spent a moment in puzzled silence. When had Jamie had the chance to speak to Clare alone? Then I recalled my shock at Sean's arrival. We'd only left the two of them together for a few minutes, but long enough.

'Why's Jamie so desperate to keep Slick's death low-key?'

'I don't know,' he said, 'maybe it has something to do with the fact that Slick's not the first.'

For a moment my brain put all sorts of connotations on that last sentence. I took an ill-advised gulp of my coffee, burning my tongue.

'The first what?' I managed.

'Bike death on that road,' Jacob said. 'You could put one or two down to stupidity but there have been quite a few more than usual so far this summer.'

'Twelve,' I said slowly, remembering MacMillan's original visit back at the cottage, when he'd thrown statistics at me to try and get me to join the Devil's Bridge Club and spy for him. 'Slick makes it thirteen.'

'Does he?' Jacob shook his head. 'I couldn't tell you

180

numbers. All I know is I don't want my lad to become number fourteen.'

'But surely, if someone's doing this deliberately – picking them off – Jamie would be safer going to Ireland than if he stayed here?' I said, testing the water. 'Unless, of course, there's more to it than that . . .'

Jacob frowned and I could see the conflict on his face. Would he come clean? Would he trust me enough to tell me?

'Look, Charlie, it's complicated,' he said. 'What with Clare and everything, I—' He broke off, sighed heavily. 'I'd just be a lot happier if I knew Jamie had someone to watch his back for him while they're over there. Will you go? Please?'

Well, that answered that question.

'All right,' I said, giving in.

'Thank you,' he said and he smiled, much closer to the old Jacob.

'You are overlooking one small point, of course,' I said, cutting across the relief on his face. 'There's no guarantee I'll pass the audition.'

Chapter Fifteen

On Tuesday evening I went back to the cottage. It seemed sad and dingy when I walked in but I was fresh out of clean clothes and, besides, the first floor walls wouldn't knock themselves down. I really needed to get on with it or I was still going to be camping on a building site come Christmas.

I left my mobile switched on all night but Sean didn't ring. By Wednesday morning I realised he wasn't going to. He would be up to his neck in the Heathrow job and it wasn't fair to expect him to be at my beck and call when he was working. He'd spared me more than enough of his time already. More than I probably deserved, given the circumstances.

I spent the day clearing up the mess I'd made at the weekend, shovelling the rubble into bags and boxes so I could cart it downstairs. I knew I couldn't put off hiring another skip for much longer.

The activity was physically hard work but required no particular cerebral participation, leaving my mind free to wander. Almost inevitably, I found myself thinking about Sean, and my father's warning.

They'd never liked each other from the first time they met. Perhaps, as far as my parents were concerned, there was always going to be an element of whoever I chose to bring home with me would never be good enough for their little girl.

It didn't help that Sean's personal transport back then

had been a motorbike. A Yamaha EXUP – the FireBlade of its day. I was on an old Yamaha 350 Power Valve, the first bike I'd bought when I passed my test.

I remember being nervous on that ride up to Cheshire nearly six years ago, as though I'd had some premonition of how it was going to go. We'd arrived in the dark on a Friday evening, so the full extent of the house was shrouded. Even so, as we'd turned onto the driveway and our headlights had swept across the imposing front facade, it didn't occur to me how it must look to him.

'Your folks live here?' he'd asked when we'd pulled up by the front steps and cut the engines. 'Which bit?'

'All of it,' I'd said. At the time I hadn't registered the significance of the question but later I realised he'd thought – hoped, really – that a house this big might be split down into apartments. It wasn't until I'd visited his mother, years afterwards, that it dawned on me her little council house on a run-down Lancaster estate would have fitted inside the garage at my parents' place and barely touched the walls.

Sean had still been a sergeant then, one of the instructors on the Special Forces course I had fought my way onto. Any obvious relationship between us would have set alarm bells ringing – as it was destined to do so catastrophically. So, we'd snuck away, leaving separately, meeting up on a motorway services.

I knew having an affair with Sean was madness but, like any doomed enterprise, once I was in the grip of it the dangers seemed worth the risk. Going anywhere together where people knew us, even my parents, was reckless at best. I suppose I was hoping that they would be as taken with him as I was.

Some hope.

My mother had prepared an elaborate meal for us and gone to town on the silver candlesticks and the starched linen in the dining room. I don't know if she was expecting to impress Sean or overawe him. At least, as an NCO, he'd attended enough formal army dinners to know his way

183

around a knife and fork with some finesse, even if he didn't look entirely comfortable while doing it. Now, he spent so much time with royalty and riches he was blasé in any company, but back then I was aware of watching him anxiously while we ate.

I wasn't the only one. My mother might have been regarding him as if he'd come before her on the bench but at least she had made an effort to be sociable. Not easy when just about every aspect of our work could not be discussed with outsiders. My father had spent the first two courses in almost silent scrutiny before he'd condescended to join in the conversation.

'You'll have been posted to Northern Ireland at some point, I assume, Sean?' he'd asked with cool detachment.

Sean had nodded cautiously. 'I've spent a little time there, sir, yes.' I knew he'd done two tours as a squaddie and three more he wouldn't talk about, even with me.

'I was there myself many years ago,' my father said casually, dabbing his mouth with his napkin. 'It was not long after I qualified as a surgical registrar.'

'The City hospital?' Sean had asked.

'No, the Royal Victoria.'

Sean had a good face for playing poker but even he couldn't prevent his eyebrows climbing at that. 'That's near the Falls Road,' he'd said, respect mingling with the surprise in his voice as he reached for his wine glass. 'What kind of surgery did you specialise in?'

'Orthopaedics. By the time I was finished I'd become quite an expert on kneecaps.' He'd allowed himself a flicker of disgust. 'Whenever we thought we'd developed a new technique for repairing the joint, they came up with a new way of destroying it.'

'Well, they're nothing if not inventive when it comes to killing or maiming people over there,' Sean had said, his voice low.

'They're not the only ones.'

Sean had heard the censure in his voice and put down his

184

glass with a careful precision that made my shoulders tense. He'd tilted his head towards my father very slowly.

'Excuse me?'

'Come now, Sean,' my father had said with some asperity. 'You can't try to tell me that the soldiers weren't just as guilty of delivering beatings – and worse – to people they thought were working against them. I've seen the results for myself.'

'And I've seen the results of a nail bomb being detonated by remote control when there was an eighteen-year-old soldier less than six feet away from it,' he said, his voice calm almost to the point of indifference.

My mother had given a soft gasp. 'Oh, but that doesn't happen any more, surely?' she'd said, shaky.

Sean had turned his head and pinned her with that dark and merciless gaze.

'It happens, just in a way that doesn't offend middle-class sensibilities so much,' he'd said. He'd wiped his own mouth with his own napkin and thrown it onto the table, sitting back.

'If you've done something to offend the paramilitaries over there, they make you an appointment to have your kneecaps done,' he'd gone on, ignoring her averted head. 'You have to turn up or, when they find you, you're dead. And trust me, they *will* find you. People used to die from kneecappings. They'd bleed to death before the ambulance got there and it would be reported in the papers – another death chalked up to terrorism.'

'But—'

'But now,' Sean had overridden her protest, rolled right over it and crushed it and kept on coming. 'Now, they call the ambulance for you first and make you wait, and when they hear the sirens approaching, *then* they kneecap you. More people survive, that's the only change. It looks better that way on the news. Somebody sat down and thought long and hard about how to do that. That's the kind of people we're up against.'

185

He'd turned back to my father who had listened to his quietly bitter outburst without expression. 'So you can't try and tell me that the occasional squaddie stepping out of line isn't understandable, isn't justified.'

'Torture is never justified,' my father had rapped back with the iron certainty of someone who had the moral high ground and wasn't going to relinquish it.

Sean had shaken his head. 'Wait until it's your family who are under threat, sir,' he'd said. 'Until then, it's nothing more than an academic exercise to you.'

We'd left the following morning, although we'd been intending to stay until after lunch. I'd been so ashamed of the way my parents had behaved that I hadn't seen them again until I was in hospital after my attack, two months later. I hadn't had to worry about my father sniping at Sean by then.

He was long gone.

The Devil's Bridge Club held their midweek meet at a pub just outside the tiny village of Watermillock, overlooking Ullswater. William hadn't been thrilled when I'd called him and asked for a chance to try out, but he hadn't shot me down in flames either. Maybe they were just expecting me to crash and burn all by myself.

I'd set off early to get up there, taking the back roads through Sedbergh and up to Kendal.

The FireBlade bounded effortlessly up the sharp incline out of the town. And when I hit the derestricted zone at the top and opened the throttle, the response was instant.

Still grinning inside my visor, I made short work of the fast open stretch of road that now by-passes Staveley, filtering down a line of slow-moving cars and flicking past a lumbering cattle truck.

At Troutbeck Bridge I turned off for Kirkstone Pass. The going was slower and trickier there, the steep gradients and acute bends making me feather the rear brake more to keep the FireBlade balanced. It was this kind of road where the lightweight little Suzuki always used to hold its own against the big bruisers and I felt a pang of regret that I didn't have it with me now.

Mind you, the FireBlade certainly came into its own once I arrived at the Watermillock Arms pub. The Watermillock was a typical Lakeland slate building with a gravel car park by the side of it that led out onto a grassed area with benches. From there you could sit and bask in the heat and admire the majesty of Ullswater in front of you and the craggy magnificence of Helvellyn at your back. When I brought my drink back outside from the bar intending to do just that, I found the bike had already gathered a small cluster of admirers of its own.

They were all young men probably around Jamie's age, wearing expensive-looking race leathers and skinned kneesliders. One even had the aerodynamic hump on his back, which I thought was a little over the top for road use.

'Hey, does your boyfriend know you're out on his bike?' he called when he spotted me. The rest of them cackled. He was short and stocky and blond-haired, with that kind of pink and white complexion that goes instantly ruddy when exposed to just about any kind of weather.

'Seriously, you never ride this, do you?' one of the others said, dubious. 'I mean, not by yourself?'

'Oh no,' I said, sweetly sarcastic, 'I usually push it, or if it's raining I take it in a taxi.'

That loosened them up a bit. I found out part of the reason for their disbelief was that the one with the hump, whose name was Mark, was on a FireBlade himself, albeit an earlier model that was rather more scuffed around the edges. I gave him some stick for owning a girl's bike – which he denied vehemently – and by the time the place began to busy up the group of us had fallen into easy conversation.

The Devil's Bridge Club arrived together, almost in formation, making a show of it. Their bikes rolled into the car park and slotted into line one after another, with Daz in the lead on his Aprilia, Jamie and Paxo in the centre, and

187

big William bringing up the rear on his lime green Kawasaki.

I don't know if he was looking anyway, but Daz spotted me as soon as he got off the bike. He hooked his lid over the Aprilia's mirror, rubbed a hand through his hair and sauntered over to us.

'You really up for it then, Charlie?' he said, challenge in his voice.

'Wouldn't miss it,' I said.

Not to be outdone, Mark stepped forwards with his chin stuck out. 'When do we start?'

I glanced at him. I don't know why I should have been surprised that he was here to try out for the Devil's Bridge Club as well. He was just the right cocky slightly aggressive type. So what did that say about me?

Daz nodded to him. 'Patience,' he taunted, smiling. 'We're just waiting for one more, then we can get on with it.'

We didn't have to wait long. Ten minutes later an old black Kawasaki GPZ900R swung into the car park and pulled up with a flourish next to the bench where we were lounging like geckos in the sunshine.

'Shit,' I muttered when the rider removed his helmet. '*Sam?*'

Sam Pickering grinned at me. 'Didn't think I'd let you have a go at this loony exercise on your own, did you, Charlie?'

'What's happened to your old Norton?'

'Nothing,' he said. 'But I thought I might need something a bit more modern, so I borrowed this from a mate.'

The other prospective member, Mark, gave a snort at Sam's description of the sixteen-year-old Kawasaki. Sam just beamed at him.

'Hi, how you doing?' he said cheerfully. He nodded to the row of parked-up bikes. 'Which is yours, then?'

'FireBlade,' Mark said with studied nonchalance.

'Oh, smart,' Sam said brightly. 'Same as Charlie's.'

Mark looked crestfallen enough at that but I couldn't resist adding a touch more salt.

'No – his is an older model.'

'All right, ladies, calm down,' Daz murmured. When I looked, his face was blank but there was suppressed laughter behind his eyes. 'If you need fuel, speak now, because you won't have time to stop. You want in, you're going to be riding a simple set course, OK? From here you're going up to the motorway at Penrith, a quick razz down to junction thirty-seven, across to Kendal, on to Windermere and back up Kirkstone to here. Got it?'

Most of it was almost the exact route I'd taken to get here. I felt my shoulders drop a fraction. At least I was going to be partly forewarned.

'That's it?' Mark said blankly. 'What's to stop us taking a short cut?'

Daz broke into a smile. 'There isn't one to take,' he said. 'And anyway, you won't be on your own. The three of you are all going to set off at the same time.'

'So it's first one back, yeah?' Mark said. I saw his gaze flick from me to Sam and back again, and he smiled. *In the bag.* I could hear him thinking from here. 'No sweat. Let's do it, yeah?'

Quite a crowd of other bikers had turned up by this time but the Devil's Bridge Club kept themselves apart from the others, sitting together like the in-crowd, ignoring the rest. *What's so special about you?*

I made sure my helmet was on straight and my jacket was zipped to the top, flexing my fingers inside my gloves, then hit the starter and the FireBlade growled into life.

Mark made certain he was first one out of the car park, with Sam close behind him on his borrowed Kawasaki. I brought up the rear, happy for now to follow the others and see what kind of breakneck pace they were determined to set.

I'd ridden out with Sam before, when he was on his Norton and I was on my Suzuki. It was a while ago, but I reckoned I knew his abilities pretty well. Mark was the unknown factor. I didn't fancy cresting a blind brow and finding he'd got it all wrong and turned his bike into a mobile roadblock on the other side.

It soon became apparent that, for all his brave talk, Mark wasn't quite as much of a have-a-go hero on the road as I'd feared. He was much more cautious than I'd been expecting through the winding roads that edged the lake.

I couldn't say I blamed him for that. The road surface was awful, rutted and bumpy so that I could feel my tyres skittering on every bend. It was narrow, too, with intrusive slabs of rock or fronds of bracken on one side and a low wall leading straight into the lake on the other to funnel oncoming traffic into the middle of the road.

Cars had a nasty tendency to appear round blind corners with their drivers' side wheels well over the white line. Too much commitment and we were in danger of smearing our head and shoulders across the front of somebody's bumper.

Where Mark did seem willing to take risks was overtaking slow-moving traffic on our own side of the road. He hopped past cars in places that made me wince and hold my breath while I waited for the crash that never quite seemed to happen.

Sam clung tenaciously to his tail, handling the unfamiliar bike with deceptive ease. I caught the duck of Mark's head as he checked his mirrors after every manoeuvre and wondered if he was dismayed to find the old Kawasaki still right up there with him.

He must have been hoping that, once we reached Penrith and turned south onto the motorway, it would be a different story. The trouble was that the GPZ might have been old but it was still capable of a hundred and fifty miles an hour. The FireBlades would top that by another twenty but neither Mark nor I quite had the bottle to max them out on the public road. Even if we'd had the room to do it.

Twenty-seven miles covered the three junctions down to Killington. We got there in less than twelve minutes. All the way I was praying there were no unmarked cars on patrol and that the camera van wasn't sitting on its favourite bridge. If they caught us at these speeds they were going to lock the three of us up and throw away the key – after they'd sent us for psychiatric evaluation, of course. As it was, I couldn't help being relieved when we thundered unmolested up the slip road by the wind farm at Lambrigg and plunged back onto the A roads again.

I'd already ridden this part of the journey on my way up to the meet and the experience had taught me to back off earlier and not go into corners quite as hot. That way I could start putting the power down sooner and slingshot out of the bends getting faster all the while.

By the time we turned off onto the road for Kirkstone Pass I was into the kind of flowing rhythm you only hit once in a blue moon. It all felt vaguely surreal. I was arriving at every corner exactly when I was supposed to, in exactly the right gear, at precisely the right speed.

I ripped past Sam, and then Mark, with the sense that I was never going to ride this well again so I might as well make the most of it. Mark was so taken aback when I slipped through on the inside of him that he let his bike come upright fractionally too early, running a tad wide on a vicious right-hander. Sam nipped the Kawasaki past while he was fighting to regain control. When I glanced back I could see the two of them neck and neck, Sam grinning broadly under his visor.

We tore through Patterdale and Glenridding, earning outraged stares from the hordes of fell walkers and tourists who thronged the narrow main street as we did so. Mark was pushing Sam hard, the two of them almost touching fairings. I hoped they'd be so busy with each other I might stand a chance of staying out ahead of them for the last few remaining miles.

Come on, Fox! Nearly there . . .

The van appeared out of nowhere.

All I caught was a big block of white that snapped out of an uphill corner so fast it seemed to have been dropped out of nowhere into my path. I barely managed to snatch the FireBlade out of its way, disrupting my tempo completely and provoking the bike into a vicious tank-slapper of a

191

wriggle that nearly catapulted me into the rocks.

It took me a hundred and fifty terrifying metres to get it straightened out again, by which time my heart was thundering and my skin was cold and clammy under my leathers.

I risked a backward glance in my mirrors but there was no-one behind me. No van, no bikes. Assailed by sudden fear, I jammed on the brakes, locking the rear wheel briefly, my smooth coordination shot to hell. I pulled tight in to the gravelly shoulder of the road and put my feet down, looking back over my shoulder.

Still nothing.

A car came sedately towards me and went past. Just as it disappeared over the brow behind me I saw the brake lights blaze on. I didn't need to be told what had caused the driver's sudden emergency stop.

Oh shit.

I paddled the 'Blade round in the narrow road, making a mess of it, and gunned back to where I could still see the tail end of the car, stationary now. I was already braking hard as I crested the rise.

The sight that greeted me was probably never going to be as bad as the one painted by my imagination, but it was bad enough, even so.

What was left of the black Kawasaki was on its side fifty metres further down the hill, with its back end on the grass verge and the front end stretching halfway across the road. It looked like it had rolled savagely end over end several times before it had finally come to rest there, fragmenting as it went. The motor was dead and a mixture of fuel and engine oil and coolant was seeping quietly into the gutter.

The other FireBlade was parked up on its stand and seemed undamaged. Mark was on his hands and knees next to it, retching violently and shivering like a whippet. I was glad to see he'd at least managed to get his helmet off before he'd lost his lunch.

When I looked at Sam, it wasn't hard to understand what had made Mark throw up.

192

My friend was sitting propped up awkwardly against the rocks at the side of the road with his legs stretched out in front of him. The left one looked relatively normal, but the right now did an abrupt ninety-degree turn halfway along his thighbone in a manner that didn't correspond with anyone's idea of correct anatomy. I could see the shattered end of his femur jutting out through the flayed skin. His foot was twisted almost completely backwards.

A vivid picture of Clare's terrible injuries sprang into my mind. *Oh no, not another one ...*

The car that had come past me was still in the middle of the road with the doors left wide open and the engine running. A middle-aged couple had emerged with creditable speed, but now they were out they seemed at a loss to know how to deal with the situation. Of the white van, there was no sign.

I yanked my FireBlade to a halt and banged the stand down almost before it had come to a complete stop. I stripped my helmet off and dumped my gloves inside, part of me totally numb.

'For God's sake call an ambulance,' I snapped to the aimless couple from the car.

As I dropped onto my knees next to Sam he reached out and grabbed my hand, squeezing hard.

'Thanks for coming back for me, Charlie,' he managed, his voice muffled under his helmet. He was trembling and breathless with the shock but I judged there wouldn't be much pain. Not yet. That would come later, and in spades.

Considering the accident had occurred less than a minute before, Sam had already conspired to lose what seemed to be half his allocation of blood. The tattered leg of his jeans was sodden with it. I could see it pulsing from the wound.

'Don't worry, Sam, we'll get you sorted,' I said, giving him a grin that I hoped wasn't as sickly as it felt.

I stood, twisting to face the couple from the car.

'Ambulance?'

The woman held up her mobile helplessly. 'There's no

service on the phone,' she said, nodding to the stark hills on either side of us. 'We must be in a blind spot. Should we go and find a call box or something?'

'No,' I said. 'I need you to back your car up to the other side of this brow and stick it in the middle of the road with your hazards on to warn any other traffic. Otherwise, if anything comes belting down here and ploughs into us we'll all be road kill.'

She nodded, pale but steady, and climbed into the driver's seat. I moved back to the FireBlade and wrenched open the rear cubby where I kept a rudimentary tool kit, grabbing an adjustable spanner. 'Mark – get yourself to the nearest land-line and call a meat wagon.'

'Er, yeah, right,' he said, dazed.

'Pull yourself together and do it right now!'

He climbed back onto his FireBlade and headed off jerkily, missing his first gearchange. I didn't stop to watch him go but stripped off my cotton scarf and hurried back to Sam.

I eased the scarf under his thigh, using the spanner to twist it tight above the wound. He sucked in a sharp breath through his teeth but made no other complaint. The flow of blood eased a little and I gently tipped his visor up. 'Where else are you hurt?' I demanded.

'Just my bastard leg,' Sam said, gasping as he tried to shift his position. 'Don't you think that's enough?'

I hid my dismay behind a reassuring grin. 'If you couldn't keep up you should have given me a shout,' I chided. 'This is one hell of a way to get my attention.'

He tried to laugh and ended up coughing. He was moving his head and neck without problem and there were no marks on the gelcoat of his helmet. I took an instant decision and started to unbuckle the chinstrap.

'Hey, you aren't supposed to do that,' objected the man from the car. 'What if he's got spinal injuries?'

I finished undoing the strap and eased the helmet off. 'Sam, is your neck broken?'

He managed a weak grin. 'No,' he said.

194

'Good,' I muttered. 'Because when you've recovered *I'm* going to break it for you – scaring the shit out of me like this.'

'Sorry,' he said on the ragged edge of a laugh. His teeth had begun to chatter now, despite the warmth of the evening. Above his beard his face was a deathly white, making those seal-pup eyes enormous.

The woman from the car walked back, carrying a picnic blanket which she handed over to me despite her husband's horrified look. I laid it across Sam's chest and tucked it in behind his shoulders with a grateful nod in her direction.

'Where the hell's that ambulance?' I wondered under my breath. I loosened the makeshift tourniquet a little so as not to completely cut the blood supply to what was left of Sam's lower leg. A fresh welter of blood flooded out of the wound. He turned his head away so he didn't have to watch himself leaking.

'I had him, Charlie,' he said, sounding unbearably tired. 'Another mile or so and he would have been sucking on both our exhausts, yeah?'

'Yeah,' I agreed. I tightened the scarf up again and hesitated before asking: 'What happened?'

'That van. Just came round the corner and wham! I was toast. Matey-boy with the 'Blade was trying to muscle his way past on the outside of me and I'd nowhere to go. Nearly got out of the way but the fucker caught my leg. Funny thing is,' he went on, voice blurring now as the pain began to kick in, 'I coulda sworn he turned the wrong way.'

His eyelids were drooping. Desperate to keep him conscious, I said urgently, 'What do you mean, Sam? Who turned the wrong way?'

'Hm?' He jerked his eyes open again. 'The van driver, 'course,' he said. 'I coulda sworn he turned into us, not away, like he was aiming right for us ...'

195

Chapter Sixteen

They carted Sam away by air ambulance, a bulbous Aérospatiale Squirrel that the pilot put down on a pocket handkerchief-sized flat spot of grass a quarter of a mile up the road, entirely without drama. I suppose, for him, this was just another day at the office.

The paramedics already on scene loaded Sam up with practised ease. I stood with the others, shading my eyes against the dust washed up by the rotor blades, and watched the lurid yellow helicopter lift off and wheel away against a bright sky.

The medics wouldn't be drawn into giving any predictions about whether they thought Sam would make it or not. I had to comfort myself with negatives. Surely they would have told me if he had no chance at all?

'Sorry about your mate,' William said quietly, alongside me.

'Yeah,' I said. 'We seem to be saying that to each other a lot lately.'

Now the responsibility for Sam's immediate survival had been lifted from my shoulders, I was aware of a grinding fatigue, manifesting itself as aching legs and a bad temper that I could feel swelling up behind my eyes.

The rest of the Devil's Bridge Club had turned up about twenty minutes after Mark had gone for help. He didn't return with them. They said he was pretty shaken up, but if the van had been as determined to run the pair of them down as Sam had claimed, I suppose I wasn't surprised.

I leaned forwards slightly to look at Daz, who was standing on the other side of William. He caught the movement and met my gaze. Just for a moment I thought I saw something haunted there.

'Another van, Daz?' I said softly. 'What is it with you lot? Did you rob a cursed tomb or something?'

'You've had a connection to everything that's happened, just as much as we have,' Paxo shot back, jumping to Daz's defence before he could answer. 'How do we know this isn't down to you?'

'Well now, let me see – could I be lying to myself?' I murmured. 'Hang on a minute, let me check . . . well, well, it seems not.'

'Heads up, guys,' William muttered under his breath. 'Cop's on his way over.'

'Crunch time, Daz,' I warned, my voice low as we watched a young copper approaching across the rough ground. 'Either you tell me what's going on or I give PC Plod over there enough ammunition to get him his sergeant's stripes.'

I was bluffing. I couldn't tell the police half of what was going on without dropping both Clare and Jacob well in it, but I was gambling on Daz not wanting to risk that. Whatever they were up to, it wasn't legal, that was for sure. And it was high stakes enough for someone to kill for it – or try to – more than once.

The policeman closed another few strides. I heard Paxo suck in his breath but I didn't take my eyes off Daz. He was the one I had to convince. Where he led, the others would follow.

He made me wait for it right up to the last possible moment. The uniform had moved close enough to touch now, pausing in front of me. One second stretched, deformed, and began to peel into the next. Still Daz kept his face blank.

197

Damn.

Anger elbowed gloom out of the way and briefly took charge. I forced my shoulders into a casual shrug as if it didn't matter either way, started to let my attention slide towards the copper who was impatiently poised to receive it.

'OK, Charlie,' Daz said, his voice quick and maybe a little uneven.

I flicked my eyes back to his face but there was nothing more to be gained from it.

'OK?' he repeated when I didn't immediately acknowledge his capitulation, making it a question this time, with just a thread of unease weaving its way through.

'OK,' I agreed, careful not to let my triumph show.

'You were with Mr Pickering when he came off, were you?' the policeman broke in, wanting to stamp his authority on proceedings. Or maybe he was just tired of being ignored. He had a slightly resigned look about him, as though he knew he wasn't going to get much out of us.

'Not exactly,' I said deliberately. 'I must have been twenty or thirty metres ahead of him when he was brought down.'

'Oh, I see.' He whistled, his eyebrows doing a little wiggle of exaggerated surprise. Just for a moment I was foolish enough to think he might be taking it seriously that Sam had been run off the road.

'Lass on her own bike, eh?' he said instead. His tone couldn't have suggested more perplexity if I'd been a fish on a multigym. He winked conspiratorially at the others. 'So, what kind of speed would you say Mr Pickering was doing when he came off.'

'I've no idea,' I snapped. 'Surely it's more relevant to ask what kind of speed the van that hit him was doing?' I shook my head in disgust. 'Have you caught up with it yet? Are you even trying?'

'I'm sure we're doing everything we can, miss,' he said. 'But considering nobody got even a partial reg number, the

198

only description we can circulate is of a white van. Good job there's not many of *those* about then, eh?'

The not-so-subtle insinuation that it was our fault for being so unobservant jarred. He smiled but I kept my face stony. I didn't need to look to know that the others had done the same.

The copper's smile dwindled. He cleared his throat and pulled out his notebook.

'I understand there were three of you riding together?' he said, frowning, making it sound like an anarchists' gathering. 'What were you doing on this road, exactly?'

For a moment I could have sworn I heard the members of the Devil's Bridge Club hold their collective breath.

'We were just out for a pleasant cruise in the Lakes on a nice summer evening, officer,' I said blandly.

He pursed his lips. 'So there wouldn't have been any kind of road racing going on then, eh?'

'No,' I said sweetly. 'Do you also ask rape victims if they were wilfully walking the streets not wearing a burka?'

He was still young enough to flush uncomfortably at that, but dogged enough not to be deflected. 'Only, we've had reports that three bikes were seen going like stink through Glenridding shortly before the accident.'

'Which three bikes?'

He frowned again, harder this time, peering more closely at his notebook as though he might have written down the answer in very small type. 'Hm,' he said. 'One was black, I believe, and the others were multi-coloured.'

'Multi-coloured motorbikes,' I echoed flatly. 'Good job there's not many of *those* about either, isn't it?'

When the police had got as much out of us as we were prepared to give them – which wasn't anywhere near as much as they would have liked – we mounted up and went back to the Watermillock Arms.

Quite a lot of the other bikers who'd turned up to watch the Devil's Bridge Club audition were still hanging around, although the atmosphere had turned a little sour, like a party after a fight's broken out.

The other FireBlade rider, Mark, was sitting hunched over one of the benches, his white fingers clutching a can of Red Bull. He looked up, saw me approaching, and made an effort to get back on track, hiding the tarnish of his shock and fear under a gloss of bravado. Then he saw the blood on my hands and the smear of it on the knees of my leathers where I'd knelt in the road beside Sam, and his nerve nearly buckled under him again.

He got to his feet, knocking back his soft drink like it had a large shot of vodka in it. Maybe it did.

'How you doin'?' he mumbled. Without waiting for an answer he turned to Daz. 'So what happens now, yeah?'

Daz regarded him flatly. 'Nothing happens now.'

'Is that it?' Mark looked puzzled. 'I mean, do we go again?'

Daz shook his head. 'No need, mate.'

And, just as Mark started to smile, Daz turned to me and said, 'OK Charlie. Congratulations – you're in.'

Mark took a step forwards, his face a tangle of disbelief. 'Hey, what about me?' he demanded. 'I mean, I finished, right? Shit, I was the only one who did! So I'm in too, yeah?'

Daz shook his head again, began to move away. 'Sorry mate,' he said, sounding totally unrepentant.

'But—' Mark broke off, plaintive, a pink flush across his cheeks. 'But I won, right?'

It was William who took pity on him. 'Who said it was a race?' he said gently.

'You—' Mark began, then it sank in that he wasn't going to win this one. 'Oh, fuck you then, right?' he muttered. 'Fuck the lot of you!' and stalked away across the car park towards his bike.

'*Wasn't* it a race?' I murmured, watching him go.

William grinned at me. 'Not necessarily,' he said. 'Wanting to get ahead is one thing. Leaving a man behind

200

is another. That's not what we're all about.'

'Very chivalrous,' I said dryly. 'If you're Porthos can I be D'Artagnan?'

William laughed out loud. Mark looked round sharply at the sound, face flushing darker at the imagined insult. He rammed his helmet on, jerked the bike off its stand and ragged it away across the car park.

William watched him go with a little smile tugging at the corner of his mouth, as though he'd been proved right about something. He gave me a playful slap on the shoulder that I tried not to reel from.

'Welcome to the Club, Charlie,' he said. 'I hope you don't regret it.'

I hitched my hip onto the edge of the nearest bench. 'So, are you going to tell me what's going on?'

Daz smiled and shook his head a little. 'What's to tell?' he said, defiant. 'We're just going for a fast weekend in the Emerald Isle – take in the scenery, sample the Guinness, chill out a little. Simple as that.'

'I could still go to the cops,' I pointed out.

'Yeah, you could – but you won't,' he said with annoying certainty. 'If there's one thing people tell me about you, it's that you stand by your friends.'

'That depends who you've been asking,' I said. 'And what makes you think you're my friends?'

The smile spread into an outright grin. 'I'm not talking about us,' he said. 'And besides, we're booked on tomorrow afternoon's boat out of Heysham. William can sort you out a ticket if you're up for it. It's your choice.'

No, I thought, *it's not my choice. It's not my choice at all.*

I looked round at the other faces. It was hard to see anything beyond Daz's bright hard smile. William was watching me with mild interest, or perhaps disinterest, like it made no difference to him one way or the other. Paxo and Jamie were the easiest faces to read. They didn't want me along, full stop, and it was a toss-up which of them wanted it less.

Daz correctly read my silence and nodded, looking almost smug now. 'Fancy a game of pool before we head back, Pax?' he asked.

Paxo gave me a last lingering look and turned away, his expression lightening as though he'd flicked a switch and I was instantly forgotten. 'You putting any money on it?'

'With you?' Daz laughed and flung an arm round his shoulders. 'You bloody hustler. I'm not that stupid. The only cash I'm prepared to lay out on a game of pool with you are the coins that go in the slot, mate.'

'What about you, William?' I asked as the other two moved towards the pub doorway. 'You going to keep me in the dark, too?'

'Dark can be good,' he said, eyebrows dancing. 'Baby, I do some of my best work in the dark.'

'Don't call me "baby" unless you want me to puke milk down your back.'

He laughed. 'Oh Charlie,' he said, shaking his head, 'I don't care what the others say. Ireland's going to be a ball with you along.'

I would have asked him more about that, but Jamie had come sidling up and was hovering nearby, looking like he had a question burning a hole in the roof of his mouth. William glanced at him and caught the urgency.

'I believe I hear the little boys' room calling to me,' he said to nobody in particular, and strolled away after Daz and Paxo.

Jamie didn't launch in immediately, just stood looking awkward with his hands in his pockets. I waited in silence for him to find his purpose. It took him a moment or two of staring out at the little boats creaming across Ullswater on a stiffening breeze.

'Don't think I don't know why you're doing this, Charlie,' he said at last, his voice quiet and meaningful.

'Oh yes,' I said mildly. 'And why *am* I doing this?'

He batted the question aside like a wasp. 'Look, the last thing I want the others to know is that my fucking parents don't think I can look after myself, all right?'

'What about Clare?' The question was out before I'd time to think about whether I really wanted to ask it or not.

Jamie's face flamed, almost as good as an answer.

'Look,' he said again, his voice as tight as the face it came out of. 'If you mess this up for me ...'

He broke off, flicking a little sideways glance at me as though he realised I wasn't likely to respond well to threats.

'If I mess it up for you – you'll do what, exactly?' I said softly, deliberately pushing him to see what would happen. I expected him to fold but to my surprise he didn't. He pushed back.

'I swear – you mess this up for me,' he said, shaking his head as though to clear his ears, 'and I'll bloody kill you!'

The Royal Lancaster Infirmary was beginning to look depressingly familiar. The receptionist even recognised me enough to give me a faint smile as I passed her on the way in. I'd taken the time before I'd left the Watermillock to wash the worst of the blood off my hands and leathers and I'd obviously managed to avoid looking too scary. I stopped to ask about Sam, only to be told that he was still in theatre.

I found Clare on her own for once. She was lying reading a magazine inside her wire and steel cage-like frame.

'Hi Charlie!' she said, sounding pleased to see me but there was something else too. Something bleeding through in the background like a slightly off-tune radio. It took me a moment to put my finger on it, then it clicked. She was nervous. My being there made her nervous. I tried not to let that hurt.

I pulled a chair up to the bedside and sat down on it, leaning close so we could talk without being easily over-heard.

'You look very serious,' Clare said, cautious. 'What's up?'

203

'I passed the audition for the Devil's Bridge Club,' I said, without preamble.

'Oh,' she said, suddenly breathless, 'so ... are you still going to Ireland?'

'I don't know,' I said. 'Especially after what's happened to Sam.'

'Sam?' Clare said with a flare of alarm. She swallowed. 'What? What's the matter with him?'

'The daft sod decided to come and try out for the Devil's Bridge brigade,' I said. 'Borrowed an old GPZ from a mate, specially, and got himself wiped out, big style.'

'Oh no!' Clare's distress knifed at me but I hardened my heart along with my resolve to keep going. 'Is he OK?'

I shrugged. 'They're working on him now,' I said. 'But his leg was pretty badly smashed.'

She paled at the picture presented by the words. After all, she didn't need much of an imagination to know what it was like to feel your bones breaking inside you.

'Oh God,' she murmured. 'What happened, do you know?'

'I was there,' I said. 'He was hit – by a white Transit van.'

'Oh no,' Clare whispered, pale as death now, a faint sheen of sweat breaking out across her forehead.

'What the hell is going on, Clare?' I said, aware that something of her anguish had transferred itself into my own voice.

She looked away. 'I-I can't tell you,' she said, her eyes filling.

'What can't you tell me?' I demanded. 'What's so terrible that it can possibly be worse than what's been going round inside my head since Sunday?'

'Please Charlie! I promised, I—'

'Promised who?' I cut in. 'Jamie?'

Clare's features went from colourless to flushed red like spilt ink in water.

'What the hell do you think you're playing at, Clare?' I

said, talking fast and low now, angry, with a wary eye out for the ever-vigilant – and protective – nursing staff. 'If you and Jamie have got something going, don't you think you owe it to Jacob to tell it to him straight?'

'He—' Clare got one word out, then stopped, her hands rising to her face, her mouth a rounded O of shock. 'Oh God, Charlie, it's nothing like that. Jamie? I hardly know him. How could you think that? He's Jacob's *son*!'

Her horrified expression was too convincing not to be genuine. The doubt collapsed and relief flooded in, making me snappy and defensive.

'So what the hell *is* going on between you two?' And when she opened her mouth I forestalled her by adding: 'There must be something pretty special because you've already lied for him.'

She flushed again, staring down blankly at the pages of her magazine as though she might find the answers written there. When she finally looked up it was straight into my face.

'He came to me last week, in trouble, needing money – a *lot* of money,' she said simply. 'And I agreed to let him have it.'

'Just like that,' I said. 'What kind of trouble?'

'I don't know.'

'You don't know,' I echoed, sitting back in my chair. 'So, you agreed to hand over ten grand to someone you claim you hardly know and you didn't even ask some difficult questions about what it was for? Come on, Clare – level with me!'

She stared. 'How did you—?'

'Know the amount?' I finished for her. 'When Sean and I threw Isobel and Eamonn out we naturally checked round to see if anything was missing. We found a bank slip for ten thousand, but no cash to go with it.'

Her shoulders came down a little, rounded in defeat. 'OK,' she said tiredly. 'Yes, I lent him ten thousand pounds and, however unbelievable you find it, I didn't ask him that many difficult questions.' She sighed, pushed the magazine aside and smoothed down the front of her nightgown. 'He said he was desperate, that he was in deep trouble, that he'd got in over his head.'

'The Devil's Bridge Club,' I said and felt the despair wind through me. 'Oh Clare, why didn't you come to me? I could have tipped the word to MacMillan and he could have picked up the lot of them before it ever got this far.'

'Picked up who?' she shot back, not entirely out of spirit. 'It's not the lads in the club who are the problem, Charlie, it's whoever's after them. Slick was the one organising the Irish trip and look what happened to him.'

'If you thought Slick was a target of some sort, what the hell were you doing out with him on Sunday?'

'You think I wanted to be there – with that creep?' Clare said bitterly. 'Oh, I know Slick's reputation. I can imagine the rumours.'

'So why did you get onto the bike with him?'

She looked guilty as well as wretched. 'I was supposed to go up to Devil's Bridge and give Jamie the money there—'

'Why at Devil's Bridge?' I demanded. 'If he was getting off the Heysham boat, why didn't he just go to the house?'

'I don't know but, just as I was about to leave the house, Slick turned up, being his usual slimy self. He said how he knew all about the money I was lending to Jamie. He made all kinds of assumptions about *that*, I can tell you,' she added, giving me a twinge of guilt for my own train of thought. 'He said how he wouldn't shout about it if I agreed to ride pillion with him. I think he just wanted to turn up with me on the back of his bike. Bragging, you know.' She pulled a face. 'I hope that was all he wanted, anyway.'

'But you left the money at home.'

She nodded. 'I-I didn't really trust him, so I said he could give me a lift up there, but that I'd get a ride back with Jamie. He agreed and, well—' she shrugged, indicating her surroundings, '—the rest is history. If I'd known

206

how deep he was mixed up in it, I wouldn't have gone within a mile of him.'

'You think whoever knocked you and Slick off did it because they were trying to stop them going? All the more reason to get Jamie out of there, surely?'

'And then what?' Clare said, strained. 'He's going to be looking over his shoulder for the rest of his life.'

I paused. 'What's Jacob's role in all this?'

She looked even more forlorn. 'He didn't know anything about it until he got back from Ireland yesterday and I-I asked him not to tell you too much,' she muttered. 'I was too ashamed.'

I stood, pushing my chair back against the wall.

'The only thing you have to be ashamed of,' I told her then, 'is not telling me the truth from the start.'

I waited until I got to the cottage before I called Sean. I'd hung around at the hospital until Sam had come out of theatre and it was late by that time, but I felt a desperate need to hear his voice. Even so, I wasn't looking forward to what he might have to say.

I'd ridden the 'Blade home sedately, thankful that the pair of us had escaped undamaged. When I'd locked the bike away in the lean-to at the back of the cottage, I went inside and picked up the phone before I'd even switched on the lights.

I called Sean on his mobile, not sure if the Heathrow job was over, or where he'd be, but he picked up on the second ring.

'Hi, it's me,' I said.

'Charlie!' he said. 'Where have you been? I've been trying to call you but your damned mobile's been off again.'

'Sorry,' I said, pulling the offending phone out of the inside pocket of my leather jacket and dropping it onto the table, along with my keys. 'I turned it off while I was at the hospital and I guess I just forgot to turn it on again when I left.'

207

'How's Clare?'

'Oh, she's OK,' I said. 'It's Sam I was worried about.'

'Pickering?' He paused. 'Tell me.'

So I told him about the Devil's Bridge Club audition and Sam's accident and my subsequent conversation with Clare.

'Call MacMillan,' Sean said right away when I was done. 'I never thought I'd hear myself say it, but he's all right for a copper. Dump it all in his lap and let him sort it out.'

'You know I can't do that,' I said wearily. 'You wouldn't do it if it was Madeleine lying there in that hospital bed, would you?'

I heard him sigh. 'No,' he said at last. 'You're right. But then, I hope she wouldn't give me the runaround to start with. Are you sure Clare's told you all she knows this time?'

'Not really,' I admitted. 'But I think it's the best I'm going to get for now. I'll have to see if I can crowbar the rest out of Jamie while we're away.'

'While you're—' The disbelief made his voice harder than normal, made me shiver. 'You're not still going to go,' he said, and it wasn't phrased as a question.

'What else can I do?'

'Don't, Charlie,' he said urgently. 'Madeleine's been doing some digging but we haven't had anything useful back yet. Until then you've no idea what you're up against or who may be after these lads.'

I shrugged, a useless gesture when you're talking to someone over the phone. 'Then that's exactly why I have to go.'

Chapter Seventeen

After everything I'd been through to get myself onto the Irish trip in the first place, I damned near missed the ferry.

I dithered over packing, even though I learned to travel light when I was in the army. Having to carry everything and still keep up with the blokes soon makes you drop out the unessentials. Besides, it was a bikers' run, for heaven's sake, not a garden party – how posh could it be? I put my washbag, first-aid kit, and anything hard into the squashy bag that clipped magnetically to the bike's tank, and packed spare clothing into my old rucksack.

I wasn't planning on coming off the 'Blade, but if I did it was better not to have anything on me that was going to make the accident worse. A mate once made the mistake of carrying his tools in a backpack and, although having some dozy old bastard in a Volvo knock him off was bad enough, then getting his left kidney punctured by one of his own screwdrivers merely added injury to insult.

Traffic was heavy and obstructive. To cap it all, just when I needed to make up a bit of time I ended up in a group of cars on the motorway who were all travelling at exactly sixty-nine miles an hour because one of them was a jam sandwich being driven by a policeman with a warped sense of humour.

The end result was that I came howling into the Port of Heysham with barely fifteen minutes to spare before they would have told me to take a hike. I gave my name at the barrier and found that, true to his word, William had sorted my ticket.

They whizzed me straight through and onto the fast cat ferry that was standing at the dockside. I watched the deck crew strap the 'Blade down, then headed for the stairwell to the passenger lounges. I found myself hoping that the rest of the Devil's Bridge crowd were already on board, or I'd no idea where I was going once I reached the other side.

Inside, the catamaran had a wide open-plan restaurant across the centre bridgedeck area with a bar upstairs and rows of aircraft-type seating at either side.

The place seemed to be teeming with bikers. I did a quick tour but couldn't see anyone familiar. A couple of times, though, I could have sworn someone was watching me. But when I turned round to scan the crowd, I couldn't see anyone paying me particular attention. Nevertheless, it made me twitchy. By the time I went out onto the small section of outside deck I was starting to get worried. It was there I found Paxo.

He was leaning on the aft railing, his leathers stripped to his waist to take full advantage of the syrupy heat. Underneath, he was wearing a white vest that was already stained with sweat and his exposed shoulders had the pink tinge of sunburn to them that was going to sting in the morning. He had a crumpled packet of Lambert & Butler clutched in his hand like a talisman. I moved alongside him.

'Hi,' I said. 'Where is everyone?'

He jerked his head towards the heavily tinted windows immediately behind us. 'First Class lounge. William pulled some strings,' he said, adding sourly, 'The rest of 'em are in there but it's no smoking.'

He gave me a look of resentment but I couldn't work out if I was to blame or it was just brought on by the prospect of a lack of nicotine in his system for four hours. Or possibly both.

The last stragglers were loaded onto the car deck beneath

210

us and the ramp was winched up like a drawbridge. There was a sign on the rail next to me that announced we were about to cross an area of special ecological interest and to do our bit not to pollute it by throwing any rubbish over the side. Then the captain eased us away from our berth and the whole view of the harbour disappeared in a belching cloud of black diesel smoke. It almost, but not quite, managed to obscure the slab-sided concrete monstrosity that is the nuclear power station next door.

Coughing, we both retreated inside and Paxo led the way through the opaque glass door into the First Class area. It was a sizeable room with windows on two sides. One of the cabin crew smiled at him and said, 'You found her, then?'

Paxo scowled back, as though it was some sign of weakness to admit he might have been looking out for me.

There were sets of tables for four all round the walls and one larger table in the centre. William and Jamie had taken that over, spilling luggage and helmets into the surrounding area. The other tables were mostly taken by serious-looking couples who'd clearly been hoping to escape the bike crowd by coming in here and didn't exactly look overjoyed when I added to their number.

The ferry cleared the harbour entrance and the jagged remains of the old wooden pier and the captain opened her up. The deck vibrations under our feet increased to a buzz as the four massive Ruston diesels began to work. Great rooster tails of spray curved up behind the stern, casting our own personal rainbow in the brilliant sunlight.

I stripped off my jacket, unzipping it from my leather jeans and draping it over the back of one of the bolted-down chairs.

'Where's Daz?' I asked, but caught the quick glance Paxo exchanged with the others. 'What? Don't tell me he's missed the boat.'

'Oh no, he's not done that,' Paxo said darkly, and his tone indicated that he thought it might be better if Daz *hadn't* made it on board.

211

Before I could ask any questions, the door to the lounge opened and Daz himself sauntered through, looking cool and handsome in his snazzy race leathers. He had that faint half-smile on his face, as though life was one big joke and he was in on it. In this case, perhaps he was right.

Behind him, also dressed in bike gear, was Tess.

I stared at her blankly, then skimmed my eyes across the veiled faces of the rest of the Devil's Bridge Club and straight away I understood Paxo's comment. Daz had not, I surmised, told the others that he was bringing Slick's widow with him. After all the arguments, I could understand their anger at this sudden apparently about-face decision.

Tess smiled brightly at the group of us, seemingly enjoying the discomfort her presence was causing. I suppose it was better than being ignored. Her glee lost a little of its shine when she spotted me, though.

I got the feeling she enjoyed the position of lone female amid a group of men and, from the way her gaze turned calculating, she was trying to work out how much competition I was going to be for their attention. If the way her expression rapidly cleared was anything to go by – not much.

'Oh, hiya Charlie,' she said, wrapping herself round Daz's arm like she was staking a claim on the alpha male and I'd have to make do with pickings lower down the food chain.

'Hello Tess,' I said, adding dryly, 'I'm glad to see you're coping so well with overcoming your grief.'

'Yeah well.' She pouted. 'Life goes on.'

'You're certainly proving that,' I said, watching Daz's obvious uneasiness with some amusement. 'I must admit I'm surprised to see you here, though.'

That injected a new smugness to her smile. 'Well, this trip *was* my Slick's idea in the first place and when the boys found out how I was the only one with certain vital—' her eyes slid over them '—arrangements at my fingertips, they realised they really couldn't do it without me. So what made them bring *you* along?'

'She was fast enough,' Paxo said shortly. It was a testament to his dislike of Tess, I reckoned, that he'd felt inclined to jump to my defence.

The ferry was out of the lee of the land now and pushing up towards its maximum cruising velocity as it struck out across Morecambe Bay. At that kind of speed the gentle swell had lumps in it like concrete sleeping policemen. As soon as we got into open water it had also begun a perceptible cindering motion, a slight corkscrewing, that always seems to come with a following sea.

I noticed Jamie was gripping the edge of the table like it was a designated flotation device. He had a sheen of sweat across his pale skin and when one of the cabin crew approached to ask if we'd like anything to eat, he actually took on a greenish cast.

'I'm just going outside for a bit of fresh air,' he managed, lurching to his feet.

'Remember to throw up on the downwind side, mate,' Paxo suggested helpfully.

'We're doing forty knots,' William pointed out. 'It's *all* down wind.'

Jamie just gave them a panicked look and fled. Tess took his vacant seat, seeming pleased with herself. I wondered if I was going to be able to stand a whole weekend of her like this.

'So where are we going when we get in to Belfast?' I asked Daz.

'Nice little hotel I found up on the Antrim coast,' he said, prompt but almost deliberately vague. 'Then tomorrow morning you have to suffer some culture by looking at the Giant's Causeway. Your reward is a trip round the distillery at Bushmills afterwards.'

'I'll try to contain my boredom,' I said.

The others slipped into a discussion on the merits of Irish whiskey versus Scottish single malt but I let it flow over

213

me. Through the tinted windows I could see Jamie standing at the railing, hunched over like a man who knows his digestive system is about to suffer a violent inversion and there's nothing he can do about it.

Most of the other people on the outside deck correctly identified the signs and steered well clear of him, but one guy strolled over to stand alongside him. He was dressed in plain black bike leathers, with a cotton scarf round his neck to keep the draught and the bugs out. Jamie glanced up sharply, recognised the figure and seemed to relax a little. The newcomer turned sideways to speak to him and then, with a jolt, I recognised him, too.

'Excuse me a minute,' I muttered, getting to my feet. 'I'm just going to check on Jamie.'

Paxo groaned. 'Not you as well,' he said, leaning back in his chair to call after me. 'Well don't come back in here if you smell of sick.'

The other occupants of the lounge stared fixedly at their newspapers and their laptops and tried to ignore him.

Outside, the wind whipped through my shirt and made me wish I'd put my jacket back on, despite the gorgeous weather. Jamie was still clinging miserably to the railing and there, alongside him, was Sean.

Sean turned to meet me as I approached. He smiled, and I wanted to run and throw myself into his arms. Aware of the audience from inside the lounge – not to mention Jamie – I contented myself with an answering smile.

'Surprise, surprise,' I said with admirable cool. I nodded to the leathers. 'I didn't know you still had a bike.'

'I don't, but one of the guys who works for me does and as a) he's out of the country at the moment, and b) I'm his boss,' he said, counting the points off on his fingers, 'he's generously agreed to lend me his Super Blackbird for the weekend.'

'Wow,' I said. 'He must really like his job.'

Sean grinned. 'Yeah, he does.'

Jamie chose that moment to start to heave and Sean and

214

I both instinctively stepped back. 'Unless you really want to watch the kid trying to turn his stomach inside out, I would suggest we take a walk,' Sean murmured. 'Where are the others?'

'First Class lounge,' I said nodding to the windows as we moved round the corner, more towards the side of the boat. 'William wangled it or I'd invite you in.'

'Madeleine sorted my ticket,' Sean said, smiling. 'I'm already in.'

I waited a beat. 'What are you doing here, Sean?'

'Watching your back,' he said. His eyes flipped down to my thin shirt. 'Although, in this breeze, your front looks pretty good, too.'

I folded my arms across my chest, defensive. 'Be serious.'

His face sobered. 'I am being serious – about your back, I mean,' he said quietly.

He glanced across but Jamie was out of sight and undoubtedly too preoccupied to be even thinking about listening in. And besides, the wind was whipping our words away over the stern as soon as they were spoken.

'We think we might have made some headway but that's not necessarily a good thing,' Sean said. 'Madeleine's being doing some searches on our friend Eamonn and it turns out he moves in some very nasty circles.'

Eamonn's words when he'd first laid eyes on Sean came back to me in a cold rush. *Now that wouldn't be a bastard squaddie I can smell, would it? Seen plenty of your type . . .*

'He's connected to the IRA?' I said, tense.

Sean ducked his head in a 'maybe, maybe not' gesture. 'More likely the other side of the sectarian divide,' he said. 'Our intelligence suggests good old Eamonn Garroway is just an old-fashioned thug, but you can't operate in Northern Ireland without the knowledge and tacit approval of the paramilitaries – regardless of your politics. The bad news is, he's heavily into the drugs trade.'

'Shit,' I murmured, my eyes straying to Jamie again.

'We were afraid of something like that.'

'Quite,' Sean said, letting his voice drawl. 'You see now why I thought you might be glad of some back-up on this one?'

'Yeah,' I said, giving him a wry smile. 'But I'm glad to see you anyway, Sean – not just for that reason.'

He raised an eyebrow, momentarily lost for words, then he laughed softly, shaken. 'Well, that's progress, I think,' he said.

Impulsively, I moved in closer so I could take some shelter from his body. He only hesitated a fraction then put his arm round my shoulders and pulled me in closer still. I tilted my head against his chest and we stood like that for a long time without the need to say anything further, watching the foaming white line of wake stretching out behind us from the ferry's twin hulls.

I could feel the heat of him seeping into my bones but it wasn't just a physical warmth. It felt good just to be near him, whatever my father's doom-ridden predictions.

Nevertheless, the memory of those words chilled me. I broke away, turned to face Sean a little. I'd forgotten how good he looked in leathers, dark and dangerous, with the wind tousling his hair. I swallowed, forced myself to concentrate.

'Did Madeleine manage to dig out anything on Isobel?' I asked, peering round the corner of the superstructure to check on Jamie. He was still where we'd left him, slumped onto the rail now, eyes shut, but at least he had more colour. Being his bodyguard, I reasoned, just meant ensuring he didn't fall over the side. It didn't mean I had to go and mop up after him.

'Some,' Sean said easily. 'She's not averse to walking a thin line when it comes to the law.'

'So maybe that receiving charge against Jacob was more down to his wife at the time,' I said.

Sean nodded. 'I think you could be right,' he admitted. 'She's been living with Eamonn – or off him, actually – for the past two years.'

216

I frowned. 'I always got the impression that she was the one with the money.'

'On paper, yes,' Sean agreed. 'It's a case of being asset rich but cash poor. She's got plenty of property but it's tied in to long-term leases. She's also got a portfolio of stuff that's up for redevelopment and *will* be worth something in the future but is worth bugger all now. Less than that, in fact, because she bought high and prices have temporarily fallen back. If this divorce from Jacob goes ahead and she has to pay him off any time soon, she's going to be financially crippled.'

'Surely they won't still have to divide everything up now, will they – not after all this time?' I said.

Sean shrugged. 'Makes no difference how long they've been apart,' he said. 'Assets are divided at the time of divorce, not separation.'

I recalled my last conversation with Clare at the hospital. 'Do you think that might be the reason Jamie got himself in deep enough water that he had to go to Clare for money?' I asked. 'If his mother's in debt, he might have thought that getting tangled up with Eamonn's business would somehow help get her out of it?'

'But instead he's got himself into a bigger mess,' Sean finished for me.

'Mm. Clare said he'd got himself in over his head and I assumed – or rather, she *let* me assume – that she was talking about the Devil's Bridge Club. But she also said it wasn't those lads who were the problem, but whoever was after them.'

'I wonder what she meant by that,' Sean murmured, almost to himself. 'Why would Eamonn be after them? What have they done?'

'Maybe nothing yet,' I said. 'Maybe it's what they're planning on doing on this trip. Could it be a territorial thing, do you think?'

'Could be,' Sean said, but he didn't sound convinced. 'Everything we've dug up on Eamonn suggests he's highly territorial.' He shrugged. 'Has to be, I suppose.'

'Is that really enough of a reason to kill Slick, badly injure Clare and then Sam, and have a go at me as well?' I said. 'Bit drastic, isn't it?'

Sean fixed me with a look. 'This is Eamonn we're talking about.'

I remembered the venom and the easy violence the Irishman had displayed that day at Jacob and Clare's. 'Good point,' I said. 'And well made.'

'Hm, I thought so,' he said, giving me a lazy smile that died away as his own memories of the same incident surfaced. His face grew hard and just as ruthless as Eamonn's, in its own way. 'Just goes to show,' he said with a smile that did nothing to warm up his words, 'you should have let me finish him while I had the chance.'

When Jamie had recovered enough to prise himself away from the railing, the three of us went back inside together. As we moved into the main cabin I got that same watched feeling down my spine and paused, scanning the crowd again.

'What is it?' Sean asked.

'I just can't help getting the feeling somebody's keeping an eye on us,' I muttered. 'It's probably just me being paranoid.'

'I don't think so,' Sean said. 'You go ahead. I think I'll do a quick recce.'

When Jamie and I walked back into First Class, the others turned and looked at us.

'Can't leave him alone, eh, Charlie?' William said. 'We saw you out there.'

'Who's the guy?' Daz asked quietly. He'd gone very still, the way some people do when they're very angry. He was staring intently at me.

'That's Sean,' I said carefully. 'I work for him. I didn't know he was coming and I didn't invite him.' *But I'm bloody glad he's here.*

'You work for him?' Tess said with scorn in her voice. 'Looking at the two of you I bet I can guess what form the interview took.'

'I bet you can't,' I bit back.

I still had the two spent nine millimetre rounds I'd put myself in the path of to save Sean's life. Two slightly flattened copper mushrooms. I had them with me now, in fact. They were in the top pocket of my leather jacket like some kind of good luck charm, but I wasn't about to show them to her.

'What's he riding?' Daz wanted to know.

'A mate's lent him a Blackie,' I said.

William raised his eyebrows. 'I say, steady on old girl,' he drawled, exaggerating his educated accent. 'Don't want to offend the coloured chappies, what?'

'OK – it's a Honda CBR1100XX Super Blackbird,' I said and he grinned at me.

'Well, the bike should be quick enough, but what about the rider?' Daz said.

'Hang on a minute. That's not the point,' Paxo snapped. 'The rest of us had to earn our place on this trip.' He let his gaze skate over Tess with hardly a flicker. 'We can't just let someone muscle in on—'

'But that *is* just the point,' Daz cut in. 'He looks like muscle and maybe we could do with some of that, hm? It doesn't mean he has to be part of anything, does it?'

'Part of what?' I said.

I almost think they'd forgotten I was there. They fell into silence that went on long enough that I was just about to growl in frustration when Jamie piped up.

'You said Sean was your boss,' he said suddenly, as though he'd only just caught up with that part of the conversation. 'Does that mean he's in close protection, too?'

I nodded, glancing round at the others, but only Tess looked surprised at this bit of news. He'd obviously told the rest of them something of the conversation we'd had outside the hospital, when I'd first broken the news to Jamie that Clare wanted me to bodyguard him. Daz's face took on a shrewd air of calculation.

'There you go,' he said, as if that settled things. 'Like I said – this boy could be useful.'

Any further discussion on the subject was cut short by the arrival of Sean himself. He picked up on the atmosphere as soon as he came into the room but didn't comment on it. On the surface he seemed friendly and relaxed. I was probably the only one who spotted the tell-tale minute shift in stance, the slight narrowing of those coal-black eyes. And then only because I was expecting to see the almost negligible controlled reaction.

Daz sat back in his chair and studied Sean as he approached, head on one side. 'So you're Sean Meyer,' he said, his voice rippling with undercurrents. 'We've been hearing a lot about you.'

'Really?' Sean said easily. 'Well, same applies.'

Daz looked momentarily discomfited, then he smiled slightly. 'I understand you're in the same line of work as Charlie here.'

'That's right.'

'So, you've been to Ireland before? Only, I expect we could do with someone who knows his way around, so to speak.'

Jamie, silent until this point, started to protest, as well he might. Daz's words were an insult to his own local knowledge – if you took them purely at face value. But Daz had been talking between the lines and he silenced Jamie with a single barbed glance.

'I've spent a little time over the other side of the water, yes,' Sean said then, softly. 'I reckon I know my way around fairly well.'

Daz nodded, as if that was the answer he'd been expecting, more or less.

'OK,' he said, giving Sean a sudden dazzling smile. 'You're in.'

Paxo made a sound of disgust at this apparent capitulation, which was echoed by Jamie. William just sat, his broad face impassive, as though he had no opinion on the subject one way or another.

'You can't do that, Daz,' Tess said, sounding furious. 'You can't just—'

'I think you'll find I can do anything I like,' Daz said. 'Everybody needs everybody else, here.'

Tess gave a noisy sigh, shot to her feet and stormed out. Her flouncy exit was somewhat spoiled by a sudden lurch from the ship, which gave her a drunken stagger halfway to the door.

Ignoring the reactions, Daz leaned across the table and nonchalantly offered Sean his hand to shake. After only a fractional hesitation, Sean took it. Their eyes met and something seemed to pass between them, some unspoken message I didn't fully catch or follow. But when Sean turned away he was frowning.

The boys had obviously ordered food while we'd been outside and the first of it was brought out at that point. Jamie lost some of his newly-acquired colour but managed to stay in his seat while they tucked in.

The conversation turned general while they ate. Daz gave Paxo grief for stuffing his face with chips and a non-diet soft drink. 'Have you any idea how much sugar there is in one can of that stuff, mate?'

Paxo broke into a smile for once. 'Good job I've got a metabolism that can burn it off quick then,' he said, undeterred.

'Yeah, won't stop you becoming diabetic, though, will it?' Daz said. 'Just wait until someone has to jab a needle full of insulin into your arse every morning and see how you like that.'

'Mate, I tell you, that's about the only thing I *would* let anyone jab into my arse!'

They all laughed. Sean sat with his forearms resting on the table and his fingers linked together, watching them

221

interact without joining in. It was as though he was conducting some kind of silent assessment. He used to do that with his trainees when he was an instructor. Without a hint of it showing on his features, he'd always been able to convey the impression that we were all somehow falling short of his expectations.

He was doing the same thing now and I could see they were all aware of it. A couple of times Daz met Sean's gaze in direct challenge, but he was the only one of them who did.

'I suppose I'd better go try and placate Tess,' Daz said with a show of reluctance when they'd all finished. He got up and strolled out.

'Have you been to Ireland before, Charlie?' Jamie asked when he'd gone. It was the first time he'd addressed me directly since we'd set off and I turned to him trying to hide my surprise.

'No,' I said, shaking my head. 'I was booked to come once, but the trip was cancelled.'

It was supposed to have been my first posting when I came out of Special Forces training. Straight into the thick of it in Shankhill. The army were conducting surveillance operations throughout the six counties and, much as they hated to admit it, women were more effective, more unobtrusive, than some big hairy squaddie who, especially in the favoured civvy garb of jeans and tan Cat boots and a bomber jacket, stood out a mile for what he was.

So although I'd never set foot there I knew a lot about Northern Ireland, but the wrong things. I knew about the soldiers killed at Warrenpoint, about the skirmishes in Newry and the running battles on the Bogside. If I dredged my memory I could probably still tell you which parts of Belfast were safe and which were no go areas. Not quite what the Tourist Board had in mind.

And, now I came to think about it, I couldn't help a prickle of unease about going there as a civilian.

*

222

If there was one thing the Devil's Bridge Club didn't do on the ferry crossing, it was sit still in one place for any length of time. Paxo announced he was going to try his luck on the slot machines he'd noticed in the bar and Jamie went with him. Sean went out shortly afterwards and although he didn't say anything I knew he was still hoping to spot whoever was keeping an eye on us. Daz still hadn't returned with Tess, so that left me and William. And I wasn't quick enough.

'I think I'll just go and see if I can find myself a good paperback in the shop,' he said. 'You don't mind staying and keeping an eye on our gear, do you, Charlie?'

Resigned, I shook my head and found myself alone in a sea of lids and backpacks.

The First Class lounge had a selection of newspapers and I grabbed one of those, scanning the headlines without too much interest. The next time I glanced outside, Daz and Sean were standing talking by the aft rail.

Actually, 'talking' was too mild a way of putting it. Sean was standing with his arms folded and his head on one side, listening intently, and Daz seemed to be pleading with him about something. There was no way I could hear what they were saying but I stared intently, knowing the dark tint on the cabin windows would mean they couldn't see in.

Eventually, Daz seemed to talk himself out. He stood, shoulders tensed, as though waiting for a judgement. Sean took his time about delivering his verdict but then, at last, he gave a short reluctant nod. Whatever it was he'd just agreed to, he wasn't happy about it.

Daz almost sagged with relief. It gave his smile a brittle, artificial brightness. He moved forwards as if to clap the other man on the shoulder but Sean froze him with a single look. Daz turned down the volume on his smile, his manner sheepish now, grateful. Instead, he offered Sean his hand again and they shook, like they were sealing a pact. Then Daz stuffed his hands into the pockets of his leather jeans and walked away quickly. As

223

though, if he stayed around, Sean might change his mind about something.

But what?

Sean stayed by the railing for a moment longer. As I watched, he turned his head and stared straight at the glass towards me. It made me draw in a sharp breath, though I was certain he couldn't see me. With Sean you could never quite tell. The normal laws of physics sometimes didn't seem to apply to the man.

After a few moments he pushed himself away from the railing and strolled back round towards the doors into the main cabin. A few moments later, he was back in First Class taking the seat opposite me.

'Well?' I demanded.

'Well what?' he said, playing the infuriating card to best effect.

'Come on, Sean,' I said, speaking fast in case any of the others walked back in. 'I saw you out there with Daz. What are they up to? What did he say to you? Come on, spill it!'

Sean regarded me without expression for a moment, then he gave me a rueful smile. 'I'm sorry, Charlie,' he said, 'but I can't tell you.'

'What do you mean you can't tell me?' I said between clenched teeth, trying to keep to a frantic whisper and stop my voice rising with outrage like an air raid siren. Even Sean looked vaguely alarmed.

'Calm down,' he said. 'Daz has just admitted something to me in absolute confidence. He'll tell the rest of you when he's ready but until then I really can't say anything – even to you.'

'But—'

'No,' Sean said, in a voice that brooked no argument. There were no buts when that voice came out. 'I gave him my word,' he said, more gently. 'Look, it's important, but it has nothing to do with why we're here.' He saw the sheer frustration on my face and smiled again. 'You're just going to have to trust me on this.'

224

Chapter Eighteen

The last forty-five minutes of the trip was at a much slower pace than the rest of the crossing. As we reached the entrance to Belfast Lough the captain throttled back to barely ten knots and ambled towards the city port.

'When they first started running the fast cat service they used to come steaming up the Lough at full chat,' William explained when Daz asked him why, 'until they discovered that the wake was actually washing dog walkers off the coastal path. Now they have to slow it down a bit.'

Just before we docked, Paxo dug in his backpack and distributed a set of walkie-talkies with headsets and microphones that Velcro'd in to the lining of our helmets.

'They'll work up to about a mile apart,' he said, 'and the mic's voice activated, so don't sing while you're riding along or we'll all have to suffer it.' He gave Sean a look of insincere apology that there weren't enough to go round. 'Sorry mate – didn't know you were coming.'

'Don't worry about me,' Sean said easily. 'I'm sure I'll manage to keep up and, anyway, I know where you're going.'

That comment netted him some sharp glances, not least from me, but he forestalled any further questions by picking up his gear and following the announcement for all vehicle drivers to return to the car decks.

Thanks in part to William's influence, we were among the first allowed off the ferry when it docked.

The Super Blackbird Sean had borrowed turned out to be a beautiful example in sparkling silver. Irritatingly, despite the fact he hadn't ridden for more than three years and it wasn't even his bike, he looked very much at home in the saddle.

We swept out of the port in convoy. Daz was in front on the Aprilia with Tess riding pillion and, in my humble opinion, wrapping herself round his back more closely than his smooth riding style strictly required. Nobody said anything about a running order but Sean naturally fell in at the rear. Maybe he just wanted to be where he could keep an eye on the rest of us.

The docks area was industrial and scruffy the way docks are the world over. On the other side of the water from the fast cat terminal the landscape was overshadowed by the huge cranes from the Harland and Wolff shipyard.

There wasn't time to do more than grab a basic impression of the city itself as we shot through it. I was too busy trying to make sure I didn't get separated at lights or cut up by other traffic. The bit of it I saw was just a city like any other. Part worn-down, part ultra modern as regeneration snuck in where opportunity let it get a skip outside the door.

Daz led the way confidently onto the M2 motorway that swung round the top end of Belfast, heading west for Londonderry. Then he veered east, taking the exit for Larne. As we bunched up at the roundabout at the bottom of the slip road, Sean came up alongside me and thumbed his visor open a crack.

'Tell them to pull over at the next available point,' he ordered, just loud enough to be heard over the bike engines. 'We've got company.'

I resisted the urge to look behind me, giving him a short nod as I repeated his instruction over my radio. There was a long pause, during which time Daz and Jamie had already

226

merged out into traffic. William launched, then Paxo, leaving just me and Sean waiting for our chance. *Damn!* Getting split up like this when we might be coming under threat was asking for trouble. My finger ends had begun to tingle with tension.

Then came a burst of static and wind noise before Daz's voice sounded casual and almost relaxed in my ear. 'What's up, Charlie – you getting left behind already?'

'Not especially,' I snapped. 'But Sean reckons we might have a problem.'

'What do you think?'

I tried to avoid grinding my teeth. 'I think we should pull over at the next available point.'

'OK, keep heading for Larne and I'll come off and wait for you at the next roundabout.'

The next roundabout was reached along a short section of dual carriageway leading up a long hill. Sean and I opened the bikes up and romped away up the incline, leaving the slower moving cars and a couple of trucks floundering behind us.

By the time we crested the brow there was no sign of the others and I felt my heart rate step up a little, squirting adrenaline into my system on a just-in-case basis. We dropped down towards the roundabout Daz had mentioned, braking hard. I checked my mirrors but could see nothing suspicious.

'We see you, Charlie,' I heard William's voice say. 'Take the first exit. Hotel car park on your right.'

Sean had moved up to my outside quarter, covering my back. I jerked my head to him to indicate that he should follow me, and peeled off left. He stuck with me all the way like a shadow.

We found the others grouped together near the hotel entrance, visors open, apparently unconcerned.

'What's the problem, Sean?' Daz wanted to know as soon as we joined them.

Sean didn't answer right away. His head was turned to

227

scan the fast main road running alongside the hotel. A dark grey Vauxhall Vectra shot onto the roundabout and carried straight on towards Larne. There were four men inside who made a big show of not looking at us as they belted past. Sean watched it go by with slightly narrowed eyes.

'That Vectra,' he said, nodding in the direction the car had taken. 'It picked us up outside the ferry terminal and he's been with us ever since.'

'Oh come off it,' Paxo argued. 'We've barely gone five miles and you're already seeing ghosts behind every rock! It's just a Vauxhall, for God's sake.'

'On tweaked-up suspension but standard wheels, with twin aerials on the back and no dealer stickers, four up,' Sean said, shaking his head. 'I don't think so.'

Daz frowned. 'So who do you think they were?' he asked.

Sean shrugged. 'Security services, cops, maybe even the paramilitaries,' he said softly. 'I was rather hoping you might be able to tell me that.'

'There's no reason for any of that lot to be after us,' William said, his voice even and apparently guileless. 'Why would there be?' But he glanced at Daz as he spoke, as if looking for confirmation that the other man hadn't told Sean anything during their little heart-to-heart.

'Really?' Sean said. 'Well, in that case, it must be me.'

At first I thought he was joking but, when he didn't smile, I realised he meant it.

'I think it might be best if I went my own way today,' he said when nobody spoke. 'I'll meet up with you at the hotel tonight.' With that he nodded, shut his visor, and toed the Blackbird into gear.

'Sean! Hold up a minute!'

He'd already begun to move off when he caught my shout and stopped again, putting his feet down. I nudged the side-stand down on the 'Blade and climbed off to go and talk to him. It was easier than having to paddle the bike round. I yanked my helmet off as I reached him and he did the same. Only difference was that I'd forgotten about the radio wire that I'd threaded down the neck of my leathers and damn-near strangled myself until I unplugged it.

'What the hell's going on?' I demanded quietly.

Sean eyed the rest of the group, who were watching us with undisguised curiosity. He flicked his eyes back to me. 'I haven't been back to Northern Ireland since I came out,' he said flatly. 'I operated here, Charlie, and trust me when I say I did some serious damage. It's been a while, but some people have long memories. That Vectra might be following this lot, or it might be following me. Better to find out for sure, don't you think?'

'But how did they know you were coming?'

He shrugged again. 'It's not difficult to find out,' he said. 'The ticket was booked in my name and that might have raised a few flags. It was only done yesterday, which might explain why they've been so clumsy about the tail – short notice.'

I thought about that for a moment. I didn't like it, but I could see the sense. 'OK,' I said, stepping back. 'I'll keep my eye on them. You take care, Sean.'

'Yeah,' he said with a grim smile, 'you too.'

After Sean had gone, heading back towards Belfast, I took station at the back and spent as much time watching my mirrors as the road ahead of me. That turned out to be easier said than done.

Daz set up a furious pace, taking no prisoners as far as making sure the group stayed together was concerned. He sliced past slower-moving traffic on his side of the road with blatant disregard for what might be coming the other way. This time, Tess's intimate grip seemed a lot more necessary. She was wrapped round his back with her head tucked in like she couldn't bear to watch.

Paxo matched him, one wild move after another, hunched over the tank of his Ducati, sliding across the seat to just about put his knee down on every roundabout.

William was less inclined to suicide and, I noted with relief, Jamie seemed content to follow him rather than try and keep pace with the lead pair. One less thing for me to worry about.

We dropped down into Larne, leapfrogging a line of trucks all bound for the freight boats to Cairnryan and Stranraer. Daz headed off up the A2 coast road, and then I had the scenery to watch as well.

I hadn't expected the Antrim coast to be quite so spectacular but in places it took your breath away. The road ran right along the edge of the Irish Sea and at one point it had actually been cut through the rock which rose over the top of our heads like a rugged gothic archway.

Eventually, Daz broke his silent concentration long enough to report, 'OK, lads, this is it,' and we pulled over into the gravel car park of a sprawling stone-built hotel overlooking a small bay. I couldn't help but be relieved that we'd all survived the first part of our journey intact and, despite Sean's concerns, unmolested.

We slotted the bikes in alongside each other and cut the engines. After the combined edgy roar of our exhaust notes, the gentle grumble of the surf rolling up onto the shingle was like a kind of furry silence.

'Nice choice,' William said approvingly, looking first at the deserted beach and then at the hotel entrance. He didn't seem at all ruffled after the energetic ride, his broad face carrying its usual impassive mask of calm.

On the other hand, when Paxo thrust off his helmet he was panting like he'd been starved of oxygen in there. His narrow face was sliding with sweat and even his mini mohican had wilted. He glared at Daz.

'Mate, what is wrong with you?' he demanded. 'You got a fuckin' death-wish all of a sudden?'

Daz turned on him with a grin that had overtones of manic about it. 'What's up, Pax?' he shot back, close to jeering. 'Never thought I'd see the day when you couldn't keep up with me when you're solo and I'm carrying ballast.' He ignored – or was too hyped up to see – the scathing glance Tess fired off in his direction. 'You losing your nerve or what?'

Paxo moved in close, bristling, the way I'd seen him do with Jamie that day outside the hospital.

'My nerve's good, mate,' he gritted. 'Can you say the same?'

'Cool it, you two,' William said. 'Not in front of the children, eh?'

It was drawlingly delivered and contrived to insult both Jamie and myself in equal measure. Jamie pretended to be too caught up in unhooking his tank bag from the Honda to have heard the comment. I had no such qualms.

'I agree with Paxo,' I said calmly. 'You're riding like an idiot. There's a thin line between brave and stupid and you're way over the other side of it. What are you trying to prove, Daz? If I'd known this trip was going to be about macho bullshit, I wouldn't have bothered.'

Instead of snapping back at me, Daz's grin just grew all the wider. 'If you can't stand the heat, Charlie . . .' he said and with that he picked up his gear and sauntered across the road towards the hotel entrance.

'Speakin' of macho bullshit,' Tess said suddenly when he'd gone, 'what happened to this tail we was supposed to have picked up?'

The others turned to look at me, challenge in their faces as they diverted their anger from one of their own to a comparative outsider.

'No one followed us after we left that car park,' I admitted reluctantly.

'So lover boy was imaginin' things back there?' Tess persisted.

'I didn't say that.'

'What, then?'

'I don't know.'

But I did. Her words brought the whole thing into focus. I was completely convinced that, if Sean reckoned the

231

Vectra had been following us, then it had. He was way too experienced and too canny to have mistaken a coincidence for a deliberate action. But either they weren't with us now, or they'd suddenly got a whole hell of a lot better at not being spotted.

Or, worst of all, Sean had been right and the tail hadn't been following the rest of us.

It had been following him.

The rooms at the hotel were large and mine had two double beds in it as well as a pullout sofa, which made me wonder about who it was really designed for. I'd half-expected that I'd be sharing with Tess, but she either had her own room or had decided on other sleeping arrangements. I didn't ask which.

As soon as I got into my room I called Jacob. My mobile didn't seem to be able to pick up a signal, which I wasn't sure was down to just being in a dodgy cell area, or whether it wouldn't work in Ireland at all. I made a mental note to ask.

I used the hotel phone instead, aware that they were probably charging me through the nose for the privilege. I caught Jacob at home and gave him a brief run-down of the trip so far. He gave me the latest news on Sam's condition, which was remarkably good, all things considered. I asked how Clare was. Her temperature was up, he told me. My father was concerned about possible infection.

'I know I'm probably biased, but she's in very good hands,' I said.

'I know that, too,' he said, still sounding anxious. 'But even so ...'

I showered and changed and met the others downstairs afterwards in the bar. By the time I arrived, everyone was there apart from Tess. I assumed she was still primping. They stopped talking when I appeared, which I tried not to let annoy me.

232

The boys had made an effort, wearing shirts or T-shirts with designer logos on the breast and, appropriately enough, a range of Nike pub shoes. Even Paxo's hairstyle was looking spruce again.

Instinctively, I'd dressed to blend in, putting on the one pair of jeans I'd brought with me plus a rugby shirt. There was still enough residual heat left in the day to make it a bit too warm for long sleeves and a high collar, but at least they hid the new bruises on my arms and the old scars around my neck.

Eighteen months previously I'd been unlucky enough to get my throat half cut and I now had a long ragged scar round the base of my neck that was my constant reminder of the incident. It was fading all the time but to me it was as obvious as a flashing neon necklace. I didn't want to have to explain to the Devil's Bridge Club how it had got there, or what I'd had to do in order to survive the experience.

'So, Charlie,' Daz said as soon as I'd perched on a bar stool and ordered a beer, 'tell us all about Sean Meyer.'

I eyed the barman, who worked on without any indication that he was listening in on the conversation, then shrugged cautiously. 'What's to tell?'

'Well, what's the story with the two of you?'

'I work for him,' I said, deliberately obtuse.

Daz made a gesture of frustration and William took over.

'What Daz means is,' he asked solemnly, 'are you shagging him?'

That brought a burst of laughter that sounded raucous to my ears, set my nerves on edge. I smiled because it was the best defence but inside I went cold and solid. I was overwhelmed by the urge to break things. Bones, mainly.

'I think that's a question you should ask Sean,' I said, sweetly. 'Only, I'd do it over the phone if I were you. It might hurt less.'

Tess appeared about twenty minutes later, in full make-up

233

and her usual array of jangling silver jewellery. She was also wearing heels and a very short skirt that revealed a pair of eye-catchingly good legs. Just about every male eye in the room swivelled in their direction. The barman even attempted to casually lean over the bar to keep them in view as she approached.

She sinuously elbowed her way into the group between me and Daz. I had to take a step back to avoid having my insteps punctured by those stilettos.

'Right, where are we going then?' she demanded.

Considering the boys had already had a couple of pints each by that time, I viewed her question with alarm, but Jamie mentioned a pub that he reckoned was within walking distance and had a pool table, bar food and some decent music.

'We can walk up and maybe get a cab back, yeah?' he suggested.

'Why not?' Daz said, eyeing Tess's heels with a flicker of amusement.

He was still smiling when we all stepped out of the hotel entrance into the still-bright evening sunshine, then his face snapped shut like he'd had a smack in the mouth.

Waiting in the car park on the other side of the road was a dark grey Vauxhall Vectra with four men inside. They were uniformly big men, and would have fitted any of the categories Sean had suggested when we'd spotted them earlier.

They'd been pulled up near our bikes and just for a moment after we appeared, they looked as shocked by the unexpected encounter as we must have done. Then the driver stamped on the gas and the car shot off, scattering gravel and snaking slightly as it hit the road again.

Shaken out of our temporary immobility, we sprinted across the road, not to give chase but to check on the bikes. We'd chained them all together like convicts and couldn't see any sign that they'd been tampered with. None of the alarm systems registered a trigger.

'Well I s'pose that answers my question,' Tess said ruefully as she joined the rest of us at a pace her footwear would allow.

I nodded. But if the Vectra was shadowing us, where the hell was Sean?

We still made the mile walk to the pub Jamie had mentioned, even though I got the impression nobody's heart was really in it any more. The pub was bright and lively and only got livelier as Friday night hotted up. Tess's attire ensured she was the centre of attention and she flirted shamelessly with anyone who had a pulse. And with one or two for whom the matter looked pretty debatable.

After we'd eaten, I stayed round the pool table playing a team game with William against Paxo and Jamie, and making a bottle of Grolsch last the evening. It didn't take long before I understood Daz's previous reluctance to take on Paxo at pool. He was a demon player. If Jamie hadn't been bad enough to handicap him, they'd have walked all over us.

'She's asking for trouble, that one,' William murmured as I straightened from a difficult pot into the centre pocket, having managed to screw the cue ball back up the table for the next shot.

I followed his gaze and saw that two local lads were sizing each other up over Tess. Their body language had taken on the aggressive posturing of two dogs circling with their hackles up before the fight starts. Tess sat on a bar stool in the middle, her legs crossed to reveal a large amount of tanned thigh. She was sipping her drink and smirking. Daz, I saw, was watching proceedings like a spectator rather than a participant. I wondered if she was trying to make him jealous.

'Do you think we ought to do anything?' Jamie murmured, frowning.

'Mm, put myself between two randy young devils and a bitch in heat?' William said, shaking his head. 'I don't think so.'

235

'Well don't look at me,' Jamie said, grinning. 'Charlie's the kung fu expert. Why can't she break them up?'

'What do you suggest?' Paxo asked. 'A bucket of cold water?'

'Oh for heaven's sake,' I muttered, handing Jamie my cue and my bottle of beer. 'Here – don't do anything with either of these until I get back.'

I walked over to the bar and leaned on it casually near where Tess's admirers were just starting to curl their lips at each other. I pulled out a fiver and waited as though to catch the eye of one of the busy bar staff.

'By the way, Tess,' I said, speaking clearly and leaning back a little so she was in line of sight. 'You didn't tell me who was babysitting your little girl while you're away?'

Tess's smug face tightened unattractively. 'She's with her grandma,' she admitted through gritted teeth.

By the time I'd got back to the pool table, the two lads who'd been all over Tess had melted away. Paxo grinned broadly and saluted me with his beer.

'Nicely done, Charlie,' he said, shaking his head. 'I mean, bitchy as hell, but nicely done!'

By chucking-out time there wasn't a cab to be had. Buoyed up by the balmy evening and the drink, the boys seemed quite happy to weave their way back to the hotel on foot, even in the dark. Tess was the only one who raised any objections but she was quickly outvoted.

The road was bordered by a grass verge on the right-hand side and a low wall leading to the rocky shoreline on the other. A shimmering moon provided the only illumination, reflected off the surface of the water. Apart from the soothing wash of the breakers, it was quiet.

The four lads drifted ahead, littering the natural sounds of the night with their boisterous laughs and shouts. I hung back, keeping my pace slow enough so that Tess could maintain it alongside me. I walked in the grass, feeling the bottoms of my jeans soon soak through with the dew.

236

Tess tottered along on the road, complaining that her feet hurt, although I would have thought the amount of Smirnoff Ice she'd been knocking back all evening would have had an anaesthetising effect.

'You're worried about 'em, aren't you?' Tess said suddenly, a moment of unexpected clarity surfacing.

I turned to stare at her in the gloom but I could barely make out her features. Ahead of us, Paxo must have tripped over something. I heard him swearing amid catcalls and laughter from the others.

'I suppose so,' I said, guarded. 'I just wish they'd level with me.'

Tess made a sound that could have been a snort. 'I don't mean that,' she said, her voice blurry at the edges but still laced with a certain cunning. 'I mean now. You're worried about 'em now 'cos they're pissed. Whaddya think they're gonna do to ya, Charlie?'

I felt a chill prickle across the surface of my skin. I jammed my hands into my pockets and tried not to rub at the goosebumps that had sprung up on my arms.

'I don't think they're going to do anything to me,' I said carefully, annoyed at her perception. Annoyed at myself for giving anything away. 'I think they'd be mad to try.'

The lights of an approaching car appeared around a bend in the road behind us, throwing drastically elongated shadows onto the road ahead. The boys were twenty metres ahead of us now and I saw them skitter for the sides of the road in the sudden glare.

I glanced back just as the car cleared the last bend. A mistake. His lights were on full beam and my retinas were instantly scorched by them. I ducked my head away quickly.

Something about the engine note was a warning, though. The car was being held in too low a gear and the revs were thrashing, harsh and high, in protest. It was also too far over to the right-hand side of the road.

Much too far.

I yanked my hands out of my pockets and grabbed Tess by one arm, swinging her round straight off her feet. She gave a single outraged squeal as she went airborne, landing with a massive thump further along the grass and tumbling to a halt.

The car shot past, its driver's side wheels kicking up a blast of gravel from the shoulder where, only moments before, Tess had been walking.

The boys jumped out of the way with shouts and curses, but the car pelted away through the middle of them.

I'd overreached to get to her in time and ended up on my knees. I got my head up fast, but the car was already disappearing and I failed to get any impression of a model or colour, never mind a number plate.

'Fuck me, are you all right?'

Jamie's voice. Now the lights of the car had gone, it suddenly seemed very dark.

It took a few moments before my eyes began to settle. Then I could just make out William and Daz picking Tess off the floor. She threw herself into Daz's arms, weeping. He froze for a moment, then closed his arms round her and started making 'there, there' noises.

'Crazy bastard,' Paxo said, glaring after the disappearing car. 'What the fuck was he trying to do?'

'I would have thought that was pretty obvious,' I said grimly, climbing to my feet and dusting off my hands on the seat of my jeans. 'The only question I have is, why?'

Chapter Nineteen

Between us, we managed to get Tess on her feet long enough to get her back to the hotel. We staggered in through Reception with her draped between us, still wailing – drunk, scared, and hurt, in equal measure.

In the light she looked terrible. Grass-stained and dishevelled. Somewhere along the way she'd lost a shoe and her shaken lack of co-ordination only accentuated the unevenness of her gait. The grass verge had been stonier than I'd realised when I'd chucked her across it and she now had a long diagonal graze across one knee and scrapes to both palms. Still, it had been a better option than the alternative.

A stick-thin middle-aged woman was working the late stint on the front desk. She took in the state of Tess and skewered the four lads with a long and suspicious glare. I think if I hadn't been with them she might have seriously considered the possibility that they'd roughed the girl up themselves. She certainly didn't seem too convinced about their furtive story of a rogue drunk driver, despite the fact that it was close to the truth.

'I've got a first-aid kit in my tank bag,' I said. 'Come up to my room, Tess, and we'll get you cleaned up.'

She took little coaxing, nodding tearfully with her lips pressed tight together like a child promised a lollipop in return for being a big brave girl. She leaned on a table long

239

enough to toe off her other shoe, abandoning it where it landed, and trailed after me.

As we reached the bottom tread of the staircase I paused and looked back, letting her go on ahead. The four of them were still standing in the reception area, stiff-shouldered with delayed shock.

'Another close one, Daz?' I murmured.

For a moment his eyes met mine, haunted, then he flicked them away and his expression shifted into devil-may-care so comprehensively that I could almost have imagined the other.

'Bar's still open,' he said, defiant. 'Anyone fancy another beer?'

'I never wanted to be here, y'know.'

I glanced up in surprise at Tess's sudden statement as I dumped another piece of TCP-sodden cotton wool into the rubbish bin. She was perched on the edge of the second bed in my room, having sat down with experimental heaviness and bounced up and down a few times, like she was thinking of staying and was just trying out the mattress.

For a moment I didn't reply. All I could think of was how hard she'd fought for the right to come along. Then I backtracked and realised Tess herself had never made that much of a fuss about it. With Gleet banging the drum on her behalf, she hadn't had to.

I also remembered how she'd told me, with apparent sincerity, that Clare had been unfaithful to Jacob with his own son. Not relevant as such, but pretty good as an indication of her inability to separate fact from fiction.

'Why's that, Tess?' I said, dropping my eyes to her knee again. I'd just about got all the grit out of it but she was going to have to stay out of short skirts for a while.

She snorted hard enough to make the bed sway and waved a hand towards herself.

'Well, look at the state of me,' was all she said.

240

'So, what *are* you doing here?' I asked, keeping my voice casual. I caught one of her hands, turned it palm upwards and started wiping dirt from the scuffed skin.

'Tickles,' she said, giggling, trying to pull it away.

'Sorry, but I really need to clean this up,' I said, not letting go, the way you'd hold onto the ear of a fractious child.

I was using a stronger solution of disinfectant than was strictly kind and it should have been stinging like hell but the alcohol was proving an effective painkiller. For the moment. Her hand had started to swell a little, too. 'You're going to have to take your rings off, Tess.'

She shook her head several times more than was necessary, then had to grab on to the bed while the room caught up with her. 'Oh no,' she said, 'they never come off, this lot.'

She held both hands up, backs towards me, to show off the rake of silver bands, adorned with glittering glass. 'Made 'em all myself. Cool, huh?' She wiggled her fingers and frowned, as though she couldn't work out why she was having trouble flexing them.

'Your fingers have already started to come up like sausages,' I said bluntly. 'If you leave it until tomorrow you'll have to get them cut off.'

She pulled a shocked face and shivered with the giggles again.

I sighed. 'I meant the rings, Tess, not your fingers.'

'Sorry,' she said, grinning inanely and making an effort to pull herself together that was only partially successful.·

But she did begin tugging at her fingers, dropping the jewellery into a pile on her lap, a purpose for which her mini skirt was not best suited. One ring slipped between her thighs onto the carpet and, when she leaned over to retrieve it, two or three others dropped, too.

Tess swore. I reached for one of the saucers from the tea-making kit, scooping the fallen rings into it and handing it to her, otherwise we were going to be here all night. She managed to peel the rest off with studied concentration and added them to the collection.

'So, if you didn't want to come to Ireland,' I said, picking up the thread again along with the cotton wool, 'why was Gleet giving Daz such a hard time about them not letting you in on it?'

'Just 'cos I wanted in didn't mean I wanted *in*, in,' she mumbled, sniggering again. Then she sobered, turning almost maudlin. 'Aw, but Gleet's been lovely to us – me an' Ashley – a proper mate.'

'Really?' I said, getting irritated with her now and trying not to show it. 'So what's he doing with Slick's bike, then?'

For a moment Tess sat and stared at me, open-mouthed, and I could see the alarm flitting about behind her eyes. God knows, there was plenty of room for manoeuvre in there.

There may have been surprise but it was not, I realised suddenly, because of anything Gleet might have done. It was because I knew about it.

'What you talking about?' she demanded, much too late.

'Come on, Tess. Slick's bike went missing after the accident and I know full well that Gleet's got it,' I said, only stretching the truth a little. 'Now why is that, hm? What doesn't he want the police to find?'

'Nothing!' she said, her voice starting to rise. 'They aren't going to find nothing.' And, as it sank in that a denial was as good as a confirmation, she added sulkily: 'There isn't nothing for them to find.'

And taken purely from a grammatical point of view, she was probably telling the truth. I squirted Savlon onto her hands and sat back on my heels, letting her rub the cream into them. She did so distractedly, in a nervous wringing gesture.

'If it wasn't Gleet,' I asked quietly, 'who *did* knock Slick off his bike?'

She looked up at me, bleary, pink around the nose like she was about to cry. 'Who says they were after my Slick?'

242

'Don't keep trying to walk me down that path, Tess,' I said softly, a warning. 'There was nothing going on between Jamie and Clare, and you know it.'

She flushed. 'He told me he was bringing her to see him,' she muttered.

'Who did?'

'Jamie. He told me Slick was bringing Clare to see him last Sunday. Didn't want his old man to find out about it. Dirty little sod.'

Realisation dawned. Not knowing about the money Jamie was borrowing from Clare, Tess had put her own perverted spin on the facts. *Well, that figured.*

'If Jacob obviously didn't know what was going on, why did you tell people he was involved?'

'I never!'

'Yes you did,' I said firmly. 'At the wake.'

'I never!' she protested again, indignant. 'Who told you that?'

'Someone I trust,' I said, crushing her. 'You said he was "on board". On board with what?'

She frowned, screwing her eyes up with the effort of recall. 'Jacob, Jacob,' she murmured, as though that was going to help. 'Wait a minute ... Jamie,' she said. 'Gnasher. I said Gnasher was on board. Jamie, not Jacob.'

'Gnasher?' I repeated. Where had I heard him called that before? Gleet. That was it, outside the hospital. I tried to work out if that's what Sam could have overheard at the wake or if Tess was spinning me yet another line. He certainly didn't seem to know Jamie – not well enough to realise the relationship between him and Jacob. *I wonder ...*

'Yeah,' Tess said, happier now she could stop the thinking that was making her vodka-addled brain hurt. 'I told Slick he was a bad idea, though, that kid. Hadn't got the cash for it until a few weeks ago. Don't know where he got it. Don't want to know, either.'

'A few weeks ago?' I said sharply, thinking of the

243

withdrawal slip Sean and I had found in Jacob and Clare's safe. It was dated days ago, not weeks.

Tess nodded, the action unbalancing her so I had to grab her arm and prop her upright again. 'Tha's right,' she said.

Her eyelids started to droop. She popped them open again only with tremendous effort, wagging a strangely naked finger in my direction. 'And the sort of people his family's tied up with,' she mumbled conspiratorially, 'you don't wanna know where he might've got it, huh?'

Her eyes were closing again. I shook her shoulder, none too gently.

'No you don't, Tess,' I said. 'No sleeping here. Back to your own room. Come on, up!'

She allowed me to drag her to her feet and waltz her, unresisting, towards the door. I'd just got it open when she suddenly snapped awake.

'My rings!'

I used her as a doorstop against the heavy self-closing mechanism while I retrieved the saucerful of jewellery, tipping the contents into her cupped hands. I was intending to just shut the door behind her but, by the dazed way she was looking round, I reckoned she wouldn't find her way back to her own room. I checked my key was still in my pocket and stepped out into the corridor with her. She instantly half-collapsed onto me.

'Need a hand?' I looked, finding, to my surprise, that Jamie was walking towards us from the direction of the stairs.

'Good timing,' he said. He held up a key. 'Daz sent me up with this so you can tuck her in. How is she?'

'I'm not deaf, y'know,' Tess grumbled, lifting her head from my shoulder.

'Well you obviously didn't hear them say "you've had enough", did you?' I muttered under my breath.

Jamie grinned at me and slipped an arm around Tess, taking the weight. 'You go ahead – number twelve,' he said. 'I've got her.'

244

Still clutching her fistful of rings, Tess threw her arms round his neck and held on like it was the last slow dance, grinding her hips against him, head buried against his chest. Jamie didn't necessarily look like he was upset by the experience.

By the time I'd found the right door, opened it and turned back, his hands had dropped to her skinny rump.

'Leave her alone.'

He looked up, eyebrows climbing at the stone-cold note in my voice. 'Come on, Charlie, lighten up.'

'She's drunk and she doesn't know what she's doing,' I said, frozen. Not an argument that works every time. I discarded it and tried another. 'And I hardly think Daz is going to be overjoyed to find you doing the nasty with Tess when she's supposed to be with him.'

'He don't want me,' Tess said, muffled and mournful into the front of Jamie's shirt. She lifted her head and gazed, sniffing, into his eyes. 'You want me, don't you, Gnasher?'

'No he doesn't,' I said grimly, disengaging the pair of them and almost shoving her into the right room. She paddled backwards and sat down on the nearest of the two beds with a thump.

'Tha's not fair,' she wailed. 'You've got Sean an' he's gorgeous an' now you want Gnasher as well, an' I 'aven't got nobody.'

'That's right, Tess. Goodnight,' I said cheerfully, and shut the door on her.

I turned to find Jamie was still grinning. 'I really feel I should stay with her,' he said, 'just to, er, make sure she's all right.'

'Leave her alone,' I repeated, knowing he was baiting me and rising to it anyway. 'Because if she regrets what she's done in the morning, I'll be the first to back her up on it, understand?'

He held up his hands in mock surrender. 'Whoa, OK, I'm sorry. I was only joking,' he said. 'I didn't think you even liked Tess.'

245

I rubbed a hand across my face, suddenly tired and flash-tempered. 'What the fuck has that got to do with it?'

The smile finally disappeared. 'I'm sorry,' he said again, and meant it this time. 'I would never take advantage of a girl.'

'Oh yeah?' I said. 'What about Clare?'

He stared at me blankly for a moment. 'What are you talking about?'

'I'm talking about the ten grand, Jamie.'

He swallowed but before he could reply we heard footsteps approaching and the murmur of voices. An elderly couple appeared, dressed up to the nines, and stopped outside a door further up the corridor while they hunted for their key.

Jamie waited until the door had closed behind the couple, then jerked his head towards the room opposite Tess's. 'Look,' he muttered, 'let's talk about this inside, yeah?'

He produced his own key out of his jeans pocket and shoved it into the lock. Inside, the room was very similar to mine, maybe a touch smaller and the twin beds were both singles. I recognised Paxo's leathers hanging on the wardrobe door.

Jamie caught my glance. 'No one wants to share with William,' he said by way of explanation. 'He snores like an industrial buzz saw. It's bad enough being in the same building.'

There was a little nervous catch to his voice as he spoke, as though he'd suddenly realised that by inviting me in like this he'd potentially put himself in harm's way.

I leaned my shoulder against the wall next to the doorway, blocking his escape route.

'Why did you need the ten thousand, Jamie?'

'Oh, um, well, I wanted to buy a new bike and—'

'Don't,' I said. The single-word command worked much better on Jamie than it had done on Sean. He shut up like I'd just hit the mute button on the remote control.

'Clare's already told me that you came to her in trouble

246

and she agreed to lend you the money,' I said. 'All I want to know is why you needed it. The truth. What's Daz got on you?'

'*Daz*?' Jamie squawked. 'No, no, no. It's not Daz who—'

He broke off, realising he'd been suckered, and gave me a smile of self-derision.

'OK,' I said, folding my arms. 'Who is it?'

He moved over to the bed and sat down nearly as heavily as Tess had done, putting his knees on his elbows and slowly rubbing his face with both hands.

'Look, I borrowed some money about a month ago from Eamonn.'

'Eamonn?' I said, trying to tone down the disbelief in my voice. 'Everyone's favourite philanthropist?'

He lifted his head, flushing. 'Yeah, I know that might seem stupid to you, but he's been an OK kind of a guy, y'know? Up 'til then, anyway. I-I needed some dosh and Mum wouldn't lend it to me. Eamonn overheard one of the rows we had about it and the next day he just handed it to me – in cash, just like that.'

'And you didn't think to ask what he might want in return for this princely gesture?'

'Of course I did,' he said, scowling. 'He just fobbed me off, y'know?'

'How long did it take him to change his mind?'

Jamie's scowl deepened. 'Couple of weeks,' he muttered. 'He was apologetic at first, then started getting creepy about Mum, said as how he didn't want this to hurt her.'

'In what way?'

'Fuck me, I don't know! You think I wanted him to spell it out for me?'

'And that's when you went to Clare.'

He nodded. 'Yeah.'

'Why did you want Clare to meet you at Devil's Bridge? Why not just go to the house?'

Jamie looked glum. 'I didn't want Dad to know about it

247

and I didn't know he wasn't at home until—' he broke off, shrugged, 'well, afterwards.'

'And did Eamonn know about this?'

'Probably – through Mum.'

I was silent for a moment, considering. 'I don't suppose there's any chance that Eamonn went after Clare – and Slick – because he wanted to keep you in his debt, is there?' I asked mildly.

Jamie's head had begun to drop but now it snapped up. He jerked to his feet, suddenly restless. 'No way,' he said, shaking his head like he could shudder the thought free. 'No. Eamonn wasn't even in the country last Sunday. He was somewhere in Europe – flew back into Manchester on Monday. Mum went over to collect him from the airport.'

I refrained from pointing out that Eamonn didn't have to be driving the van himself in order to be responsible for it.

'So how did they know about the crash?'

'I spoke to Mum on Sunday night,' he muttered. 'I told her then. She must have told Eamonn when she picked him up.'

'And they decided they'd see what they could nick from the house before Jacob got back,' I said.

I looked up in time to see a guilty expression flirt across Jamie's face and suddenly I put it all together.

'But there wasn't anything to nick, was there, Jamie?' I said quietly, 'Because you'd already been into the safe and grabbed the money before your mother arrived. All that stuff she came out with about us being after the same thing. She just wanted the cash and, when she realised I either didn't have it or wasn't going to let go of it, she set Eamonn onto me.' I saw by his face I'd got it nailed and the realisation fired my anger. 'Didn't you give a shit about what had just happened to Clare?'

Jamie stopped pacing in front of me, put his hands on my arms. 'Look, Charlie, I—'

At that moment there was the rattle of a key in the lock. The door swung open and Paxo walked in. He stopped abruptly when he saw the two of us, frozen like that, and a sly grin spread across his face.

'Oops – sorry,' he said, totally unrepentant. 'Didn't know I was interrupting anything. You want me to go and come back later, mate? Or can I stay and join in?'

Jamie's hands dropped away like he'd just had his fingers burned. I levered myself off the wall.

'I was just leaving,' I said, stalking out past Paxo with as much dignity as I could manage. 'And anyway, Pax, I hardly think I'm your type – for a start, I'm not inflatable.'

Back in my own room I was too tired to spend much time turning over what Jamie had told me. I stripped off my clothes and cleaned my teeth before climbing straight into bed. There'd be time to dissect it all in the morning – when Sean was back.

The realisation of just how much I missed him, needed him, came to me right on the edge of sleep. It was my last conscious thought before I pitched into the comforting darkness.

I woke. The room was still blacked out and the building was silent but I knew something was different. Something was wrong.

I sat up and was about to reach for the bedside light when there was a quiet slither from across the other side of the room. The small lamp on the chest of drawers by the TV clicked on. I winced at the sudden glare, screwing my eyes up until they'd had a chance to adjust.

Sean sat in the chair next to the drawers. He was wearing his leather jeans, a T-shirt, and his bike jacket was laid across the bed next to mine. He still had his hand on the lamp switch and, when I was able to focus again, I saw that he was smiling.

'Don't you ever knock?' I demanded, surprise and the sudden awakening making me grumpy. 'How did you get in?'

'Not if I can help it,' he said easily, 'and you really

should remember to use the security chain. That lock was hardly much of a challenge.'

'Sorry to disappoint you,' I said.

He got to his feet, untucking the T-shirt and starting to gather it upwards from the hem. My heart started to thunder so hard I almost had to raise my voice to be heard over it.

'What are you doing?'

He stilled in mid-undress. I had to force myself not to stare at the expanse of smooth flat skin already on show.

'Making use of your spare bed,' he said. 'It's too late to check in – even if they'd held a room for me – but I didn't want to climb in until you'd woken up. You'd probably have killed me.' He was only half joking.

'Oh, well in that case, make yourself at home,' I said, trying for casual.

He smiled. 'Thanks.' And with that he disappeared into the bathroom.

I lay down again and stared at the ceiling. I knew I should have been thinking about what Sean might have found out after he split off from the rest of us, but the fact that the Vauxhall had turned up at the hotel shortly after we did seemed to answer that one.

Instead, my brain was being ruled by my body. By the opportunity presented by having Sean in the bed next to mine. *What if ... ?*

The bathroom door opened and he clicked off the light. He'd stripped down to his shorts and now he draped his leathers across a chair and turned back the covers on the other bed.

Go on. Ask him. Invite him ...

He moved across to the light by the TV and reached for the switch.

'Sean—'

He paused, glancing back to me. His eyes were in shadow and I couldn't read his face.

'What is it, Charlie?' His voice was gentle.

250

My nerve failed me.

'Um, goodnight,' I said.

'Goodnight, Charlie,' he said softly, and plunged the room into blackness again.

The next thing I knew I was sitting bolt upright in bed with my breath coming fast and shallow and my eyes wide open. I had no concept of the passing of time. It seemed I'd only just let my head fall back and it had bounced me straight up again.

For some reason this second disturbance of my sleep brought with it a burst of unreasoned rage. I froze, listening for a repeat of the sound that had woken me, prepared to lash out. Then it came again and, with a sense of profound shock, I recognised it for what it was.

Someone was crying.

The realisation snuffed out my anger instantly, dried my mouth yet threatened to wet my eyes. Slowly, I swung my legs out of bed and sat there, gripping the edge of the mattress. The silence went on long enough for me to imagine it must have been part of a dream, where nothing comes as a surprise. Not even the idea of a man like Sean Meyer weeping in the night.

And then I heard it. Little more than a gasp, a catch in his breath, brim full of anguish and pain. My night-dilated eyes could just make out Sean's restless figure amid the snarled-up sheets only a metre or so away. For a moment I did nothing more than watch him sleep and listen to him dream.

The dream was hot enough to make him sweat, savage enough to send his heart rate soaring, and dark enough to force out quiet whimpers from between his clamped lips. Trapped in slumber, his subconscious was free to torture him at will.

I had nights like that myself.

I leaned over and stole a hand across the bedclothes. I found his twisting fingers and crept my own between them.

251

He gripped tight, blindly, not knowing I was there. Instinct taking succour where it was offered, like a frightened child.

I suffered from my own nightmares. It had never occurred to me that Sean must have his monsters to face, too.

On the surface he seemed so calm, so solid and, despite what I might have thrown at him in anger, so in control. I'd never considered his doubt or pain. Yet here he was, crying out in his sleep and needing comfort of his own. Did I really have anything to offer him that hadn't been irreparably damaged in transit?

Hesitant, I stood, pushed back the sheets and slid into bed alongside him, reaching out to him. His body was heated, febrile, so that where our skin touched I almost expected it to sizzle. For a second he resisted, tried to push me away. If he'd continued I think I would have let him, but he didn't.

He seemed to rise a layer out of the hell where he'd been burning. Not enough to wake, but enough to recognise me. Or somebody like me.

He let me slink under his arm, sneak my head onto his shoulder and wrap my limbs across his shuddering body, anchoring him in this reality. His roughened chin skimmed the top of my head. I could feel his breath in my hair, slowing.

I lay awake and listened as his body began to drift, as his pulse climbed down. And I decided, fiercely, that I would give as much as I was able to. As much as Sean would take. Two broken halves could not necessarily be put back together to form a whole, but I had to try.

For both our sakes.

Chapter Twenty

When I opened my eyes the following morning, it was to find Sean lying on his side facing me, arm bent, head propped on his hand.

'Hi,' he said quietly, giving me one of those slow-release smiles.

'Hi yourself,' I said, feeling my breath hitch, my heart stutter. I stretched, hiding a yawn together with my self-consciousness behind my hand. 'What is it with you and watching me sleep?'

He laughed, little more than a bubble of amusement, and reached to smooth a tangle of hair out of my eyes, using that distraction to neatly dodge the question. 'You're very peaceful when you sleep.'

'Not always,' I said. I paused. 'And neither are you.'

The smile faded and Sean rolled away onto his back. The light filtering through the thin curtains touched on the healed scar at his shoulder and just for a moment I wished all his injuries had been merely physical. Instead, the one that had hurt him the most was the savage blow to his psyche and, as I well knew, treating those wounds could be a much more hit-and-miss affair.

'Ah,' he said. 'I wondered what had brought you all the way over here from your own bed.'

'You don't remember?'

He shook his head, frowning. 'Nothing specific,' he

said. 'I never do unless something wakes me in the thick of it, so to speak.'

I passed over the admission of frequency. For the moment. 'And then?'

He shrugged and it was my turn to rise up and lean over him. 'Talk to me, Sean.'

A long sigh, a slow letting of breath. 'Yes, I have nightmares,' he said at last, closing his eyes briefly. 'Gut-wrenching vicious bloody nightmares.'

'The same one, or different?'

'Variations on a theme usually,' he said, using that flat emotionless voice I'd heard from him so many times before. 'I'm either watching people die and doing nothing, or I'm killing them myself.'

'Who?'

He opened his eyes and flicked them sideways to meet mine. I saw him calculate whether to tell me the truth or just a version of it. Finally, he said frankly, 'People I know. People I . . . feel strongly about. People I was in the army with, my friends, my family. The number of times I've slit my father's throat in my sleep, the old bastard. Trouble is, I slit my mother's alongside him without distinction. And then . . . there's you.'

I laid a hand on his chest and told myself it was purely for balance. Under my palm his skin was taut and hot, a slightly elevated heart rate the only trace of his distress.

I stayed quiet, let him find his own way. 'It's like something's trying to tell me that I'm only going to end up hurting you, Charlie,' he said then. 'And not just you, but anyone I care for. It . . . worries me, sometimes.'

That was a dramatic understatement, I knew, but getting this kind of confession out of him at all was an achievement so I let it pass.

'Dreams are just a way of coping with the dross that's going round in our heads,' I said at last. 'I have them, too, y'know? I get to relive what happened to me in glorious Technicolor – the four of them, the dark, the cold. And it's

254

so powerful I can't shake the reality of it. I can wake up freezing in the middle of a heatwave. And sometimes, yes, there are weird twists.' I hesitated, but he was being brutally honest, so why shouldn't I? 'Sometimes the only face I can see is yours.'

He winced. 'Christ,' he murmured. 'I'm not surprised you knocked me flat on my back the other night. I guess I was lucky you *didn't* kill me.' He brushed a fingertip across the mark on his cheekbone and allowed his lips to twitch in bitter self-contempt. 'God knows, I showed you enough ways to go about it.'

'Yes, but it does *not* have to be this way,' I said, angry with the effort of trying to keep the anguish out of my voice. 'We can do something about it if we want to.' His eyes were on mine again, black like sorrow, and I couldn't read a glimmer of his thoughts beyond them. 'All we have to do is want to enough.'

'Oh, trust me, I want to,' he said with quiet feeling. I caught the gleam in his eye only a fraction before he reared up and tumbled me back onto the pillows. He swooped for the hollow of my neck like a vampire, muttering almost to himself, 'Of that you can be quite certain.'

My hands clutched convulsively at the bedclothes while he feasted at the jagged pulse that raged beneath the scar at my throat, robbing me of breath along with logical thought and any willpower I might have once possessed. Flames ignited like arson along every nerve-ending until they threatened to engulf me totally.

At last, when I thought I'd go crazy under him, he came up for air. Both of us were gasping. His mouth traced lazily across my shoulder and my hands came together of their own volition to meet at his spine, delicately sketching the ripple of muscle beneath the skin. I felt him quiver under my touch. So tough, so strong, so vulnerable.

He shifted suddenly, rolling onto his back again and this time taking me with him, hands firm at my waist. I ended up sprawled along the full length of him, leaving me in no doubt just how badly he wanted me. But there was reticence about him, too, a shadow of restraint.

He was holding back to let me make all the running, I realised, doing nothing that was going to trip any alarms. Not this time. I put a fist either side of his shoulders and arched my back so I could look down at his face.

'I never thought of you as the kind of guy who'd lie back and think of England,' I said, and my voice was husky.

Sean laughed softly. 'Oh, it's not England I'm thinking about,' he said. The laughter fell away in the face of his sudden intensity. 'It's you, Charlie. It's always been you.'

His hands lightly braceleted my wrists, then skimmed upwards to my shoulders and I felt my elbows almost buckle. When those long clever fingers finally brushed across my collarbones and dropped to my breasts, my arms gave out completely. I sagged into him.

Infinitely slowly, he nudged my chin up and kissed me. Something spun and shattered behind my closed eyelids. His hands moved lower down my body, his deft touch causing a trail of devastation.

My illusion of being in control was fragmenting, like the last few seconds before the crash when you still have the faint vain hope that you can ride out of this intact but you're already beyond redemption. I knew I had only moments of sanity left before little things like consequences wouldn't matter a damn.

I wrenched my mouth free and heard a mewl of protest that could possibly have been me. Robbed, Sean went for the pulse-point at my neck again and the haze of his breath against the shallow indentation below my ear was almost my undoing.

'Sean,' I managed, even as my vision bulged and distorted. 'Wait—'

He gave a low groan of protest but immediately stilled. I didn't have to ask him twice.

'Um, you weren't ever a Boy Scout by any chance, were

256

you?' I asked, pulling back a little and trying to force the shakiness out of my voice.

I saw by the quick flash of his grin that he'd caught on right away, even if he was going to make me work for it. 'No, but I got chucked out of the Cubs for fighting when I was seven,' he said lightly. 'Does that count?'

'No. Have you got . . . ?' I said, annoyed to find myself so tongue-tied. 'I mean, I wasn't expecting . . .'

He took pity on me. 'Inside jacket pocket,' he said, nodding to where his leathers hung on the chair next to the bed. He lifted up and nipped at my lower lip with his teeth. His hands had begun to coast again, making bolder forays that wreaked havoc with my concentration. 'You don't have to be a Boy Scout to be prepared, you know.'

I twisted under his touch, gulping in air like it was my last breath. 'So sure of me, were you?'

'Sure? Never,' he said. 'Hopeful? Always.'

Sean stretched out for the pocket he'd indicated. I've never been so glad to see a condom. He stripped the foil packet open without a fumble but still it was all taking much too long. The need was a brutal chanting in my head now, a roaring in my blood that echoed burning in my belly.

Desperate for relief I scraped against him, growling in sheer frustration, limbs slick with sweat. Then his fingers were grasping my hips to hold me steady, ready, poised, but at the last second he hesitated. I could have wept.

'Christ, I don't want to hurt you,' he gritted out. 'I'm not sure, if we go much further, that I'll be able to stop.'

'Then don't,' I said, swept with certainty as my voice cracked. 'Don't stop, I mean. Oh God, please don't stop.'

And somehow he knew that I was way past the point where I needed gentleness from him. His hands jerked downwards.

I came the instant he was inside me.

There was a moment of suspension, then I was flooded by an overwhelming barrage of sensations, a sweet rush so sharp it could almost have been pain. It surged up through my body and burst out of the top of my head, scattering my brains, exquisite and unbearable.

My last coherent thought was a fierce affirmation. This was right. It was meant to be. Sean and I.

And to hell with everyone who tried to tell us different.

Next thing I knew, someone was hammering at the door to the room. Groggy and disorientated, I had no idea how long we'd lain together.

I felt Sean slide out from under my cheekbone almost before I'd come to. He yanked his T-shirt over his head and pulled on his shorts, checking me briefly over his shoulder as he moved to the door.

I just had time to sit up in bed and clasp the sheets primly around me as he slipped the chain and opened up.

'Wakey wakey, Charlie! Come on, you'll miss breakfast and—'

William's voice broke off suddenly as he registered Sean in the doorway. Embarrassingly, the rest of the Devil's Bridge Club also peered in through the gap. Only Tess was missing – if I had to be thankful for small mercies.

Paxo pushed to the front and led the way into the room, glaring at the obvious signs that Sean and I had shared the same bed. As if that wasn't confirmation enough, I flushed painfully, feeling the glow of it suffuse my face right up to the roots of my hair.

Paxo's outraged gaze went from Sean to Jamie and back again. 'Jesus H Christ,' he said, his voice cruising with disgust. He jerked his head towards me. 'Is there a fucking rota or something for her I don't know about?'

Sean's face never changed. He took a step forwards and closed in on Paxo, butting up against him, forcing the smaller man to retreat until he was hard up against the wall to the bathroom. Sean's shoulders were angled towards me, his body blocking the movement of his hands, but suddenly Paxo's colour bleached out and his eyes bugged.

258

'I'll pretend – for now – that you didn't say that,' Sean said, his voice soft and pleasant. 'But if you're ever foolish enough to try and repeat it, Martin, we may have to have this little chat again, OK?'

He stepped back and Paxo started to double over very slowly, like a tree falling. He got far enough down to brace his fists on his thighs and stopped like that, fighting tears and asphyxia. He was wearing his bike jeans and the thick leather should have afforded him some protection. But – in this case – nowhere near enough.

The others stood frozen, unsure exactly what it was that they'd just been witness to. Sean turned back to them and smiled.

'If you wouldn't mind giving us half an hour to get sorted,' he said politely, 'we'll meet you downstairs, OK?'

Dumbly, they nodded, began to file out. William looped an arm round Paxo's shoulders but Paxo shrugged him off. He straightened with an effort and staggered out, red-faced, coughing. Daz was last to move. His eyes met Sean's and clashed silently, then slid away.

Sean shut the door firmly behind them. 'Not quite the discreet assignation I had in mind,' he said, his expression rueful. 'Sorry.'

'It doesn't matter,' I said and was surprised to realise that it didn't. Not any more. 'I assume that Martin is Paxo's real name?'

He nodded. 'Martin Paxton. Manages a bar in Lancaster. Daz – Darren Henderson – runs some kind of craft centre just outside Manchester, and William Lacey works for the ferry company. Madeleine dug out the gen on them and I didn't think it would do any harm to scare Paxo a little.'

'On top of halfway castrating him, you mean?'

Sean shrugged. 'You would have done the same,' he said with the barest hint of a smile. 'I just got to him first.'

He moved back across to the bed but as he did so his foot

259

kicked something that was hidden just under the valance. He bent to retrieve it and when he stood he was holding an ornate silver ring between his fingers.

'Yours?'

'Damn,' I said. 'It must be one of Tess's. She was here last night.'

His eyebrows went up. 'Wow,' he said. 'So Paxo was right about you. Girls as well – I'm impressed.'

'*Oh please*,' I muttered, trying to keep my face stern and failing miserably.

He snagged a corner of the sheet and whipped it out of my hands, ignoring my yelp of protest. 'Come on,' he said, grinning. 'Out of bed, you. You can fill me in while you're in the shower.'

He showered quickly first, then shaved while I showered. I felt surprisingly relaxed amid the unfamiliar domesticity, helped by the fact that we were talking all the while. I ran through the events of the evening before, from the reappearance of the Vauxhall to Tess's near miss and what both she and Jamie had told me.

When I emerged, it was to find Sean absently turning the ring he'd found over in his fingers, looking at the pretty cut of the stone against the light from the window.

'So we still don't know why Jamie borrowed the money in the first place,' he said, sounding distracted.

'No,' I said, rubbing a towel vigorously over my hair. Although I kept it roughly in a bob, no longer than my jawline, there wasn't the time to dry it properly and after a day scrunched under a helmet I knew it was going to be uncontrollable. 'But I reckon he might fold if I keep nagging at him. I'll have another go ... what is it?'

Sean was holding Tess's ring up and something in his face had changed.

'What do you make of this?' he asked, throwing it across to me so I had to let go of my towel to catch it. I rolled the ring in my fingers for a moment and shrugged, frowning. 'What about it?'

'Unless I'm very much mistaken, that stone is a genuine diamond. A big one.'

'You're joking!' I said, but knew even as I spoke that he was not. He had no reason to. I looked again, still doubtful. 'But it's huge.'

'Mm,' he said. 'Best part of a carat. Beautiful clarity and hardly any occlusions.'

'Occlusions?'

'Flaws. You value diamonds on the four 'c's – carat, cut, clarity and colour. This is hitting all the buttons.'

'And you know this because . . . ?'

'I've done some work out in Africa and there are a lot of these rocks about. It pays to know what you're looking at.' He smiled. 'Plus, I've just spent twenty-four hours with that very chatty and knowledgeable Dutch gemstone courier and I was interested in what he had to say.'

'Tess told me she'd made it herself,' I said, remembering how drunk she'd been. Too drunk, I would have thought, to have lied convincingly.

'She probably did make the setting,' Sean said, peering inside the band. 'It's not a bad effort but there's no hallmark and it doesn't do justice to the quality of the stone.'

'How the hell can she afford a diamond this size?' I wondered.

Sean shook his head. 'Officially, she can't,' he said bluntly. 'She's supposed to be a jewellery maker but she just about lives on state benefits more than she works – as far as the taxman is aware, anyway.'

'She had a fistful of rings like this one,' I said slowly. 'If they're all real she must be draped in a fortune. So where's she getting the money?'

'I think that's something we need to determine – and sooner rather than later,' he said, his face grim. 'I don't know about you, but I've no desire to find out the hard way that the reason I'm along on this jaunt at all is to play minder to a load of drug mules.'

*

261

By the time we got downstairs and checked out, the others were all waiting for us – rather pointedly, I thought – in the car park. The sun was already burning brightly and they sat and sweated inside their leathers.

They had unchained the bikes and were sitting on board. Daz even had his Aprilia ticking over. While Sean and I got ourselves strapped down and zipped up and sorted, he blipped the throttle repeatedly. The bike's exhaust made an impatient gruff bark of sound but I refused to be rushed through my preflight checks. I knew, once we set off, I wasn't going to get the chance to put right any minor irritations like a rucked-up sleeve or a wayward piece of fringe in my eyes.

I'd been hoping I'd get the opportunity to give Tess her ring back and ask her about it, but she was already mounted up on the back of Daz's bike, helmet on. If anything, she seemed reluctant to meet my eyes, never mind talk to me, and she certainly didn't look like someone who's just lost a massive diamond. I left the ring in my jacket pocket. There'd be time later.

Once we were on the road it was clear that the boys were taking their temper out on their machinery. Daz set off as he meant to go on, with scant regard to Tess clinging on for dear life behind him. Paxo was right up there dicing with him, almost goading him to greater excesses. Every now and again I caught the mutter of cursing over my headset when sheer stomach-churning adrenaline made maintaining radio silence an impossibility.

I tried not to give the FireBlade too much pain until the engine had warmed through. Then I clicked my visor fully closed and dropped everything down a gear.

I shot past Jamie almost at once and ended up hard on William's heels. The big guy had abandoned his usual laid-back riding style and let the devil take command. He was a natural rider, surprisingly quick for someone whose movements never seemed hurried, and whose natural bulk acted like a permanent drogue chute.

By the time we had covered the few miles up the coast to Glenarm I was actually enjoying myself. In my mirrors I kept getting the occasional glimpse of Sean holding station on Jamie's rear quarter, like he was shepherding him along at a slower pace. And behind them, nothing.

Then, as we passed the road that turns back to Ballymena, a dark grey Vauxhall Vectra flipped out of the junction and fell in behind us.

I saw Sean react, dropping back slightly, coming off his line for corners and allowing the gap between Jamie and the Blackbird to widen. I knew he was putting himself between Jacob's kid and the threat. He did it immediately, without any hesitation, and suddenly that very fact terrified me.

'Daz,' I said abruptly into my voice-activate mic, 'Hey Daz, we've got company. That Vauxhall's back on our tail again.'

'So what?' Daz's voice came back, tight with concentration and bravado, both at the same time. 'Let him follow us if he wants. We've got nothing to hide.'

The Vauxhall driver stayed with us, neither closing up nor significantly dropping back, until we turned off onto the steep and twisting coast road at Cushendun. Then he braked hard and pulled over, as though he knew where we were heading. As though he knew he had us cornered.

The thin film of anxiety took the shine off the rest of the ride. I should have been admiring the staggering scenery and the view of the Mull of Kintyre across the flat-calm water of the Irish Sea. Instead I spent too much time watching behind me and got a couple of corners badly wrong. Enough to jerk my heart rate up, to start my hands sweating inside my gloves and to make the FireBlade seem brutishly unwieldy under me.

By the time we turned off into the car park at the Giant's Causeway I was relieved to be stopping. Daz and Paxo were already off the bikes with their lids on the bars and their leathers open to the breeze coming up off the water, revealing sodden T-shirts underneath.

Paxo dragged on a cigarette like an asthmatic at his inhaler. Tess was sitting on the grass with her legs stretched out in front of her, looking slightly shell-shocked by the experience. Daz looked from one to the other and grinned triumphantly as William and I pulled in alongside him.

'You lot are riding like a bunch of old women,' Daz jeered.

'*Old women?*' Paxo said, his voice an outraged squawk that made his cigarette jiggle between his lips. 'I was right up your arse all the way here, mate.'

'At least the rest of us stand a chance of surviving long enough to get to be old,' William said as he unbuckled his helmet and ducked out of it. His voice was placid but the sweat ran down his temples and beaded across his upper lip.

As I took off my own lid I ran a hand through my hair and realised that my prediction about the state of it had been on the optimistic side. I looked like a wet traveller's dog and felt worse.

Jamie and Sean were last to arrive. The twisty roads had given Jamie a better chance of keeping his smaller bike close to the pack than long fast straights would have done, but still he looked exhausted. Sean yanked his lid off and, although I could tell by the muscle jumping in his jaw what he thought of the pace Daz was setting, he held his tongue.

'Who's for an ice cream?' Daz asked brightly. Before anyone could answer, he headed off towards the café. As he walked away from us he was clicking his fingers together nervously, like he was on edge and couldn't keep them still. I wondered seriously if he was on something.

As though the same thought had occurred to them at the same time, William and Paxo exchanged silent glances and followed Daz to the café. Jamie muttered about finding the loo and went after them.

Sean stripped off the top half of his leathers and leaned against the Blackbird to let the sun and the wind dry him off. He seemed relaxed but he had angled himself, I noticed, so he could keep an eye on the approach road.

I went across and sat beside Tess on the grass, digging in my pocket.

'By the way – I think you dropped this in my room last night,' I said, holding the ring out to her. The diamond sparked and flared in the sunlight.

I was watching her face carefully enough to see the spasm of horror that passed across her features, quickly damped down into something approaching mild relief.

'Oh brilliant, thanks,' she said, taking the ring from me. She dug in the inside pocket of her leathers and produced a clear plastic bag full of her remaining jewellery. I assumed her fingers were still too sore to get the rings back on. Small wonder she had hardly noticed one of them was missing.

'It's a lovely ring,' I said, cautious. Out of the corner of my eye I saw that Sean had stilled, listening, even though his attention seemed for all the world to be elsewhere. 'It must be worth a bit.'

Tess laughed a little too loudly and for a little too long. 'Nah, I told you – I made it myself,' she said. She swung the bag round her finger, casually, so the contents jingled together.

'So, what's the stone?' I asked, guileless. 'It's a nice-looking cut.'

'Mm, I liked it,' she said, still distracted by the way the rings danced in the light. 'Shame it's only paste.'

She looked up as she said it and I knew she'd realised full well that she didn't have me fooled. And she didn't care either. She caught my momentarily dumbfounded expression and laughed again.

'What? You never thought this lot was real, did you?' she demanded, shaking the bag and still grinning. 'Oh yeah, right – like I'd walk round drippin' in diamonds! Money comin' out of my ears, me.'

For what it was worth, I would have pressed her further

but the boys reappeared at that point.

'Oh good, ice creams,' she said unnecessarily. 'Hey! Mine's the one with the Flake in it.' She jumped to her feet and trotted over to them, stuffing the bag of rings back into her pocket as she went.

I got to my feet to follow, but Sean caught my arm as I went past and shook his head.

'Let it go, Charlie,' he murmured. 'For now. You won't get anything useful out of her.'

After a moment's hesitation, I nodded reluctantly, leaned my hip against the FireBlade, and waited for the boys to reach us.

Apart from Daz, they were carrying two ice cream cones each, all of which had chocolate Flakes in that had already semi-melted in the heat. Jamie had given one ice cream to Tess and William passed me another. That left Paxo with the one for Sean, a fact that had him scowling more furiously than usual. He practically handed it over at arm's length, snatching his fingers back like he was expecting the other man to bite them. Sean just smiled his predator's smile, unnerving him further, and accepted graciously.

'Come on then,' Daz said, bouncing on his toes. 'We're here to see a bit of culture, so let's go have a look-see at this causeway.' He picked the Flake out and sucked the ice cream off it. 'Any ideas who built it?'

William rolled his eyes. 'Nobody built it, you jackass,' he said. His sweat moustache had now been replaced with a vanilla ice cream one but he didn't seem to care. 'It's made up of basalt. The rock forms that shape naturally, without any interference from anyone else.'

There was a bus ferrying people down the steep incline to the beach but we chose to walk, eating our ice creams as we went. The landscape was alien and deeply strange. A tangled pile of curious hexagonal stones, stacked and jumbled like someone had pushed them off the edge of the cliff above with a JCB and left them where they fell.

We joined the other tourists who were walking and

clambering over the rocks. Close up the stones looked a little like interlocking concrete sections. It wouldn't be hard to be convinced that the whole structure was man-made.

'Breathtaking, isn't it?' William murmured, staring across the formation.

'Yeah, suppose so,' Paxo said, looking around him with a totally nonplussed expression on his face. He checked his watch. 'Now then, where's this distillery, mate?'

He glanced round automatically for Daz as he spoke, but discovered the other man was standing a little apart from the others, tense, wired. Sean was close to Daz, watching him as though he was about to break.

We converged on the pair of them in time to hear Sean say, 'Tell them, Daz. It's time. Tell them or I will. You can't go on like this.'

Daz threw him a panicked look but we were too close by then and it was too late to say more if he didn't want the rest of us to hear it, too.

'Tell us what?' Jamie asked, worried. 'What's going on?'

'Daz has something he needs to tell all of you,' Sean said, stressing the *need*. Not *want*, I noted. It was clear that whatever secret Daz had confessed to Sean, the last thing he wanted to do was share it any further.

'What is it?' Paxo demanded. He came forwards, slinging his arm round Daz's shoulders and giving him a friendly shake, grinning. 'Come on, mate! We're all in this together, aren't we? You can tell us anything. How bad can it be?'

With a final desperate glance at Sean, Daz swallowed and shrugged helplessly.

'OK,' he said. 'You see, guys, the thing is ... I'm gay.'

Chapter Twenty-one

Is that it? So what?

The words formed in my head but I didn't let them out. In fact, for a moment the only sound was the rush of the surf against the rocks and the raucous cries of the gulls circling overhead. It sounded like they were laughing at us.

Then Paxo snatched his arm away, flushing furiously. He took a step back and gave a splutter of laughter that died in his throat.

'Ah, mate, come on!' His eyes swivelled from face to face, looking for the first chink in the practical joke. 'Don't kid us about!'

'I'm not,' Daz said calmly, more confident. It was like, now it was done, the act of coming out had lost its terrors for him. 'It's true. I'm gay.'

William nodded slowly. 'Well, good for you, Daz,' he said. 'I know that must have taken some doing, telling us that. I admire you for it.'

'Oh for fuck's sake,' Paxo wailed. 'Not you as well?'

'What's the big deal?' Jamie said, nonplussed. 'So, he's gay. So what?'

'Plenty – if you're completely homophobic,' Daz said, body tense.

'Why did you wait until now?' Paxo demanded. 'I have to tell you, mate, your timing on this stinks.'

Tess, I realised then, had been standing silent in the

268

background. But when I glanced at her I found she was wasn't entirely still. She was trembling. As I turned towards her she took a couple of quick steps forwards and launched a long telegraphed right at Daz's jaw, regardless of her swollen fingers. He ducked away easily enough and her punch hit his shoulder.

'You bastard!' she cried, flailing at him then. 'You only wanted me along on this trip as cover!'

Jamie grabbed her arms and pulled her off and, after a moment's struggle, she turned her face into his chest and burst into tears. He led her a little distance away and sat her down on a short basalt column, holding her hands and shooting reproachful glances in Daz's direction.

'Is that right?' Paxo demanded, watching them. 'You told us she wouldn't be left behind, that you didn't have a choice but to let her tag along. And all the time—' He threw up his hands and spun away.

William raised an admonishing eyebrow. 'I realise it's difficult, but you could have handled this better,' he said at last. 'It's not what you've done, Daz, it's the way that you've done it.'

'Yeah well,' Daz muttered, flicking his eyes to Sean. 'Maybe I didn't have much of a choice about that.' And he too walked away, stumbling slightly over the rocks, in the opposite direction to Paxo.

'I guess from that that you forced his hand somewhat?' William said to Sean.

Sean shrugged. 'He was doing his best to break his neck proving what a man he was,' he said. 'And he was going to get round to bringing it out in the open at some point. I just hurried him along a little.'

'Best part of ten years I've known Daz,' William said sadly, shaking his head. 'And I'd never have guessed.' He paused, gave Sean an assessing glance. 'How did you know?'

'I've learned to be a good judge of people,' he said. 'It goes with the territory. Besides, there were one or two things in Daz's background that made it a possibility and then on the ferry there was something about him so I played along and he—' Sean shrugged '—revealed himself, shall we say.'

Sean had always a sixth sense for, not weakness exactly, but people's secrets. I'd never successfully been able to hide much from him, that was for sure. But even so . . .

'Revealed himself how?' I demanded and thought, unbelievably, that I saw a faint slash of colour across his cheekbones. 'What? What did you do?'

Sean's eyes flicked from me to William and back again, a slightly pained expression on his face.

'You made a pass at him, didn't you?' I said, incredulous, and saw the pink darken round his neck. 'You did!' I concluded. 'So that's what you found out when you were out on the back deck together,' I said. 'I'm not surprised you wouldn't tell me.'

'I just wanted to be sure,' he said, nodding, still looking a little sheepish. 'I gave him my word that I wouldn't say anything – that I'd let him tell you and the others himself. If he hadn't been riding like he had a bloody death-wish I would have left him to it, but this was getting beyond a joke. Someone was going to get killed.'

William's gaze had tracked over Jamie, still crouched with the upset Tess, and to Paxo, a hundred metres away sucking furiously on a cigarette. 'Still,' he said, his voice mild, 'Paxo and Tess haven't taken it well. Might have been better to have left it until we got back, don't you think? Instead of pushing him out of the closet now.'

'Why?' Sean said. 'What's so special about this trip?'

William just smiled and shook his head again, as though Sean wasn't going to catch him out that easily.

'If you're so good at this intuition business,' he said, 'why don't you tell me?'

'Don't worry,' Sean said, favouring him with a tight little smile of his own. 'We will.'

*

270

Tess refused to get back on Daz's bike for the few miles from the Giant's Causeway down to the little village of Bushmills. Paxo wouldn't take her and, although Jamie offered, he was struggling to keep up solo. Neither Sean nor I wanted the added encumbrance, just in case of trouble, so in the end it was down to William to pat his pillion seat and give her a ride. She scrambled onto the Kawasaki behind him and wrapped her arms round his waist like she was using him as an oversize comfort blanket.

Daz just shrugged, fired up the Aprilia and resumed the pace he'd been setting all morning. If anything, I suppose he felt he had even more to prove now than he did before.

Either way, Paxo wasn't about to be outridden by his mate, regardless of his sexual preferences. The two of them goaded each other to ever greater risks, scything past what little traffic we encountered and carving through bends on totally the wrong side of the road.

'Hey guys,' I said at last over the radio. 'Remember Sam? This is going to end with somebody going home in an ambulance.'

Nobody replied.

Jamie and I were in the second wave with William, making progress but still going a lot more cautiously than Daz and Paxo. I occupied the small part of my mind that wasn't tied up with the mechanics of riding the bike, with the problem at hand. Daz's announcement explained a few things about his behaviour, but not everything. So, he'd been keyed up and worried – quite rightly, as it turned out – at how some of his mates would react. But that told nowhere near the whole story.

My eyes flicked ahead to where I could just make out Paxo, hunched over the tank of his Ducati. Paxo might be angry enough to be less cautious than William, in which case we might get something useful out of him. Not that Paxo had a very high opinion of me, but perhaps he was scared enough of Sean to tell him something. It was worth a try.

We all of us made it the short distance down to Bushmills intact, with no sign of the Vauxhall behind us. The road was teeming with other bikers and I started to get a stiff neck from all the friendly nodding I was doing.

Bushmills village itself was small and picturesque. The only odd note was the little local police station, which was bristling with razor wire and CCTV cameras. It seemed out of place in such a peaceful rural setting. That and the sprawling distillery on the outskirts.

Paxo was still sulking during the tour of the distillery but he didn't unleash his outright hostility until we got to the tasting at the end. Then he couldn't resist a dig about such fine whiskey being wasted on Daz – what with him being more of a Babycham man.

For a moment I thought Daz was going to rise to it, but then his shoulders came down a little and he smiled, wryly. 'Well, I seem to remember it was you who got smashed out of your skull on Snowballs when we were in the third year at school together,' he said.

Tess was watching Paxo with her fists clenched by her sides like she was hoping they'd start brawling. She came close to getting her wish, then Paxo gave a bitter smile of his own and raised his tasting glass in reluctant salute. Whether it was at the reminder of his own previous drinking habits, or just how long they'd been friends, I couldn't be sure.

'*Touché*,' I murmured.

'I think you'll find that's *sláinte*,' Jamie pointed out, aiming for light relief.

'*Na zdoravye*,' Sean put in. Of course, he would know the Russian.

'Cheers!' William said.

But Daz just pinned Paxo with one of the brilliant smiles he occasionally produced and raised his glass in very deliberate provocation.

'Bottoms up,' he said.

Knowing that the next leg of the journey was a run right the way down to the south end of Strangford Lough, I sought out the loos before we left Bushmills. The way Daz was behaving I wasn't sure he'd stop on demand and nothing disrupts your concentration on a bike like a full bladder. Besides, some of the Irish roads were so bumpy it could have been disastrous, not just uncomfortable.

Just about everybody had the same idea. When I got back to the car park, it was to find only Sean was ready and waiting, and he was frowning.

'What is it?' I asked as soon as I was close to him.

He nodded across the busy car park to where there was a line of other bikes. 'That Suzuki over there,' he said, indicating an old GSXR with Lucky Strike paintwork. 'I'm sure I've seen that one a couple of times already so far this trip.'

I shrugged, scanning for the grey Vauxhall. 'Hardly surprising,' I said. 'There were a lot of bikes on the ferry and they all seem to have had the same idea when it came to routing.'

'Hm,' he said, ducking his head slightly and pulling a face. 'Maybe.'

'If you're bothered,' I said. 'Why not give Madeleine a call with the reg number and see what she can find out?'

Sean patted the top pocket of his jacket, where I could see the slight bulge of his mobile phone.

'Already done.'

'What did you make of Tess's reaction to the ring earlier?'

'Oh, she was definitely lying,' Sean said casually. 'The interesting question is why?'

I took the opportunity of the stop to give Jacob another try. This time my mobile phone was playing ball and it connected right away. It seemed absurd to have such a clear line when it felt like we were in another country, regardless of official boundaries. When I'd asked after Sam and Clare I filled Jacob in on events so far, including Daz's revelation.

'It's an odd setup,' was all Jacob said, rather sadly, when I told him about Daz's revelation. 'But apart from these blokes following you, there hasn't been any sign of any trouble?'

'Someone tried to run us down last night,' I said. 'It was too dark to see if it was the Vauxhall crew or not.'

'And you think it was definitely deliberate?'

'I don't know,' I said. 'It had that feel to it ... It would help if they'd come clean with us about what they're up to. It turns out that Tess is wearing a fortune in diamonds and we've no idea where the money for that came from. I'm sorry, Jacob, but if it's drugs, Sean and I are out of here.'

'I'm sure it won't be,' Jacob said quickly. 'Jamie wouldn't be so stupid as to get himself mixed up in something like that, I promise you.'

'Maybe,' I said, still dubious despite his reassurances. 'We're down to Portaferry next, apparently. We'll see if we can prise any more information out of the lads then about what's going on. Who knows? When they've had a few drinks they might be a bit more forthcoming.'

The others arrived back in dribs and drabs – Paxo first, then William. Jamie and Daz arrived together.

'You not worried about being seen coming out of a public toilet at the same time as him?' Paxo asked Jamie, his tone sour.

Daz's face twitched like he'd finally had enough. He rounded on his mate, jaw set.

'Look, Pax, you weren't accusing me of shagging anything that moved yesterday, were you? So, what's changed, huh?' he snapped, almost but not quite hiding the hurt in his voice. 'OK, so I've admitted I'm gay. That, given a choice, in the right circumstances, my preference would be for a guy rather than a girl. That doesn't suddenly make me a slag, does it?'

Paxo's lips twisted in disgust. 'Frankly, mate,' he said, wheeling away, 'I have no idea quite *what* that makes you.'

'I knew he'd be like this,' Daz said, not quite hiding the bitter note in his voice. 'When I was in art college down in Manchester it was practically the norm. Get further north and it's like some people still don't know it's legal.'

It was a relief, once Tess had reappeared, to get back on the road. The Suzuki rider hadn't shown up to claim his bike and it was still sitting there when we pulled out of the car park and headed south.

We ran down through Ballymoney and dropped into the top end of Belfast on the urban motorway. I noticed signposts off for the Falls area and wondered how my father had felt, working there when the Troubles were more or less at their height. Apart from that one occasion during dinner with Sean, he'd never talked about his time in Northern Ireland. Mind you, he wasn't exactly the reminiscing type, good or bad.

Eventually, we crossed the River Lagan and started heading east, past the Stormont parliament building, for Newtownards. Daz seemed to have settled now. He let Paxo overtake him and, when the smaller guy realised that he wasn't going to get a battle out of him, he calmed down a little, too.

At Newtownards we turned off onto the smaller A road that skirted the eastern side of Strangford Lough. The ride took us through more stunning scenery as we wended our way through Comber and Greyabbey.

I'd no idea the place was so pretty. Not exactly a side to it you ever used to hear about on the evening news, where the only images you ever saw were of six-year-olds hurling Molotovs at burning APCs against a backdrop of balaclava'd funeral salutes and paramilitary murals on the ends of terrace houses. The reality was a revelation.

Even our tail seemed to have backed off. The Vauxhall

was notable by its absence and, though I looked hard at all the bikes we met, I didn't spot the Lucky Strike Suzuki among them.

By the time we reached Portaferry it was six o'clock and I was beginning to feel the effects of my largely sleepless night. I was glad when we finally turned off the road into a small private car park by a cosy-looking hotel right on the harbour side.

There was an awkward moment when we checked in, owing to the number of rooms that had originally been booked against the number of people who'd actually turned up. That and who, in the light of the day's events, was prepared to share with who.

William's snoring was obviously preferable, in Jamie and Paxo's eyes, to the alternative of sharing with Daz. The clearly confused girl on the reception desk handled it all with remarkable patience, nevertheless.

Eventually she managed to allocate a family room that had two twin beds and a pullout sofa for the three lads, and two single rooms for Daz and Tess. Then she looked at Sean with a resigned expression on her face. He smiled at her. 'We'll just have a straightforward double,' he said and I realised I'd been holding my breath.

We unloaded the bikes and carried our bags upstairs. Nobody seemed to have brought more than a small tank bag, a rucksack, or throw-over panniers. No point when we were only here for another two days. It struck me then that half the trip was nearly gone already and so far the Devil's Bridge Club hadn't done anything that might require them to need a pair of bodyguards in tow.

Tomorrow we were due to cross the border for the run down to Dublin.

What the hell did they have planned then?

The bar at the hotel was small – too small for the seven of us to sit round in comfort. Instead, once we were showered and changed into our civvies, we headed out into the evening sunshine and walked up the steep main street in search of another watering hole.

'At least this way,' Tess said, puffing out a breath as she eyed the climb, 'we'll be going downhill on the way back.'

'Yeah,' Paxo put in, grinning at her. 'Have too much to drink tonight and we can just roll you back down to the hotel instead of having to carry you.'

We found a pub at the top of the hill which, after an initial moment of restraint, proved welcoming. Nevertheless, Sean and I steered the group to a corner table with a clear view of the door. We also made sure we grabbed the chairs that meant we could keep an eye on the rest of the room without making it obvious.

We chose from the menu and Daz went to order the food from the barman and get the first round of drinks in.

'You must have come across a load of queers when you were in the army, eh?' Paxo said to Sean. He was watching Daz move across the other side of the room like he was trying to spot the difference in the way he walked.

'They've only just changed the rules to allow it,' Sean said calmly. 'When I was in, the Powers That Be took a very dim view. If they found out you were gay, you were out. Counted as "dishonourable conduct", apparently.'

'Maybe it's because they didn't do pink camouflage,' Tess said, waspish.

'The Spartans positively encouraged homosexuality in their soldiers,' William said reflectively. 'They reckoned it made them fight more fiercely alongside each other.'

'Yeah,' Paxo said, 'and look what happened to *them*.'

'One of the guys who works for me now is gay,' Sean said, making me automatically do a mental review of his staff, trying to work out who. 'It makes no difference.'

'A gay bodyguard?' Paxo repeated. He shook his head in disbelief. 'Ah mate, what kind of a bloke would want someone protecting them who might make a pass at him?'

'What's the guy's sexual orientation got to do with how well he does his job?' Sean asked, sounding impatient now.

277

'Charlie's a bodyguard. Are you trying to tell me she can't protect men for the same reason?'

'Yeah, but she's not gay,' Jamie said with a grin. 'I mean, if she was, would a woman want her looking after them?'

'Now *that* would be different,' Paxo said with a hint of glee, flicking his eyes from me to Tess and back again. 'Everyone knows lesbians'll shag anything in a skirt. Bring it on!'

'My sister's gay and she's been in a steady relationship for the last eight years,' William said, his voice suddenly cold. He fixed Paxo with an icy glare and watched his confusion for a couple of beats before adding, 'Confucius say: when in hole, mate, stop digging.'

'Well how was I supposed to know?' Paxo muttered, still rather pink around the ears. 'I thought they were just flatmates.'

Daz came back with the first of the drinks and raised his eyebrows at Paxo's scowling face and William's equally stony expression.

'Well,' he murmured, wry. 'This looks like being a fun-packed evening, doesn't it?'

The first signs of trouble lit up about an hour later. The boys had come to an uneasy truce and, after a couple of beers each, the conversation had relaxed back onto something like its old footing. Tess now seemed to be making a play for Jamie and he wasn't resisting too hard, although he did keep shooting little worried glances in Daz's direction, as if just making sure he really didn't object.

The pub had filled up gradually and all the tables were now occupied. The demographic was younger than I'd expected for such a sleepy little place, mostly young men who could well have been other visiting bikers. Out of leathers it was hard to tell.

Sean subjected everyone to the same casual scrutiny

278

when they arrived and, sitting next to him, I could tell the moment something changed.

'What is it?'

'There's a table of lads over near the far window,' he said to Daz. 'Without making it obvious, can you have a look and tell me if you know them?'

To his credit, Daz made a reasonably convincing job of glancing around as though to check the location of the gents' but, when he turned back, he leaned forwards conspiratorially. The others did the same and I saw a flicker of annoyance on Sean's face.

'Not a clue, mate,' Daz said. 'Why, what's the problem?'

'They keep looking over here and nudging each other,' Sean said, his voice low. 'I think we should drink up and find another bar.'

'Suits me,' Paxo said, shrugging as he reached for his beer and sat back.

I let my eyes pass over the group Sean had indicated. I hadn't noticed anything amiss about them but, now I looked more closely, I could see they were quietly egging each other on. Question was, to what?

It didn't take long to find out.

Before we'd had time to polish off our current round of drinks, the biggest of the group got to his feet and came swaggering across like he had a six-shooter and spurs. The others followed a few paces behind and what worried me was the fact that, although they'd finished their drinks, they hadn't put down their bottles and glasses. As unobtrusively as I could, I eased my chair back.

'So, which one of you fuckers is the fucking queer?' The big man spoke with an aggressive local accent.

For a moment there was utter silence. It lasted for maybe no longer than a year – or it felt that way, at least. During that time a whole string of interconnected thoughts whipped through my brain. Everything from the way the group moved, both individually and as a whole, to who else had noticed what was going on. The barman had frozen like a terrier that scents a fox, instincts honed by years of dealing with belligerent drunks.

Then there came the hollow scrape of a chair going back. I flicked my eyes sideways and found, to my surprise, it was Paxo who'd got to his feet, hands clenched and chin thrust forwards.

'Who wants to know?' he demanded.

The big Irishman grinned nastily. If he'd been able to pick which of us he'd wanted to take on, Paxo would probably have been his first or second choice.

Before the man had the chance to express his glee, another chair went back. This time it was William who got to his feet. I saw the Irishman take a mental step back as William rose to his full height. William's dark face was the same ominous mask he'd worn when I first encountered him at the hospital.

William didn't speak, just stood with his arms folded, rocked back on his heels slightly, head a little on one side. A second later Jamie was on his feet next to him.

'Whoa, hold up guys.'

Daz put down his drink and stood, looking shaken. Nothing to do with the challenge, I realised. Everything to do with the response.

He faced the Irishman, defiant. 'You got a problem with me?' he asked, his voice quiet.

'So you're the fucking queer, then?' the man said, glancing back to make sure his mates were right behind him before he took the final step.

'That's right,' Daz said.

'Me too!' Jamie threw in, his voice a little high and wild. He sounded breathless, but that would be the adrenaline shot. The fight was almost inevitable now and his system was cranking up for it, the tension racking his nerves tight as rigging.

'No, no,' William murmured, 'I think you'll find that *I'm* Spartacus.'

280

The Irishman laughed without understanding the joke. His mates joined in, the sound loud and primitive, pumping them up, driving them on. Then Sean stood up and they stopped laughing.

You couldn't deny there was something inherently violent about Sean. It wasn't just the size of him or even the way he moved, it was the way his thought processes were wired. There were times when, in some subtle way, he could make them show on the outside. It was what made people step into the gutter to avoid a confrontation with him when he was walking down a narrow pavement.

But now I noticed his stance was different. He was keeping it open, hands up a little, fingers outstretched. Hardly anyone in that room would have noticed that he could have turned passive appeasement into aggression in an instant. *Walk away now and I'll do the same*, he was saying, *but take me on and I will flatten you.*

The Irishman was either too drunk, or too inexperienced, to respond to this escape route when it was offered to him. He took another step forwards.

'OK now lads, let's have this outside,' the barman called across. 'Go on, in the street with you – I'll not have you brawling in my place! The police are on their way.'

It was the perfect opportunity for a climb-down and, just when I thought the Irishman might still be just sober enough to take it, Daz took a step forwards.

'You heard the man,' he said softly to the Irishman. 'You up for this, or what?'

The fight kicked off almost before we were all out of the door. The pub had no car park, so the entrance spilled us all straight onto the heavy slope of the street, across a metre of pavement, then into the road.

Daz went for a pre-emptive strike, launching a fast but amateur blow to the Irishman's head. After that, it was a messy free-for-all. I grabbed Tess and got her out of the firing line, then stayed on the outskirts. Sean saw what I

281

was doing and gave me the slightest fraction of a nod in response.

Group fights are hard and fast and dirty and you're as likely to get thumped by one of your own team as you are by the opposition. You need a sniper who can stay on the periphery and only join in when things are going badly for your side.

So, when the guy who Daz had hit waded in using his empty beer bottle as a club, I edged in behind them and kicked the back of the guy's knees out from underneath him, then ducked away again.

Paxo had clearly done martial arts of some description. He fought with more balance and style than I would have expected, but made the mistake of getting too fancy and took a nasty couple of hits to the ribs as a result. As soon as his opponent had his back to me, I slammed a couple of short hard shots into the guy's kidneys. He grunted but by the time he had the breath to look round, I was gone.

William was relying on brute force and sheer weight, swinging his fists wildly and missing his target more than he was hitting it, but at least his swatting fists kept the blows away from him.

Jamie had seemed to be holding his own, but I saw him go down out of the corner of my eye. Next thing he was curled on the ground with two of them getting stuck in. One was laying in with his boots, but the other had picked up a piece of smashed glass.

'Sean!' I shouted and, despite the chaos, he turned instantly, unaffected by the usual tunnelling of sight and sound. The guy he'd been fighting was on the floor at his feet. He saw Jamie down and jumped for one of his attackers. I abandoned my detached stance and went for the other.

My opponent was bigger than I was but hampered by his instinctive reluctance to hit a woman. He'd also already been giving it his all for more than thirty seconds and, in a brawl, that's a long time. Boxers spend their whole life preparing for the ring, yet are exhausted after bursts of action lasting only a couple of minutes. And this guy wasn't a professional fighter.

I ignored the wicked piece of jagged glass in his hand and took his nose out sideways with my first sweeping blow, aiming to water down his vision and distract him with the pain. After that I could choose my target. I hit him, just once, at the vulnerable point on the side of his jaw where his moustache would have come down to meet his chin, had he been wearing either. I put my bodyweight behind it. He overbalanced backwards and went crashing.

The lad who'd been facing Sean lost his nerve at that point and ran. Sean checked to see I was coping, then took off after him. When I'd made sure the guy I'd hit wasn't going to get up again in a hurry, I went after them both.

Not that I didn't have confidence that Sean could tackle the man he was chasing. That wasn't what worried me.

I was scared that he could tackle him only too well.

Chapter Twenty-two

The guy Sean was chasing had plenty of incentive to escape but he was just about spent from the fight and he didn't have Sean's predatory instinct. He'd headed downhill as his best chance of survival, arms windmilling for balance as he ran, then skidded round a corner and disappeared from view.

Sean shot after him, gaining ground with every stride. By the time I'd rounded the corner myself, Sean had the guy on the ground down by the wall of a building and had hit him just to the outside of his left eye, hard enough to quell his struggles, to frighten and hurt him rather than put him out. Sean glanced up as I approached. I caught something in his face and gave him a single nod to show I was prepared to follow his lead.

The guy on the floor was in his early twenties, dark-haired and solidly built. He might have been brave when he was hunting as part of a pack, but now he was singled out and down and on his own his courage seemed to have deserted him. He was gasping for breath and sweating hard enough to stain through his shirt, his hands spread in front of him as though to ward off another blow.

'Don't hurt me,' he begged, his accent local. 'Sweet Jesus, don't hurt me.'

'Now why would I want to do that, you wee fucker?' Sean said, perfectly slipping the slant and rhythm of East Belfast into his voice.

I thought the guy on the ground was going to have a heart attack, or wet himself, or both. His face buckled completely as he recognised the tones and made all kinds of wild and unsubstantiated connections.

'Sean,' I murmured, deliberately allowing a trace of unease to slide through. 'You can't kill him – not here.'

'And why not?' Sean said. 'Didn't your man here and his pals have it in for us?'

'We didn't!' the guy yelped. 'Honest to God, we didn't! No one else was supposed to get hurt.'

'What about the young lad you had on the ground between you?' Sean demanded roughly. 'You looked to have it in for him, right enough.'

'OK, OK,' the guy said, squirming backwards until his shoulders were hard up against the brickwork. Not a good idea if Sean decided to hit him again, but clearly he was too scared to think straight. 'Look, we were told to do him over, right? To break something – stop him getting on a bike, or something. I don't know any more than that. Honest to God!'

Sean and I exchanged glances.

'Now who would tell you to do a thing like that?' Sean said softly.

The guy's eyes swivelled as though searching for an excuse he thought we might swallow. He failed to come up with one before Sean had straightened and made a big show of drawing back his fist.

'OK, OK!' the guy shouted, flinching his head away, hands still up. 'I don't know who it was, all right? Davey got this phone call earlier tonight, telling him this group of English bikers'd be in Portaferry and to look out for them. Said one of them was gay. We didn't know someone like you'd be with them or we'd have stayed well clear.'

'Davey's the big feller who came over?' Sean surmised. 'So who would be calling him about that?'

'I don't know!' the guy squawked, tension making the tears squeeze out and roll down his cheeks. 'Davey works

285

as a bailiff. He knows all kinds of folk. Sweet Jesus, that's all I know!'

I believed him. He was too frightened to be inventive.

After a moment's consideration Sean stepped back and jerked his head. 'All right, you be on your way now,' he said, his voice still quiet, laced with contempt. 'But I don't want to see your face again, you understand me? Not ever. Or I'll do more than tell your pals you cried like a girl.'

The guy scrambled to his feet, never taking his eyes off Sean just in case of a double-cross. As soon as he was upright again, he bolted. We watched him dive into the gap between two buildings and disappear from view.

'Well now,' Sean said then with a lazy grin, shouldering back into his own skin. '*There's* a part I haven't had to play in a while.'

'You're very convincing.'

'Mm, well,' he said. 'At one time, I had to be.'

We started walking. Staying put was foolish, as was going back to the pub. We had to assume that the boys had managed all right on their own so we headed downhill, back towards the hotel. I jammed my hands into my pockets.

The light was starting to go now, dusk softening the edges of the trees on the far side of the Narrows. The tide was running in fiercely, funnelling the water through the restricted gap into the Lough. The regatta of little boats clustered near the shoreline had all swung on their moorings to face into it.

'So who on earth rang this Davey bloke and told him to duff one of us up?' I wondered.

'That is an interesting one, isn't it?' Sean said. 'Our friend Eamonn has a fair amount of rental property and would undoubtedly know a few bailiffs.'

'But he's living with Isobel. Why would he want to beat up her son?'

'Who says Jamie was the target? They could have been indulging in a bit of queer-bashing and got the wrong man.

286

After all, our boys didn't make it easy for them to spot him.'

For a few moments we walked in silence. Then a sudden thought occurred to me. 'If it was Eamonn, how did he – or those lads in the pub – know about Daz coming out? Now, apart from telling you on the ferry, he only made that one public this morning. So is this a new threat, or a continuation of the old one?'

'Good point.' Sean nodded. 'Though without knowing what the hell it is they're up to,' he said, 'it's hard to know who might have it in for them.'

When we got back close to the hotel we found the rest of the Devil's Bridge Club sitting on a bench on the edge of the harbour, licking their wounds.

They looked pretty sorry for themselves, even though the group who'd set about us *hadn't* succeeded in their aim to put one of us out of commission.

We might have come to Jamie's rescue but he'd still taken a pasting. He was sitting with his arms wrapped gingerly around his body as though his ribcage would spring open if he let go of it. Tess was next to him, her arm across his shoulders. Daz sat a little apart from the others with his head tilted back and a wad of tissue pressed against a bleeding eyebrow.

'Well, well, where the fuck did you two piss off to?' Paxo demanded, flicking his cigarette butt over the harbour wall into the water.

'Finding out who that lot were who attacked us, and why,' I said.

'And did you?'

'The kiddie you picked a fight with was a bailiff called Davey,' Sean said to Daz. 'It seems he had a phone call telling him all about you and instructing him to make sure somebody wasn't in a fit state to get on their bike tomorrow.' He let his eyes pan over their shocked faces, then added, 'Any ideas why that might be?'

287

Of all of them, Tess looked the most shaken but perhaps I was just being unkind to her. Even living with Slick she probably hadn't been witness to too many skirmishes close up.

'Who would call this bloke and tell him to go after us?' she said, swallowing to firm up her voice. 'That's ridiculous.'

'Somebody did,' Sean said, eyeing her. 'Someone who knew about Daz. You tell me.'

She threw her hands up in frustration and anger. 'We were all there when he admitted what he was!' she snapped. 'Grow up, Sean – it wasn't me.'

'He never said it was,' I said blandly. 'Guilty conscience, Tess?'

'So did everybody in this fucking place know about you before you told your mates, then?' Paxo wanted to know. 'Laughing behind our backs, were you?'

Daz rolled his uncovered eye in Paxo's direction but before he could answer I noticed a police car appear at the far end of the harbour and start to cruise slowly in our direction.

'I would suggest we continue this conversation inside,' I murmured. 'Seems a waste to pay for a hotel bed and then spend the night in the local nick, doesn't it?'

Once you had a room key you could enter and leave the hotel by a side door that opened out into a stairwell leading directly to the rooms on the upper floors. At least it meant we didn't have any explaining to do to whoever was on the reception desk. Paxo was limping slightly on his right leg as we walked in and Daz's eye was still bleeding.

'You ought to get that sorted out,' Sean said to him.

Daz's eyes flicked in the direction of his mates for a moment, then back again. 'Yeah, well, it'll be fine.'

'I've got my first-aid kit upstairs if you want some help?' I offered.

He hesitated for a second, then nodded, looking grateful.

'OK,' he said then. 'Thanks.'

We took Daz to the room Sean and I were sharing. It had been recently renovated by the looks of it, with striped wallpaper and antique pine furniture, and there was still a faint smell of new paint. Daz eyed the double bed but sat down on one of the armchairs by the window while I fished my kit out of my tank bag. Sean filled the small kettle on the side table and started putting together coffee from the little packets provided.

Daz threw the sodden tissue into the waste paper basket and folded up a fresh piece. He watched me unpacking disinfectant and Steri-strips and his lips twisted.

'You not going to put gloves on before you deal with me?' he wanted to know, his tone taunting. 'The others seem to have developed a sudden strange reluctance to get my blood on them.'

'Sit back and shut up if you want that eye looking at,' I said.

The cut was small and just above his eyebrow where it would tend to bleed a lot and look worse than it was. I managed to clean it up for long enough to get the Steri-strips to stick and hold the sliced edges of skin together.

He sat without complaint while I worked on him, not taking those startling blue eyes off me. It was like being watched by a Siamese cat.

'There you go,' I said at last. 'Try and let the air get to it tonight, but I'd put some sticking plaster over it before you try and get your lid on tomorrow morning.'

He delicately traced the repair with his fingers and nodded his thanks.

The kettle boiled. Sean poured water into both mugs and handed one to me and the other to Daz. I perched on the corner of the bed while Sean took the chair opposite Daz and sat leaning forwards with his forearms resting on his knees and his hands relaxed between them. There was a scrape across the middle two knuckles on one hand, I saw. Other than that he bore no signs of having been in a fight.

'What's going on, Daz?' he asked gently then. 'People are getting hurt. One of you's been killed. Is it worth it – whatever it is?'

It was neatly timed. Daz was physically at a low ebb, felt

289

isolated from his friends, and we'd just patched him up and been nice to him. Classic interrogation techniques.

He shrugged, still pigheaded despite everything that had happened.

I sighed. 'Look Daz, you're in the shit and we can protect you. It's what we do,' I said, trying to be persuasive rather than exasperated. 'But we can't do it if you won't tell us what we're trying to protect you from.'

'Who says we need protection?'

I stood up, frustrated into action, but with three people in it the bedroom was too cramped to pace. 'I'm only here because I made a promise to a friend,' I said, turning back to him. 'And Sean's only here because I am. But you need us, whether you like it or not. Tonight should have proved that. For God's sake – what do we have to do to get you to trust us?'

'We do trust you,' Daz said. 'Otherwise you wouldn't be here.'

'Ha!' I said, scathing. 'Where's "here", Daz? Because from where we're standing the only place we are is in the dark.'

He let his breath out in a huff and sat up. 'OK,' he said, sounding weary, like we'd finally battered him down into submission. 'We're here because we've made a deal to buy something over here and bring it back to the UK.'

I was aware of a sickly taste in the back of my mind. 'What kind of a deal?' I demanded, unable to keep the disgust out of my voice. 'Drugs?'

'Fuck, no,' Daz said quickly. 'We may be many things, Charlie, but there's no way we'd have anything to do with shit like that and that's the truth.'

'So what kind of shit *are* you into?'

Daz shrugged. 'Diamonds,' he said.

'Diamonds?' I repeated blankly, glancing at Sean. I checked Daz's face carefully for any sign of guile but it was clear and open. I sat down on the corner of the bed again. 'Why the hell have you made a deal to buy diamonds?'

'For my work,' he said, sounding almost surprised that

I should have to ask. 'A lot of the stuff I do is ceramics and glassware from local artisans, but I deal with jewellery makers all the time. Didn't you know?'

I shook my head slowly. Diamonds. After all our fears and speculation, it was almost an anticlimax. When Sean had said Daz ran a craft centre I'd expected something a little more homespun. It never occurred to me that he might be dealing with precious gems. From the look on his face, Sean hadn't made that connection, either.

'So, did you provide Tess with the stones she's wearing?' Sean asked. 'The ones she's trying very hard to pretend are not real?'

The surprise showed on Daz's face. 'You spotted that one, then?' he said, rueful. 'No, that was Slick.'

'Convenient to pass that one over to someone who can't refute it, isn't it?'

He flushed. 'That's not what I'm doing,' he said quickly. He sighed heavily, took a drink of his coffee. 'Look, in the last year I started to buy in some secondhand jewellery and I was getting in loose diamonds to replace lost stones. I was using Tess to do a bit of that repair work for me.'

'Why Tess?'

'We were at art college together,' he said. 'She dropped out to have the kid, Ashley, and we lost touch for a while. Then one day she came into the shop with this boyfriend of hers, Slick. We chatted, you know how it is, old times. She'd been keeping her hand in, making her own stuff, and she was interested in doing more, so I got her doing some work for me.'

'And what about the diamonds she was wearing?' I asked. I took a sip of my coffee but the little packets of UHT milk the hotel supplied had done little to cool it down.

'The first time she came in I'd noticed the rings she had on, of course,' Daz said. 'She showed them to me as examples of her work and, well, you couldn't miss rocks like those, could you? So I asked about them. She told me Slick had a contact who could get stones and was I interested?'

'And it didn't occur to you that there might be something ever so slightly underhand about all this?' Sean said, keeping his voice mild.

'Of course,' Daz said. 'But I asked around in the trade – discreetly – and no flags came up that they were stolen, so I bought them. They were a mixed bag of cut stones – circular and pear-shaped brilliants, mostly. The biggest was about point-eight of a carat. I used it to replace a poor quality solitaire emerald in a ring I'd bought in cheap because it was damaged. I sold it on for less than it was really worth, but I still made a fat profit. The customer got a decent stone at a bargain price and everybody went home happy.'

'What happens when the customer goes for an insurance valuation at some later date,' Sean said, 'and discovers just how much of a bargain he's got?'

'What's he going to do – come back and complain?' Daz jeered. 'Human nature, mate. He just thinks he's got a wonderful deal and he keeps his mouth shut. I've never had one back.'

Sean was silent for a moment, digesting that one, then he said, 'And what was different about this time? This deal?'

Daz took another swig of coffee and spent a few moments turning the cup in his hands, to the point where I thought we'd lost him.

'The scale of it,' he said at last and his shoulders relaxed a little, as though he was relieved to finally get it out in the open. He looked up. 'Slick kept coming back with more gemstones and I kept buying them until, a month ago, he told me about this contact he had in Dublin who had a job lot to get rid of. Only Slick didn't have the cash to buy them up front. Shit, the kind of money he was talking about, neither did I. It's not exactly the sort of thing you can go to the bank about, is it?'

'So you went to your friends,' Sean said quietly.

Daz rubbed a hand across his face, forgetting about the eyebrow, and winced. 'Yeah,' he admitted. 'I remortgaged my flat and scraped together as much as I could, and Slick

292

managed to put some up, and then I got William and Paxo involved, and Jamie wanted in as well. They all put in an equal share.'

'Ten grand a hit,' I said. 'They must really trust you.'

His eyes flicked to mine, then slid away, guilty. 'Yeah, they did.'

'So how much have you put up, altogether?'

'Eighty grand,' Daz said.

I tried to keep my face as blank as Sean's but I couldn't prevent a small twitch. *Eighty grand. People had killed for less. A lot less.*

'For diamonds worth how much?' Sean asked.

'When I'm done with them – about a quarter of a mil,' Daz said, and there was a hint of a thrill in his voice. 'Imagine it! All we had to do was meet with the contact in Dublin and carry the stones back to the UK. No taxes to pay, no import duties. I promised the boys I'd double their money and it would be a blast.'

'And then Slick died,' I said deliberately, watching the excitement fade, wanting to remind him this wasn't all fun and games.

'We still don't know it wasn't an accident,' he said quickly.

'Not at the time, maybe, but what about afterwards? What about when that van chased me after Slick's wake? When possibly the same van wiped out Sam Pickering? Did it not occur to you then to call the whole thing off?'

'Of course it did,' he muttered. 'But it was too late then. Part of the money had been paid and none of us could afford to lose it – least of all me. Besides, Tess still had the contact in Dublin and she was up for it.'

'Hm,' I said, thinking of her drunken candour. 'She wanted you to get the diamonds but she wasn't keen on actually coming with you, was she? It was her pal Gleet who was pushing for that.'

'Well, if she wanted the rewards she was going to have to take the risks as well,' Daz said. 'As for Gleet – he lent

293

Slick part of his stake money. That's his angle. And he modified the bike for him.'

'Modified?'

'Yeah, he grafted in a false silencer can onto the exhaust to carry the stones.'

'Ah,' I said, 'so *that's* why Gleet nicked the wreckage of Slick's bike back after the crash – he couldn't afford to have the police taking it apart.'

'How did you—?' Daz began, then seemed to give up trying to figure it out. 'Yeah,' he said then. 'He did.'

'But you haven't added on anything to your Aprilia,' I said. 'How are you going to carry them?'

He grinned. 'Well I'm not planning on swallowing them, if that's what you mean,' he said. 'No – waterproof bag dropped into the tank.'

'Hm, they'll never think of looking *there*,' Sean murmured and, louder: 'So, when do you meet this contact? And where?'

Daz hesitated again, tried to cover it by finishing the last of his coffee and putting the mug down on the window ledge. 'We're going to do the deal on Sunday,' he said. 'We'll meet up with him sometime after the track day.'

'Track day?' I repeated.

'Yeah, it's a free-for-all at Mondello Park circuit – the one just outside Dublin,' Daz said. He paused, taking in our blank faces, and grinned suddenly. 'Did nobody tell you about that? Shit – I hope you both brought your driving licences then, or they won't let you out on the track and you'll be missing a treat. They only resurfaced it last winter.'

He got to his feet but only made it a couple of strides towards the door before Sean stopped him.

'One last thing, Daz,' he said. 'Who's been tailing us since we got here?'

Daz frowned. 'We haven't seen that Vauxhall since this morning,' he said. 'I thought they'd given up.'

'What about the guy on the Suzuki?'

294

'What Suzuki?' His surprise seemed genuine enough.

'With Lucky Strike paintwork. It was on the ferry yesterday, came past us on the road up to the Giant's Causeway
this morning, and was in the car park at Bushmills.'

Daz's face cleared and he shrugged. 'No idea, mate. You
worry too much,' he said. 'Look, I'll see the pair of you in
the morning, yeah? Just do me a favour and don't tell the
others what I've told you.' He gave a rueful smile. 'Old
Paxo's sulking enough with me as it is.'

It was only after he'd closed the door behind him that I
stood and turned to Sean. 'Why is he lying about knowing
who's on that Suzuki?'

'Who knows?' Sean said, getting to his feet himself. He
collected the empty coffee mugs and put them back on the
tray with the kettle. 'I reckon he's probably given us most
of the full story there, but he's still holding back.'

'Are you going to call Madeleine and see what she can
dig out on any hooky diamonds?'

'Mm,' he said, distracted, moving across to flick on the
bedside lamp and slip the chain onto the door. 'I'll do it
first thing tomorrow morning.'

'Tomorrow?' I glanced at the bedside clock in surprise.
'It's not that late. Why not do it now?'

'Why?' Sean echoed softly, closing in on me with such
plain intent that my mouth dried even as a sliding heat
drenched slowly through my belly. 'Because I've been alone
in a room with you, Charlie – and a bed – for *seconds* now
and yet, strangely enough, we both seem to still be dressed.'

He backed me up until I bumped against the wall by the
door with a breathless laugh. Suddenly his hands had infil-
trated my shirt without me ever knowing how he'd undone
the buttons. 'That's why,' he murmured against my tipped-
back throat.

'Really?' I managed, my voice a gasp as my eyes went
blind. 'You must be losing your touch . . . *Oh*, maybe not . . .'

Chapter Twenty-three

The next day, Saturday, we rode down to Dublin. We left Portaferry just after breakfast, took the five-minute ferry trip across the Narrows to Strangford, then climbed through the spectacular Mourne Mountains to cross the border at Newry.

I'd been expecting more of a checkpoint but instead all I saw were the signposts suddenly swapping into kilometres, an extraordinary number of adverts for fireworks, and billboards proclaiming the innocence of the Colombian Three.

The main N1 road to Dublin was not dual carriageway for the most part, but it was wide enough for easy overtaking and, I was surprised to discover, most of the slower moving traffic obligingly put two wheels onto the generous hard shoulder to let you zip past with minimal exposure. Only the tourists seemed to stay out and hog the white line.

We made good time over the ninety miles or so, stopping only once just outside Balbriggan for fuel and a break in a little roadside café. We dragged two tables together and all sat, apparently a united group, but I could feel the divisions snake and rip between us. The tension was so manifest it practically needed its own chair. Nearly all the boys bore the marks of last night's scuffle and Paxo was still limping slightly.

Sean went to the counter for the pair of us and came back with two bottles of mineral water so cold the outside of the glass ran with condensation. As he put mine down in front of me he reached out and casually brushed a strand of hair back from my face.

I froze at the simple intimacy of the gesture, without immediately knowing why. Then it hit me. In all the time Sean and I had been together before, we'd had to hide that fact from the outside world. In the army, regulations had forbidden him from fraternising with his trainees – certainly on the kind of level we'd risked.

And afterwards, in Germany and in America, we'd been doing our best to pretend that all we had between us was a working relationship. This openness was a new and vaguely disturbing development and, I realised as I gave him a belated smile, it was going to take some getting used to.

Paxo was still barely speaking to Daz. As soon as he'd finished his drink he muttered about going outside for a fag, colouring furiously as his unintentional *double entendre* sank in.

Daz sighed and would have followed him, but William put a hand on his arm.

'I'd leave him be, if I were you,' William said, his voice bland. 'His preconceptions of you have taken a bit of a battering of late, but he'll come round.'

Tess made a noise under her breath and pushed her own chair back, following Paxo outside. A moment later Jamie rose with a smile and went after her. Through the café window we could see Tess cadging a cigarette from Paxo as the three of them lurked together in the car park.

'Are they plotting my downfall, do you think?' Daz murmured.

'Well, somebody is,' I said. 'We still need to find out who set Davey and his gang onto us in Portaferry. And we need to find out before you make this pickup on Sunday.'

William's eyebrows climbed over the rim of his mug of tea. 'You let them in on it, then?' he said evenly to Daz.

'I didn't really think I could keep them out of the loop any longer, mate,' Daz said, sneaking a sly sideways glance

297

at Sean as he spoke. 'Without them we would have been in real trouble last night.' He rubbed ruefully at the plaster on his eyebrow.

William considered that one in silence for a moment, then nodded. 'Fair enough,' he said. He eyed me assessingly. 'You cut in on the cash, too?'

'Not interested,' Sean said briskly, speaking for both of us. He flashed a quick smile. 'Although if it will make you feel better about it, I'll invoice you for our professional services when we get back.'

William smiled in response. 'Hey, who says I was feeling bad about it?'

We were back on the road ten minutes later. William must have passed on the news about Sean and me as we were getting suited up again in the car park. I didn't hear how William put it but Paxo suddenly muttered a short sharp curse and threw down his gloves in disgust.

'In some circles,' Sean told him in a lazy drawl, 'that would be taken as a challenge to a duel.'

For a moment I watched Paxo fight the urge to tell Sean what he could do with himself, in graphic detail. But the memory of their encounter in the hotel in Co Antrim was painfully fresh in his mind. He stood seething for a moment longer, then bent and snatched his gloves up again, yanking them onto his hands in black silence.

'Why are you doing this?' Tess demanded then, her thin face tight with suspicion. 'I mean, what's in it for you two, eh?'

Sean paused in the middle of fastening the strap at the neck of his leathers and flicked his eyes over me. 'We gave our word to someone,' he said. 'Nothing more than that.'

Jamie had tensed at the direction the conversation was going, I saw. He caught my eye with a look that was half plea, half threat.

'So you're doing all this out of the goodness of your hearts, huh?' Tess said, her voice ripe with sarcasm. 'Well, I just think it's pretty convenient that until you two appeared on the scene we wasn't havin' no trouble. Now look what's happened.' And with that she jammed on her lid, effectively slamming the door on further argument or denial.

William was in the middle of lifting his own helmet. He paused and threw us a dubious glance as Tess climbed onto the back of his bike. 'Much as I don't like to admit it, the lady has a point,' he said. 'After all, anything you get for free these days is usually free for a reason – because it's not worth having. So, are you two half as good as you seem to reckon you are?'

Sean didn't respond immediately, just swung his leg over the Blackbird, twisted the key in the ignition and thumbed the engine into life. 'Well,' he said then with a swift fierce grin, 'let's just hope you never have to find out ...'

Compared with the kind of pace Daz had set north of the border, we had an almost leisurely cruise along the toll road round the western side of Dublin. It was just fast enough to keep a cooling draught rolling up over the FireBlade's fairing. Every time we slowed I could feel the heat building inside my leathers and bouncing up at me from the shimmering tarmac. If the temperature didn't let up a little tomorrow, I decided, this promised day at Mondello Park was going to be unbearable.

Since I'd acquired the FireBlade I'd done several track days with it – at Oulton Park in Cheshire, mainly, which wasn't much more than an hour from my parents' place, even allowing for traffic. I'd even had a day at the Superbike school at the new Rockingham circuit near Northampton, learning to lay the big bike down far enough through every corner to kiss my knee-sliders across the kerbs. It wasn't as manoeuvrable as my little Suzuki, but with any luck this previous experience meant I wasn't going to make a complete fool of myself out there tomorrow. If only that was all I had to worry about.

From Dublin we headed slightly southwest and as we got

closer to Naas, we started to pick up signs for Mondello
Park. The number of bikes had increased into a swarm so
that it was almost impossible to spot if the Suzuki with the
Lucky Strike paintwork was still shadowing us, but I had
faith that, if he'd been there, Sean would have spotted him.
There was no sign of our friendly Vauxhall-driving thugs,
either.

Naas itself seemed to be strung out along either side of
a single main street and at first we struggled to find our
hotel. There was a fair amount of reasonably good-natured
banter over the radio from the lads about Daz's duff navi-
gational abilities.

'Are you absolutely sure you're bent, Daz?' I heard Tess
demand when we'd made yet another U-turn. 'It's just I
thought it was only *real* men who would never ask for
directions.'

When we did finally find the right turnoff it was to
discover a massive modern hotel lurking at the end of what
seemed to be an industrial estate. The building was all
stainless steel and glass, artistically interspersed with
dramatic swathes of stonework. As we pulled up in a line
near the fountain by the impressive main entrance, I was
aware of the sinking feeling that I hadn't packed anything
remotely suitable to wear at such a venue. Mind you, by
the look on Tess's face, neither had she.

As soon as we walked into the granite and marble-lined
lobby I could tell it was a proper high-class hotel – rather
than merely one with high-class pretensions – by the reaction of the staff. There wasn't one. The polished
professionalism of the chic-looking woman manning the
reception counter never missed a beat as she smiled a
welcome to this dusty bunch of fly-splatted reprobates and
handled our check-in.

The room Sean and I were given matched the rest of the
place – all sleek modern styling around a huge bed and a
claw-footed bath in the *en suite*. As well as the usual
mundane trouser press and in-room safe, you were given a

300

DVD player and a PlayStation as well. We'd only been in there five minutes when there was a knock at the door from a member of the housekeeping staff offering to turn the bed down for us.

When she'd gone I said ruefully to Sean, 'I don't think I even *own* anything that would make me fit in here and, if I do, I certainly haven't brought it with me.'

He grinned. 'We're going to have to do something about that when we get back,' he said. 'Don't take it the wrong way, but you're going to need to blend in a bit more with the kind of people who've got the money to hire close protection personnel.' The grin took on a wicked tint. 'Perhaps I should get Madeleine to take you on one of her infamous shopping raids on the West End.'

Madeleine and I got on much better now than we had done initially, as Sean well knew. But we still didn't have the kind of girlie friendship where I could see myself squeezing into a changing cubicle with her at Versace in my underwear.

I grinned back and went into the bathroom. It was only once I was there that the true import of what he'd said sank in. Sean had assumed, almost automatically, that I was coming back to work for him.

I shut the bathroom door behind me and leaned back against it, momentarily staring at the limestone tiles on the opposite wall.

'*Stay involved with Sean Meyer and you* will *kill again*,' my father had said. '*And next time, Charlotte, you might not get away with it . . .*'

I turned my head away, eyes squeezed shut as though to avoid having to see the words in front of me. My future was irrevocably bound up with Sean's, I knew that. But, despite my brave words to my father, did that mean I was necessarily destined for a permanent career as a bodyguard?

Had I learned nothing from the disaster in America?

I opened my eyes. The hotel bathroom reasserted itself. I couldn't avoid a wry smile as I realised that these very

301

surroundings were an indication that no, I hadn't learned anything. Here I was, on another assignment, another country, another babysitting job.

Besides – if I didn't do this, what else was there for me?

Sean was just finishing a call on his mobile phone when I came back out.

'Speak of the devil – that *was* Madeleine,' he said as he folded the phone shut and put it back in his pocket.

'Well, you know her best,' I said sweetly. 'And?'

'No large amounts of loose cut diamonds have been reported stolen anywhere in Europe,' he said, ignoring my jibe. 'And the Suzuki with the custom paint is registered to one Reginald Post. It's a Lancaster address. The name mean anything to you?'

I shook my head slowly. 'No, I don't think so.'

'Mm, back to square one, then,' he said, pulling a wry face. 'I hope you're not planning on sampling too much Guinness later though, Charlie,' he added, 'because I think maybe tonight we should keep our wits about us.'

Perhaps with the previous night's unplanned entertainment in mind, the boys opted to stay and eat in the hotel bar that evening, which made keeping an eye on them somewhat easier. By prior arrangement, Sean and I took it in turns to make some excuse to leave the group and do a number of quick and apparently casual sweeps of the hotel's public areas.

Around ten-thirty I murmured something about the little girls' room and strolled out of the bar. There was a widescreen TV over in one corner that had been tuned to one of the satellite sports channels. The highlights of that day's Moto GP qualifying had just come on, so I didn't think I'd be missed.

I started on the upper floors and worked my way down, passing through the foyer and sticking my head into the restaurant, before taking the stairs to the basement car park.

The underground car park was a maze of concrete on a single level, brightly lit and, if the number of empty spaces was anything to go by, far too large for the current capacity of the hotel. For the most part there were far more bikes than cars. The hotel must have been the favoured choice for those attending Sunday's track day.

And there, in a line of others, tucked in a far corner, I found the Lucky Strike Suzuki. I approached it carefully, tried to remember if I'd noticed it earlier and couldn't decide. But when I poked my fingers through a gap in the fairing, the engine casing was still warm to the touch.

I hurried back upstairs to the reception desk and asked nonchalantly if my old mate Reg Post had checked in yet. The young guy on the desk tapped away at his computer, frowning for a few moments.

'I'm sorry, Miss, but we don't have anyone of that name registered,' he said, looking crestfallen at having to disappoint me. 'Let me just check for you if he has a reservation . . . no, it doesn't look like it. I'm really sorry about that, Miss.'

'No problem,' I said quickly. 'He must be booked in somewhere else.'

The guy raised his eyebrows as though, in his opinion, there *wasn't* anywhere else to stay in the area, but he was much too polite to actually say so.

I walked back across the foyer and hit the stairs to the basement again. Just as I pushed the heavy door open at the bottom, I heard the echoing roar of a bike engine bouncing off the bare concrete walls as it was revved up through a gear.

Instinctively, I broke into a run. As I did so I caught the flash of coloured fairing and the Lucky Strike bike shot past me, heading for the exit. I increased my stride, sprinting diagonally now to try and get ahead of him but by the time he was halfway to the redline in second I knew I was already beaten.

All I managed to see was a set of black leathers and

helmet on a big figure who was hunched over the tank as he sped away. The brake lights flared briefly just before the sharp upward sweep of the exit ramp, then he was gone.

I slowed, cursing under my breath, knowing it was pointless to pursue him any further. Who the hell was he? And what had he been doing here if he wasn't checked in?

Just in case, I made a quick detour to check over our bikes which we'd shifted underground after we'd checked in ourselves. They were still chained together in a line and nothing seemed to have been disturbed.

I stood, catching my breath and, in that moment of stillness, heard one of the doors out of the car park slam shut on its self-closing mechanism. My head snapped up and I silently berated myself for being stupidly slow. If I couldn't get hold of the mysterious Mr Post, the next best thing was to find out exactly who he'd been here to see.

I belted back for the door and eased it open but the stairwell inside was empty. I went up as fast and as softly as I could, keeping to the outside of the walls. I didn't hear footsteps on the tiled steps but suddenly the noise from the bar grew louder and quieter again, as someone passed through the door into the foyer.

Abandoning any pretence at stealth, I pounded up the last half flight and yanked the door open. The foyer area was empty. There wasn't even any sign of the young man on the reception desk who'd been so helpful before. *Damn.*

Admitting defeat, I walked straight back to the bar. The majority of the Devil's Bridge Club were still where I'd left them – only Tess was missing. Sean was lounging on one of the vast leather sofas facing the entrance. He had his arm resting along the back and a bottle of beer swinging lazily from his other hand.

But the relaxed attitude was a blind, as I was well aware. So was the beer. He'd barely drunk half of it over the course of the entire evening. He kept taking the bottle with him to the bar whenever he bought a round and coming back with the same one, still barely touched.

The result was that he was a lot sharper than the others. He looked up, took in my face and got to his feet immediately, steering me out of earshot round the far side of a pillar.

A waiter hurried past, heading for a small group who'd been celebrating a birthday on the far side of the bar. He was carrying a dessert with two lit sparklers stuck in the top of it and Sean waited until he was gone before leaning in close.

'What's happened?' he demanded.

I filled him in briefly. 'I didn't see who it was,' I finished. 'Have any of this lot moved?'

Before Sean could answer there came the click of heels and Tess appeared from the direction of the ladies' room, still rearranging her short skirt. She smiled slyly at the pair of us as she went past and I had to control the urge to distance myself a little from Sean. *Come on, Fox, you don't have to hide this any more.*

'Well, *that* answers that one, I suppose,' I said, wry, watching Tess totter back to her seat. 'But whoever was in the car park then went up the stairs like a rat up a drain-pipe. No way could she have done that in those shoes. Anyone else?'

'Just one,' Sean said, and his face told me I wasn't going to like it.

'Who?'

'Jamie.'

Getting Jamie on his own to ask him about his involvement with Reginald Post was no easy task. Tess seemed to have latched herself onto him and every time he went to get the drinks in she was with him. She certainly didn't want to leave him on his own with me, that was for sure. Eventually, Sean took over distracting her long enough for me to slide in alongside him at the bar.

'So, what's with you and Reg Post?' I asked quietly while the barman had gone off to fetch more bottled beer.

'What?' Jamie had been watching the bike racing on the

305

TV and only pulled his gaze back to me with an effort. Again the resemblance to his father hit me square in the chest. 'Who the hell is Reg Post?'

'Remember the Lucky Strike Suzuki that's been tailing us?' I said. 'That's him.'

'What about him?' Jamie said, making a good job of sounding casually disinterested now. 'We haven't seen any sign of him since Bushmills.'

I shook my head. 'He's here,' I said. 'I saw him in the car park less than half an hour ago.'

'Car park ... ?' Jamie repeated slowly, then gave me a slow smile. 'Are you checking up on us?'

'Of course,' I said, allowing mild surprise to coat my voice. 'I promised Clare and your dad I'd look out for you, and that's what I'm doing.'

He shook his head, still wearing a look of bemused amusement at my actions. 'I don't know anyone called Reg Post and I don't need you looking over my shoulder all the time.' He flipped a couple of euro notes at the barman and picked up the drinks. 'You want to mollycoddle anyone, try Daz,' he said over his shoulder. 'He seems to be the one who's losing his bottle with this ...'

We didn't learn anything more during the evening, despite the fact that the boys should have drunk more than enough to loosen their tongues. In fact, I began to wonder how they were going to be sober enough by morning to find their way *to* a racetrack, never mind ride around it.

I was very surprised that everyone made it down to breakfast on Sunday looking more or less fit. Even so, there was a lot of strong coffee being drunk and not many fry-ups being eaten.

'So, what's the plan?' I asked when the serving staff had cleared away the plates and brought another pot of coffee for the table.

'We have to have a plan now?' Paxo asked with a groan,

306

clutching his head with one hand and reaching for the coffee pot with the other.

'Bearing in mind what you're up to, it might not be a bad idea,' Sean said, sitting back in his chair.

Paxo tried to bristle at the remark but couldn't find the energy.

'We get to Mondello Park, get out on the track and have some fun. Don't forget to take your driving licence, by the way, or they won't let you on the track,' Daz said, deliberately obtuse. 'And don't wear your radio and headset, either. They don't allow them inside the circuit – they interfere with the communications gear between the marshals and race control, or something.'

I glanced at Sean but it was a moot point for him – he didn't have a radio anyway. He shrugged.

'Better leave it behind,' Daz said. 'If they catch you with it they'll probably confiscate it, whether it's switched on or not, and besides,' he'd added with a grin, 'I would hate you to trash it if you drop the 'Blade.'

'And here was me about to throw the bike up the track if you hadn't said that,' I muttered, sarky.

'So, what about the exchange?' Sean said, not to be deflected and it was Daz's turn to shrug.

'We meet this guy and make the exchange back here this afternoon – after we get back from Mondello,' Daz said, matter-of-fact, as though he was describing a far more conventional shopping trip. 'Then we get back on the ferry tomorrow and go home. Back to work on Tuesday morning, eh lads?'

'Just like that?' I said, trying to keep my tone level. 'Do you know him by sight – this guy you're meeting? If not, how will you recognise him?'

Jamie's eyes flicked to Daz as though he, too, wanted an answer to that one.

Daz just smiled and indicated Tess with a wave of his coffee cup. 'Tess knows him,' he said airily.

Tess smiled slightly and said nothing. She was very quiet

this morning, sitting hunched in her chair drinking coffee. I wondered if she was having second thoughts about this whole idea. She had managed, I noticed, to get her rings back on today and they glittered on nearly every finger.

'What about the money?' Sean asked and, once again, the boys exchanged unreadable glances. 'How are you going to handle the hand-over of that without being fleeced?'

'It's already been handed over,' Daz said, his eyes flicking around, never still. 'Don't sweat it, Sean. It's all taken care of. You worry too much.'

'Sounds like you've got it all wrapped up,' Sean said, putting his own cup down so precisely onto its saucer I could tell the depth of his anger. 'How many times have you done this before?'

Daz's smile slipped a little. 'We haven't,' he said quickly.

'Exactly,' Sean said tightly. 'I've negotiated with terrorists and freedom fighters, guerrillas and rebels, from Afghanistan to South America. And they're all the same in one basic respect – they're crooked. They want what you've got and they'll cheat it out of you if they think they can possibly get away with it.'

We left the hotel at a little before nine-thirty. Despite all my and Sean's arguments, Daz remained stubbornly convinced that his purchase of the diamonds was going to go smoothly and he refused to let us in on the details. I could feel Sean's frustration like my own.

It wasn't far to Mondello Park. We followed the signs from the motorway and wound through the countryside into a thickening throng of bikes.

When we stopped at a fuel station a couple of miles outside the circuit the forecourt was a mass of brightly coloured cow hide, Kevlar and plastic and the air rang to the roar of dozens of exhaust pipes that had not been chosen primarily for their silencing abilities.

As soon as we stopped Jamie and Paxo abandoned their bikes and shot off to the gents', which was in a little block to one side of the kiosk. Either they were still trying to settle their stomachs after the beer of the night before, or their nerves at the prospect of getting stuck in to the track.

Sean pulled the Blackbird up alongside me as I edged the FireBlade towards the pumps.

'Our tail is back,' he said through his open visor.

'Which one?'

He smiled. 'We picked up a white Merc Sprinter van almost as soon as we left the hotel,' he said. 'He's just pulled over about a hundred metres further up the road but the driver hasn't moved. He's waiting for us.'

I glanced in the direction he'd indicated and could see the van sitting between two parked cars. It was too far away and at too much of an angle to see the occupants but I had no doubts that Sean was right about their intent. The Sprinter was bigger than a Transit and correspondingly more solid. I couldn't suppress a shiver at the memory of my last escape.

I paddled the 'Blade forwards half a metre to repeat the information to William, who was just in front of me in the queue.

William paused for a moment. It was difficult to tell how he was taking it when all I could see of his face were his eyes. After a moment, though, he nodded and leaned over towards Daz, who was slightly in front of him. As he did so I was sure I caught sight of a wire disappearing into the top of his leathers from underneath the back of his helmet.

The sight of that wire sent a flare of uneasy temper through me. It could only mean that William was still wearing his radio. And if he was, that meant Daz and the others probably were, too. But they'd specifically told me to leave mine behind.

There were several reasons I could think of why the Devil's Bridge Club would suddenly not want me to be able to listen in on their conversations. On today of all days.

And none of them were good.

309

Chapter Twenty-four

Mondello Park circuit was, as Daz had predicted, a blast. The organisers had obviously run so many of these events before that it was an easy and well-practised routine for them. We arrived, signed on, listened to the brief and laconically-delivered instructions on track etiquette and how the flag system worked, then were given our wristbands and the time of our session.

Even the weather seemed to be with us, the temperature considerably lower than yesterday. Modern bike engineering will stand up to Saharan operating temperatures, but I wasn't so sure about the riders.

The sessions were graded according to ability. I knew Daz, Paxo and William would automatically go for the most experienced one. I put myself into the intermediates, as did Sean. When I raised my eyebrow at that he just smiled.

'Employee or not,' he said, 'it's not my bike.'

I was a little concerned at where Jamie would pitch, bearing in mind my promise to Jacob and Clare to keep him out of trouble. When we came out of the marshal's office on the upper floor of the building over the pits, I spotted him below us with the rest of the Devil's Bridge Club standing round like they were ganging up on him.

I nudged Sean's arm. 'Maybe they're having a go at him as well,' I murmured.

By the looks of it, whatever they were telling Jamie wasn't

going down too well. He stood with his arms folded and his shoulders tense. Eventually he spun away from them and stalked towards the stairs up to the office. As he reached the top he saw us and must have realised that we'd witnessed the exchange. He paused, then came on scowling.

'What's up?' I asked.

'They want me to go out with the fucking novices,' he said, his flash of temper surprising me. 'Like they don't think I can hack it with the big boys.'

'We're only in the intermediates,' I said, hoping to mollify him but he only glowered all the harder.

'I know,' he snapped. 'If you were all in the top group at least that might mean *I* could move up one.'

'Just go out and give 'em hell in whatever session,' I said, aiming to be encouraging. 'Better to be way out in front than getting lapped.'

Jamie didn't reply to that one, just disappeared into the office looking ready to pull the arms and legs off somebody's teddy bear.

'They've been pushing him to keep up all the way here,' Sean said, watching Jamie go with narrowed eyes. 'I wonder why the sudden attack of conscience now?'

'Look on the bright side,' I said. 'At least it means we don't have to worry about him while we're out on track.'

'Bloody hell,' I said half an hour later. 'It's going to rain.'

We were sitting in one of the stands overlooking the track, watching the early novice session warm up. The smell of two-stroke oil was heavy in the air.

William eyed the clouds overhead. 'How can you be so certain?'

'I can feel it in my bones,' I said, rubbing at the dull ache in my left arm. 'The pressure's dropping.'

He raised a disbelieving eyebrow but didn't contradict me outright. 'Should make life more interesting, if nothing else,' he said and his eyes slid to the track as Jamie's Honda came ripping into view.

311

Jacob's genes were showing big time out on the track. Jamie zipped round the outside of another two stragglers as he came past us, riding like a man possessed, eyes locked on the next corner, totally in the zone.

'The kid's got some talent,' Paxo admitted, watching him disappear.

'Mm,' I agreed. 'Too much to be in with this lot. It makes it look like he's just showing off. He ought to be up a group.'

Daz shrugged. 'Well, he can always move up this afternoon,' he said casually. He checked his watch. 'You two ought to be getting ready for your session. As soon as they've finished scraping those baby Aprilias out of the gravel trap they'll be starting on the intermediates.'

Dismissed, Sean and I went to reclaim our bikes, lining up with around twenty others in the pit lane. Once the last group was all safely back in, they started letting us go out onto the track two at a time to avoid carnage in the first corner. Sean and I edged up towards the front of the group. My heart started to pump harder. Two more pairs in front of us, then one.

I clicked my visor down and started to let the 'Blade's clutch out until it was almost biting, upping the revs, holding it with two fingers tucked round the front brake. The bike felt as though it was bunching its muscles underneath me. The marshal waved us away.

Show time.

I must admit there was a part of me that had wondered how hard Sean would ride, bearing in mind I knew just how fiercely competitive he could be. It was something of a surprise, then, when he slotted in behind me at the first bend and stayed there.

After a few corners it became apparent that he had no intention of overtaking me, so I stopped worrying about him tangling me up and concentrated on reeling in the guys ahead.

312

I had the feel of the bike now, and the advantage of being about two-thirds the weight of most of the other riders. By the time we were halfway through the twenty-minute session, we were only four away from leading the pack.

And then the rain started.

I did my best to overlook the first few splashes on my visor, but once the track had turned dark with it I couldn't ignore it any longer. The contact patch with the road on a bike is so much smaller than a car's that you really have to have ultimate faith in the compound of your tyres to go balls-out in the rain. I really didn't have that kind of confidence.

I backed off the throttle and felt rather than saw Sean ease off behind me. Hard on our heels was a guy on a Yamaha R1 who'd been very upset when we'd carved past him a lap earlier. Now he was only too happy to regain his track position. For a second I debated on contesting his challenge, then let him go.

When the marshals brought out the chequered flags to signify the end of the session, we'd dropped back another two places. But, we were still up on our starting position and at least we hadn't suffered the indignity of ending up in the kitty litter, as someone had, big style, with what had begun the day as a very nice Ducati 999.

Sean finally came up alongside me on the cooling-down lap, tipped his visor open and grinned at me through the gap.

'What happened to you, you wimp?' he shouted across. 'We were right up there 'til you chickened out.'

'Hey, I was just giving you a way out with honour,' I retorted. 'You're the one who's on a borrowed bike.'

We cruised back into the pits and carried on through back into the paddock, along with the rest of our group. The rain was coming down harder now, the wind picking up restlessly under it.

We left the bikes parked up and took shelter in one of the open pit garages, listening to the inevitable post-session

313

post mortem. The guy who'd dropped the Ducati took some good-natured stick but didn't seem unduly bothered by the prospect of going home by recovery truck with what remained of his pride and joy.

There was no sign of any of the other Devil's Bridge Club members, but I assumed Daz, William and Paxo would be getting ready for their turn on the track. As for Jamie, he was obviously still sulking and was nowhere to be seen.

The rain eased back to a light spit, enough that our leathers were adequately waterproof to venture out in it. Sean and I grabbed a coffee and a burger and found a seat in the stands to watch the boys do their stuff.

As expected, Paxo and Daz went through their grouping with single-minded determination, riding too aggressively for most of the other riders to cope with. In fact, they were so clearly racing each other – despite all the warnings that this was *not* a race – that I was amazed they didn't get themselves black-flagged.

William was more circumspect but he still cut through the field with an efficient lack of drama. Despite the fact that this was supposed to be the session for the most experienced riders, the standard varied a lot. By the end of it Daz was just coming up to lap some of the tail-enders for the third time. He cut round one so close that he frightened the poor guy into a shimmy that nearly sent him off the track altogether.

Even Paxo didn't have the stomach for that kind of suicide. He dropped back and the two of them finished with one other bike in between them. William was two places further down the order.

We strolled down to meet them as they came in. I half expected Jamie to be there, too, but he was still absent.

'I haven't seen him either,' Sean admitted when I voiced my concern. 'And there's been no sign of Tess practically since we got here.'

The Mercedes Sprinter van had seemingly followed us as

314

far as the circuit entrance, and then kept going, making it difficult to tell if it really was tailing us or not. I'd felt secure inside the perimeter, among the crowds, but now I started to get an uneasy niggle at the back of my mind.

When we got to the pits, the boys were rowdily celebrating their performance. Daz in particular was in ebullient mood. He'd been trying so hard that he was bathed in sweat. When he unzipped his leathers his T-shirt was soaked through with it.

'What did you think?' he crowed when he spotted us. 'Not bad, huh?'

'Indescribable,' Sean said shortly. 'Where are Jamie and Tess?'

William had just grabbed a few bottles of mineral water and he returned at that point, handing one over to Daz with the faintest shake of his head.

'Why?' Daz said, still pumped up and cocky, taking a swig. 'They not with you?'

'You know they're not,' Sean said. I glanced at him. His voice had gone quiet and his body had that coiled look about it. And with a sudden clarity I knew why.

We'd been had.

Daz's story of meeting the courier later, at the hotel, was just so much smoke. We'd been deliberately kept out of the loop. That was why they'd made Jamie go out in the lower grade session. It explained perfectly why he'd been so pissed off that Sean and I had chosen to go for the intermediate group. Daz and the others had wanted to make sure we were occupied so Jamie could slip away. If we'd gone for the same session as the others, Jamie could have moved up into the intermediate one and still been on his way while we were all occupied on the track.

And, wherever he'd gone, it had to have something to do with the diamonds.

Daz just grinned at us without replying as he watched the realisation take hold of both of us. Sean sighed, took a quick step forwards, wrapped his fists into the front of

315

Daz's open leathers, and simply swung him off his feet. He rammed the other man up against one of the pit garages with casual violence, all too fast for the others to react. They just stood and gaped. The only reaction from the nearest bystanders was to scuttle out of the way.

'Where have they gone, Daz?' he demanded tightly.

'I don't know what you—'

Sean lifted him so his feet were barely on the ground and shook him viciously.

'Oh no, no bullshit. Not any more. Tell us now.'

Daz's gaze swivelled briefly across mine. Anger kept my face cold and hard and he didn't like what he saw there any better than he had done with Sean. There was the sound of running footsteps behind us but I didn't turn round to check. I willed Daz's nerve to break. We only had moments left.

'All right, all right!' he said. 'He went to meet the courier, OK? To make the exchange. He should have called by now.'

'Where?'

Another hesitation. Another hard jolt. 'The fuel station we stopped at on the way in. He was supposed to meet him there.'

'Now then, lads, what's all this about, eh?' asked a voice behind us. I finally turned to find one of the pit lane marshals behind us. He was a big guy, rolling his shoulders reflexively inside his orange coveralls.

Sean relaxed his grip slightly and let Daz back down onto his heels. Daz jerked his leathers out of Sean's hands and slid out from under him, angry and scared. And most angry that he'd been scared.

'Is the big feller causing you trouble, then?' the marshal persisted, nodding towards Sean.

For just a moment, Daz hesitated. If he said yes, the chances were Sean would be thrown out of the circuit and Daz must have known that I would go too. I could see the debate flitting through his brain on whether that would alleviate or exacerbate his problems. Jamie – and Tess, presumably – had gone for the diamonds and had not returned. He might just need us ...

316

'No, everything's fine,' he said, giving the marshal a bright smile. 'He's just jealous 'cos I rode rings round him.'

The marshal eyed them both for a few seconds, face layered with doubt, then he shrugged.

'A bit of friendly rivalry is good,' he said, his tone a warning. 'Just as long as it stays friendly, all right?'

'So, would you care to tell us what's *really* going on, Daz,' Sean said tiredly when we were all out into the paddock and they'd parked up near to our bikes. 'And for fuck's sake make it the whole story this time.'

Daz had the grace to flush a little, hunching his shoulders. The adrenaline generated by the track was dissipating now and the cooling sweat made him shiver. It had started to rain again and that didn't help.

'All he was supposed to do was go meet with the courier and Tess was supposed to verify the diamonds wore kosher,' he said.

'When?'

'We rang the guy when Jamie came back off his session,' Daz admitted, flicking nervous glances at William and Paxo for support. 'The two of them went to meet him while you were both out on track.'

Sean didn't reply right away, just stood with his hands on his hips staring from one face to another as though he couldn't believe their naive stupidity. He wasn't the only one.

'You bloody fool, Daz,' he said quietly at last.

'It was a straightforward exchange,' William put in evenly, coming to his friend's defence.

'Yeah – for a shit-load of diamonds you've already paid for,' I shot back. 'Did it not occur to you that they might try and keep the cash *and* the diamonds?'

'Er, actually, they don't have the cash,' Daz said, not quite meeting our eyes as he confessed to yet another lie. 'Not all of it, at least.'

317

Sean rolled his eyes. 'So where's the rest?'

'In the safe in my room,' Daz said. He caught the look of outright disbelief on our faces and flushed again, deeper this time. 'Look, all Jamie was supposed to do was check the gear over with Tess, yeah? Then he was supposed to give us a shout over the radio and we were going to take the guy back to the hotel and give him the rest of his money. Now we can't raise him, so he must have gone out of range. I don't understand what's gone wrong. It was supposed to be so easy.'

Sean flipped him a bitter and cynical smile. 'Yeah,' he said, 'that's what they always say.'

It took us less than ten minutes to get back to the fuel station where the clandestine meet was to have taken place. It was nearly twelve o'clock now and the forecourt was still bustling with bikers either on their way to the afternoon sessions at Mondello Park, or coming back in to refuel from the morning.

Beside the small squat kiosk itself there was the brick-built toilet block Jamie and Paxo had used earlier, and a large rutted car park at the rear. Two cars were parked on the rough gravel, an elderly battered Fiesta that looked as though it belonged to the kiddie serving in the petrol station, and a nearly new Audi A8 on Dublin plates. Was that, I wondered, the kind of car a dodgy diamond courier would drive?

Of Jamie's little Honda, there was no sign.

We pulled up alongside and climbed off the bikes. Sean turned a slow circle, eyes narrowed as he surveyed the scene.

'Spot on, isn't it?' he said to me.

'No overlooking houses and the CCTV only covers the pumps,' I agreed quietly. 'Yeah, it probably is.'

Sean indicated the door to the ladies' loo. 'You want to check in there for any sign of Tess while we do this side?' he said.

I nodded and did a quick sweep. Inside, the ladies' had a cracked tiled floor, a grubby stainless steel handbasin and two cubicles with planked wooden doors. Neither of them were occupied.

I came out just in time to see Paxo come rushing out of the gents' and vomit into the weeds by the side of the building. I didn't stop to ask him what was wrong, just pushed the door open and went in.

The gents' toilet was bigger than the ladies', with a row of four cubicles as well as the usual urinals along the wall opposite. It stank to high heaven – not an uncommon state of affairs for public loos. But in this case the smell was overlaid with another, more rancid tone.

Blood.

Oh shit. Oh please, not Jamie ...

As I came in, William backed out of the largest cubicle right at the end of the row, clutching at the door jamb for support. Daz followed him out so fast they nearly tripped over each other's feet. He looked up in alarm when he saw me approaching.

'Charlie, no!' he said. 'Don't go in there—'

I didn't bother to explain to him that, whatever was in there, it was unlikely to be the first time I'd seen it. Or something very like it. I pushed past him, gathering myself for the shock, but it wasn't what I was expecting.

The dead man was a stranger. He was sitting fully clothed on the pan with his body propped against the cistern and his head thrown back. The pose revealed the gaping wound across his throat, like he had a second mouth that was silently screaming.

The blood had soaked down through a good suit that had once been dark grey. His knees were together but with the feet splayed apart, revealing slender ankles in pale grey silk socks. His hands dangled straight down at either side. If he'd been wearing rings or a watch, they were gone. To one bloody wrist was chained a leather briefcase that was lying open and empty on the flooded tiles.

Sean looked up as I entered. He was crouched just out of reach of the blood, staring at the dead man with cool detachment.

319

'One ex diamond courier, I presume,' I said with as much composure as I could manage. It wasn't the first time I'd seen someone with their throat cut and the memories that returned now were both abiding and abysmal.

'I would say so,' Sean agreed, rising. 'Well, he's no diamonds on him now, so that probably takes care of the *why* he was killed but, the question now is, who by?'

'Jesus, man, how the fuck can you two stand there and calmly discuss this?' Daz demanded, his voice a strangled squawk. 'I mean, Jesus!'

'Good point,' I said to Sean, my voice bland. 'We should get out of here.'

'Mm.' He nodded shortly, turned to the others. 'Have you touched anything?'

They shook their heads but I carefully ripped out some paper hand towels from the dispenser and wiped the door jambs on both sides, just in case. I flushed them down the loo in the next cubicle, operating the lever with my elbow.

Outside again, the rain suddenly smelt fresh and clean, despite the petrol station fumes close by. Paxo obviously felt far enough away from the pumps to light up and when we emerged he was hovering next to his Ducati, puffing on a cigarette with all the fervour of an expectant father in a hospital waiting room.

'Right,' Sean said, swinging his leg over the Blackbird. 'Back to the hotel.'

'Why?' William demanded with a trace of bitterness. 'What the hell difference does that make?'

Sean just looked at him. 'Does Jamie know you brought the rest of the money with you?'

The boys exchanged glances, then Daz said, 'Well, yeah, of course he does. But it's locked in the safe in my room.'

Sean jerked his head back towards the toilet block and its grisly secret. 'After this,' he said grimly, 'do you really think he's going to let a little thing like that stop him?'

Chapter Twenty-five

Jamie cannot have done this.

All the way back from Mondello Park to the hotel, that was the only thing I could think about.

That, and what the hell was I going to tell Jacob and Clare? They'd trusted me to look after Jamie. To keep him out of trouble. You couldn't get any deeper in trouble than a vicious killing and, one way or another, he was up to his neck in this one.

At the same time, part of my brain just couldn't accept that he had actually done the deed himself. I remembered tackling him in the hallway of the house in Caton. His instinctive response to the fright of his discovery had been to take a swing at me. But that didn't mean he could slash someone's throat, rob them, and leave them propped on a toilet.

No, that was much more Eamonn Garroway's style.

The thought started as a niggle and grew into a monster as we thrashed through the countryside back towards Naas. Jamie might not have murder in his psyche, but his mother's boyfriend certainly had.

The question was, how big a part had Jamie played in his schemes?

I backtracked. We'd been followed off the ferry by someone who knew we were coming. They hadn't bothered trailing us to the hotel, but had turned up later. Then they'd

321

been waiting for us on the road to the Giant's Causeway the following day. How had they known where we were going, if not because someone had been tipping them off?

But, even as the thoughts came whizzing towards me like a summer midge swarm, I did my best to swat them away. After all, why had somebody tried to run Tess down when she was needed to make contact with the diamond courier? Why had somebody arranged for Davey and his mates to attack us in the pub at Portaferry? Who was the guy on the Lucky Strike Suzuki?

And, even before we'd ever got to Ireland, who had deliberately run down Slick and Clare, and then tried to do the same to me after Slick's wake? Not to mention what had happened to Sam during the Devil's Bridge Club audition. But however hard I tried to slot it together, nothing fitted.

Nothing at all.

We didn't bother with niceties when we got back to the hotel, abandoning the bikes right outside the front entrance and just about running through the foyer. Daz stabbed at the call button for the lift a couple of times and, when it failed to miraculously arrive, headed for the stairs with a muttered curse.

We burst out of the stairwell at the fifth floor, some of us rather more out of breath than others, and thundered down the corridor to Daz's room. He fumbled in his leathers for his key card, but when he swiped it through the reader, it flashed the red light at him and stubbornly refused to disengage the locks.

Daz tried it several more times, then Paxo snatched it out of his hands and tried too, also with no success.

Daz swore at some length. 'I'll have to go back down to reception and get another,' he said, trembling with nerves now. 'What was wrong with a good old-fucking-fashioned key, for Christ's sake?'

'OK,' Sean said. 'Charlie – go with him.'

'What's the matter?' William said sharply. 'Don't you trust us?'

'No,' Sean said, not bothering either to glance at him or pull his punches. 'The rest of us will wait up here. Which are your rooms?' he asked the others. William nodded towards the door opposite. When he dug out his own card, it operated the lock without a glitch.

Daz and I headed back to the foyer. Going down the stairs was easier than coming up but Daz was still gasping for breath by the time we reached the ground floor. As we reached the door at the bottom I grabbed his arm.

'Hang on,' I said. 'Take a moment, calm down and think about what you're going to say. If you go up to them in a panic they're going to be suspicious. And, right now, we can't afford too many awkward questions, hm?'

He looked set to argue but then he nodded, fighting to regain some self-possession. He didn't make a bad job of it considering his whole world must have seemed like it was coming down around him.

'You almost sound,' he said with a shaky smile, 'like you've done this before.'

'Yeah well, I suppose that's because I have.'

We managed to approach the front desk with something like a saunter in our stride. I feigned an interest in the spa treatments on special offer while Daz waited for the bloke on the desk to finish on the phone. They must have had an infinite number of staff members at that hotel, because I don't think I'd ever seen the same one twice. Certainly, the man who put down the receiver and smiled politely at us now was a stranger.

'I wonder if you can help me, mate. I seem to be having a bit of trouble getting back into my room,' Daz said, managing to produce a smile of his own as he held up the offending key card.

'Oh, and I'm very sorry about that, sir,' the man said, sounding for all the world as though he meant it. 'What room would you be in?'

He tapped away at his computer terminal as he spoke, but when Daz gave his name and room number, the man's smile became a puzzled frown. There was a betraying stiffening of his neck and he flicked his eyes covertly back up to Daz.

'Um, would you mind if I was to be asking you for some identification, sir?' he said, adding hurriedly. 'Just for security purposes, you understand.'

'Er, no. Not at all,' Daz said, digging his wallet out of an inside pocket and folding it open to show his driver's licence. His voice was commendably calm, but when he leaned on the desk the fingertips of his left hand tapped a jittery rhythm against the polished granite surface. I moved in close and put my hand over his, giving him my best simpering smile even as I crushed his fingers into immobility under mine.

'Is there a problem?' I said innocently.

'No, no! Er . . . but I think I'd better be calling security,' the man mumbled, looking mortified as he reached for the phone again.

I saw the alarm flare in Daz's eyes and nipped the knuckles of his middle two fingers together hard enough to keep him quiet.

'Don't you think it might be a good idea to tell us what the trouble is first,' I said, taking a flyer and putting the ominous note of the disgruntled guest into my voice, 'and we'll be the judge of whether it can be sorted out here and now, without all the hassle of going any higher up the chain?'

The man hesitated a moment, then put the phone down again. 'Well, I had another guy come to me, less than an hour ago, and didn't he say just the same thing – gave me the same name and the same room number and told me that his key card wouldn't work. It happens sometimes – people put them next to something in a pocket and it wipes them. So I programmed him another card up, quick as you like, without asking him to prove who he was and I think I'd

324

better get security to come up to your room with you now, just so you can check there's nothing missing or—'

'No!' Daz yelped. I gripped his fingers again and he took the hint to modify his voice before he went on, sounding less panicked, 'I know who that was and there won't be anything wrong. Honestly! There's no need for security.'

The man looked unconvinced. I leaned over the counter and lowered my voice confidentially. 'It was almost undoubtedly one of our lot – he fancies himself as a bit of a practical joker,' I said, rolling my eyes to invite him in on the secret. I jerked my head towards Daz. 'It's Daz's birthday, you see. Now if I know good old Jamie, he'll have been in there and decked the place out with balloons, ready for us getting back.'

The relief on the man's face was almost comical. 'Oh well, that's all right then,' he said, his hand fluttering at his chest. 'And here was I, imagining the worst . . .'

The corridor was deserted when we got back up to the fifth floor but, as soon as Daz ran the new key card through the lock, the door across the hallway opened and the others piled out.

The room was the same layout as the one Sean and I were sharing on the next floor up. The in-room safe where Daz had stowed the rest of the money for the diamonds was tucked away in the bottom of the little wardrobe area just as you went in, opposite the bathroom. It didn't need a close inspection to spot that the door was standing open and the safe was empty.

Daz stuck his hand in anyway, just in case, like that amount of cash in used fifties could somehow still be lurking out of sight at the back. When he'd finished his fruitless search he sat back on his heels with a groan.

Paxo and William stood around watching him with slightly dumbstruck expressions on their faces. Sean, meanwhile, did a circuit of the room, giving it a fast check over, moving with intent economy. On the far side of the bed he bent down and lifted a helmet off the floor.

Right away, I recognised it as Jamie's.

Sean nodded shortly to me. I was still standing by the entrance, and as I was nearest, I ducked my head into the bathroom.

And froze.

'Sean,' I said, my voice strangely flat. 'I think you need to see this.'

The others knew from my tone that something was very wrong but they seemed unable to react more than to stare blindly at me. Sean pushed them aside and stepped past me, opening the bathroom door wide.

Tess was lying in the bath, fully clothed, with one leg folded back underneath her and both arms draped over the sides. She looked small and fragile and rather childlike. Her head was turned at an unlikely angle and her eyes were open. It didn't take a genius to work out that her neck had been broken.

'Ah ... shit,' Sean murmured under his breath.

'This wasn't Jamie,' I said quickly, like I was abruptly short of breath. 'It can't have been. He would *not* have done something like this. Not to Tess.'

Sean moved in and bent closer, eyes inspecting the body with cold precision. The others seemed to come out of their trance at that point. Daz took one step over the threshold and stopped with something approaching a whimper.

Sean barely turned his head. 'If you're going to be sick, do it somewhere else,' he said shortly.

I forced myself not to turn away from Tess, even though the sight of her made my heartbeat struggle painfully inside my constricted chest.

'Her rings are gone,' I said, suddenly noticing her naked fingers dangling over the rim of the bath. 'She was wearing them again at breakfast but they're not there now.'

'Her left arm's broken just above the wrist, so she must have put up a fight,' Sean said quietly. 'But this is what

326

killed her, look – she was hit with something, hard, across the side of her neck here, under her ear. You can see the bruising. One blow,' he went on, a strange sympathy in his face now, velvet on stone. 'I doubt she would have known much about it.'

I glanced around. 'Whatever it was they used, they must have taken it with them.'

'Mm,' Sean said, straightening. 'You got a bruise very like that across your arm, remember?'

A fast picture of that wicked extendable baton unfolded in my memory. Sean saw from my anguished face that I'd connected the two. It seemed a bitter confirmation of my earlier fears.

'Eamonn?'

'I wouldn't be at all surprised,' he said, turning grim.

You should have let me finish him while I had the chance. Sean's words came back to taunt me. It was a testament to his will power that he didn't feel the need to repeat them himself.

'So, what the fuck do we do now?'

It was Paxo who spoke. He sounded somewhat subdued, defeated even. The most interesting thing was that the question was directed towards Sean.

The Devil's Bridge Club members had put themselves totally into his hands. William had retreated into a blank silence so that it was difficult to know what he was thinking, while Daz was clearly in shock.

We'd shepherded the three of them back to Paxo and William's room across the hallway, carefully hanging the Do Not Disturb sign on the door to Daz's. It wouldn't prevent Housekeeping from making their nasty discovery but it would delay them, at least.

'I'm not entirely sure you can do anything other than call the *gardai*,' Sean said, leaning on the wall by the window and folding his arms across his chest. 'Whether he was the driving force behind it or not, it would seem Jamie's done

327

the dirty on you. He took Tess to meet the courier, who's now dead and minus the gems. He then brought her back here, and now *she's* dead and the money's gone as well. Face it – you're in the shit. But it'll make it ten times worse for you if you run.'

'What about the diamonds?' Daz said, his voice plaintive now. The three of them were sitting on one of the beds, slumped and dejected.

Sean shrugged. 'Forget them,' he said, brutal. 'If they were nicked we could try and drop Jamie in it with the authorities. I know a guy in Amsterdam who loves to track down and recover stolen gems. There might even have been a reward. But, even though I can't believe they're entirely legit, I've already run some checks and they don't show up as stolen.'

Daz shifted uncomfortably. 'They're not stolen, exactly,' he admitted. 'They just didn't get here through the usual channels.'

Sean stared at him for a moment, face bleak. He'd taken on that stillness I recognised. He only wore it when things were raging all around him, or he was trying to contain it within. 'As soon as I found out they weren't stolen, there was really only one logical explanation,' he said quietly. 'You bought blood diamonds, didn't you?'

Daz flushed. 'At the time, I didn't know that's what they were,' he protested.

'Not at first, maybe,' Sean said, and there was a danger-ous softness to his voice now. 'But it didn't take you long to find out, did it?'

'Wait a minute, what the fuck are blood diamonds?' Paxo demanded.

'They're also called conflict diamonds,' Sean told him but his eyes were still on Daz. 'They're smuggled out of the mines in places like Botswana and Sierra Leone by the workers – who'll be shot if they're caught, incidentally. The rough stones are traded on the black market, cut in the backstreets of India, and peddled into Europe usually to finance the drugs trade,' he said, glacial. 'Good job there was " no way you'd have anything to do with shit like that", right Daz?'

Daz wouldn't meet his eyes as Sean threw his own earlier disavowal back in his face.

'We trusted you!' Paxo jumped to his feet and rounded on Daz. 'You promised us a good laugh and a double-your-money deal. It was supposed to be a "victimless crime" right?' he spat. 'Now look at it – all gone to fuck.'

'I don't like it any better than you do, Pax,' Daz said, voice rising. 'And I had a hell of a lot more cash at stake!'

'Fuck that!' Paxo shouted. 'Christ. You don't get it, do you? Two people are dead! We could all go to fucking jail because of you. And getting fucked in the showers every morning by some hairy-arsed armed robber and his mates might be your idea of fun, mate, but it fucking isn't mine, all right?'

'Hey, back off,' William said, without heat or volume. 'OK, so he's been a bloody fool, but having a slanging match now isn't helping. The question is, what can we do about it?'

'Depends what you mean by "do about it"?' Sean said. 'Our best plan is to contact the local police. We've already delayed longer than they're going to like but I think we can explain some of that away. Leave it much longer and it starts to smack of conspiracy.'

'There's always Superintendent MacMillan,' I suggested. 'I know it's way out of his jurisdiction but he might be persuaded to intervene on our behalf. And he did ask me to look into this in the first place.'

'*What*?' Paxo squawked. 'You were going to sell us out to the filth? You little cow!'

'No, actually,' I said coldly. 'He asked, and I told him to go take a running jump.'

'So what good's he going to do us now?'

'Well,' I said, still smarting enough to be harsh about it, 'he might make the difference between a couple of years for smuggling, and life for murder.'

329

'The other thing to consider is that even if these diamonds don't show up on the official stolen list, they've almost undoubtedly been siphoned off by somebody,' Sean said, cutting in then. 'If I drop the word in enough of the right ears your pal Jamie might find life suddenly gets very ... difficult.'

'Don't,' I said immediately, even though I could still see Tess's lifeless face staring out of that bathtub at me. The trouble was, I could see Jacob and Clare's faces, too, back in the hospital in Lancaster, pleading with me to keep Jamie out of trouble. I didn't think I could have failed at that in any more spectacular fashion.

I became aware that everyone was watching me. 'We don't know if Jamie's on his own in this, or if he's having his strings pulled by Eamonn,' I said quickly. 'Don't you think it might be a good idea to find out before we feed him to the sharks?'

'Sharks are too fucking good for him,' Paxo muttered. 'I want to feed him to something with really blunt teeth so it hurts like fuck when he's being ripped in bits.'

'What do you suggest?' William asked me, ignoring Paxo.

'Well, for a start, where's his bike?' I said. 'He would never have left his helmet if he was planning on riding out of here, so how else did he leave? Maybe you've got it all wrong and he and Tess were ambushed on their way to meet the courier. Maybe he's not to blame for this.'

Nobody looked convinced but Sean was frowning. 'We need to see if the bike's down in the car park,' he said. 'We should go and do a search now, before we call anyone.' He checked his watch. 'Another ten minutes isn't going to make much difference, one way or the other.'

Everybody stood, started heading for the door. As I made to follow them Sean tapped me on the shoulder and I paused, waiting until they'd gone on ahead.

'You do realise,' he said gently, 'that if Jamie *isn't* a willing participant in this enterprise, then once they'd got the diamonds and the money they might not have had any further use for him?'

'I know,' I said, trying to suppress a shiver. 'I'm trying not to think about what we might find down there.'

Once we hit the underground car park we split up to cover the ground faster. I found myself automatically checking underneath and in front of all the parked cars. The kind of spaces where you might conceivably dump a body.

I was just peering into one of the big industrial waste bins near the service entrance when I heard a deep shout from William. I let the lid clang shut and spun round.

I must have been furthest away because by the time I arrived the others were already gathering next to a shiny black pickup truck just across from the exit ramp. As I rounded the front of the truck I saw Sean crouched by the body of a man lying sprawled alongside it and my skin shrank instantly at the sight of him. Sean glanced up.

'It's not Jamie,' he said immediately, reading my fear, although the logical side of my brain had already processed that information. The man was too big and his leathers were plain black rather than Jamie's more garish colour scheme.

Now I looked more closely I could see his dark hair was shorter, too, but it was difficult to tell under the blood that was matting the back of it. A small pool had formed around his head like a halo, staining the dusty concrete almost black. Sean slipped two fingers against the man's neck, just under his ear.

'Is he . . . ?' Daz asked, his voice hesitant.

As if in answer, the man lurched like Sean's touch had burned him, starting to thrash. Sean put his hands on the man's shoulders and braced against him.

'Hold still,' he said sharply. 'We're here to help.'

He had to say it several times before the man quieted down. By the way he was moving it was clear the blow to the head hadn't done him any serious damage, so we rolled him fully over.

331

'Bloody hell,' William said in surprise, almost his first sign of emotion since we'd found the courier's body. '*Gleet?*'

It was hard to recognise the man who'd hosted Slick's wake in the field behind the farm in Wray. It seemed a long time ago. One side of his face was coated in dried blood where it had rested on the ground, giving him the wild-eyed look of a tribal warrior.

Sean got an arm under Gleet's shoulders and helped him to sit up. He did so with a groan, suddenly clutching at his right elbow with his left hand and cradling it across his body. From the way his right hand drooped, his arm was pretty badly busted.

'What the fuck is he doing here?' Paxo demanded of no one in particular.

'Let me guess,' I said when Gleet himself didn't respond. I had a brief flashback of Daz in the hotel room at Portaferry when we'd told him about the Lucky Strike Suzuki. He'd known exactly who the rider was and hadn't seen him as a threat. Now I knew why. 'The name on your driver's licence wouldn't be Reginald Post would it, by any chance?'

Gleet looked up briefly with eyes that struggled to centre but I thought I saw a sliver of recognition in them.

An engine started up somewhere behind us and moved off. We instinctively gathered round Gleet, obscuring him, as a car went past and disappeared up the exit ramp.

'We need to move him away from here,' Sean said, tense. 'Gleet! Come on, man, stick with me! Can you stand up?'

With Sean and William supporting him, we managed to get the big biker on his feet and steer him a slightly staggered course across the car park towards the lifts. On the way we passed the Suzuki that Gleet had been riding to follow us through Ireland. It was parked at a haphazard angle, like he'd stopped suddenly and just jumped off.

Daz rushed ahead of us, jabbing at the call button for the

lift. I held my breath as I watched the floor indicator dropping towards us and the doors opened, but nobody was
inside. I reckoned we might have difficulty finding an
explanation for Gleet's macabre appearance if we did bump
into another guest, but our luck held.

I went to fetch my first-aid kit from Sean's and my room.
By the time I returned to Paxo's room they had Gleet sitting
down on the closed loo seat in the bathroom and had
mopped the worst of the blood away from the wound on his
head. It turned out to be little more than a tear in his scalp
that had bled more alarmingly than its severity warranted.
Nevertheless, it had been enough to knock him cold and,
even now, it was taking him a while to come round fully.

When William let me back in, though, Gleet at least
looked up and more or less focused on me. Daz had the
kettle on and Gleet blinked rather than nodded his thanks
when he was handed a mug of sugary tea. They'd got his
jacket off him somehow and his right arm was resting
across his lap, lifeless apart from the unconscious twitching
of his swollen fingers.

'You must have the skull of an ox,' Sean said to him. 'I
don't know many people who could have taken such a belt
across the back of the head like that and lived to tell the
tale.'

'Yeah well, shame I ain't got bones to match,' Gleet
said, lifting the shoulder of his injured arm with a wry
smile that didn't hide the pain he was in.

'What the fuck happened?' The question burst out of
Paxo like he'd been doing his best to contain it until now
but it had finally got away from him.

'Where do I start?' Gleet murmured, closing his eyes for
a moment. He opened them again. 'OK, Tess asked me to
come over and keep tabs on you lot. Where is she, by the
way?'

The casual question took us by surprise so that no one
had a chance to prepare a face against it. Gleet took a sip
of his tea, eyes darting round us. He caught our dismayed

333

expressions and lowered the mug very slowly, his face going through phases of denial, shock and anger before finally settling on a deep abiding sorrow.

'Oh no,' he muttered, almost to himself. 'I knew it was gonna be bad when I saw them taking Jamie, but ... oh Jesus, no. Not Tess ...'

He choked into silence, head down, his left hand clutched round the half-drunk mug of tea like it was his only anchor. After a moment his shoulders began to shake and I realised he was weeping.

I glanced up. The boys were standing around uncomfortably in the tiny bathroom, all squeezed in together, trying not to touch or meet each other's gaze. I saw Sean take a breath to ask Gleet questions and, however desperately I knew we needed answers, I couldn't let him do that to the poor guy. Not right now.

'OK. Everybody out,' I said, herding them through the door into the bedroom. When Sean would have argued, I added, 'Give him a minute, for pity's sake.' And I shut the door firmly behind them.

When I turned back Gleet was openly crying, tears sliding down through the dried blood on one cheek, leaving smeared greasy tracks.

'I loved her,' he said, more to himself than to me. 'And I never got the chance to tell her.'

'Oh Gleet – she knew,' I said softly, but couldn't have explained my certainty.

'I would have done anything for her,' he said, running straight on as though I hadn't spoken. 'I even lent Slick part of his share of the dosh for this caper.' He gave a harsh snort that never quite made it into a laugh. 'Should have known he'd mess it up. He never had nothing he didn't trash, that lad. So I talked Tess into coming along, just to make sure she got her share. And now—'

He broke off, mouth compressed into a thin line with the effort of damming back the floodwaters. His lips quivered under the strain and finally broke banks.

'It's all my fault,' he said, oozing bitterness like a polluted beach. 'I knew the kind of people Daz was getting himself mixed up with and I didn't warn him or nothing.' He looked up, seemed to focus on me properly for the first time since my return. 'I might as well have killed her myself.'

Chapter Twenty-six

'So, what happened, Gleet?' Sean asked.

I'd let Gleet pull himself together for a moment longer before we went out. He'd heaved himself upright and, awkwardly with one hand, had splashed cold water onto his face first. He didn't bother to dry it, just shook his head a couple of times like a wet dog.

Maybe he thought it might obscure the fact that he'd been crying – enough to be worth the pain it clearly caused him to move his head so abruptly. Nobody who looked at those red-rimmed eyes could make any mistake about that, but I didn't think it kind to say so.

When we emerged to the others' scrutiny, Sean's question was gently put. As though he was only too aware of the pain it was going to cause to go over the events again, now Gleet knew that Tess was dead.

It was strange. In the past I'd watched Sean kill without compunction, without a hint of hesitation or regret. And yet here he was, behaving with such compassion towards a man he barely knew.

'I followed you all down to Mondello this morning,' Gleet said, sitting down carefully on the edge of the bed and shuffling back against the headboard, hunching his shoulders so his elbow didn't bump against the woodwork. 'I met up with Tess down in the car park last night and she told me the plan.'

I looked at him in surprise. 'That was Tess?' I said. 'I knew someone had been down there with you but I didn't think she could get up the stairs so fast in those heels ...'

Even as I said it I realised there wasn't any mystery. She'd just taken them off to scamper up the smooth concrete steps and across the polished lobby floor, and put them back on to walk back into the bar. Not exactly a difficult trick.

Paxo shot me a dark look, like I was side-tracking Gleet unnecessarily, and waved him on with some impatience.

'Seeing as I knew what was going on, I just hung around near the main gate at the track and waited for the pair of them to leave, like. Only I thought I'd got more time so I went for a bit of a wander. I thought the bunch of you would all be in with the advanced mob and you'd send Gnasher – Jamie – out with the intermediates.'

That flat grey gaze swept over Sean and me, cutting the others out. 'He must have been spittin' feathers when you two decided to drop down a group and force him in with the novices, but they needed you out of the way so Jamie could slip out with Tess, like,' he went on. 'They shoulda been there and back inside twenty minutes and you'd never have been any the wiser, see?'

'Yes,' Sean said, ominous, 'we do see.'

Gleet paused a moment as though the long speech had tired him. His skin had that waxy pale tinge and he'd started to sweat. He had his right hand tucked under his left forearm and was gripping it tightly, as though he could squeeze the pain away. From this angle it was pretty clear that his elbow joint was smashed and, from the scars, it probably wasn't the first time.

'So,' Gleet went on, labouring a little now with the distraction, 'I was in the wrong place. I was watchin' the action from in the stands when I saw his bike leavin'. Took me a little while to get back to the Suzi and set off after 'em, like. By the time I got to the petrol station, it was too late. They'd already gone.'

'And you didn't see anyone else?' Sean asked.

Gleet started to shake his head and stopped, wincing. 'No, nobody. Nobody except all the lads who were fillin' their bikes up for the track. I stuck my head into the bog, but there didn't seem to be nobody there, neither. I thought I must have missed 'em on the road, but I knew I hadn't.'

Sean and I exchanged a quick look. Had Gleet seen the dead courier? It would seem not. He had no reason to lie if he had. *Should we tell him?* Sean shook his head slightly. *No point.*

'So, what then?' he prompted instead.

'Well, I shot back here and cruised round the car park a coupla times, but I couldn't spot that little four hundred of Jamie's anywhere, so I was just about to hightail it back to Mondello – feeling a right plonker if you must know – when the lift doors opened and there he was,' Gleet said, eyes focused inwards, remembering. 'He was struggling like a bastard, I'll say that for him, but two of 'em had a hold of him and they knew what they were about – bouncer types.' His gaze snapped back, skimmed over Sean and took in the size and the way of him, recognising something of what he was.

'Struggling?' Daz said, frowning. 'But we thought Jamie was the one who—' He broke off abruptly as Gleet's head swung in his direction.

'Who what? Who did for Tess, you mean? No way,' Gleet said, stony. 'Not the way he was fightin' and yellin', like. Whatever they'd done, he didn't look like he wanted to be any part of it.' And he went quiet because now, unlike then, he knew exactly what it was that Jamie had not wanted to be a part of.

'So why were they taking him at all?' I wondered. 'And where?'

Gleet forgot himself long enough to attempt a shrug, then had to pause to catch his breath. He'd begun to rock a little, almost unconsciously, in self-comfort.

'Search me,' he said at last. 'But he didn't want to go, that's for sure.'

'So, what did they do with him, these men?' Sean asked, repeating my question.

'They had a big white van near the exit,' Gleet said. 'Merc of some kind, I think. They started trying to bundle him into the back of it, but he didn't want to go. Eventually, one of them pulled out one of those extending night-sticks and thwacked him one.'

Sean's eyes flicked to mine again. *Eamonn?* I wouldn't give him an answer.

'They hit him?' Paxo said, sounding puzzled. 'But we thought he must have been in it with them . . .'

'No way,' Gleet said. 'I saw them hit him and it wasn't no friendly tap, neither. He went down like a sack of spuds.'

'And what happened to you?'

'I hopped off the bike and waded in, like,' Gleet said, rueful. 'Should have waited until they put that damned stick away first, though. Took one on my arm, first whack, then got lamped round the back of the head and that was me out of it. Next thing I knew, you lot were standing over me.'

'We still don't know why they were taking him – or where,' Sean said, almost to himself. He glanced at me. 'If they were going to kill him, why bother to take him with them at all?'

'They don't seem too fussed about leaving a trail behind them,' I agreed.

'Oh, I don't think they were out to kill him,' Gleet said and all eyes turned in his direction. 'Well, just as the first bloke clouted Jamie, the other one grabbed his mate's arm and yanked it back, like. Told him to "go steady" or "go easy", something like that. I didn't catch it right. Sorry.'

So, who would want the kid in one piece? Sean's gaze flicked towards me and I saw the same answer that had been forming in my mind.

His mother.

339

'It's got to be,' Sean said, as though I'd spoken out loud.

'Shit,' I muttered, suddenly replaying the conversations I'd had with Jacob since we'd arrived in Ireland. His questions. My answers. I'd kept him up to speed and thought no more about it. 'Isobel must have made a deal with Eamonn. And I know just how she's been getting her intel.'

'You weren't to know, Charlie,' Sean said, almost without censure.

Paxo had been following the brief discussion backwards and forwards like a tennis fan, scowling. 'Hang on. Are you trying to tell us that Jamie sold us out to his mother?' he said, voice rising. 'The little shit.'

'I don't think so,' Sean said. 'They thumped him and chucked him in the back of a van. Hardly the way you'd treat a co-conspirator, is it?'

'So why *have* they taken him?' William asked.

'I've no idea,' I said, grim. 'But I think I might know someone who can answer that.'

I crossed to the phone and followed the instructions for dialling out international. Everyone's eyes were riveted on me, with the exception of Gleet. He'd allowed his head to sag back against the pillows and his eyelids had sunk into a doze like someone had flicked a switch.

'Who are you calling?' Paxo demanded as the call connected and rang in my other ear. 'Come on, Charlie, don't—'

I held my hand up to silence him as the phone was picked up at the other end.

'Hi Jacob,' I said. I was aiming for a light tone but my voice came out tight and ever so slightly angry. Which was hardly surprising, given the circumstances.

'Charlie!' Jacob said, sounding just as tense. 'What's happening?'

'We were rather hoping,' I said, 'that you could tell us that.'

He paused a fraction too long. 'What do you mean?'

I sighed. 'Just let me talk to Isobel,' I said tiredly. 'I

340

know she's there. Just tell her the courier's dead, Tess is dead, and Eamonn's boys have taken Jamie, but that if she thinks that cold-hearted bastard is going to let the boy live after what he's seen, she's kidding herself.'

For a whole five seconds I stood there clutching a silent telephone then Jacob said, quiet and subdued, 'Hold on a moment,' and all the background noise at his end abruptly disappeared.

I closed my eyes briefly. I suppose that right up until that point I'd been hoping Jacob would blow up at me again for getting it all wrong. Instead all I felt was the stab of betrayal in my side, like a vicious stitch.

There was some crackling at the other end of the line. 'Jamie is Isobel's son as much as mine. I'd no right to keep her out of it,' Jacob said then, his voice sounding more distant, echoing. 'I've put it on speakerphone. Go ahead, Charlie. Isobel's right here.'

'Have you told her what's happened?'

'Yes,' Isobel's voice sounded uncharacteristically wavery. She seemed to take a breath and said, more firmly, 'Yes, he has.'

'I don't know what kind of a deal you cut with Eamonn, or what promises he's made you, Isobel,' I said, harsh, 'but he won't keep them. He can't. As soon as he's got what he wants, your son is history.' I paused, and couldn't resist adding, 'And you as well, probably.'

Even the poor reproduction of the phone system couldn't hide the gasp my words provoked, although I couldn't have told you which of Jamie's parents it came from. But it was Jacob who said, hesitantly, 'Can you ... do anything?'

'We can try,' I said. I looked up, met Sean's gaze and took what I needed from it. I shut my eyes briefly. Maybe there were times when Sean was in danger of being close to the monster my father claimed, but who else would be so willing to walk with me into situations like this without balking? 'We need to know where they're taking him.'

'I don't know,' Isobel said, faltering. 'Eamonn didn't tell

me exactly what he had planned. Just that he was going to take the diamonds after the courier had handed them over.'

'Well, the poor bloke didn't exactly hand them over. They had to cut his throat first,' I snapped, infuriated by her vagueness. 'Come on, think, Isobel! You know the man. Where is Eamonn likely to have taken Jamie?'

'Er, well, he has an industrial unit at a place just north of Newry. Used to be a farm,' she said. There was a reluctance to her, as though she was still loath to sell Eamonn out, in spite of everything. But once she'd begun the words seemed to pick up their own momentum and she gave me detailed directions on how to find it. 'But you wouldn't stand a cat in hell's chance of getting in there unannounced,' she added, more like her old brisk self. 'It's out in the middle of nowhere, isolated. You can see anyone approaching over a mile away. And he won't be alone.'

I thought of the men we'd seen following us from the ferry. Were they the same ones Gleet had encountered, or did Eamonn have more muscle at his disposal?

I covered the receiver and relayed the information to Sean. He shook his head.

'We haven't got the time or the equipment to mount an assault,' he said. 'Our best chance is to take them on the road.' He checked his watch. 'They've nearly an hour head start on us but if they've any sense they won't want to risk getting stopped for speeding.' He flashed me a quick hard grin. 'If we don't hang about we should be able to catch them before they hit the border.'

I lifted the receiver back up to my mouth. 'Jacob?' I said, my eyes still on Sean. 'We'll do what we can.'

'Thank you,' he said, heartfelt, like he knew we were his last chance.

'Just one more thing,' I said, hearing Isobel start to speak and deliberately cutting across her. 'Don't let Isobel make any phone calls.' And I hung up on her outraged squawk.

342

'Hell of a time to get caught without a gun on me,' Sean said, rueful. 'I didn't think I'd need one for this trip.'

'Can you get hold of one round here?'

He laughed shortly. 'You can buy anything just about anywhere if you know where to go,' he said, then shook his head. 'But not without wasting time we haven't got. We'll just have to improvise.'

Almost in step, we started for the door.

'Hey, just hold on a minute, guys!' Daz's voice halted us. We turned back to find the Devil's Bridge Club members eyeing us in varying stages of dismay. 'What about us?'

'What about you?' Sean echoed, cold. 'You'll have to stay here and say your bit to the Irish police.'

'While you two go and try to ambush a moving van from two motorbikes?' William asked calmly. 'Not very good odds, are they?'

Sean shrugged. 'We've had worse,' he said.

'Why go at all? Why not let the little sod get what's coming to him?' Paxo said bitterly. He'd began to shiver like he was freezing, his thin frame vibrating with delayed shock.

'Can't do that,' Sean said. 'Besides anything else, we've given our word to his father that we'll get him out of this.'

'And what about the rest of us?' Daz demanded, his voice low.

Sean didn't reply to that one, just stared the other man down. He didn't need to spell it out that Daz and the others had lied to us, if only by omission. That, if they'd come clean earlier, two ugly deaths might have been avoided.

Daz dropped his eyes and looked away.

'What about the cops?' Paxo demanded. 'You said yourself that running would only make things worse.'

'For you, yes.'

'You need us,' Daz said, intensity holding him still now. 'Let us go with you.'

'Why?' Sean said, folding his arms and allowing that

343

obsidian gaze to slide over them in turn. 'How much experience have you had at ambush techniques?'

'How much has she?' Paxo threw in, jerking his head in my direction.

'More than you think,' Sean said mildly. 'More than the rest of you put together, that's for sure.'

They fell silent. For a long couple of seconds nobody spoke, then William said quietly, 'We might not be as expert as you – and Charlie – at this kind of thing, but we can still help.' He took a deep breath, let it out through his nose, flaring his nostrils. 'Let us help. We *want* to help. God knows, we've made a balls-up of things so far. Give us a chance to put things right.'

I saw Sean hesitate.

'What about the police?' I said.

'Don't worry about the local fuzz. I'll stay and tell 'em what happened.'

I turned, surprised, to see Gleet was awake again and sitting upright on the bed. He gripped his broken elbow a little tighter and gave us a wan excuse for a smile. 'I don't think I'd be much good to you for anythin' else, like, would I? And I reckon you need all the help you can get ...'

'OK,' Sean said. 'You're clear what we need?'

'Yeah,' Daz said, listing on his fingers as we hustled into the lift and headed downwards. 'Glass bottles – preferably with screw caps – sticky tape, sugar, paint. Any preference on colour?'

'I hardly think it matters,' William said, rolling his eyes. 'After all, we're not planning on redecorating the place.'

'So, what *is* he planning on doing with that lot?' Paxo wanted to know. 'It's like something out of the fucking *A-Team*. Suddenly he's turned into Hannibal Smith. Hey, Charlie could be that token chick, whatever her name was; Daz can be Faceman; I could be Howling Mad Murdoch and—'

'You can stop that right there,' William said sharply as

344

we hit the ground floor and the lift slowed and stopped. 'I absolutely refuse to be that tosser Mr T, all right?' He waited a beat, scowling as the doors opened, then muttered under his breath, 'Fool.'

Sean didn't join in the banter but that didn't mean he disapproved, either. He understood, better than most, that it was just tension finding its own release.

In the foyer we split off in our prearranged directions, only too aware of the clock ticking. William stayed in the lift and headed for the maintenance area in the car park, while the others disappeared in the direction of the bar and kitchens.

I trotted over to the front desk and, using my best smile, managed to snaffle a roll of brown packing tape. The same guy who'd sorted Daz's keycard out was still on duty and he was still feeling guilty enough to be accommodating.

By the time I'd got back to the lift, Daz and Paxo were already there, clutching half a dozen empty one litre bottles between them. I looked at them in surprise and Paxo grinned at me.

'There was a big plastic skip of them near the bar, so we just helped ourselves,' he said. 'We found three with lids on.'

'Good enough,' I said. 'Where's Sean?'

'Here,' Sean said, appearing. He had a one-kilo bag of sugar in one hand and a small metal tube in the other which he held up and shook at me. 'Remember those little short sparklers in the dessert last night?' he said.

'Fuses,' I said, smiling. 'Perfect.'

Right before we left, I used the hotel phone to place an international call to Detective Superintendent MacMillan.

'Hi there, Superintendent,' I said, breezy and reckless, when the police switchboard put me through. 'You remember you asked me to find out what that group of bikers were up to?'

There was a long pause at the other end of the line. I

345

stood there, holding the phone to my ear while the Devil's Bridge Club members stood around and tried not to look offended. Besides anything else, now they'd made their choice to go with us, they were mostly too apprehensive to react to my admission.

Gleet was still on the bed, propped up with pillows. We'd folded a bath towel into a makeshift sling around his arm. His eyelids were heavy again and he was fighting to keep them open.

Then MacMillan said in that familiar clipped voice, 'Why do I get the distinct impression I'm going to regret saying "yes" to that?'

'Well, make a choice,' I said, matching my tone to his. 'I don't have much time.'

There was another pause, shorter this time but, if silence could have a tartness to it, this one had much more of that.

'All right, Charlie,' he said eventually, with a heavy sigh. 'I'm listening.'

'I'm in Ireland,' I began, baldly. 'There are two people dead.'

I heard the hiss of his indrawn breath. 'What is it with you?' he muttered tightly, then, louder: 'All right. Tell me.'

'One we think is a diamond courier, murdered in the gents' toilet of a petrol station just outside Naas. The other was Slick Grannell's girlfriend, murdered in a hotel room nearby.'

'Grannell's girlfriend?' he said sharply. 'Wait.' And he hit the silence button at his end without waiting for my acquiescence.

I did as I was told, listening to the static. The boys waited with me, most of them so tense I don't think they'd remembered to breathe. Only Sean looked at all relaxed and that, I knew, was deceptive. It seemed to take a long time before MacMillan came back on the line.

'Mr Grannell was doing some deals with some nasty people involved with smuggling gemstones out of Africa,'

346

he said without preamble when he returned. 'Since his death we've had a few enquiries in from other forces and from Interpol. I'm not at liberty to discuss the details with you, Charlie, but I would strongly advise you, for what it's worth, to contact the local police, to co-operate with them fully, and leave it to them,' he said, spelling out each word very precisely as though someone else might be listening in. 'I did try and warn you but, trust me, you do not want to get yourself any deeper involved with this one than I fear you have done already.'

I shook my head. A useless act since he couldn't see me do it. 'It's not as easy as that,' I said. 'After they killed Tess they grabbed one of the lads – Jacob Nash's son, Jamie.'

'Ah,' MacMillan said, not needing to be told about the strong bond I had with Jacob and Clare.

'We think we might know where they're taking Jamie, and we're going to see if we can catch up with them,' I said, deliberately cagey. The last thing I wanted was for MacMillan to try and intercept or divert us. Or, for that matter, ask too many questions about how we intended to go about our task.

As if he could read my mind MacMillan paused again and then said, 'Is Meyer with you?'

'Yes.'

He made a humph of sound. 'So, why are you telling me this – apart from to make me a possible accessory to whatever it is you're going to do?' he said, the sarcasm sharp in his voice now.

'We've a man injured,' I said, eyes trailing over Gleet where he lay against the pillows, his face still partly clotted with old blood. He'd lost his battle with sleep again, his head lolling sideways in a way that echoed starkly how Tess's had been. 'He tried to stop them taking Jamie and they laid into him. When the police get here, it would help if there was someone who could vouch for him, otherwise I think they're going to give him a pretty hard time of it.'

347

'And why can't you vouch for him yourselves? No, on second thoughts don't answer that,' he interrupted quickly before I had chance to speak. 'I really don't want to know.' He sighed again, an annoyed release of pent-up breath. 'All right, Charlie. If they call me I'll put in a good word for your friend. What's his name?'

'Officially he's Reginald Post, but he's known as Gleet,' I said.

'Ah, that wouldn't be the same Gleet who runs a custom bike workshop from his sister's farm near Wray, would it?' the policeman asked.

It was my turn to pause, taken aback. 'Yes, it is. How do you know that?'

'We wondered where he'd got to, and that sister of his is doing sphinx impersonations – or should that be gargoyle?' MacMillan muttered. 'We raided his place yesterday and discovered the remains of Slick Grannell's bike there. I could do with a word with the mysterious Mr Post myself.'

'I'm sure if you can get him away from the *gardai* unscathed, he'll talk to you all you want,' I said.

'Hm,' was MacMillan's only reaction to that. 'Oh, there is one thing you might be interested to learn,' he went on. 'Once we'd recovered Grannell's motorcycle we were able to compare paint traces we found on a Transit van abandoned the day after the accident. Of course, we'll have to wait for the lab to do their stuff for it to be definitive, but our lads are pretty sure they'll be a match.'

He paused again, as though carrying out some internal debate on how much more to tell me. Eventually, when I didn't interrupt him, he sighed and said, 'The van was reported stolen, as you would expect. But, interestingly enough, the registered owner is a property company based in Northern Ireland – the director of which is one Isobel Nash. In light of what you've just told me I think we might well be having a word with Mrs Nash in due course.'

'I think the person you should really be aiming to talk to

348

is her boyfriend, Eamonn Garroway,' I said. 'And watch your step when you do. His idea of a conversation tends to hurt.'

Sean tapped his watch and I nodded to show I understood.

'Sorry, Superintendent,' I said, brusque, 'but we need to get moving.'

'All right, Charlie,' MacMillan said, resigncd. 'I should know by now that trying to talk you out of whatever it is you're going to do is a pointless exercise so I'll save my breath, but ... good luck.'

'Thank you, John,' I said gravely. 'We're going to need it.'

Chapter Twenty-seven

We were just on the outskirts of Dundalk, less than ten klicks from the border, when we finally caught up with the van that had taken Jamie. If it hadn't been for Isobel's information, I would have begun to believe we were heading in totally the wrong direction long before then.

As it was, William and Daz voiced their doubts several times during the frantic ride north. When they had the breath to do it, that is. It made no difference to the pace Sean set. He'd abandoned his previous laid back style and was going like a lunatic. I tried to work out where the rustiness had worn off his riding abilities. Somewhere between the ferry to Belfast, and here, Sean had shed his inhibitions like a second skin.

Now he went for hairline gaps in traffic that made me wince, surviving on gut instinct and sheer brass neck. The rest of us followed him with a kind of reckless faith that where he could get through, so could we.

Nevertheless, all I could hear in my ear-piece was Daz swearing as he missed yet another collision by fractions. Paxo was probably being quite vocal with his opinion, too, but nobody could hear him. He'd given Sean his headset and radio before we set off.

'You're going to need this more than I am,' he'd said, dumping the whole lot onto the seat of the Blackbird. Jamie's headset had been still in his helmet, but the radio itself was missing, otherwise we would have had a spare.

Sean had looked up from carefully packing the bottles we'd prepared into his tank bag. We'd loosely wrapped them in more towels filched from the hotel bathroom to stop them clashing together.

'You'll need this, too,' Paxo had said and handed over his Zippo lighter. 'And it's my favourite, so don't lose it, all right?'

'Thank you,' Sean had said, and meant it. 'I won't.'

Paxo had nodded and rammed on his helmet, cutting short any further talk. He'd slotted the Ducati in behind me as we roared out of the car park. I'd glanced up at the hotel just once as we'd ridden away past the front of it.

Gleet had said he'd give us a half-hour head start before he called the cops. As we howled round the outside of Dublin and headed north, that time seemed to be trickling away. And the further we went without any sign of the Merc van, the faster the minutes seemed to be running out on us.

Unless you wanted to go the scenic route, the only clear way from Dublin up to Newry was the N1, the same road we'd taken on the way down. It was largely fast and open and what little traffic there was on a Sunday was moving quickly on it.

'That's the one!' Sean's voice sounded loud in my ear, edged with triumph as he recognised the registration number Gleet had given us. 'Just overtake and don't look at it too much,' he warned. 'We need to get ahead of him and we don't want to tip him off.'

The Merc driver was doing a steady sixty-five and not looking as though he was pushing hard to keep that up. We slipped past trying not to give the van more than casual attention and accelerated away hard afterwards, putting some distance between us.

I couldn't resist a brief glance sideways into the cab as I drew alongside, taking in an almost subliminal flash of

351

three figures spread across the front seats. None of them were Jamie.

The driver was in short sleeves and had a chunky gold bracelet around the hairy wrist nearest to the window. He had the glass wound halfway down and he was smoking. He didn't look at all like a man who's just been part of kidnapping, theft and murder.

We'd already been cruising in bursts over a hundred but Sean stepped it up for the next few miles, then eased off as we passed the signs for a lay-by coming up.

'That should do it,' he said. 'We'll stop up ahead.'

We all backed off accordingly. Paxo overshot me before he got the idea, braking hard to make it into the lay-by itself.

The road was almost straight at this point, slightly raised up on an embankment that dropped away sharply at either side to a stout post-and-rail fence and then into grassland. For our purposes, it couldn't have been better.

The only worrying factor was the wind. There was no sign of the rain that had dogged us at Mondello, but the wind had picked up and was gusty, particularly over the exposed piece of road. It was going to make things that bit more tricky.

There were no other vehicles parked up but, even so, Sean checked round before he unzipped the tank bag and handed out the three bottles containing the gloss paint William had found in the hotel basement. They were the bottles without lids, so we'd smothered the top of the necks with packing tape.

'Now, you all know what you're doing?' he said in that calm, almost soothing voice he'd always used to inspire confidence in terrified new recruits on their first live-firing exercise. The Devil's Bridge Club members nodded, keyed up and anxious. 'Switch your lights off so you don't attract his attention as you're coming up behind him. You're going to have to fling these things pretty hard to get them to break, all right? Glass is amazingly tough stuff. It's not like you see it in the movies. Aim for the windscreen if you can. The gloss will smear better than emulsion and they won't be able to clear it, OK?'

'What then?' Daz said, giving up trying to wedge his bottle somewhere into the Aprilia's fairing and carefully stuffing it down the front of his leathers instead. Paxo and William did the same.

'You get the hell out of Dodge,' Sean said sharply. 'Trust me, Charlie and I will be right behind you.' He handed one of the other bottles across to me. I stood it in the top of my tank bag, making sure it was packed upright so as not to spill, but accessible enough to retrieve easily when the time came.

'What about afterwards, if – when – the van stops?' Daz said.

Sean flicked his eyes to me and I saw the question in them, *Are you ready for this?* I nodded, just once. *As I'll ever be.*

'I think you'd better let us worry about that,' he said. 'Just get far enough ahead not to get caught up in anything, then pull over and wait for us there. You've got Jamie's helmet? Good. With any luck, he'll need it soon.'

Paxo had been staring back over his shoulder, waiting for the van to catch us up.

'Here they come!' he said now, his voice high and strangled. 'Let's do it, yeah?'

As soon as the van flashed past our position, the three of them launched out of the lay-by, gunning the bikes up to speed in seconds. A moment later, Sean and I followed.

We hung back behind the others, keeping station while we waited for the boys to do their stuff. If they failed there was still a chance we could stop the van but Eamonn's men would be ready for us and things would be so much more difficult.

I felt the nerves knotting my stomach into a tight hard ball. I swallowed, tried to breathe evenly, but that only seemed to make things worse. Reacting to circumstances was one thing, I realised. I could do that without a qualm. But actually instigating an attack was something different again. And especially with such untrained troops. I felt the enormous weight of the responsibility for their safety lying on me.

Does Sean feel the same? I glanced sideways, noted the tension in his arms, the stiff set of his neck as he kept his eyes riveted on the events unfolding ahead. *Of course he does.*

The FireBlade was a reassuringly solid presence under me, with the Super Blackbird keeping easy pace alongside, like two cavalry horses picking up to a canter before the final charge. *Into the valley of death rode the five ... well, let's hope not.*

I glanced ahead and saw the boys tight up behind the Merc. They'd clustered together where they would be almost out of sight of the van's mirrors, hiding in his blind spot.

I saw them nod to each other, their signal. Almost as one man, they reached into their leathers and pulled out their bottles full of paint.

Paxo went first, shooting up the left-hand-side of the van. He flung the bottle awkwardly back over his right shoulder with his left hand as he drew level.

The bottle hit the front end somewhere without breaking and bounced up over the roof-line to land twenty metres behind the rear bumper. There it did finally smash, splattering pure brilliant white gloss paint all over the road. Sean and I had to swerve to avoid it.

Daz and William spurted up the right-hand side of the van as soon as Paxo began his run. But, as the first bottle hit, the Merc driver braked hard enough to lock one wheel, sending up a puff of smoke. The van lurched to the right, forcing the other two bikers to swing wide.

William was just at the point of his pitch and the sudden change of direction threw his aim out completely. The bottle landed hard enough to break this time, but too low and to the left.

354

'Shit!' I heard him shout. 'Direct hit on the radiator grille, but nothing on the glass. Sorry guys.'

The van straightened as the driver fought with the wheel, the high back rocking violently. As William pulled away, Daz glided in almost close enough for van and bike to touch, controlling the big Aprilia with delicate precision. I held my breath as he seemed to keep it there for an eternity. The slightest sideways twitch from the Merc, or heavy gust of wind, and he was going to be history.

Then Daz stood up on his footpegs and backhanded the bottle he was holding straight down onto the windscreen directly in front of the driver, like he was christening a battleship.

Even from our position, we saw the paint spray up.

'Bull's-eye!' I heard Daz yell. 'He's all yours!'

The Merc had began to snake wildly, scrubbing off speed until it was down to less than fifty. We dropped our own speed back to match and I held my breath hoping the van would stop of its own accord. After a few seconds it was clear that wasn't going to happen. They must have known this was an ambush now, and their only chance to avoid disaster was to keep moving.

'Looks like we're going to have to do this the hard way,' Sean's voice said in my ear. 'You ready?'

'Lead on,' I said, terse.

Sean ripped away the tape holding Paxo's Zippo lighter to the headstock of the Blackbird. He already had a row of the mini sparklers we'd taken from the hotel dining room jammed in around the bike's clocks, where the rake of the fairing would keep them more or less out of the buffeting wind.

In this comparatively sheltered zone, Sean persuaded the Zippo to hold a flame at the third strike. He thrust his hand in among the forest of sparklers and kept it there until half a dozen of them had fizzed into life. We'd timed them back at the hotel and knew you got an average twenty-second burn out of each of the magnesium-coated rods.

355

He swung his bike in on my right, close enough to hand over two of the lit sparklers. I leaned across to grab hold of the stems with my left hand. Even though I knew it was just about impossible for the wind to extinguish them, I ducked my hand into the shelter of the 'Blade's fairing, just in case.

'OK,' Sean said, seemingly right inside my head. 'Remember Charlie, eight seconds' maximum, OK?'

'OK,' I repeated.

'Sure?'

'Oh for heaven's sake, Sean,' I growled, 'let's just do this thing and go home, all right?'

I glanced sideways as I spoke and realised he was grinning at me. In spite of everything.

I grinned back and touched the burning end of the sparkler in my hand to the one poking half out of the bottle top in my tank bag. For a moment nothing happened, then it flared and caught in a glittering shower of tiny shards of light.

One thousand, two thousand . . .

I grabbed the bottle and yanked it free with my left hand, snapping the power on with my right and shifting my body-weight to guide the FireBlade up the passenger side of the van as I did so. I felt rather than saw Sean doing the same on the driver's side.

Four thousand, five thousand . . .

As I pulled alongside the cab window, I could see through it to the smeared mess that was the front screen. The guy nearest me turned to stare as he caught the high rev of the 'Blade's engine, his mouth rounding in panic as he saw what I was holding.

Seven thousand, eight thousand . . .

I pulled past, twisting in the seat to lob the bottle clumsily over my right shoulder as I did so, in much the same way that Paxo had done. The difference being that I wasn't relying on the impact to shatter the glass.

We'd pushed the sparklers halfway down inside each

356

bottle, which we'd filled to about the two-thirds level – partly with petrol drained from Gleet's Suzuki, and partly with the sugar Sean had appropriated from the hotel kitchen.

Petrol in liquid form doesn't burn easily. It's the vapour that's highly inflammable and we'd left a good-sized air gap at the top of each bottle to allow it to build up. The long ride up from Dublin, sitting on top of a hot motorbike with the sun on it, had done the rest.

As soon as the sparks from our improvised fuses dipped under the taped-down caps, the petrol fumes went up. A fraction of a second later, the burning vapour ignited the liquid fuel, creating an unstoppable twin-stage explosion of dramatic proportions. The sugar helped, of course. It made the petrol burn hotter and faster, which was part of the reason we'd added it.

Both bottles detonated with a thunderous incendiary clap, the second coming almost as an echo of the first.

Mine went up first. It had already hit the left-hand side of the front end when it disappeared in an instant supernova of heat and light. I felt the concussive blast at my back, even as I whacked the 'Blade's throttle right round to the stop and catapulted out of the way.

Despite his own instructions, Sean had held onto his bottle a second or so longer. The modified Molotov cocktail went up, still in the air, less than a metre from the driver's side of the front screen. The deadly mixture was already a scorching boiling mass when it plastered itself onto the glass.

I held the FireBlade at full chat for another two seconds, peripherally aware that the front end of Sean's bike had popped up level with my knee. It was only then that I backed off long enough to risk putting my head into the vicious slipstream to glance in my mirrors.

The Merc van was on fire. The whole of the front end seemed totally engulfed in dirty orange flame, even the tyres. That was the other reason for the sugar. It glued the blazing petrol to whatever it touched, like napalm.

As I watched, the van swerved violently onto the other side of the road, into the path of a truck heading in the opposite direction. The truck locked up and the trailer stepped out, narrowly avoiding a jack-knife.

The Merc locked up, too, broadsided, skidding back across to its own side of the carriageway and carrying on without stopping. It shot straight across the hard shoulder and bounced violently down the short embankment, crashing through the wooden fence at the bottom and ripping out half its front suspension in the process. It finally came to rest, still on fire – and, remarkably enough, still on what was left of its wheels – about a hundred metres into the field.

As soon as we saw the van was going to crash, both Sean and I had grabbed for the brakes. I'd always thought the cross-drilled discs on my Suzuki had been good until I'd found out just how amazing the FireBlade's brakes were. I felt the compression in my arms as the front forks dived, my belly wedging hard against the back of the tank.

The road was wide enough to swing round, even on a modern sports bike with no steering lock to speak of. We flashed back to the point where the van had left the road, pulling the bikes to a jerky stop on the hard shoulder. A car had already stopped there and the elderly man inside was just climbing out as we roared up. He asked us something but we didn't stop to find out what it was.

The embankment was steep enough that Sean and I had to slide and slither our way down it, vaulting the fence at the bottom and breaking into a flat run across the field. Sean outstripped my pace easily, unbuckling his helmet as he went, yanking the radio wire out of his leathers and stooping to place rather than throw it down onto the ground. I followed suit.

The front of the Merc van was still ablaze. It was surface burn, not close to touching the inside of the engine bay or the fuel system, but Hollywood has implanted the idea that any vehicle on fire is likely to explode at any moment. I could hear shouts and screams from the men inside.

Just as we reached the van the driver's door was flung open and a burning apparition lurched out, bleeding from a dozen deep shrapnel wounds. I realised to my horror that, when Sean's Molotov hit, the driver must have been partially leaning out of the window, possibly trying to see round the obscured windscreen.

Now, he was coated in flaming petrol that, as it was intended, had welded itself to his skin as it burned. The stench of his flesh and hair on fire almost made me gag. He rushed at us, flailing his arms and shrieking like the damned.

Without the faintest hesitation, Sean pivoted on one leg and kicked the Merc driver high in the chest. The man's legs swept out from underneath him with the force of the blow and he landed hard on his back on the ground. Sean immediately stripped off his own leather jacket and smothered the flames, pinning the man down as he put him out.

As he did so, one of the other men from the front of the van appeared through the smoke billowing round the bonnet. He barely glanced at me as he came past, dismissing whatever threat he thought I might present, all his focus on Sean.

Sean was crouching by the driver, still stifling the flames as the man thrashed and screamed. I knew I couldn't let the driver's accomplice get to him in such a vulnerable position.

This new player was smaller than the driver, thin and wiry, with dark hair and a couple of days' beard growth. He didn't quite fit Gleet's description of a bouncer type but, when he reached inside his jacket, I saw why he didn't need to rely on muscle to get the job done for him.

His right hand came out of his pocket holding a baton like the one Eamonn had used, in the closed position. He moved around me, still advancing, and snapped his arm down and back and away from his body to telescope the two inner segments of the baton into place.

I darted sideways, eyes on the hand that held the weapon. I jerked up with my left hand behind the man's wrist as I punched down hard with my clenched fist on the back of his elbow joint.

Normally the elbow is one of the strongest joints in your body because it's well protected by the surrounding muscles, but not this time. The man's arm was straight to the point of hyper-extension from the action of opening out the baton.

I heard the splintering crack of his elbow joint popping apart, even over the driver's cries.

His arm seemed to instantly disconnect from the rest of his body, taking on a dead rubbery quality. The baton dropped from fingers he suddenly had no control over. He had time to turn his head in my direction, eyes wide with a kind of hurt surprise, as though I'd cheated somehow.

I didn't give him time to get used to the idea.

I snatched up the baton on its second bounce, reversed it into my hand and slashed at his right kneecap with it, putting him down and out of the fight.

Aware that there had been three men in the front of the Merc, I spun round, tensed, the baton gripped tight in my fist, to find William, Paxo and Daz staring at me from about ten metres in front of the van. The third man was slumped on the grass at their feet. There was enough blood on his forehead to suggest he'd knocked himself about in the crash and they'd just dragged him clear.

I shut my mind to the horrified fascination on their faces.

'Don't just stand there,' I shouted, my own shame making my voice harsh. 'Jamie's still in the back. Get him out!'

There was a second's immobility, then Paxo broke it, making quickly for the rear of the van. The others were close behind him, wrenching the doors open just as I reached them.

Inside, the back of the Merc had been panelled out to make a flat-sided plywood box. Jamie lay crumpled in one of the front corners, hard up behind the cab. His hands were roughly tied behind him and to his ankles, so his knees were bent right back.

The fear on his face when the doors were thrust open took a moment to change to relief as he screwed up his tear-riven eyes against the sudden flood of light.

'Christ,' he said on a gasp that was almost a sob. 'Oh, thank Christ.'

I jumped up into the back, unzipping my jacket pocket and pulling out my faithful Swiss Army knife to slice through the packing tape they'd used to secure him. They must have got through half a roll of it, wrapped round and round his limbs until it had become one twisted sticky brown band.

'What about his bike?' William asked as we cut the last of the tape free and Jamie unfolded himself with a grunt.

The little Honda had been shoved into the back of the van and lashed to ring-bolts at one side. It was leaning precariously but the webbing straps they'd used had held. Good job too, or the bike would have toppled right on top of Jamie during the crash.

'Forget it,' Sean said from the rear doorway. He jerked his head in the direction of the road. 'We'd never get it back up the embankment and we've attracted too much attention as it is.'

Jamie was too shaken up even to protest about abandoning his ride but he had other things on his mind. 'Hey, what about the money and the stones?'

'Leave them – leave them all,' I snapped as Daz and William half-dragged, half-carried him out of the back of the van, the blood-flow to his legs still fighting the constriction.

The driver was out, in both senses of the word. Wisps of smoke still rose from his skin and clothing, but there were no actual flames. Sean had left him in a semi recovery position sprawled on his side in the grass. The man the others had rescued was still unconscious, too, but the one I'd hit

361

was sitting up a few metres away, clutching his broken elbow in a way that reminded me sharply of Gleet.

And suddenly I had a series of vivid mental images, not just of Gleet with his shattered arm, but of the diamond courier sitting propped on the dirty toilet with the gaping wound in his throat, robbed of his dignity along with his life. And of the fear captured immobile on Tess's face as she lay dead in the hotel bathtub. The driver might or might not survive his injuries, but he was a casualty of battle. The others had been little more than executions.

I stopped briefly alongside the man with the broken elbow. He looked up at me with a dull hatred in his eyes that only served to fan my anger.

'Tell Eamonn this ends here,' I said, my voice cold. 'But if he wants to take it further we *will* finish it – and him. Understand?'

The man paused, not wanting to give me an inch. Then his gaze flicked round the faces of the others, all silently intent on him, and the precariousness of his position seemed to dawn on him. He nodded, not meeting my eyes. I leaned in close. He struggled with himself not to lean away from me.

'And if you should think about changing your mind later,' I added quietly, 'I swear I'll come back and break your other arm.'

Chapter Twenty-eight

By the time we'd got Jamie back to the bottom of the embankment – Sean and I retrieving our helmets as we went – a small crowd had gathered on the road above us. A couple of the braver onlookers ventured down the steep slope and made for the van and the men lying around it. Their sideways glances as they passed made it clear that they knew we were to blame for what had happened, but nobody quite wanted to call us on it, even so.

Jamie was mobile enough to climb back up unaided, though he was still pale and unsteady when we reached the top. The rest of the crowd parted silently and let us pass. Anyone who was thinking of mounting a challenge took one look at our set faces and quickly changed their mind. We hurried through them back to the bikes.

The Devil's Bridge Club had left their machines scattered across the hard shoulder near where Sean and I had stopped. Now we all jumped back on board, Jamie climbing on behind William, who handed him his helmet.

We took the couple of seconds required to plug our radio headsets back in before we all jammed our lids on and fired up the motors. As we pulled away I looked back over my shoulder, down towards the Merc van.

The flames had died back and mostly gone out as the petrol exhausted itself. The paint was blackened around the front end and had largely burned away from the glass where

Daz had scored his direct hit on the windscreen.

The bystanders who'd gone to help were clustered around the driver but their movements seemed uncertain, as though they'd very little idea of what to do for him. He was going to need years of plastic surgery – if he survived. And we'd done that to him.

I tried to feel sorry, but it wasn't something that came easy.

'So, what do we do now?' It was Daz who voiced the question over the radio and I realised that we hadn't talked about what happened after we intercepted the van. All our efforts had been focused on getting Jamie back.

'We head for the next ferry,' Sean said, pulling out smoothly to overtake a farm tractor, getting back into a rhythm. 'Any ideas, William?'

'We've missed the Belfast to Heysham boat, but there should be one coming in to Larne in less than an hour,' William said after a moment's consideration. 'I know the guys on board and they should be able to squeeze us onto it. That'll take us across to Troon.'

'Good enough,' Sean said. 'Anywhere away from here will do.'

Compared to our earlier pace, we rode almost sedately round the outskirts of Belfast and headed up the A2 for Larne. I was bringing up the rear of the group and all the way I had one eye on my mirrors, watching for signs of pursuit. None came.

By the time we dropped down into the harbour at Larne and saw the reassuring bulk of the ferry waiting there, I couldn't help a small sigh of relief. As William had predicted, he was a known face to the ticketing staff at the gate. He negotiated our way on board without any real fuss and the bikes were slotted in to one side of the car deck.

'Might be a rough crossing today,' one of the crew told us. 'We'll make sure they're well strapped down for you.'

We clattered our way up the metal staircase to the passenger deck and William led the way towards the First

Class lounge at the stern, charming his way in with a friendly greeting to the smartly-uniformed woman in charge.

'You're lucky – we're so quiet today I think you'll have the place to yourselves, William,' she said. 'I think everybody's heard the weather forecast and decided to give it a miss.'

'Thanks, Jo,' William said gratefully, dumping his helmet onto the nearest table. 'I think we could do with some peace.'

'Busy trip, huh?' she said brightly.

'Yeah,' he said, giving her a tired smile, 'you could say that.'

I pulled out my mobile, only then noticing I'd missed three calls during the mad ride up from the south. When I checked, all of them were from Jacob. I tried calling him back but his answering machine cut in. I left him a brief message to say Jamie was safe and we were on our way back.

After the adrenaline rush of action that had pumped up our systems ever since we'd gone chasing away from Mondello Park, the climb down left all of us slow and lethargic. I was aware of a slow creeping headache starting up from the back of my neck and I rolled my shoulders, trying to relieve the pressure.

Only Sean still looked wired, keeping an eye on the door and reacting minutely every time it opened and the cabin crew bustled about their pre-sailing tasks. It wasn't until the bow doors had shut and the vibrations through the deck picked up to signal we were moving off that he seemed to relax a fraction.

'Is that it?' Paxo demanded softly, glancing at him. 'Is it over?'

Sean returned the look without smiling. 'Oh no,' he said dryly. 'It's only just beginning. We've left a trail of bodies halfway up the damned country. Whether we were actually responsible for them or not, the fallout from this is going to be practically nuclear.'

365

Paxo just groaned and closed his eyes, letting his head fall back against his seat.

I turned to find William watching me intently.

'What?' I said. 'What have I done?'

'I don't know how you can ask that,' William said quietly, 'after what you did back there.' His eyes flicked to take in Sean as well. 'Either of you.'

'We did what was necessary,' I said, a bit sharper than I'd intended but I was getting past caring. 'What would you rather we'd done?' I went on, jerking my head in Jamie's direction. 'Left him?'

'I'm not talking about that,' William said, still in that infuriatingly even tone. 'We watched you break a guy's arm – his *elbow* – just like that.' He clicked his fingers. 'Like it was nothing. What would you have done if they'd broken Gleet's leg instead?'

'I didn't plan it that way.' I let my breath out through my nose. 'Besides, these were not nice people we were dealing with, William,' I said, trying to hold back my temper. 'You give them an inch and they'll take your bloody head off. You can't play by the same rules as everyday life. They just don't work.'

William looked wholly unconvinced. 'I was right about you, Charlie,' he said, a little sadly. 'You're one scary girl.'

He stood and headed for the door but was barely halfway there when Sean's voice stopped him.

'You can't do that do her,' he said and I was surprised to hear the thread of underlying anger. 'You can't pick Charlie up when you need her and throw her down again when you're done.' He met my eyes and I saw a challenge there that was not just intended for William, but maybe for me as well. 'We're who we are. What we are. And, like it or not, you needed someone like us to sort out the mess you'd got yourselves into. Don't lay your guilt on us now it's done.'

William didn't immediately respond, just paused a

moment, ducked his head in a way that was neither acceptance nor denial, then pushed the door open and walked out.

Daz stood, too, looking awkward. 'Look, we know what you've done for us. We're just not . . . used to this like you are,' he said, hunching his shoulders. 'Shit, I'm still shaking to think about it. I'm going to wake up seeing it for months. You two just look like this is, well, *normal* for you. I'll talk to him.' And with that, he went after William.

As Daz pushed open the door, he nearly collided with a woman who was just walking in. He stepped round her without looking and kept going, but as Sean and I recognised her we both came to our feet, tense.

'Isobel?' I said, incredulous. 'What the hell are you doing here?'

'What did you think I was going to do?' she threw back, brusque as she advanced, her eyes locked on her son. 'As soon as you'd finished talking to Jacob I drove up to Troon and got straight on the first ferry. I saw you driving on board so I never got off. Did you honestly think I was going to sit by and do nothing while my boy was in danger?' And with that she enveloped Jamie in a big bear hug that he didn't look entirely comfortable with.

Sean and I exchanged glances. If Isobel had found us so easily, what about Eamonn? The anxiety that had almost dissipated after our fight and flight was suddenly at full rev again.

'We'll leave you to your reunion,' Sean murmured. Mother and son were too preoccupied to answer him. I glanced at Paxo as we went past but his head was still tilted back against the seat and he seemed to be asleep. We left him undisturbed.

As soon as we were outside the lounge, Sean said, 'We need to do a quick sweep of this place, just in case we've any other surprise visitors. You take the starboard side, I'll go port. OK?'

I nodded and moved away.

The ferry had cleared the coast now and was moving

367

into open water. I looked out of one of the large side windows and saw the sea flecked with white horses. The motion had become more violent and I had to match my stride to the roll of the ship. People were already gathering up their sick bags and one or two looked as though they were just about ready to use them. I wondered how Jamie was faring.

I found nothing untoward as I checked the bar and restaurant areas, the shop and the amusement arcade. I spotted Daz and William out on the deck, standing close by the rail with their backs to me. Daz was doing the talking, waving his hands as he spoke. I didn't feel inclined to interrupt them.

I tried to be annoyed at William's comments but what I really felt, I realised, was hurt. Hurt that he could look at me and see someone who would cold-bloodedly target the man's arm purely in revenge for Gleet's injury, when I hadn't done so. I'd just reacted to circumstance. Hadn't I?

And, with a jolt, I recognised that maybe that was why Sean had responded badly when I'd tackled him over his treatment of Eamonn that day at Jacob and Clare's place. I'd accused him of going in too hard and he'd taken offence. Now I could begin to understand why. Not only that, but it dawned on me slowly, unpleasantly, that other people looked on me in just the same light.

Sean was already waiting for me outside the First Class lounge when I got back there. He cocked his head on one side.

'What is it?' he asked. 'You look a bit fazed.'

'I suppose I am,' I said, rueful, pulling the door open for him to walk through first. 'I was just—'

We both stopped dead.

The lounge seemed empty apart from the cabin crew member William had called Jo, who was sprawled across the floor in front of us, as though trying to crawl towards the doorway. Her tights were torn at the knees and her neat pillbox hat was askew. There was a trickle of blood rolling

368

down the side of her face and she stared up at us with unfocused eyes that were wide with shock and fright.

Sean stepped round the pair of us as I crouched in front of her. 'Jo! Are you all right? What happened?'

'I-I don't know,' she said, her speech slurring a little. 'I don't—'

'Charlie,' Sean cut in. I caught the urgent tone and glanced up. He was over by the seating, kneeling over something – or someone – hidden from my view behind one of the tables.

'I'll be back in a moment, Jo,' I told the woman with what I hoped was a reassuring hand on her shoulder. 'Just lie still. We'll get you some help.'

I hurried over to Sean. As I rounded the end table the first thing I saw was a pair of bike boots, leading up to leather-clad legs. The sight filled me with a sense of deep foreboding. If the state of an innocent bystander like Jo was anything to go by, I knew what I would see at the other end of this wasn't going to be good.

I was right.

Paxo lay on his back on the polished wooden decking with his hands spread slightly out from his body, palms downwards like he was having to hold on to stay there. A pool of blood haloed his head from some unseen wound. There was a lot of it, spreading fast.

Oh shit.

'Paxo,' Sean was saying calmly, not letting alarm leak into his voice. His self-control always had been better than mine. 'Martin, can you hear me?'

Paxo's eyes opened, very slowly, but he didn't move his head. His breathing was shallow and seemed to require conscious effort.

I started to turn. 'I'll get someone,' I said. 'They must have a medic on this damned ship.'

Sean glanced up at me and shook his head, just once. *We're too late.*

At that moment the door opened and Daz and William

369

walked in, jerking to a stop as they spotted Jo just inside the doorway.

'Go find a medic,' I snapped at them. '*Now!*' Daz took one look and bolted. William squatted down to comfort Jo.

'Come on, Martin,' Sean said. 'Don't give up. Stay with me, man!' Paxo didn't seem to hear him. He was gasping now, the gaps between inhalations growing longer, more laboured. I could see his skinny chest vibrating with the stress every breath was causing him. His limbs began to shake, one heel dancing.

I looked at Sean again, helpless, my vision blurring.

I heard movement and then William dropped to his knees alongside me.

'Aw Jesus,' he muttered, raw pain in his voice. 'What *happened*?'

Paxo's lips moved and Sean leaned closer.

'I guess,' Paxo whispered, 'you better keep that lighter . . .'

And then he simply stopped breathing.

'Oh, no. No you don't,' Sean growled, and I felt his anger rising like my own. He twisted to rip open the zip on Paxo's leathers, exposing the front of his T-shirt, and brought his clenched fist down hard, twice, on Paxo's sternum, trying to shock his heart back into action. 'Come on, you little bastard, you don't give up on me that easy!'

With a kind of controlled violence, he linked his hands and began cardiac massage on Paxo's chest, the force of each compression making the smaller man's body jerk and twitch. I took over while Sean pinched Paxo's nose and tilted his head back in a desperate attempt to breathe life back into him.

We kept going like that right up until the ship's doctor arrived at a run and told us, gently, that we were wasting our time. The back of the skull had been fractured like an eggshell, causing catastrophic damage that even a fully-equipped hospital would not have been able to deal with.

Paxo was dead.

*

370

Daz took it hardest. Despite their differences on this trip, he'd been Paxo's oldest friend. He slumped down on one of the corner seats, put his head in his hands, and wept. William had gone back over to Jo, who had also been moved onto the seating and was having her head wound dressed.

I stood with Sean, feeling sick with despair and guilt. That we'd left Isobel with Jamie and so left both him and Paxo unprotected. But we'd thought the danger was over, hadn't we?

The ferry's crew quickly decided to herd the rest of us out of the lounge and close it off, leaving Paxo's body undisturbed for the police when we docked in Troon.

We were ushered out into the corridor outside with our gear. Our names were taken and then we were left almost to our own devices. We were almost ignored in the general air of controlled panic. This was not, I surmised, an eventuality for which the crew had received much training.

William came out, giving Jo his arm to lean on, then handed her over to a couple of the crew who led her away. He watched them go, then came back over to us with his face grim.

'She says she walked back in on it,' he said quietly. 'Pax was already down and this guy was just about to belt Isobel. Jo thought he was using a walking stick, but it sounds like one of those extending batons.'

'Did she describe the man?'

William shook his head. 'The only thing she noticed about him was he had plaster across his face, like his nose was broken ...'

The shrill warbling tone of a mobile phone started up and I realised we must still be close enough to land to pick up a signal.

Daz had sunk down onto the nearest row of seating as soon as he'd come out of the lounge, still looking dazed. Now we turned to see him slowly come out of his stupor long enough to dig automatically in his pocket, pulling out

371

his phone and staring at it as though he didn't know what the noise meant. It was William who went across and took it out of his hands, pressing the receive key. He listened in silence, then turned back, holding the phone out.

'Charlie,' he said, nonplussed. 'It's for you.'

Equally puzzled, I walked across and took the call. 'Hello?'

'Well now, I was right about you, wasn't I, Charlie?' said a soft voice at the other end of the line, hardly audible over the background noise. 'You have got some fire in your belly, haven't you?'

'It's all over, Eamonn,' I said, earning myself sharp glances from both Sean and William. 'What do you hope to gain by this?'

'I want my diamonds.'

'Do you really. And who says they're yours?'

Eamonn laughed, a sound entirely without mirth. 'Well, they're certainly not yours,' he said. 'Let's just say that Isobel here promised them to me in return for cancelling certain debts. And I always collect what's owed to me.'

'We don't have them,' I said.

'Oh, I think you'll find you're mistaken, Charlie,' Eamonn said easily. 'Let's hope so, or good old Jacob's not going to need to bother with a divorce, is he now? Tell me, do they still bury family members in one grave these days?'

'We don't have them,' I repeated through gritted teeth.

'Don't lie to me, you little *bitch*,' Eamonn snapped, his lazy drawl snuffed out like a flame. 'I'll give you ten minutes to come to your senses, or these two start dying. And trust me, unlike your friend there, I won't make it quick ...'

The phone went dead in my hand. My face was bloodless as I turned to Sean.

'Eamonn wants the diamonds,' I said through lips suddenly stiff. 'In ten minutes or he's going to start killing them. But we don't have the bloody diamonds!'

Sean said nothing, just turned his gaze very slowly

372

towards Daz. As if he could sense the weight of it, Daz lifted his face out of his hands, eyes darting from one of us to the other.

'*Do* we have them, Daz?' Sean asked then, his voice quiet and cold.

Daz flushed. 'They were in the glovebox of the van,' he admitted at last, little more than a mutter. 'I got the money back, too. Well, there was no point in just *leaving* them, was there?'

Sean moved in on him. Daz hesitated for a second, then reached inside the jacket of his leathers and pulled out a black pouch, dumping it into his outstretched hand.

With his back to any passers-by, Sean undid the drawstring and tilted the bag up. A shower of sharply defined stones, glistening and brilliant, dropped into his cupped palm. Sean rolled them a little, so they sparked and scintillated as they caught the light. He looked at Daz, his face bleak.

'If they weren't blood diamonds before,' he said in that deadly calm voice of his, 'they certainly are now.'

Daz tore his eyes away from the diamonds as though breaking thrall.

'Take them,' he said bitterly. 'Do what you have to.'

Sean bagged the gems up again and slipped them into his pocket, zipping it shut.

'William,' he said, 'Charlie and I have just swept this ship from the bow backwards and didn't see any sign of Eamonn. You know the layout. Where could he be hiding?'

William frowned in concentration. 'We were outside on the starboard after deck and I'm sure we would have seen Jamie and Isobel being hustled past us,' he said. He nodded to the set of doors nearest to us. 'If they went out on this side, and went aft, I suppose they could have got back down to the car decks. But the doors will have been locked off as soon as we left harbour.'

Sean glanced at the Breitling on his wrist. 'You'd better call Eamonn back and tell him we're willing to do a deal,' he said to me. 'I don't know how much longer we'll have cell coverage.'

I nodded, scrolling through the mobile phone menu until I found the list of received calls and hitting the dial key. It connected and rang out four times before Eamonn answered the call.

'So, changed your mind, have you?' he said slyly, by way of greeting. 'Thought you might.'

'We're prepared to make an exchange,' I said, clipped. 'When and where?'

'Engine room,' Eamonn said. 'I get the gems, you get Isobel and that brat of hers, and we all walk away happy.'

'As simple as that,' I said, not bothering to hide the scepticism. 'What guarantees do we have that you haven't already pushed them over the side?'

'Oh, don't tempt me,' Eamonn said, almost jovial again. 'Here.'

There was a pause, then Jamie's voice came on the line, high in his distress. 'Charlie! I'm sorry, I—'

'OK, that's enough,' Eamonn said, cutting in. 'They're both fine – for the moment. It's up to you how long they stay that way. Engine room, Charlie. You've got four minutes.'

I stabbed my thumb on the End key even though Eamonn had already finished the call.

I swore under my breath. 'How the hell does he think he's going to get away with this?' I muttered. 'He must know that we'll ring ahead and as soon as the boat docks in Troon the police will be all over him.'

'So we plan for the worst,' Sean said, grim. He picked up his helmet and ripped the ear-piece and microphone for his radio out of the lining, reattaching it to the rest of the unit inside his jacket and draping it round his collar. William, Daz and I quickly followed suit.

'OK, William, I want you to stay on the outside, in case this all goes pear-shaped,' Sean said to him. 'Eamonn's got to be planning a double-cross, but at the moment we don't know what. You're known to the crew. If it all sounds like it's going bad you're probably the best person to get us some help. Daz, you're with us. OK?'

They nodded, faces tight with apprehension. They must have thought, after the strike on the van, their brush with danger on this trip was over.

We were all wrong.

We pushed the outer door open and went out. The outer deck smelled of salt and diesel and chip fat from the extractor vents out of the restaurant kitchen. It was driven into our faces by the fierce wind whipping up off the Irish Sea and I was glad I was still wearing my leathers.

The sea was lumpy and getting worse. There were only a couple of the hardier passengers braving the elements and we kept an eye on them as William led us through a low gate that was clearly marked as Off Limits. From there we broke into a half-jog, half-stagger towards the stern, trying to compensate for the lurching of the deck under our feet.

Gouts of spray were being thrown up over the railing. I glanced at the increasingly rough dark green swell and hoped that, whatever Eamonn had planned, it didn't involve any of us ending up in the water.

On a day like today, anybody going over the side wouldn't stand a chance in hell.

Chapter Twenty-nine

William led us confidently to a heavy steel door in the superstructure that opened into a steep stairwell. The inside was never intended for passenger eyes. It was industrial in its construction, lined with padding to prevent injury in rough seas like these were increasingly becoming. The ferry's stabilisers were working hard to compensate for the motion but we held on tight to the handrail all the way down, nevertheless.

At the bottom William indicated another doorway into the engine control room. It was loud down there, and hot enough to break me out in a sweat under my leathers. William opened the door slightly and peered cautiously through the crack. He glanced back, frowning.

'There should be at least a couple of crew down here,' he said, keeping his voice low as he pushed the door wide. 'I don't know where—'

As the door swung open we caught sight of two men in ferry company uniform, slumped on the floor.

'Well, it looks like we're heading the right way,' Sean muttered, derisive. 'You want to know where Eamonn is, just follow the trail of bodies.'

He crouched by the two men, checking for pulses. One of them stirred at his touch, groaning.

'The engine room's through there,' William said, jerking his head. 'The lever operates the door.'

'OK,' Sean said, straightening. 'Do what you can for these two and then get topside. I've a feeling we might need you up there.'

William nodded, eyes sliding over us from an impassive face. 'I take it all back, what I said earlier,' he said, stony. 'If you get the chance to kill that bastard, take it.'

If the engine control room was hot and noisy, that was nothing compared to the engine room itself. The place was crowded with pipes and wires and the steel grate flooring vibrated hard under our feet. Huge cooling fans were fighting a losing battle to circulate the sweltering stale air and the stink of engine oil overlaid everything, thick enough to taste.

We found ourselves on a mezzanine walkway overlooking one of the massive diesel engines that drove the ferry. The top of the engine casing itself must have been three or four metres in length. There was no sign of any crew, or of Eamonn.

Sean nudged my arm and indicated we should go forward and keep our eyes peeled. I jerked my head to Daz and we moved off. There was little point in trying for stealth. The racket of the engines running covered any sounds we might have made.

'Ah, there you are now. I was beginning to think you'd decided these two weren't worth giving up a small fortune in diamonds for,' Eamonn's voice called out above the clamour. 'Not that I'd have blamed you, after the trouble they've caused.'

We stepped forward to the railing to see Eamonn down on the engine room floor below us, previously hidden by the bulk of the engine itself. He had forsaken the suit he'd worn during our last encounter for jeans and a flying jacket.

The extendible baton he'd used to kill Paxo was in his hand, the lethal metal tip resting lightly on his shoulder. Another like the one Sean had taken away from him at Jacob and Clare's, and the one I'd taken away from the man in the Merc van. I wished I'd kept hold of it.

Jamie and Isobel had been handcuffed to each other's wrists, face to face, around a steel support pillar. Jamie was on his knees, hugging the metalwork, his eyes closed and his face drenched with sweat. For a moment I wondered what the hell Eamonn had done to him, then I remembered his acute queasiness on the outward voyage, when the sea had been almost glassy compared to this. The plunging of the ship and the lack of a visible horizon was making even me feel unbalanced, and I didn't suffer from seasickness.

'I hardly think they're the troublemakers round here, do you?' Sean said, his voice loud enough to carry but icily controlled. 'They haven't quite extended their range to common murder.'

Eamonn smiled nastily at us from beneath the plaster that stretched across his nose, partly obscuring his face. He took a step sideways and circled the shackled mother and son like a shark.

'Oh but now that's not true,' Eamonn declared. He stopped, pushed the edge of the baton under Isobel's chin and forced her head back with it. 'Is it now, Isobel my darlin'?'

Isobel stayed stubbornly mute, pressing her lips together into a thin line and glaring at him with pure hatred in her face. Eamonn studied her dispassionately for a moment, then lowered the baton and moved round to Jamie, grasping his hair to lift his slack head up and wedge the baton across his throat. Jamie's eyes flew open as he began to choke.

'Tell them,' Eamonn goaded, gaze locked on Isobel.

Up on the walkway we saw Jamie begin to struggle in Eamonn's hands and moved forward instinctively. Eamonn's head jerked round towards us.

'Hold off or I'll snap his neck in a heartbeat and there won't be a thing you can do to stop me,' he commanded. We stopped. He turned his attention back to Isobel. 'Tell them, or your lying face will be the last thing your little boy sees.'

'All right,' Isobel said from between clenched teeth. 'I killed him, is that what you want to hear? Well, I admit it and to hell with you!'

'Not good enough,' Eamonn said, tightening his grip. Jamie was panicking now, hands jerking so that Isobel was forced hard up against the other side of the pillar. 'Tell them, Isobel,' Eamonn taunted her. 'Tell them the kind of woman you really are. They're prepared to die for you and this worthless brat of yours. Don't you think they're entitled to know?'

'I-I killed Slick Grannell,' she said, her voice wobbling. 'It was an accident. I wasn't aiming for him. I just wanted to stop that scrawny bitch from giving Jamie the money.' Her scornful gaze swept over her former lover. 'I was trying to keep my son out of all this. To protect him from *you*.'

'You were trying to kill Clare?' I couldn't stop the shocked question bursting out. All the time the Devil's Bridge Club had been slyly trying to point the blame for the accident that had claimed Slick's life towards Clare, and they'd been right. I remembered my last phone call with MacMillan. The van that had hit Slick had been registered to Isobel and I'd ridden right over that fact and jumped straight to the conclusion it must have been Eamonn or one of his men driving it instead.

Eamonn took one look at the shock in our faces and released his grip on Jamie, who slumped forwards, coughing. When he could speak again he stared up at his mother with a kind of horrified disgust on his face.

'So that's why you wouldn't loan me the money in the first place,' Jamie said and there was no mistaking the sneer in his voice. 'You live with this crooked bastard but you wanted to keep *me* out of it?'

'Oh she would have been in there like a shot if she'd had the chance, wouldn't you, Isobel?' Eamonn mocked. 'Truth is, though, she's broke. Wasn't that your real reason for trying to run Jacob's blonde bimbo down? No imminent wedding means no divorce and you wouldn't have had to pay the old man off, now would you? A nice little side benefit.'

'So why did you go along with all this?' Sean slung at him. 'What was in it for you?'

'Oh I found out about the little deal your man there was putting together,' Eamonn said, nodding to a white-faced Daz. 'It sounded too good to be true, so I thought I'd cut myself a slice by staking young Jamie. I must admit it was a bit of a surprise when his father's jail-bait threw a spanner in the works by giving him the cash to try and pay me off.'

'Her name is Clare,' I said with a brittle precision that hurt my jaw. 'And she's twenty-seven. Hardly jail-bait.'

'She's still young enough to be his daughter,' Eamonn returned. 'She was a thorn in my side, I know that much. That "accident" was a mixed blessing. When Isobel admitted to me what she'd done I thought she'd blown the whole deal by killing Slick. I thought he was the only link, but Tess had the same contacts, so all was not lost.'

'So why try and run Tess down on Friday night?' I said, although even as I spoke I knew the answer.

'Oh that was Isobel's boys again. Getting inventive, weren't we, my darlin'? Getting desperate, too. Thought that if you lost your contact, you'd give it up.'

She curled her lip at him but Eamonn just grinned back at her.

'And that bunch who jumped us in the pub at Portaferry,' I said. 'Isobel again, I assume?'

'Oh yes,' Eamonn said cheerfully. 'You see the kind of mother she is – prepared to have her own son beaten up to keep him away from the thick of it?' He tutted and shook his head. 'Evil and vicious. My kind of woman.'

'So she knew you were planning on hijacking the diamonds as soon as the exchange was made,' Sean said. He'd gone very still, his only movement an unconscious counterbalance against the crashing of the ship. 'Why wait until then?'

380

Eamonn shrugged. 'Because without Tess, and the boy wonder here, we couldn't flush out the courier. All we had to do was keep tabs on you until the rendezvous and we'd get the diamonds without having to lay out a cent. And all *I* had to do was promise Isobel my lads would get her little boy out of there before the shit started flying,' he said, smiling broadly like it was all so simple.

'You two were the only possible fly in the ointment, but their own greed made them keep you out of it, otherwise we might have had more of a fight on our hands,' he went on, darkly now. 'And it turned out I was right about that, wasn't I? I knew you were trouble right from the start.' He touched a tentative hand to the plaster on his nose. 'My lads did their best to get rid of you, Charlie, but it seems you've a habit of surviving.'

A brief and graphic snapshot of the van that had chased me from Slick's wake, and Sam's accident sprang into my mind. I doused it quickly.

'You must know that as soon as we reach Scotland they'll be waiting for you, don't you, Eamonn?' I said instead.

Eamonn's smile blinked out to turn his face cold again. 'I'm tired of listening to your yacking,' he said. He glanced at his watch. 'I have a schedule to keep to. Hand over those gems.'

Sean unzipped his pocket with a show of reluctance and produced the pouch. Eamonn's eyes locked greedily onto the prize.

Sean paused, nodding to Isobel and Jamie. 'Release them first,' he said.

'You're in no position to dictate terms to me.'

'Neither are you,' Sean said.

Eamonn's face was murderous, then he smiled again. 'Why not?' he said. He produced a set of keys from his jacket pocket, held them up for a moment, then deliberately let them fall. The keys hit the grating at his feet and slithered through into the dark void below.

'There you go, now,' he said. 'It won't take you more than – what? Two minutes to reach those? And I can't take them back either. Fair's fair. Now give me those stones.' He stepped closer to Jamie again. 'I can still kill the boy, if that's what you're after?'

Sean sighed and started to move towards the nearest stairwell. As he passed me his eyes slid sideways, little more than a flicker. I followed his gaze and saw a set of tools on the wall behind us, each clipped into its own place. Right in the middle was a large pair of bolt-cutters. I blinked at him, just once, to show I'd got the message.

'I don't think so,' Eamonn's voice called out. We both froze, as though Eamonn had caught the gesture and divined its meaning.

Eamonn was shaking his head. 'Not you,' he said, eyes narrowed on Sean. 'You must be joking if you think I'd want to be getting close to you again for a while. And she's just as bad. Give the stones to the wee faggot. He can bring them.'

Daz flushed at the insult but said nothing as Sean handed over the bag of diamonds to him. He made his way down the steep open-tread steps and approached Eamonn warily, fiddling with the pouch in his hands.

Eamonn held out his hand for the stones, his expression as arrogant as a man with his nose plastered all over his face can manage.

'Charlie! Sean! Can you hear me?' William's voice sounded tinnily from my collar. 'Er, I think we might have a problem up here.'

'What is it?' I muttered, lifting the mic nearer my mouth as casually as I could manage.

'A big nasty-looking guy's just come through the Off Limits gate and broken the lock off the fire control room,' William said.

'The what—?' I began, just as Daz reached out to give the diamonds to Eamonn.

At the last moment Daz flipped the untied bag upside

382

down and the stones showered down onto the metal grating like hail, disappearing into the same dark space that had swallowed up the handcuff keys.

'You want the diamonds,' Daz cried wildly. 'Here, take them. It won't take you more than a couple of hours to get to them!'

'You stupid bastard,' Eamonn roared, bringing the baton slashing down towards Daz's head.

Even as Daz blocked the blow with his forearm, Sean had jumped for the stairs, sliding down the handrails rather than bothering with the narrow treads.

Before he could reach the bottom Eamonn had lifted a small walkie-talkie to his mouth and shouted, 'Are you in position, Michael? Hit the bastards! Hit them now!'

There was a delay of perhaps three seconds, during which time I'd started to dive for the board that held the bolt-cutters. Sean had landed at the bottom of the stairs and taken a stride for Eamonn. Daz had fallen and was rolling out of the way, hugging his injured arm to his chest.

I'd almost begun to believe that whatever nasty surprise Eamonn had planned had backfired on him when the big cooling fan next to me suddenly lost impetus and started to spin down. A piercing alarm siren wailed into life, backed by a blinding flashing light.

The engine room lights all went out, leaving only the warning light strobing in the darkness. Then the emergency lighting clicked in.

'William,' I snapped into the radio, shouting over the siren. 'What the hell's going on?'

'Oh shit,' William said. 'He's hit the manual override on the fire control system. Get out of there, Charlie! You've got thirty seconds before the compartment seals.'

'What?' I yelled, wrenching the bolt-cutters off the wall and racing for the stairs. 'What the hell happens after thirty seconds?'

'The whole of the compartment floods with CO_2. It takes less than two minutes.'

383

Oh shit, I echoed silently. I jumped the last half-dozen steps, landed badly and staggered on.

The vibrations through the deck had changed, I realised, the engines were shutting down as well. As our forward momentum dropped, the stabilisers began to lose effectiveness. The ferry had already been pitching in the swell but now it began to roll more violently as well.

'Shut it off, William,' I managed. 'Jamie and Isobel are stuck down here. Shut it off!'

'You can't,' William said, anguish twisting his voice. 'Once it's been activated, that's it. It's supposed to be a last resort if there's a fire. Anybody still in there when it goes off is as good as dead. Just get out!'

'Daz,' I shouted. 'Get to the door. Wedge it open!'

'With what?' Daz demanded, lurching to his feet.

'Anything you can damn well find!'

Sean had cornered Eamonn by this time. Eamonn took one look at the deadly intent in Sean's face and tried to bring the baton up, but the confined space was against him. He backed up and prepared to make a stand but Sean just swatted the baton aside and put one hard deliberate blow straight into the middle of Eamonn's face, shattering his already broken nose. Eamonn gave a squeal of pain and dropped to the grating with his hands to his face.

Sean didn't bother trying to finish the fight. He'd heard my brief exchange with William on his own radio and now he spun back to where Jamie and Isobel were tied.

I braced myself steady against the railing to operate the big bolt-cutters. They sliced straight through the inside band of the handcuffs without any fuss. Jamie was still on his knees and I had to cut him loose from Isobel completely so Sean could hoist him to his feet.

Isobel gave a gasp. We turned to find Eamonn was back on his feet with a length of heavy chain in his hand and blood running freely down his face.

Sean dumped Jamie's almost senseless body onto me. 'Get him out,' he said.

The fear grabbed me by the throat but there wasn't time to argue. I half-carried, half-dragged Jamie to the staircase, shouting at him until he put one foot in front of the other and began to climb.

We reached the upper walkway. I glanced back briefly as Eamonn launched a frenzied attack on Sean, just had time to see Sean dance out of the way, agile despite the heaving floor under him, and kick Eamonn's legs from under him.

'Come on, I don't know how long it will hold!'

Daz was by the doorway. He'd found a small pallet truck and had jammed that into the door aperture. The door itself was attempting to close on hydraulic rams that were designed to seal the engine compartment in the event of disaster, come what may. Over 2000psi of pressure was slowly and inevitably crushing and distorting the legs of the pallet truck. Our last exit was shrinking with every passing moment.

And then, our thirty seconds were up.

I heard a hissing noise from above my head. A series of pale green pipes with flat nozzles was strung across the ceiling of the compartment. Now, gas was spraying out from each nozzle. The carbon dioxide, heavier than air, cascaded down into the engine room like misted water.

Desperation lent me strength. I heaved Jamie over my shoulder with a thankful prayer that it wasn't William I had to lift. Gritting my teeth, I charged for the doorway, almost throwing Jamie through the gap into Daz's waiting arms.

I turned. Isobel was staggering along the walkway about six metres behind me but of Sean – and Eamonn – there was no sign.

'Come *on*!' I bellowed, starting to gasp now as the carbon dioxide flooded in, and trying not to let the panic show. 'Time's up!'

Sean's head appeared from the other side of the engine. He scrambled up onto the massive diesel, ran along the top of the casing and jumped for the walkway near where I was standing. I grabbed his forearm as he landed, but his grip was tight. He vaulted over the railing in a flash and dived for the steadily closing doorway. I followed him through, dimly aware of hands grasping me and hauling me clear.

'Who else is inside?' demanded a man alongside me. He was in uniform like a naval officer and carrying a walkie-talkie. Through the haze of little black dots that the carbon dioxide had starred across my vision, I realised that Isobel wasn't right behind me.

'Two,' I said, still panting for breath, just as one leg of the pallet truck buckled with a terrible graunching noise and the door lurched a little further closed.

'Mum!' Jamie cried, coming out of his nausea enough to realise who was left behind. 'Where is she?'

As I watched, Isobel's head and shoulders appeared through the gap. Two crew members grabbed her arms and started to pull, but she was suddenly yanked backwards with a dreadful wailing cry. Eamonn's bloodied face thrust out of the doorway instead.

Jamie flung himself forward and Sean and I grabbed him before he would have tried to force himself back into the engine compartment. He struggled wildly in our arms, tears streaming down his face.

The crew, meanwhile, started to pull Eamonn clear without making any judgements on who deserved to be saved. The door was edging towards its goal all the time, the pallet truck little more than a compressed and twisted mass of scrap metal. But Eamonn was nearly out, only his legs remained inside.

I could see the triumph blooming on his face but then the triumph changed to horror. He began to yell, struggling against something still inside the engine room.

Through the ever-diminishing gap I could just make out Isobel's face, teeth bared. She'd abandoned any last hope of making it out of there, but she had a death grip on Eamonn's shins and she wasn't for letting go.

'Mum!' Jamie cried again.

'I'm sorry,' she said calmly. 'Tell your father I'm sorry, too.'

Eamonn's struggles unintentionally loosened the crew members' grip on his arms and Isobel managed to drag him another few inches further backwards. His eyes met mine and for a second I saw resignation and defeat in them.

'Was it worth it?' I asked him.

Eamonn didn't reply. At that moment the structural integrity of the pallet truck finally failed. It folded up completely. With that last piece of resistance gone, the hydraulic ram on the compartment door achieved its aim, quietly and without fuss.

Isobel still had Eamonn's legs pinned inside the engine room when the door closed. The steel plate cut through both his thigh bones, just above the knee, as neatly and as precisely as a guillotine.

Epilogue

'It was a mess,' I said. 'They airlifted Eamonn back to Belfast and they reckon he'll live, but they had to take what was left of his legs off completely, just below his hip joint. He'll be lucky if he can even wear prosthetics.'

Clare, who'd come so close to amputation herself, blanched in sympathy inside the framework surrounding her hospital bed.

'And Isobel?' she asked with a mix of emotions running through her voice.

As she spoke she glanced warily across at Jacob who was sitting on the other side of the bed. I'd already told them who was responsible for the accident that had claimed Slick's life, and so nearly cost Clare her own legs. Jacob had not taken the life or death of his estranged wife well.

I shook my head, shifting a little in the plastic visitor's chair. 'The carbon dioxide system is designed to totally douse a major engine fire, apparently,' I said. 'Usually it's the captain who has to take the decision to set it off but, as William said, it's a last resort. Anyone left in the engine compartment simply suffocates.'

That had been Eamonn's great escape plan all along, we'd realised. He'd intended to get out while we were still scrabbling for the keys to unlock Isobel and Jamie, as one of his men manually overrode the CO_2 system from the rear fire control centre on the deck above.

As it had done, he knew the stricken ferry would eventually limp back into Larne, its nearest port. There Eamonn had intended to slip away in the confusion, leaving the rest of us dead in the engine room to tell no tales.

And if Daz hadn't decided to scatter the diamonds instead of handing them over, it might just have worked.

'You were so lucky, Charlie,' Clare said, sober.

'Yeah,' I said tiredly. 'But it doesn't feel like lucky.'

We sat for a moment and said nothing. I thought of Slick, dead under the wheels of Isobel's van. Of the diamond courier, and Tess, Paxo, and finally Isobel herself. Not to mention Jamie, who'd watched his mother die, and little Ashley, who'd lost both her parents inside a week. So many casualties that might have been avoided. So much damage left behind.

The driver of the Merc van had survived but lost his eyesight. Perhaps that was for the best, so he'd never see children crying in the street at the sight of his disfigured features. Sam was going to need further surgery on his shattered leg and Gleet was in line for a replacement elbow, when the police were done with him. As for Clare herself, my father was fairly confident she would regain full use of her limbs. But it was going to take months, if not years, to put it right.

'And what will happen to Eamonn?' Jacob asked.

'He's hired a fancy legal team who are using his injuries to delay like mad,' I said. 'But MacMillan is pretty certain he'll go down for what he's done. They're just manoeuvring about the length of his sentence.'

If the authorities hadn't been so delighted to be handed Eamonn on a platter, the rest of us would have faced some serious charges over our ambush on the Merc van. As it was, they were prepared to overlook our somewhat unorthodox methods in return for evidence that would help to convict Eamonn on a whole host of charges. I suppose it didn't do our case any harm that we'd also handed over a rather large quantity of conflict diamonds. Although they'd be tearing up the grating in the ferry's engine room for weeks before they found them all.

'You'll be interested to hear that you'll get most of your ten grand back,' I said, my voice bland. 'After we ran the Merc van off the road, Daz grabbed the money along with the diamonds. It isn't quite the return on your investment that Jamie promised you, but at least you won't lose everything.'

Clare's face registered a kind of startled hurt. 'As if that matters now,' she muttered.

'It must have mattered at one point,' I said, keeping my voice even and non-confrontational only with a supreme effort. 'Because you knew right from the start, didn't you, what Jamie was up to?'

Clare's jaw dropped as she stared at me. Her eyes flicked sideways towards Jacob but I don't know what message passed between them. I didn't take my eyes off her pale face. One of the nurses bustled across the ward behind me, chattering with a colleague. I ignored them.

Eventually, Clare said, 'Yes,' so muted she was almost inaudible.

'So, why didn't you tell me the truth back then?' I said quietly, aware of a lancing pain. 'What difference did you think it was going to make?'

She shrugged, awkward. 'You see everything so black and white, Charlie,' she said, finally looking up at me with eyes that shone bright with unshed tears. 'You see the right thing and you do it. No doubts. No deviations.' She stopped, swallowed determinedly. 'You saved my life once and damned near got yourself killed in the process and you've never blamed me.'

Jacob reached out and silently took one of her hands in his, entwining their fingers together. 'How can I ever live up to that?' Clare went on, her voice breaking slightly. 'How can I live up to the fact that you were prepared to make that kind of sacrifice for me.'

I stared at her a little blankly. *Oh, if only you knew the*

390

demons that ride me. 'You've got it all wrong, Clare,' I said. 'I don't expect you to be worthy of anything. You're just you. My friend.' *At least, I thought you were.* 'I just wanted the truth from you. I would have gone to the wall for you regardless.'

Jacob sighed. 'It was a mistake,' he admitted with a weary smile. 'And I'm sorry for it, Charlie. We both are.'

I got to my feet, stood a moment. 'Yeah,' I said, 'so am I.'

I started to head for the door but found I couldn't leave it there. At the foot of the bed I turned back, took in the pair of them. They hadn't moved, still sitting with their hands grasped together.

'You should have trusted me,' I said, and walked out without looking back.

The Royal Lancaster Infirmary still looked and smelled the same as I made my way along the corridors to the front entrance and out into the breezy sunshine. I paused outside the doors, letting the sun warm my face, the wind comb the taint of the place out of my hair.

A black Shogun swung into the car park and stopped alongside me. I got in and closed the door behind me, fastened my seatbelt and leaned back against the headrest, briefly closing my eyes.

'You OK?' Sean asked.

I opened my eyes again, found him watching me with that faint little half-smile hovering round his lips.

I sighed. 'I suppose so,' I said, giving him a rueful smile in return. 'If only they'd trusted me ...'

'Trust's a funny thing,' he said softly. 'Sometimes people make you wait for it longer than you think they ought to.'

He put his hand on the centre console between us, palm upwards. After a second I put my own down on top of it, felt his fingers close around mine. And I was suddenly aware of not being quite so alone in this any more. I sat up, squared my shoulders.

391

'Let's get out of here,' I said.

'Where to?'

'Anywhere away from here,' I said. 'Find me a job, Sean. It's time I went back to work.'